Above the Fog

by
Karen Lynn Nolan

FIREFLY
SOUTHERN FICTION
LIGHTHOUSE PUBLISHING OF THE CAROLINAS

ABOVE THE FOG BY KAREN LYNN NOLAN
Published by Firely Southern Fiction
an imprint of Lighthouse Publishing of the Carolinas
2333 Barton Oaks Dr., Raleigh, NC 27614

ISBN: 978-1-946016-62-1
Copyright © 2018 by Karen Lynn Nolan
Cover design by Elaina Lee
Interior design by Karthick Srinivasan

Available in print from your local bookstore, online, or from the publisher at:
ShopLPC.com

For more information on this book and the author visit: karenlynnnolan.com

Brought to you by the creative team at Lighthouse Publishing of the Carolinas:
Eddie Jones, Eva Marie Everson, Lindsey Brackett, Christy Distler, Shonda Savage,
Christy Callahan, and Evelyn Miracle

Library of Congress Cataloging-in-Publication Data
Nolan, Karen Lynn
Above the Fog/Karen Lynn Nolan, 1st ed.

Printed in the United States of America

PRAISE FOR *ABOVE THE FOG*

Thirteen-year-old Coreen Shell's hardscrabble life will resonate with all readers, young and old. Set in Kentucky's Appalachia coal mining country, Karen Lynn Nolan's cast of characters bring a new meaning to storytelling. Their voices are unforgettable. Reading *Above the Fog* reminds readers of the importance of community and humility, leaving them raw with emotion and wanting more long after the story is finished.

~Ann Hite
Author of the award-winning Black Mountain series
and the upcoming nonfiction narrative, *Roll the Stone Away*

Karen Lynn Nolan lifts us from the depths despair with her beautiful words as her rich characters rise above the fog of confusion and hatred.

~Stephen M. Vest
Kentucky Monthly

Above the Fog hits the nail on the head. Nolan captures the hard culture of the Appalachian Mountains. Born and raised a mountain girl, Nolan depicts the deep heart and realism that was coal country, giving us characters that we not only love but want to invite over. Above the Fog shows us how uncertain faith becomes solidified. I look forward to more.

~ Cindy K. Sproles
best-selling author of
Mercy's Rain and *Liar's Winter*

In *Above the Fog*, Karen Lynn Nolan gives us a satisfying novel about hope, love, and reclamation. Set in a Kentucky mining camp, it is the coming of age story of Coreen Shell as she begins her thirteenth year and realizes that her life is about to change, and that change is not always easy. Nolan's attention to the nuances of life in the rural South will make readers believe they are right there with the Shell family, and her characters are rich and full. This debut novel tells a troubling story well, and long after its conclusion, readers will hold Coreen Shell and her family close to their hearts.

~Raymond L. Atkins
Author of *Set List* & *Sweetwater Blues*

Filled with twists and turns that resemble the mountain roads Karen Lynn Nolan writes about, *Above the Fog* takes us on a journey through heartache, a life-changing flood, an unexpected murder, and seemingly insurmountable circumstances. But through it all, hope reigns as a broken family discovers that even the dark fog-filled moments of our lives are always in God's hands. You'll love this fresh new voice in Christian fiction!

~Michelle Cox
Author of the *When God Calls the Heart* series and *Just 18 Summers*

ACKNOWLEDGMENTS

A book is the result of a lifetime of experiences, memories, and relationships. I am thankful for them all—good and bad—because of what they taught me. It would be impossible for me to name every person who has played a part in my journey to write *Above the Fog*, but a few dear souls stand out. Without them, this book would never have been written.

If not for Andrea Dresdner, my first writing instructor after I moved to Atlanta, and her unique writing prompts, *Above the Fog* would never have become a book. I never imagined a simple assignment to write a one paragraph scene would burst into flame and become Coreen and Sarah's story.

Ann Hite, author of a fabulous Black Mountain series of Appalachian novels that captured my imagination, blessed my socks off by inviting me into her fabulous Critique Group. Her writing and the group's positive critiquing and encouragement of my work kept me moving forward. Ann became my mentor and guided me to improve my story. Then, she sat me down and commanded me to "just submit it already." Some of the best advice this heel-dragging perfectionist had received.

Special thanks to my group of readers, Karrisima Walker, Joanna Kidd Lindsey, Marbara Stivers, Michelle Welch, and Jennifer McGehee, who were willing to read the entire manuscript, critique it, and answer an extensive list of questions about it before I submitted it for consideration. Their honest insight and encouragement provided the courage I needed to take it to the next step.

It still thrills me that someone I hold in such high regard, Eva Marie Everson, read my first 1,500 words in her fiction class at Blue Ridge Mountains Christian Writer's Conference and said, "This is good." Even though her words were spoken with an air of surprise, I took it as encouragement to finish the story. The next time she read my first page and said, "Of course, you know I love this." When I approached her for advice on how to continue my journey, I did an internal happy dance when she asked me to submit the manuscript to her and Firefly Southern Fiction. After much practice for patience, I received the email that changed my life forever. Thank you, Eva, for having faith in me and this story. You made my childhood dream finally reach fruition.

No book is complete without the guidance from a fabulous editor. Lindsey Brackett graciously led me through the process of tightening, expanding, and improving my story. I truly loved the process. Thank you, Lindsey, for the hard work and insight. And thank you for your patience as we both learned about the friendship between Appalachian dialect and the publishing world.

One non-writing-world person made this book and the unbelievable hours at the computer possible—my chiropractor, Dr. Rickey Allen. He tortured my back and hammered it into submission and reduced my pain enough to spend the needed time in my chair. Thanks, Dr. Allen, for your magical hands and your humor. Do I get a discount now?

You will find bits and pieces of my Harlan County, Kentucky family and friends sprinkled throughout the book. My memories have become a kaleidoscope of personalities, character, struggles, hopes, and dreams—surrounded by mountains and hollers. No matter where I go, my heart still lives in those blessed mountains. But special thanks to my church family at the Loyall Church of Christ who taught me about God's love by how they loved me and made me one of their own.

The Lord gave me the passion for telling stories, the seed for telling Coreen and Sarah's story, a reason to keep writing when I doubted myself, and brought my work to fruition. I am truly grateful and humbled that He entrusted their story to me and with it fulfilled my childhood dream of writing for Him.

DEDICATION

To Awesome Son
You are my hero.
On those days when my writing went well, you allowed me to ramble
on about the lives of my imaginary friends without a complaint.
On days when I griped and hit the delete key repeatedly, thinking
I must be crazy to think I could write a book, you tolerated me.
On days when my life fell apart, fear overwhelmed me, and
I thought I could never write again, you inspired me and urged me
on. You took my hand when I was scared and wanted to give up.
You loved me unconditionally and guided me through the dense fog,
up the mist-covered mountains, and into the sunshine above.
Because of you I know that above the fog, the sun still shines.

Chapter 1

If there really is a God, then let the roof of the mine collapse on Daddy today and send him to hell, where he belongs.

Coreen plucked a chenille thread from the faded bedspread and flung it into the dark space behind her cot. Tears blended with sweat and slid across her face. Stained curtains fluttered as a steamy breeze blew down the holler, through the coal camp, and into the dining room that served as her sleeping quarters.

The room seemed gloomier than usual. Dark shadows lurked in the corners and threatened to swallow up the buffet, discarded by a family who could afford something better. Its sagging drawers and chipped paint made her sad. The shadows closed in on her too as she lay on the metal cot, tucked into the corner like the Christmas gift nobody wanted.

Springs squeaked as Coreen turned away from the room and stared out the window. Mountains rose in every direction, like prison walls around the mining camp. She ran her fingers across a fresh bruise. If only she could escape. Especially today. Especially after what he did this morning—and what he said he planned to do tomorrow. But no matter how hard she tried, no answer came to mind.

A low rumble echoed through the hollers. The odor of dirt mixed with coal dust seeped through the window. A storm was coming. Coreen twirled her ponytail, nearly the color of the faded-yellow chenille bedspread beneath her, and wrapped it into a bun. A gust of wind whipped the curtains into the air, slapping her damp skin in a torturous dance.

A raindrop plopped onto the tin roof, then another and another until the sound resembled an approaching coal train. The intensity mirrored Coreen's anxiety. She lay there listening, thinking about a solution to her problem, dreaming of a happy ending—until her eyes flickered and closed.

* * *

A boom exploded. Windows rattled and the cot shook. Coreen shot up with a gasp. An eerie yellow tint filled the room. Her heart pounded. "Mama? Mama? Where you at?"

All was silent except for the rumbles of thunder and the concussive pounding of rain on the roof. Across the room, light framed the door to her parents' room. She listened. No sounds inside the house. Did it mean he wasn't home yet? Was she safe for now?

Lightning sizzled outside her window and filled the house with pulsing flashes. A gust of wind picked up the rain-soaked curtains and slapped Coreen across the face. The thunder cracked with such violence, it seemed to lift the house into the air and drop it.

"Mama!" she screamed as terror wrapped itself around her.

Coreen bounded off the bed and ran to her mother's room, her bare feet smacking the wooden floor. She flung open the door. "Mama, why didn't you answer me? Did ya hear the thunder? It 'bout skeered me to death."

Her mother raised her eyes from the stained pages of a gothic romance novel and sighed. Silver clips encircled her head, forcing coal-black hair into pinned curls. "You knew where I's at," she said in her slow mountain drawl.

"But it skeered me. I—"

"For goodness sake, you're twelve years old. You don't need nobody to come running 'cause they's a storm outside. What's wrong with your clothes? Did you pee the bed?"

"No." Coreen shook her head as she looked down and ran her fingers across the damp shorts and shirt. "I guess it rained in on me."

"You're so stupid. Why didn't you close them windows up when it started raining? Now you made a mess. I bet your bed's soaked through." Mama lowered her eyes to the book, then raised them again and glared at Coreen. "Go on. Get in there and get them windows closed up. And rip off them blankets and hang 'em up on the line to dry. Your daddy's gonna beat your butt when he gets home. And he probably won't stop with you."

A tear welled up as Coreen turned. She lowered her chin and padded to the door. The clock on the dresser made her stop and look back at her mother. "Ain't he s'posed to be home already?"

"Be glad he ain't," her mother mumbled as she went back to her book.

Coreen's shoulders relaxed. He hadn't come home yet. She plodded to the dining room, searched for the string that dangled from a bare bulb, and clicked it on. The room filled with dim light. As she reached across the bed to pull off the bedding, her thighs leaned against the metal frame. It felt good against her skin. She lingered a moment, enjoying the only cool thing she'd felt since the dog days began.

Coreen balled up the soggy bedspread and sheets and carried them to the clothesline stretched from the front window frame to the kitchen doorframe.

The line bounced and bowed toward the floor as she tossed the linens over it and stretched them out to dry.

Coreen closed the windows and ventured out to the front porch to watch the storm—and think. The screen door slammed shut with a metallic *boing* of the spring. Her Mountain Feist dog ran to greet her from under the settee.

She leaned down to give him a pat. "Hi there, little Patches. Eww, you're all wet. So am I—so I guess it don't matter none. Come on, you want to swing with me a bit?"

Patches jumped into the swing and laid his head across Coreen's lap. She rocked her feet back and forth on the bare wood, swinging slow enough to keep the dog relaxed and content. Her teeth gnawed the swollen spot on her bottom lip. Occasional lightning pulsed across the sky and revealed the outline of the mountains, followed closely by a resonate boom. Rain beat its rhythm on the stone steps. Sheets of water rushed from the roof in a waterfall-like cascade and crashed onto the ground below, sending a cool mist onto the swinging friends above.

"I ain't never seen it rain this hard before, Patches. It looks like it's midnight out here, but it's only about eight o'clock. It's kind of scary looking. But you ain't gotta worry none. I'll protect you."

She ruffled the squirrel dog's black, white, and brown patches of fur then plopped a kiss on his wet nose. Patches moaned the way loved dogs moan and shifted in the swing to expose his tummy. Coreen smiled and obliged the request as her mind wandered. Thoughts of her last moments with her father caused a storm to rally inside her—much greater than the one around her.

"Why's life got to be so hard? Why can't I have the kind of life I read about in them books?"

The metallic taste of fresh blood caused her to stop chewing her lip and wipe it with the back of her hand. As she pulled her hand away, she noticed the fresh bruises on her wrist. She flinched as she gently touched them with her fingers and then moved on to the older ones farther up her arm, now turning varying shades of yellow and green.

"Sometimes I wish I could find a way to stop all the hurtin'. Maybe I could jump into the river and drown—or lay down on the train track and let the big engines squash me. Nobody'd miss me."

The swing glided forward and back. Patches looked up at her and whined.

"I don't think I'm brave enough to do it though. Maybe somebody could take care of it for me the way they do in them Agatha Christie books I read." She leaned down close to the dog's ear and whispered, "Better yet, maybe somebody could take care of Daddy for me."

Patches bayed softly and then sneezed. Coreen chuckled. "Don't worry my little puppy, I ain't gonna leave ya."

Her smile slumped into a frown. Rain pounded the ground and splashed onto the porch. Mist rose up in the hollers, obscuring the mountains from view, much like the thoughts in Coreen's mind. The chains of the swing squeaked. Thunder crackled.

"What am I gonna to do, Patches? What am I gonna do?"

Chapter 2

Sarah awoke with a gasp. Still propped on her pillow, semiprone, she jerked her head to look at the bare pillow next to her. A crick in her neck sent a shockwave of pain down to her shoulder, causing her to poke her fingers into the tender spot to relax the muscle. She glimpsed at the clock on the dresser and did some mental math.

Vernon should have been back from his shift thirteen hours ago.

He'd never missed dinner before. Something must have happened. A rock seemed to grow inside her stomach as she dwelled on the possibilities. She wasn't worried about him, heaven forbid, but she couldn't make sense of it.

The unfinished book lay open beside her. Her heart raced as she grabbed it and stuffed it under the mattress so he wouldn't see it. The last time he caught her reading, he ripped out the pages in a rage and told her reading was a waste of time. Later, when she took the destroyed book back to the bookmobile lady, she blamed it on the dog. Vernon would probably have sent her to the hospital again if she'd told the truth. Of course, she would have lied about why she went to the hospital too.

She tried to remember if she had ever felt guilty about the lying.

The rumble of thunder rattled the windows. The springs squeaked as Sarah scooted off the bed and pulled back a faded blue curtain to see if Vernon's old Chevy was parked out front. It wasn't. She exhaled slowly as the beat of the rain transported her into a world of dark castles where a handsome knight rescued her from torture and impending destruction.

Sarah flung the curtain back into place, and with it the dreams she knew could never come true. There were no knights or princes. Life could never be like the books she read. She would always be trapped in her miserable, and definitely not romantic, life.

Thoughts buzzed through her mind like flies in summer. Where could Vernon be? Did he cross the county line to where drinking and gambling were legal and decide to stay? Maybe he found somebody new to torture. Or he got drunk and drove off the mountain on the way home and lay all bloody and mangled in his car at the bottom. The hint of a smile stretched her lips and then relaxed away.

She glanced at the bruises on her arms. Some were fresh and deep purple. The rest were varied shades of green, blue, and yellow. She knew not all bruises were visible. At least she'd gotten one night of peace.

A crack of thunder snapped her out of her pondering. As she slid her feet into raggedy slippers, she caught her reflection in the mirror above the dresser. The woman staring back at her from the distorted glass surprised her. It should show an innocent, carefree girl of thirteen, not a dried-out, hardened shell of a twenty-seven-year-old woman, empty and without hope. The memory of the past thirteen years held nothing more than a haze of pain and loneliness. Her fingers reached up to stroke her face. All she saw were the bruises and scars. A tear almost formed. She shook it off and shuffled through the house.

The kitchen radiated heat, but she needed coffee anyway, even if it meant building a fire. Besides, he would demand it if he came home now. She pulled some kindling out of the dented lard can on the hearth and put it into the firebox of the cook stove. He could afford an electric stove like the other women in the coal camp owned, but he refused to buy one. She supposed he spent the money on booze and gambling. She also figured he wanted her to be miserable. As long as he got his dinner, he didn't care how much she suffered.

Fire flared in the tinder box. She added enough coal to get it going strong. As the flames grew, so did the heat. Sweat trickled down her face, neck, and chest. She gathered up the tail of her cotton gown and wiped the moisture away.

As the coffee brewed, she fanned herself with a funeral home fan. Her tongue played with a raw spot inside her cheek as she stared out the window. She sighed and sipped her coffee, then absently chewed on the spot until a metallic taste stopped her.

The blue teacup clock ticked on the wall as the coffee perked. Vernon should have started his shift thirty minutes ago. Did he? She smacked the fan onto the table, almost snapping the thin wooden handle. Jesus' face stared up at her from the back of the fan. A snarl ripped from her throat as she threw the fan onto the table, inhaled down to her toes, and marched to the wall phone. Her fingers trembled as she dialed.

"Red Diamond Mines."

"Edith ... it's Sarah Shell. I's wondering if Vernon happened to—"

"Sarah, I's getting ready to call y'all. Ain't Vernon coming in today?"

"What d'ya mean? He ain't there?" Her toe poked at a chipped piece of linoleum where the worn floorboards peeked through. If he wasn't at the mine, then where was he? She peered through the house and out the front door. No car. Her chest raised and lowered like she'd been running.

"No, honey. The men waited around for a bit, but he never did show up this morning. They went in without him. We's wondering if he's feeling sickly … or something."

Sarah hesitated, then closed her eyes. "Edith … I ain't seen him since yesterday morning. Did he show up there yesterday for his shift?"

"Yeah, he worked yesterday. But nobody's seen him since they came out of the mine at five. Where in the world d'ya think he is?"

"I ain't got no clue," Sarah spat. She made a fist with her free hand as heat flushed through her. "Edith, if he comes in, please don't tell him I called. Okay?" He would be furious if he knew she'd called and checked up on him.

"I'll keep my mouth zipped shut. I promise."

"Thanks, Edith. I don't want to … embarrass him or nothing." Embarrassing Vernon could send her to the hospital. A wave of lightheadedness made her grab hold of the wall. She had made a big mistake, but how could she get out of it now? "You know, Edith, he probably went out with some of the men, and they got rained in or something."

"You're probably right. I ain't never seen it rain like this before, won't let up at all. I saw water all over the roads this morning. Didn't think I's gonna make it past Moo-Cow Curve. I hope I can get back home tonight. Vernon's got one of them little Chevys, ain't he? Maybe he just couldn't get through the water. I'm sure there ain't nothing to worry about."

Would Edith never shut up? This mistake of a phone call made Sarah's hands tremble and her head hurt. "I ain't worried. I's … wondering."

"Maybe you should call the sheriff and make sure there ain't been no wrecks or nothing."

"I don't think I need to. I'm probably overreacting, and he'll pull up to the house any minute. If he happens to come there though, could you quietly give me a call?"

"No problem, hon."

"Thanks. And don't forget—"

"I know, I know, I won't say a word. Bye, hon."

The smell of fresh coffee intoxicated her. She filled the chipped Hawkins Garage mug and took a quick sip. The molten liquid made her flinch as it touched the raw spots in her mouth. After two more sips, the pain subsided and the effects of the coffee calmed her. If she believed God would listen to her, she would have asked him to make sure Vernon didn't know she called around about him.

Sarah picked up the fan, turned the Jesus picture away from her, and absently whisked it back and forth with one hand while she drank. The rain still pounded on the roof and poured off the eaves in a thick sheet. As she stared at the water, she waited, wondered, hoped, and dreamed he would never come home again.

* * *

Coreen woke in a daze, wondering why she was smothering. She fought off her offender, realizing the afghan from the back of the couch fell on top of her during the night. Rain continued to beat heavily on the roof. Outside the screen door, early-morning light barely filtered through the curtain of rain. Rather than make a run for the outhouse in such weather, she decided to visit the slop jar in the corner of her room. Then, still in a morning haze like the thick layer of fog usually hanging heavy on the mountains, she followed the fragrance of coffee to the kitchen.

"Mornin', Mama."

Her mother stared out the window, slurping coffee and fanning herself. Coreen glanced up at the clock.

"Why didn't you wake me up? I missed the bookmobile. My books are gonna be late now, and I won't have no new ones to read this week."

"It didn't come." Mama gazed into the mist and muttered in monotone.

"Didn't come? Why not? Today's Monday, ain't it?" Coreen lifted one brow and frowned.

"'Cause it rained all night. The whole place is flooded out there. They'd a got stuck in mud and water. 'Course they didn't come."

The words sent chill bumps down Coreen's back. Seemed everything she said made Mama mad. Getting out of sight offered the only way to avoid getting hit.

"Flooded? I'd better check on Patches."

The floorboards bowed as she ran to the front door. Mama called after her, "Don't go out in the water."

The screen door banged as she crossed the porch and stopped at the edge. Deep, fairly clear rainwater covered the ground.

"Wow, look at all the water. Patches, Patches, where are ya?" Coreen turned to search. On the settee, a confetti of paint layers peeking through the worn areas, she found the dog curled up on a brown paper poke with the Ford Commissary logo in faded red ink.

"There you are, boy. Did you see all the water out there? I guess you won't need your water bowl filled today, will ya? Ya hungry?"

The feist lifted his head and moaned in response. Coreen gave him a hug, ruffled his ears briskly, and kissed his nose.

"I guess you are. I'll be right back." She picked up the gnawed-on margarine tub, banged it on the floor to dislodge any pesky ants, and went back into the house. Humming and swinging the dish in one hand, she swiped the other hand across the still-damp bed linens on the line. Her feet, wet from the rain on the porch, collected coal dust from the floor and left a trail of smudged footprints.

"Sure rained a lot out there. Looks like a big lake. I bet it'd feel good and cool to swish around in."

Sarah continued to stare out the window as Coreen opened a can of dog food, used the sharp edge of the lid to slice half of it into the dish, and diced it into small chunks. Then she tore off a square of used tinfoil from a stock on top of the refrigerator, stretched it over the can of leftovers and put it into the refrigerator for later.

"Make sure you don't get in the water. It'd be my luck you'd get bit by a cottonmouth or drown or get 'lectrocuted by a bolt of lightning."

"I never thought about snakes in the water." Coreen shivered. "Don't worry. I sure don't wanna git bit." Coreen walked to the kitchen door, stopped, and turned to her mother. "Did he come home?"

"Nope," she spat without turning from the window.

"D'ya think, maybe, something happened to him?"

"Don't talk silliness. It'd be too easy."

Coreen chewed on her lip as she stared at the floor on her return trip to the porch. She put the food on the floor and sat on the swing. Mist obscured the mountains completely. Even her grandmother's house next door hid behind a gray veil. Her tongue explored the hills and valleys of tender spots inside her cheeks and on her lips, remembering each one. Remembering … like she couldn't stop remembering her prayer. Wouldn't they know if he died though? Wouldn't somebody have called to tell them?

A blast from an approaching coal train made her squint and stick her fingers in her ears. Patches lifted his head from the food bowl and howled in hound-dog fashion. Train wheels screeched as metal rubbed against metal. The camp house vibrated. Coreen watched the train as it passed, carrying a heavy load of black blocks in the open cars.

"One, two, three, four, five engines this time. It's gonna be a long one, Patches."

The dog licked the empty bowl to get every last morsel. Finding none, he licked his face, gave a burp, and trotted over to jump onto the swing.

"I wish I could get on a train and ride out of these mountains forever. Mammaw told me L&N means Louisville and Nashville. I wonder if I could take it to Nashville where the Grand Ole Opry is?"

Coreen swung and petted Patches' tummy as she watched the train cars pass. "I'd love to sing at the Opry. Someday, Patches, I'm gonna be a famous singer and songwriter. I'll make lots of money, and I'll never have to live in a mining camp—or with anybody who hates me—ever again. But don't worry. I'll take you with me. After all, you're my best friend. You're my only friend."

Patches gave her wrist a lick. Coreen smiled and rubbed his tummy as he snuggled into her lap. "If they won't let me ride the train, maybe we could get on the tracks and walk to Nashville." She snorted. "Eh, I'm dreaming. I couldn't walk from eastern Kentucky to the World's Fair in Knoxville right now, so how do I think I could make it to Nashville?" Sighing, she added, "Besides, I ain't got nowheres to stay when I get there. Maybe my prayer'll be answered and I won't have to leave yet."

Coreen snuggled tightly and breathed in Patches' dogginess. "I gotta do something. I'm thirteen today. Daddy said I'm a woman now." She bit her bottom lip until she tasted fresh blood. "At least, after he comes home I will be. I ain't got much time left."

The caboose clacked past until it disappeared into the mist and rain. Coreen sang the song she'd written about a caboose passing by. She sighed down to her empty spirit and turned to look in the direction of the railroad crossing. No cars entered the camp.

Yet.

Chapter 3

"Is Sheriff Mayhall there?"

Sarah's breathing quickened as she practiced in her mind what she should say. She needed to be careful or Vernon would find out she called. This was crazy. As she decided to hang up, a voice came on the line.

"Sheriff Mayhall here. What's the problem?"

His professional tone made her heart stop. She couldn't say anything. When she spoke, she sounded weak and unsure. "DeWayne, it's Sarah Shell. I'm—uh—wondering if you've heard anything about any wrecks—or anything." She shook her head at how stupid she sounded.

His voice immediately softened. "Good morning, Sarah. Wrecks? You mean Vernon?"

"I's wondering if maybe he'd ... you know ... been in one." Sarah stared at the ceiling and shook her head again. The two cups of coffee seemed to agitate inside her like the old Maytag wringer washer on the back porch.

"We've gotten a few people who thought they's smarter than they are and tried to cross flooded-out roads and got stuck. But no real wrecks. And I don't think any of them involved Vernon ... Why?"

"I—well—DeWayne, I need to know if you've seen Vernon anywheres."

"What happened, Sarah?" His calm and controlled voice made her knees weaken.

"Nothing I know about. He never come home yesterday, and Edith out at the mine said he didn't show up for his shift this morning either. I need to know what's going on so I can ... be prepared." She blew out the breath she'd been holding and felt drained of energy.

"I ain't heard nary a thing. I'll check around for you though, and call you back. Okay?"

Sarah curled the phone cord around her finger. "I'd appreciate it. I don't want to cause a fuss. You know how he can be."

"Yeah, I know. But you're right, this ain't normal—even for him. I'll check around and see if anybody knows anything. Don't worry none."

"Thanks. You're about the only friend I got. 'Course, I can't let him know that." Sarah smacked her forehead. She shouldn't have said that.

DeWayne stayed silent for a few seconds. "Uh ... your mama treated me like a son. Y'all probably got real tired of me hanging around your house all the time. She was a real good cook though. I timed my visits for supper." He laughed. "Or dessert."

"So you only hung around because of the food?" A smile crept across Sarah's face.

"N-no," he stuttered. "Food was a benefit. I really came around because ... uh ... because Larry and Junior were such good friends. And you, of course."

Sarah's cheeks warmed. "I enjoyed having you around. You treated me nicer than Larry and Junior."

"They loved you. When I came home after my first tour in Nam, I promised 'em I'd keep my eyes on you and your mama. We didn't know I'd be too late. I'm sorry I let you down." His voice dropped to nearly a whisper.

"It weren't your fault."

"I shoulda stayed home and took care of you. They hadn't even called me up yet. But I thought it'd be a great adventure and a way to go to school later. Little did I know."

"DeWayne, you couldn't have stopped what happened with Vernon. But I could use your help now. Please don't tell nobody I's asking about him, okay?"

"I won't. I'll say he didn't show up at the mine today and leave it at that."

Sarah hung up and walked back to the window. Many a night he came home drunk and mean. Nights she ended up with bruises and spilled blood. Could she finally be free? She knew she'd never be totally free as long as the girl was here.

Lightning crackled. Thunder rattled the kitchen windows. Maybe a bolt of lightning struck him dead and burned him to a pile of ashes and nobody would ever find him.

* * *

The houses of the mining camp rested like ducks on a pond. Clear water now covered the third step. Coreen sighed from her perch in the swing and wished she could've gotten a new book to occupy her thoughts instead of dwelling on the last time she saw her daddy. She picked up her notebook and pencil and studied on writing a new song about the rain and an evil man who drowned and died a horrible death. She concentrated on the water for inspiration.

"Look at the water now, Patches. I wonder how deep it's gonna get. It looks so cool. I wish I could jump in and swim around." Patches looked up at her and moaned. Sometimes she believed he could understand what she said. "'Course

I can't swim, so I'd sink to the bottom and drown. It's so hot out here though." Coreen stared into the water. "It ain't too awful deep. I can see all the way to the bottom, and there ain't a single snake out there."

She twisted her ponytail into a tight corkscrew and stretched it over her right shoulder and down to her waist. After doodling a few words, she scratched them out. Then she tried a few more, sighed, and thumped her pencil on the arm of the swing.

Her mind wandered back to the older girls in school and what they said about boys. She chewed on the pencil eraser. Is that what Daddy ... No. She shook her head. Daddy wouldn't do that—even if he hated her.

"I wonder where he is, Patches. The wondering's making my tummy hurt. I guess it's the not knowing makes me so flustrated."

Patches jumped down from the swing and walked to the screen door. Mama flung it open and smacked him out of the way.

"Come in here and help me put kettles out. Rain's dripping all over the place. Hurry up."

The swing shook as Coreen catapulted herself out of it and went inside. She tossed her notebook and pencil on the couch and followed Mama as they maneuvered around the puddles, gathered up the largest kettles and bowls from the kitchen, and placed them strategically throughout the house. Water plop-plop-plopped into each one.

The phone rang in the kitchen.

"Here, take the rest of these pans and set 'em out. Then get the mop and clean up the mess in the floor." Mama ran to answer the phone.

Coreen took the pans and searched for more leaks. One large drip happened to be right over Daddy's side of the bed. She briefly considered placing the smallest bowl a tad off-center. She thought better of it, sighed, and thrust a larger bowl where he'd lay his head. With the drips contained, she headed to the kitchen for the mop.

Her mama turned away from her to talk on the phone. Coreen grabbed the rag mop leaning against the back-door frame and went back into the dining room. She stopped outside the kitchen door, out of view, and listened.

"Did they check the hospital ... and the morgue ... How about Gertie's over the county line ... No, I didn't call 'em. DeWayne, I ain't calling that demon mother of his and asking her nothing ... Okay, thanks. I can't handle her today.

"Yeah, we're okay. I can tell it's raining hard. But it's clear rainwater out there. The river ain't never got close to us before, so I don't think we have anything to worry about."

Coreen peeked around the door. Mama's face looked sad as she gazed at the

13

floor and wrapped the phone cord around her finger. Coreen's heart felt heavy in her chest.

"Now where would we go? And how in the world would I get Mother out of her house and up to the road? She can't climb a mountain and the camp's already full of water, so we can't get out by the road. It's up to our third step ... We'll take our chances. Besides, if we did leave and Vernon come home and we's gone ... I don't even want to think about it."

Coreen shuddered. She didn't want to think about what he already promised to do when he got home.

"The church? You mean the one in Mt. Pleasant? DeWayne, there's no way we could get her there. It's about two miles. I know, I know. If it's the only choice, we'll have to find a way. I don't think we need to worry about it. It'll probably stop raining any time now. I mean, how much rain can there be?"

Coreen leaned back against the wall and imagined the rainwater covering up the house and drowning them all. At least she wouldn't have to worry about Daddy hurting her anymore.

"No. I don't want you to send somebody to get us. It'd take a boat anyway. Our road's a mess. Okay ... I promise. I'll call you if I need you. And thanks for looking for him. Let me know if his mother knows anything. Don't let her know I'm the one asking though."

Coreen, hearing the phone hang up, rushed to sop up the puddles so Mama wouldn't know she'd been nosy. Why could nobody find Daddy? Even more important—what would happen when he finally got home?

"I got as much as I could, Mama. I'll wring out the mop in the rainwater."

Mama stepped into the kitchen doorway. "You're dripping all over the place. Hurry up. And keep an eye on the water level out there."

"Okay."

Coreen stopped at the screen door and turned back. "They didn't find him, did they?"

"Did you put something under every drip to catch it?"

"Yep, including the one on Daddy's pillow." She turned away with her chin up and walked out onto the porch. "Mama, the water's up to the fourth step now. Only three more to go."

She dipped the mop into the clean rainwater and swished it around. A pool of black grew and then dissipated as she pushed it against the step and repeatedly pumped it in and out of the water. Then, with all her strength, she twisted and squeezed the water out of the mop like it was her daddy's neck she was wringing.

* * *

Estelle Kincaid favored her right hip. With one hand clinging to a cane and the other hand steadying her on the wall, she hobbled toward the ringing phone. The noise stopped as she snatched up the receiver and put it to her ear.

"Hello?"

"Mother, you okay over there?"

"Yeah, as okay as possible." She dropped into her La-Z-Boy, a Christmas gift from her eldest son. "I ain't seen Vernon's car over there since yesterday morning. What's going on?"

"I don't know. Nobody ain't seen him since he left the mine yesterday."

"Well, he's prob'ly holed up somewhere dry having a good ole time." She chuckled. Probably drunk out of his mind with some woman, more than likely. "Made any phone calls?"

"A couple."

"Did you call his folks?"

"'Course not. I'd never want to know anything bad enough to ask her. And if he's there, she can have him. Got any leaks in your ceiling?"

Estelle followed her daughter's change of subject. "Yep. I got pots lined up through the whole house. This stinking place is full of holes. It's a wonder it's still standing. But you gotta take what life gives you and make the best of it."

"I know, I know. I've heard it all my life."

Estelle's heart ached for her baby daughter and that fool of a husband. "Well, it was a hard life, Sarah. But I survived and so have you."

"Survived? I wouldn't call it survival, Mother. I'd call it hell on earth."

A tear threatened to roll down Estelle's cheek. If only she could change that day. The day that led to her baby's life of hell. "We all got some hell days. It don't mean they all are—"

"Mother, d'ya need me to send Coreen over there to help you with them drips?"

Estelle sighed. "No. Don't make that sweet child come out in this rain. Have you heard anything about how high the water is?"

"DeWayne said it's getting up there and seemed to be worried about the river overflowing the banks and making its way over here to us. I can't believe it'd ever make it this far."

Estelle leaned over and pulled back the curtain enough to check the water level. Surely it wouldn't get high enough to reach the porch. It never had before.

"He said we should get out of here and go to higher ground. Now where in the world's he think we'd go? I can see you climbing the mountain to get to the main road."

"Poo." Estelle laughed as she rocked. "It's only a little rain. Now, some of them folks right down on the riverbank might have a problem, but it ain't gonna get all the way over here. Mercy, we got the train tracks built up between us and the river."

"I'm gonna go now. If Vernon tried to call, he wouldn't be able to get through—and you know how much he'd like that."

"Okay. I don't want you to take any chances."

"Call me if you need anything."

"I will, honey."

The phone clicked into silence. Estelle sat, holding it in her hand, as she pondered. Images of Sarah's constant bruises and cuts made her heart ache down into her gut. If only she could do something to help. The last time she tried, it landed her in the hospital, near death. The damage he did to her hip, and now the arthritis that had set in, reminded her every minute of the day how powerless she was against him. She instinctively reached her hand to her hip and tried to rub away the pain.

Annoying beeps from the disconnected phone brought her back. She hung up the receiver and began the ritual of standing up. With her hands on the armrests, she rocked herself back and forth a couple of times and pushed her body up with a groan. She grabbed her cane and hobbled through the house, emptying the water from each pot, pan, and bowl into a bucket. Pain seared through her back, hip, and leg as she dragged the bucket to the front porch to empty it off the edge. After putting the empty bucket by the door, she sidled herself to her cane rocker, a gift from her daughter Shirley, and collapsed into it.

As she watched the rain crashing around her, Coreen came out of the house next door and yodeled to her with a wave, "Yoo-hoo, Mammaw."

"Yoo-hoo right back, little Co-reen."

Estelle watched as Coreen swung. Her smile relaxed back into the wrinkles of her face and her eyes sagged. That poor child. Such a delightful child shouldn't have to live with so much pain.

Her eyes closed as she lowered her chin. *Lord, it's in your hands. Please help my girls. Protect them from evil.* She looked out at the rainwater. *Wash their lives clean, Lord. Wash their lives clean.*

Chapter 4

Patches opened his eyes and stretched out his legs, releasing a noisy yawn, his tongue hanging out like a strip of half-cooked bacon. After he maneuvered himself out from under the settee and shook out a cloud of dust and debris, he made his way to the edge of the porch and stared down at the steps. Wrinkles appeared above his eyebrows. He cocked his head to look at Coreen, lifted his muzzle in the air, and howled.

Coreen chuckled. "What's wrong, little Patches? You gotta go potty? Poor thang. You've gotta go somewhere. Go ahead." She pointed at the steps.

Patches gave Coreen a sideways glance, moaned, and looked at the water, now up to the fourth step. He stepped down onto the top step with his front paws, rear sticking up the air, and glanced at Coreen again.

"Go on, you can do it."

As if approaching a hiding possum, Patches crept down the steps and through the splashing runoff from the roof until he reached the last one still above rainwater. He leaned forward and sniffed it, opened his mouth, and lapped up a generous portion. Then he did a little dance of sorts on the step, hiked his leg precariously, and added a little yellow to the clear water.

"Good boy." Coreen praised the dog as he bounded up the steps, shook off the rain, and shared it with her.

"Okay, okay. Thanks a lot for soaking me, boy. Yuck."

Coreen swiped the dog water from her face, arms, and legs, laughing at the dog's glee. As she turned her head back toward the front yard, she noticed something unusual. The water approaching the house, which had been mostly clear, showed a dark-brown muddy patch in it, much like when she put vanilla flavoring into a cake batter and stirred it up. As she watched the muddy patch grow closer and wider, she slid out of the swing and walked to the edge of the porch. Her heart thumped faster as she also noticed the fifth step now under water. Only two steps to go before it would be on the porch.

"Mama! Mama, you really need to come out here," Coreen hollered.

Footsteps pounded through the house. The screen door flung open.

"What you hollering about? Your daddy coming?"

"No, Mama. Look." Coreen pointed to the muddy patch as it approached.

"Heavens above, the river's coming. Coreen, go out the back door, up the hill, and over to your grandmother's house. We gotta get her out of there. I'm gonna grab some stuff and meet you both out on the hill in back. Now hurry."

Coreen grabbed a piece of rope from a table on the porch and tried to tie it to the collar on Patches' neck. Her fingers trembled, and she couldn't make them work right.

"What d'ya think you're doing? Leave that dog here. Now hurry up!"

"No. I ain't leaving him here to die. I'm taking him with me, and if I can't take him, then I'm staying here with him." Coreen struggled to get the rope tied as tears rolled down her face.

"We ain't got no time to argue about this. Go. Now." Mama threw her arms up and hurried inside the house.

With the rope finally tied, Coreen dragged the confused dog to the door. "C'mon, Patches, we gotta go."

The dog sat his butt on the porch and refused to go any farther. Coreen realized it was hopeless since Patches learned years ago dogs never enter the house or they get whipped. She leaned down and hefted up her friend and carried him into the house and through the maze of blankets, into the kitchen, and out the back door. Since the back of the house sat against the side of the hill, there were no steps and only shallow puddles on the ground. She put Patches down and fairly dragged him across the hillside, slipping in the wet weeds with her bare feet as she hurried to Mammaw's house.

Coreen stopped to tie the dog's rope to the pump handle and burst into the house screaming, "Mammaw, Mammaw, hurry. The river's coming. We gotta get outta here."

* * *

Estelle grabbed her cane propped up against the nearest wall and struggled to get out of the recliner. After a few false attempts, she grunted and rocked back and forth, finally freeing herself from the chair as Coreen pulled on her. With one hand rubbing her hip, she made her way to the front window and looked out at the approaching waters. "Lord, protect us."

"We gotta hurry, Mammaw. It's coming really fast." Coreen tried in vain to pull her grandmother to the back door.

"I gotta get my medicine."

"I'll get it for you. Where's it at?"

"It's on the table by my bed. And be careful not to trip over them pots in the floor."

The warning came too late. Coreen yelped in pain as she tripped over a big pot and sent it clanging across the room.

"My pictures. I can't lose my pictures."

Coreen carried the pill bottles to the dining room as Estelle grabbed her black pocketbook with the metal snap on top, opened the buffet drawer, removed a stack of family photos and a pile of papers tied with a faded lavender ribbon, and stuffed them into the bag. Coreen dropped the medicine into the pocketbook and snapped it shut.

"Come on, Mammaw. Let's get outta here. Mama's waiting for us on the hill."

"The hill. How am I gonna get up that hill?"

"I'll help you. Come on. Let me carry your pocketbook for you. And I've got to get Patches."

"Patches?"

"Yeah, he's tied to the pump. See? Here we are, Patches. It's okay. Let's go."

* * *

Coreen hung the oversized bag on one shoulder, wrapped the dog's rope around her hand, and tried with all her might to help her grandmother up the hill and across to meet up with her mother.

Mammaw's foot slipped on the grass. She yipped and grabbed hold of a narrow tree.

"Coreen, honey, I can't go so fast. I gotta rest a minute."

"I'm sorry. Here, let me hold you up a little. Hang on to this here tree. Take your time. We'll make it. One step at a time, Mammaw." Coreen looked behind them at the approaching water. Her heart pounded in her chest. "We need to hurry, Mammaw."

"Okay, honey. I know."

"Maybe it'll be easier for you if we walk more across the hill instead of straight up it. Here we go."

"Coreen!"

Coreen turned to see Mammaw's rump hit the wet weeds. As she fell, her cane flew from her grasp and slid down the hill and into the water that now swirled around to the back of the houses.

"Hug the tree real tight. I'll be right back." She tossed the pocketbook onto Mammaw's lap and dragged Patches with her back down the hill, mostly sliding.

"Be careful. Don't fall in the water. It ain't worth it."

She ignored the warning and splashed into the edge of the water where she saw the cane sink. She knew what she had to do, but her body shook with fear. The water swirled closer to her. It was now or never.

With her heart pounding, she took a deep breath and jumped into the now-muddied water. She sloshed around with her hands, frantically searching. Her lungs burned. She lifted her head out of the water and blew out the air. Gasping, she made herself take another deep breath and try again.

God, please help me find it. Mammaw won't make it up the hill without it. Right when she thought her lungs would explode inside her chest, her hand latched onto something smooth and straight. She splashed up out of the water, Spluttering, then coughing.

"I got it." She held it in the air like a trophy. Patches, who stood on the hillside and kept the rope taut during the search, stuck his nose in the air and bayed the victory.

* * *

Sarah emerged from the back door with her pocketbook stuffed as full as she could get it with family photos, a change of underwear for mother and daughter, important papers, and the romance novel from the bookmobile. She heard Coreen holler and looked around for her.

"Coreen. Where's your mammaw? What are you doing in the water? Are you crazy?"

"She fell and lost her cane. She's up there." Coreen pointed up the hill at Estelle sitting on the ground, hugging the tree, with her head lowered.

"Come help me get her up." Sarah carefully made her way across the slickness as Coreen arrived with the cane and Patches.

"Mother, are you all right? What happened?"

"I slipped. I'm okay, thanks to Coreen. Here, honey, take this pocketbook so I can get up. Can you two help me a little bit?"

They latched onto her arms and tugged. The slight woman barely budged. Sarah leaned down and wrapped her arm around her mother's waist and hefted her with all her might. They all grunted as they struggled. Her mother reached out and grabbed hold of a tree and pulled. Finally upright, she clung to the tree as the three of them heaved gasping breaths.

"Mama, I think we better hurry. Look." Coreen pointed at the brown swirling water as it slapped against the hillside like a hungry bear.

"Okay. It's time. Let's go."

They continued the slow, steady climb in the unrelenting downpour. The steady rise of the angry waters below them kept them moving when they wanted to rest. Sarah's head pounded as she struggled to keep her mother on her feet through the tangled brush, wet and slippery, interspersed with slimy mud patches. All three clung to young trees along the hillside for support as they pulled themselves up and tried to keep from falling. Sliding into the water now would be fatal.

They reached a path of sorts, worn into the hillside and leading to the main road above. Slick with mud, Sarah knew it would be too dangerous to attempt. Instead they walked alongside in the weeds. There were no trees to hold onto here, so they needed to be extra careful. Sarah's chest heaved as she pushed to keep them moving up the mountainside. She could hear the labored and wheezy breaths of her mother. Their pace slowed.

One last push up the hill brought them to a leveled-off place. The main road lay within sight. Sarah turned to look back down the hill. They were a safe distance now.

Between them and the road stood a huge moss-covered boulder that had dislodged from the mountaintop years ago and bounced its way to this spot. Sarah didn't know if it stopped here because of the ancient maple tree it now leaned against or because of some power stronger than the tree, which decided to spare the lives at the bottom. For a brief second, she wondered whether those lives were spared today.

"Mother, let's sit on this here rock and rest a bit. I'm wore out, so I know you are. We'd better check it first to make sure there ain't no copperheads or rattlesnakes or nothing under there. All we need. Coreen, get that dog over here. He'll let us know if there's something there."

"C'mon, Patches, let's see if there's a big bad snake under here. You smell anything, boy? Snake? Possum? C'mon, sniff. Good boy." She gave her protector a couple of pats on the head as he turned away from the rock and sat down. Coreen scrunched her nose and slung the water off her hand.

"Eww, you're so wet. I think it's okay. He didn't act like there's anything there at all. Especially not a squirrel."

They perched on the rock, adjusting themselves until they found the most comfortable position. Each attempted to wring the rainwater out of her hair and clothes. They used the tails to wipe the rainwater off their faces. The rain continued to crash onto them, even through the thick foliage of the maple tree above. Patches sat in front of them and panted.

In silence, Sarah looked down into the camp, her home since birth. Her mother and Coreen watched in silence too. From her vantage point, she could see where the river overflowed the banks, rose above the railroad tracks, and then traveled down the dirt lane to their homes. She watched the muddy waters swirl in anger as it overtook everything in its path. Reminded her of Vernon.

A burning fist squeezed Sarah's heart. Her old life was dead, just not in the way she expected. Would her new life be even worse? What would happen to her now? Would Vernon blame her for the flood too? And where could he be? All she had was questions. No answers.

Sarah saw the sadness in her family's rain-soaked faces as they stared down the hill in silence. Loss was loss—even when they didn't have much to lose.

The furious river shook the houses from their foundations, rocked them to and fro, twisted them, and finally tipped them into the raging rapids. Everything they could call their own disappeared from sight. They watched as the life they knew ended, leaving them with … nothing.

After what seemed a lifetime, Coreen wriggled on the rock. "My tush is numb—and I bet my underwear is brown and muddy."

"I brought a fresh pair, Coreen."

"Oh, Lordy." Her mother threw her hands to her cheeks. "I forgot to bring clean step-ins." Then she chuckled. "Ain't it awful? We just lost everything, and the one thing I'm worried about is clean underwear."

Mother leaned forward and slapped her knee. She kept laughing. Sarah couldn't help but laugh too. Then Coreen giggled. They sat on the rock, rainwater dripping from their hair, until they finally burst into gut-wrenching laughter. They laughed until they grabbed their stomachs.

Tears, hidden within the rain, flowed down Sarah's cheeks. Sweet release. "Like you always say, Mother, you gotta take what life gives you and make the best of it."

Chapter 5

Patches jumped up and yanked on the rope still in Coreen's hand. His yips interrupted the laughter as he stiffened his hackles and moved to the edge of the hillside. The yips became a series of warning barks, with a growl or two thrown in for good measure. Faint voices sounded in the distance. A capped head bobbled into view, followed closely by a bouquet of water-soaked white-blonde heads.

"JT, Pat, is that you?" Mammaw called out.

"Yeah, it's us Miss Estelle. Howdy, Sarah, Coreen." JT spit brown juice into a nearby bush, and Coreen snarled her nose. "Glad to see y'all are safe."

JT supported his wife's arm as she carried the baby and dragged a toddler with the other. Three children followed, slipping on the wet grass and practically crawling up the hill. Their white-blonde hair clung to mud-streaked faces even the downpour of rain couldn't clean. Coreen wondered if they knew about soap.

"Where's Vernon? I figured he's with you since he didn't make it to his shift this morning."

"He never come home yesterday," Coreen piped in.

"He never? Where'd he go?"

Mammaw gave Coreen the evil eye. "Maybe you oughta get Patches quiet, Coreen. He might bite somebody."

Coreen shimmied herself off the rock. "He ain't gonna bite nobody, Mammaw. He's doing what a dog's supposed to do. Patches, be quiet. They're friends. Shush."

Mama stretched out her arms. "Here, Pat, give me the baby for a spell. It's a little drier under this tree."

Mama took him into her arms and smiled down at the chubby cheeks as she rocked him gently. Coreen felt a pang in her heart. She wished her mama would smile at her that way.

Pat rubbed her arm and then shook out her fingers. The children gathered around Patches, hugging him and tussling with each other to get the most pats and licks.

Mammaw shifted on the rock. "Y'all barely got out in time, didn't ya? It was pretty close for us."

"Yeah, it shore was scary. I thought we's gonna be goners. JT barely made it home in time to help me with the young'uns." Pat glanced over at JT as he stared down the hill in silence, his head lowered and shoulders slouched.

"D'ya know if anybody else got out?" Mammaw shifted on the rock and winced.

"I did see the Doepels hoofing it up the mountain about a half hour before us. I reckon they's heading for shelter."

Coreen wrinkled her nose. She hoped they wouldn't meet up with them Doepels. They were always doing something mean to the others in the camp. One son, Argo, even tried to steal from the commissary. Rotten to the core. All of them.

Pat sidled over next to JT. Coreen and Mama joined them at the edge and watched the river below churn with foam as it raced through the camp and took everything loose hostage. The ugly brown soup lunged at the trees and anything else in its path. Like a deadly monster.

The whirling brown water now hid the roofs of the houses from view. Trash latched onto tree limbs as the water rushed past. Empty milk bottles, plastic bags, roof shingles, lawn chairs, and disposable diapers swirled in the agitated waters and floated away.

After a few quiet moments, Mama whispered, "You know, we better find some place to get inside. It's gonna be dark soon, and these kids is already hungry and tired."

"Yep, I reckon we better. Ain't nothing here no more." Pat released her grip on her husband and turned her attention to getting her kids off Patches. "But where we gonna go? Everybody I know lived down there."

Coreen watched the muddy water and wondered if everybody got out. She pulled on her bottom lip with her fingers and lowered her head. Suddenly, losing everything didn't seem so important. They all made it up the hill alive.

Well, except Daddy.

"Sheriff Mayhall told me this morning the Baptist church is opening its doors to people. It ain't too fer a piece. Guess it's worth a try." Mama bounced the baby on her hip and turned toward the road.

JT turned away from the flood and scuffled over to the rock. "Here, Estelle, let me help you off there."

He held on to her arms as she wiggled herself off the rock and stood on solid ground again. She leaned over to stretch her muscles. Coreen wondered how she could possibly make it to the church when walking to the outhouse had always been a chore for her.

Mama hitched the baby on one hip and her pocketbook on her shoulder. Coreen grabbed Mammaw's bag and put it over her shoulder and wrapped the rope around her hand again. Pat's arms were filled with a groggy toddler. The remaining children followed Patches wherever he went. She felt a bit like the Pied Piper. They stepped onto the gravel road and headed toward Mt. Pleasant.

Lightning flashed. Thunder rumbled. Trees, heavy with moisture, bowed over the road, tunnel-like. Rain mixed with a dense mist enveloped them.

Coreen turned to look behind her on the road. She half expected to see Daddy tromping toward them, madder than a wet hen. He wasn't there. She blew out a breath.

Not yet. What would he do when he found them?

Chapter 6

Estelle chose her steps carefully. Massive puddles hid the dips and debris hiding beneath the muddy water. She forced herself to keep going as JT held on to her now-numb right arm. Tears ached in her chest. If only she could give up. Instead, she clamped her jaw tight and kept sloshing through the water.

Sarah kept moving the baby from one hip to the other. Even Coreen quieted down and slowed her pace. A tree stump on the side of the road caught Estelle's attention. "D'ya think we could take a little break here?"

"'Course we can, Miss Estelle. Here, let me help you sit on this here stump. It ain't gonna feel so good, but it's better than standing up, I reckon."

"Thank you, JT. You're a blessing."

Rain continued to sting their skin. Everyone found a place to rest for a bit. Their faces drooped and their shoulders sagged. She tried to hide the throbbing pain in her body, but she doubted she would make it to Mt. Pleasant. Her chest heaved from exertion and anguish. To give up sounded so sweet.

"Mother, are you rested up yet? We need to get moving. The kids are looking awful tired."

"And my tummy's growling." Coreen splatted her hand on her stomach. "D'ya think they'll have some food at this church?"

"I sure hope so." Pat looked down at her towheaded crew.

"JT, if you'll help pull me up from this here stump, I'll try to get going again." Estelle hung onto his arm. In her mind she kept repeating words from the Bible. *The Lord is my strength. I can do all things through Him who strengthens me.* She hoped the good Lord would listen to her, because every step she took made her believe the words less and less.

"I shore wish this rain would let up some. I can't hardly see where I'm going." Sarah shifted the baby again.

"And I wish all this water on the road would soak in or drain off. I bet my feet are so wet even my toenails are wrinkled."

"Mammaw, you're so silly." Coreen giggled as she stood up from a rock barely above the water.

A brief smile lightened the mood, if only for a moment. Estelle breathed in deeply and took a step.

Thunder rattled the skies as lightning crackled around them. The rain hadn't let up at all. She felt her eyes droop and her shoulders slouch. Her whole body vibrated and buzzed. She slowed down until she couldn't tell if she still moved.

"Mother, you okay?" Sarah whispered as she came close.

"How much longer is it? I feel like I been walking a 'coon's age."

"We'll make it. Just take your time."

The air was so muggy from the heat and rain, Estelle felt like she would drown when she drew a breath. She knew everybody felt the same, but they were younger and not so beat up. The children started fussing, and a few licks were struck. So much water stood on the road now, nobody found a place to sit and rest.

Estelle breathed in as much air as she could and rubbed her raisin-like hands over her face, eyes, and hair. Would this day ever end? "I wish it'd stop raining. I'm tired of all this water in my eyes, and my skin's all wrinkled up like a shucky bean."

Coreen gave her a hug. "But we're gonna make it—eventually."

Estelle gave her hip a rub, trying to get the circulation moving and calm the pain.

The group moved much slower than before. Even the youngest gave up splashing as they walked and whined more often.

Estelle's arm ached from leaning so hard on the cane. Like her hip and legs. Tears tumbled down the grooves in her aging and rain-soaked face. She wanted desperately to give up. Every muscle in her body screamed. She wanted to lie down in the grass and forget about it. Tears became sobs. Her body wanted to melt into the muddy puddles.

"Miss Estelle, you okay?" JT whispered.

All she could do was shake her head from side to side as the sobs continued.

"Come over here and let's sit you down a spell."

"It ain't no use. I can't do this no more." Her knee buckled, and JT grabbed her around the waist before she could hit the ground.

"Mother! Coreen, take the baby." Sarah thrust the child into Coreen's arms and rushed to Estelle just in time to keep her from hitting the ground. "Mother, are you okay?"

"I ain't got no more strength in me. Leave me here and go on without me."

"No. I ain't leaving you. I'm staying right here till you can walk some more."

"I can't do it," she whispered, not able to hold up her head. She didn't want to die in a puddle of muddy water.

"Yes, you can. It ain't much fu'ther. We're gonna make it. Don't you dare try to give up now."

"I can't."

"What have you always told me? Take what life gives you and make the best of it. We're gonna do exactly that. You rest and we'll go a bit more."

Coreen sloshed over to her. "I love you, Mammaw. You're gonna make it, you know. You got to." She leaned over and kissed a wrinkled cheek.

Estelle closed her eyes and silently prayed for help. She knew her body couldn't make it any farther. She wouldn't admit to giving up; she was facing reality. Sarah wouldn't leave her there. The only solution required a God-sized answer. As she asked for a miracle and whispered her amen, one of the children yelled, "They's a car a-comin', Mammy."

"They ain't no car, young'un," JT grouched.

"Yeah, they is. See." The oldest boy stood up and pointed his finger toward Mt. Pleasant.

Through the rain, the outline of approaching car lights grew closer. The group gathered as the sheriff's Jeep crept up and came to a stop. The door flung open almost immediately, and DeWayne Mayhall burst from the car and ran to them.

"They said the river wiped out the camp. I'm so glad to see you. I's worried sick. Is there anybody still down there?"

JT spoke up. "If they is, it's too late."

DeWayne ran over to Estelle, wrapped his arms around her, and nearly lifted her off the tree. "Miss Estelle, I'm so glad you're okay. I'm sorry I didn't get you out of there in time. Did you climb that mountain?" Amazement showed all over his face as he looked at her and hugged her again.

"I'll forgive you if you'll let me sit in your car. I'm a mite tired." Her voice sounded as weak as she felt.

"Here, let me help you. You can sit up front with me." He carried her and placed her gently into the front passenger seat and closed the door.

Estelle leaned back into the soft cushions, smiled, and said, "Thank you, Lord. I knew you could do it."

* * *

Sarah's heart softened as she watched DeWayne take care of her mother. Such a tender man.

Nothing like Vernon. Sarah stared at the muddy water covering her feet. Like her life. Filth.

Another car arrived with lights flashing. When the young officer stepped out of his car, DeWayne called out, "Chucky, turn them lights off. This ain't no

29

crime scene."

"I like the lights." Coreen smiled.

"Hey, munchkin." DeWayne patted her soggy head. "Well, I see you're traveling with a friend there."

"Yep. I weren't gonna leave without Patches."

"'Course not."

Rainwater dripped off DeWayne's wide-brimmed hat and onto his bright yellow rain coat.

"You folks okay? Sarah. I'm sorry I didn't get here sooner."

"Late's better than never." Her heart skipped a beat as she stared at the water around her feet.

"I reckon so." He dropped his gaze to the water covering his shoes. "Your mama looks a little beat. She need a doctor?"

"I think she'll be okay. She needs to rest. And maybe to dry off and eat something. Actually, we all need it."

"I'll take you to the Baptist church down the road. They're still taking people in. Nice folks there too. They'll take good care of you. Let's pile into the cars and get out of this rain."

"Hot diggity. You mean we get to ride in police cars? Can you make the lights flash? And turn on the sirens?" Coreen squeezed her hands together and held them to her chin.

"For you, munchkin, I might be able to arrange it. Sarah, you want to ride with your mama?"

Sarah headed to the car. "Come on, Coreen, and bring the dirty beast with you. DeWayne, you do realize your car's gonna stink to high heaven after we get out."

"Don't worry none. You wouldn't believe all the stink I've had in that car." He laughed as he turned to JT. "You and your family can ride with Chucky. He does have a pretty good driving record, so don't you worry none. He'll get you there safe. The water's not too deep up here. Just big puddles."

JT herded his kids toward Chucky's car. "Thanks, Sheriff. I shore appreciate your help. The kids are about wore out."

Everyone stuffed themselves into the police cars, dripping onto the floorboards and fogging up the windows even more. Sarah watched DeWayne fiddle with his mirror so he could see Coreen in the back seat and smile at her. Then he looked over at Sarah and winked. She felt her heart jump a little and turned to swipe away a spot on the foggy window so she could stare outside. DeWayne turned on the flashing lights, flipped the switch to make the sirens wail, and splashed through the water.

* * *

Coreen pooched out her lips when DeWayne turned off the sirens as they rounded a curve and stopped. A small limestone building, covered on one side with ivy and with a steeple on top, sat on the right.

"Is this it? Are we here?" Coreen swiped the fog from the window to see better.

"Yep, this is New Hope Baptist Church, munchkin."

"Woo-hoo. We're here, Patches." She ruffled the dog's ears and he barked.

Mammaw swiped a small clear patch on her window up front as they pulled into the parking lot. "Lord-a-mercy. Steps."

"Don't worry none. They got a ramp. I'll get as close to it as I can and then I'll help you to the door. You don't need to worry none."

The other car pulled in beside DeWayne and parked. DeWayne opened the back door, and Coreen scooted off the wet seat and back into the heavy rain. "Come on, Patches. We're here."

"Come on, Miss Estelle. We got it made now." JT took Mammaw's arm and helped her out of the car.

DeWayne came around and took the other arm. As they practically carried her up the ramp, the rest of the group followed behind them like weary sheep.

DeWayne pushed a button beside one of the dark-green doors and then pushed a button on a fancy metal handle, and the door creaked open. They stepped inside and closed the door. A sense of peace settled over Coreen. Apparently, everybody could feel it because nobody said a word, not even the smallest child.

Coreen walked over to some double doors. They opened into a large room filled with white wooden benches covered in thick red cushions. She wanted desperately to lie down on one of those soft pillows and sleep for a couple of days.

At the other end of the room, some steps led up to a higher floor with a wood box in the middle and two chairs on each side that looked like thrones. On the wall behind them a window looked like a crazy quilt of different colors with a wooden cross in the middle.

Footsteps creaked on the floorboards beside them. Patches yelped as the group jerked their heads toward the sound. A tall man in dark-blue pants and a light-blue shirt bounded into the room from stairs hidden in the back corner.

"Hello. I'm Bob Turlington, pastor here." He smiled at them. "Hello, DeWayne. Good to see you again."

"D'ya have room for my friends here? They're from Dodge Camp."

"We have plenty of room downstairs. A few of your neighbors are here too."

"Mammaw!" Coreen shrilled as her grandmother slumped between DeWayne and JT.

"I think I need to sit a spell."

Coreen rushed to Mammaw. Tears welled up in her eyes as she hugged her.

The pastor took DeWayne and JT by the arm. "Can you gentlemen help me get her downstairs? We could create a fireman's chair and carry her down. Here, let me hold her up for you."

He held her upright as the two men interlocked their hands and made a seat for her. Pastor Bob lowered her down onto their hands and took her cane so she could grab hold of their shoulders.

As they walked toward the stairs, a smiling woman trotted up to get out of their way. Coreen thought the woman's tightly curled gold hair made her glow like an angel.

"Do you need any help, dear?"

DeWayne and JT, holding their passenger on their hands still, moved toward the stairs and slowly carried her down step by step.

"This is my wife, Loretta." The pastor smiled at her. "They're taking Mrs. Kincaid downstairs for a rest. She's had quite an ordeal today. Could you figure out a way to take care of our most unique guest?" The pastor wrinkled his nose at Patches and then grinned at his wife.

"His name's Patches." Coreen couldn't help but smile at the angel.

"Well, Patches, I think I know the perfect spot for you." Loretta leaned over and patted the dog's soggy head and smiled the sweetest smile Coreen ever saw.

"And for the rest of you, we have cots set up. We also have a clothes closet filled with clean, dry clothes. I'm sure you'll be able to find something to fit. Some ladies from our church have food cooking too—and gallons of ice tea and Kool-Aid. Sound good?"

The children squealed and clapped their hands.

"What about Patches?" Coreen ignored her own growling stomach and kneeled down to her friend and held him close. She doubted they would have dog food in the church.

"I'm sure I can round up something yummy for Patches to eat. We live next door and have a fenced backyard—and a porch so he can be out of the rain."

Coreen screwed up her face. "Are you sure he'll be okay over there?"

"You can come with me to get him set up. We can give him food and water and a blanket to sleep on. Acceptable?"

Coreen jumped up from the floor. "Come on, Patches. You're gonna have a nice place to sleep tonight. Let's go."

Coreen followed Loretta, who held a pink umbrella over the two of them. It seemed rather silly to her since she was already soaking wet, but she appreciated the kindness. They walked in harmony together down the steps and across the grass to a bright white house surrounded by a matching white wooden fence.

"You got a real nice house. It don't look nothing at all like mine—well, especially now. Mine's under the river."

"I'm so sorry, Coreen. I'm sure this is a tough time for you—and your family. But don't worry, you'll be okay—and Patches too." Loretta smiled her glorious smile again.

The three entered the backyard, closed the gate, and crossed to the porch. "Well, Patches, I reckon I can take this rope off now. You're free." Coreen flung her arms wide.

Patches, realizing his freedom, barked as he ran wildly around the yard. After a moment, he slowed his pace and began sniffing out his new surroundings. Loretta and Coreen laughed at his antics and then entered the back door to the house. Coreen stared in awe at the wallpapered walls, furniture that matched and looked new, family photos, and a vase of real flowers on the eating table.

This must be the most beautiful house in the world.

Loretta took two bowls from a cupboard and walked over to a tub stuck in the top of the counter. When she pulled up on a silver handle, water came out.

Coreen squealed and opened her eyes wide. "You got water inside the house?"

"Yes, we do." Loretta blinked at her and smiled again. Coreen loved that smile. "Here, can you carry this to the back porch while I get some food for Patches?"

She carefully maneuvered the bowl across the kitchen and out the door, being extra careful not to spill a drop on the rugs. "Here, Patches, I got you a drink."

Coreen came back into the house as Loretta opened the refrigerator door and took some chicken, vegetables, and a slice of cheese and put them into the bowl. "There. I imagine this will be a gourmet meal for Patches."

Coreen wondered what *gourmet* meant, but she didn't ask. They walked outside with the food. As soon as Loretta put it on the floor, Patches ran up and sniffed it. Almost immediately, he attacked the food.

"You's hungry, weren't ya?"

"I'll go inside and get a blanket for him. Be right back, okay?"

Coreen sat on the porch as Patches finished off the meal with a few licks of his face and a doggy burp.

"If you'd slow down a bit, you wouldn't always burp. Now, I gotta leave you alone for a while. You'll be okay. Loretta's gonna bring you a nice blanket to sleep on tonight. And you have a big yard to play in. It's been a rough day so you get some rest, okay?"

Patches climbed into Coreen's lap, curled up into her arms, and let out a long sigh. Coreen caressed him as she sang one of the lullabies she had written.

One small blue bird
Sings his sad song.
He hopes someone will hear him sing
And answer him.

He sits alone
Day in and out.
He only leaves to eat and sleep
Then back again.

He won't admit
His song is lost
Amidst the trees of loneliness
And so he sings.

One small blue bird
Sings his sad song.
He sits upon a quiet limb
All the day long.

Chapter 7

Sarah's shoes squished and squeaked as she stepped onto the tile basement floor. She slowed her pace and stepped gently, hoping the noise wouldn't draw the attention of the entire room of people milling about. The pastor led them past a darkened area where cots were lined up in rows, each topped with a folded blanket, a pillow, and random personal items.

Beyond the cots, bright lights made her squint at the rows of tables stretched across the room. Several people sat at the tables or stood talking. Children of all ages chased each other with the squeals of play or clung to an adult's leg, whining to be picked up. The noise made her want to run from the room. She hated racket.

She scanned the room and found her mother already seated at one of the tables, holding a cup of what she reckoned held coffee. Coffee would be next on her list of things to do, as soon as she changed into dry clothes. She relaxed some when she saw familiar folks from the camp. At least there were other survivors.

"I'll show you to the clothes closet first so you can get into some dry clothes." The pastor led them to one of the small rooms on the side and opened the door.

"You're welcome to whatever you can find. When you're ready to change, there are some rooms on either side of the kitchen, one for the ladies and one for the men. There are also some towels and hangers in there so you can hang up your wet clothes to dry. Please feel free to take whatever you need. That's why it's here."

As the pastor left them alone, they stood staring at row after row of clothing, neatly arranged for men, women, and children.

"I don't know about y'all, but I'm really anxious to get out of these wet things and into something dry." Sarah walked over to the first rack, searching for something appropriate for her mother and herself.

"You bet." Pat walked over to the children's section. "My skin's all wrinkled up from the rain. I look like a bleached-out prune. Come over here, kids. Let's see what we can find. There's boxes of undies here—and some diapers."

They gathered up complete changes of clothes, including skivvies. Pat rushed off with her kids all in tow as Sarah stopped by to collect her mother.

"D'ya think you can make it to the changing room over there to put on these dry clothes?" She could tell by the look in her eyes Mother neared exhaustion. But she needed to get her out of those wet clothes and get her settled with some grub.

"I'll try. Can you hand me my cane?"

After considerable effort on both their parts, they sported fresh clothes much fancier than any of their homemade items now lost to the flood. Sarah checked herself in a mirror on the back of the door. A smile pulled at the corners of her mouth as she raised her shoulders higher. Her fingers worked through her wet hair, straightened by the rain, as it hung almost to her waist. She sighed and gave up on making it presentable. "I sure wish I brought a comb. This hair's a mess."

"Let's get out of here and sit down again. I'm ready for some food too. The cup of coffee hit the spot, but it made my stomach feel emptier." Her mother grabbed her cane and took Sarah's arm. Pat and the kids followed close behind as they entered the main hall.

"Well, don't you ladies look marvelous." Pastor Bob stood with his hands on his hips and smiled at them.

Coreen and Loretta joined the group. "He's right, Mama. You and Mammaw look right purdy. Where can I get something to wear?"

Loretta touched her on the shoulder. "I'll show you, sweetie. Bob, honey, why don't you show them where to get some food while I take care of Coreen?"

* * *

As Coreen entered the clothes closet, the choices overwhelmed her. She giggled with glee, scrunched her shoulders up, and clapped her hands together. She searched through everything in the ladies' section, fingering each piece, oohing and aahing.

After several minutes, she decided on a pink floral summer dress with ruffles. "How about this one, Miss Loretta?"

"I think it's perfect. There's a box of undies over here too. These should do fine. Now, let me show you where you can change."

Outside the dressing room, Coreen stopped and whispered, "Miss Loretta, I think before I change I should take a little trip to the outhouse."

"We don't have an outhouse. We have indoor restrooms with toilets and running water."

Coreen wrinkled her face. She'd never heard of such a thing.

Loretta smiled at her. "Let me show you."

She followed Loretta into a room marked "Ladies." Coreen's eyes grew wide when she saw her first "in-house." Wallpaper with lavender flowers covered the walls. She touched everything in the room—the walls, the glistening porcelain of the toilet tank, and the soft roll of paper attached to the wall. "This ain't nothing like our outhouse at the camp. Or the one at the school either. At least it had two holes in it. But this is beautiful—and clean."

She ran her fingers gingerly across the fixtures and sniffed a bar of pale-green soap in a dish. A soft green chair sat in the corner of the room. Coreen ran her fingers back and forth across the seat. She'd never felt such a soft fabric before.

Loretta demonstrated the features of flushing and then washing up at the sink with the soap and running water. Coreen smiled when Loretta showed her the paper towels to dry her hands.

"Wow, this is the greatest thing I've ever seen. You don't have to go outside with all those bugs and spiders—and sometimes snakes. And it smells so good in here. You're so lucky."

"I'd say fortunate. But I never realized it before today."

Loretta showed Coreen how to lock the door so no one would accidentally come in on her and then left her alone. Coreen's first flush startled her, but washing her hands and face with warm water and the fancy soap was a luxury she'd never known. She smiled, heaved an energizing sigh, and went to the dressing room.

After she changed into the new dress and hung up her wet clothes, she stood at the mirror and smiled at herself as she moved from side to side, smoothed the sides, and fluffed the ruffles. For the first time in her life, Coreen looked like a lady. She left the room with her head held high and her chin slightly raised.

She walked over to Loretta and did a little twirl. "This is the most beautiful thing I ever wore in my whole life. Thank you, Miss Loretta." She flung her arms around her in a tight squeeze.

"You're welcome. You look pretty special, you know."

"I do? Nobody's ever said I looked special before." For a moment Coreen forgot about her house and all her possessions, few though they were. She even forgot about Daddy. Her entire insides glowed with a warmth she liked.

"Are you ready for some dinner now?"

"You bet. I'm starving to death."

Loretta pointed to an open window stretching across the back wall of the hall. "All you have to do is go up there, and they'll fill your plate for you. The silverware and napkins are at the end, and drinks are on the little table right there."

"Thanks."

Coreen swung her arms as she walked and made the ruffles dance. At the counter, Sheriff Mayhall walked up to her and put his hand on her arm. She looked up at him and smiled, but he didn't smile back. He acted like he didn't even know her.

"Hi, DeWayne." She hoped he would notice how beautiful she looked in her new dress.

"Where's your mama?" DeWayne's coldness made her smile disappear.

She chewed on her bottom lip and looked around the room. Coreen pointed. "She's standing by that table over yonder."

Without saying a word, the sheriff let her arm go and walked across the room. Her chest tightened and goosebumps popped out all over her body. Something didn't feel right. She turned away from the food and watched as DeWayne touched Mama's arm, leaned down, and whispered something into her ear. The color faded away from Mama's face as if she'd seen a ghost. Coreen's body buzzed with an electric charge. Something was terribly wrong.

Mama's knees buckled ever so slightly as she reached for DeWayne's arm. He quickly grabbed onto her arms, set her down into a chair, and got on one knee in front of her.

The room grew misty and silent as some force drew Coreen like a magnet across the room. She threw herself at Mama's feet. "Mama? What's wrong? Please, please, tell me."

With eyes blacker than the night sky at new moon, she stared right through Coreen. "He's dead."

Chapter 8

Sarah stared into the dark nothingness that enveloped her like a shroud. Sleep would not come since the three of them lay down on their makeshift beds. At least the pastor moved their cots into a separate room to give them more privacy. She appreciated being behind a door and away from prying eyes. They probably expected her to cry.

The only tears she planned to shed were tears of joy.

At least in here, she wouldn't feel the judgmental eyes watching her, expecting her to act like the grieving wife. But why couldn't she sleep? Maybe she was too tired. Or maybe because the cot felt more like sleeping on the porch swing.

Every so often the whimper of a child and the soothing hum of a parent's voice wedged their way through the darkness. A group of voices muttered nearby. A man laughed. Then several voices joined the laughter. Were they laughing at her?

The lingering odor of food and coffee made her stomach contract with nausea. She carefully rolled to her side on the narrow cot. Outside the window of the small room, she heard the drip … drip … drip … of rain as her mind raced. Little movies played in her thoughts.

What did DeWayne say? Vernon must've tried to cross deep water. Just like him—stupid man. Didn't have a lick of common sense.

They thought the car got stuck. Did he sit there and wait for the water to trap him? Maybe he dared it to block him. Why else would he stay in the car?

Sarah fluffed the flat pillow and tried to get comfortable. Funny how her old bed came to mind. At least it was comfortable. When he wasn't there.

Darkness closed in on her. Is that what it's like in the mine? Trapped in the dark, no way out, no light. How would she find her way out? Would she ever find the light? She pressed her hands to her chest. Her heart felt like it had been forced through the meat grinder. Raw. Left to rot in the dark.

She didn't have a home. No money. No job. No clothes. Nothing. Except Coreen. The constant reminder of all that's wrong with her life. Sarah turned to her side and hugged the pillow. She got what she wanted—freedom from Vernon. But she had no idea what to do with that freedom.

Be strong. Don't give up. That's what her mother would say. If only she had the freedom to be weak—to fall apart—to give up.

For a moment, in her mind, she became that innocent girl of thirteen with hopes and dreams. A tear escaped her eye and streamed across her face and onto the pillow. She remembered dreams of falling in love. Being a famous singer. Laughing. Living happily ever after. Vernon ripped those dreams into shreds and stomped them into the ground the moment she met him. Were they gone forever? Her body trembled as tears tumbled across her face.

The tears weren't for Vernon.

Maybe she cried for the child Sarah, the tortured and abused Sarah, or the unknown Sarah of tomorrow. Outside the window, the drip … drip … drip … of the rain droned. Was it too late to ever be happy again?

*   *   *

Estelle's muscles screamed in pain as she attempted, in vain, to find a position allowing her to sleep. Even her pain pills seemed to have no effect on the abuse she put herself through today. She needed sleep. Tomorrow would be a challenging day. A lot of challenging days were coming. But her body refused to relax. What could she do? She couldn't sleep on a cot in the church basement forever.

Sarah refused to talk to her about it. Could she be in shock? Maybe she didn't feel anything at all.

Or she's glad he's dead.

The day she got the news of her Jack's death, her whole world crashed around her feet. The fear of surviving with four young'uns terrified her. The worst part was the loss of their deep and pure love.

Not like Sarah and Vernon.

A veil of emptiness washed over Estelle. She still missed him after all these years. Would Sarah and Coreen ever miss Vernon?

Estelle closed her eyes to the darkness and begged God to protect her girls. She also prayed the Lord would draw them to Him and show them He loved them. Her prayer would not be easy to answer. It would be much easier to take care of their physical needs than their spiritual ones. Before saying her amen, Estelle asked for enough relief from the pain to get some sleep.

When she heard Sarah moving around on her cot, she asked for sleep for her baby girl too.

Estelle wiggled around, tightened her muscles, and then relaxed them. She glanced toward the window and thought she could see a star in the sky. The last thing she remembered was the drip … drip … drip … of the rain from the gutter outside the window.

* * *

Coreen absently fingered the ruffles on her new dress as she lay on her bed. The air felt hot and stuffy. With a sigh, she flung the thin blanket off into the oblivion of darkness. Darkness. Her mind wouldn't slow down enough for her to think clearly. She grabbed thoughts at random as they raced past her.

Her daddy's dead. Did that make her an orphan now? Her mama didn't cry a tear. She wouldn't talk to anybody either. She didn't blame her. All those nosy people kept asking questions that weren't any of their business.

Coreen rolled to one side on the cot, careful not to roll off. Her eyes refused to stay shut. Somebody dropped something heavy, and it bounced on the floor in the main room where everybody else slept.

What would they do now? Where would they live? Why didn't she feel anything? She should be crying. Shouldn't she?

Somebody laughed. If only she had something to laugh about—besides her daddy being dead and not able to do what he said he planned to do. Funny how she didn't feel like laughing about it right now. At least he couldn't hurt her anymore. Did that make her bad? Was this her fault because of the prayer she prayed before the rains?

Did God hate her now?

She blew out a breath and smacked her hands on the cot. Daddy deserved it. He was mean and evil. He deserved dying. Didn't he?

Coreen flopped over on the cot. She wished it would cool off. Another baby cried somewhere. Why didn't somebody make that baby hush up? At least she was safe now. She shuddered. Not even her mama knew what he'd done—or promised to do.

Would Mama even care?

She raised up on her elbows and peered into the darkness. Could haints come into a church? If only Patches could be with her.

Out of sheer exhaustion, and for the first night since Coreen could remember, she closed her eyes and slept without shedding a single tear. The last thing she remembered was the drip … drip … drip … of the rainwater outside the window.

Chapter 9

Coreen opened her eyes to blinding rays of sunshine coming through the window. She jumped off the cot and squealed with delight, causing Mama and Mammaw to jolt from their night of restless sleep.

"What's wrong with you, girl?"

"The sun's shining, Mama! Look, ain't it beautiful? It's stopped raining." She squealed again. "I need to check on Patches. But I think I need to go to the in-house first."

"In-house?" Mammaw stirred.

"Yeah. Instead of an outhouse, they got an in-house."

"Lordy, girl. It's called a bathroom, not an in-house." Mammaw grunted and the wrinkles on her face tightened as she wiggled her feet off the side of the cot. "I bet I'm a mess after all the tossing and turning I did last night. I'm gonna need some help getting up from here. Can you girls help me?"

With a bit of grunting of their own, they heaved her off the cot and helped her stand until she got her bearings.

"My body ain't cooperating this morning. I feel like I been dragged down the railroad track, bumping every single tie, by a big ole black bear, and left for dead."

"It's no wonder, Mother. You climbed a mountain, walked in a downpour for pert' near two mile. What d'ya expect?"

"I think you're pretty amazing, Mammaw. I'm proud of you."

"Bless your little heart." She gave Coreen's cheek a couple of pats. "My body's not so proud of me. It's complaining big time. Where's my handbag? I need to take my medicine so I can at least walk to the bathroom today."

"Here it is, Mammaw."

As she reached out for the bag, Mammaw squinted at a ray of sunlight. "What a beautiful morning it is out there. Look at that sunshine. The fog's still laying on the mountains, but the sun shore is peeking through. At least it'll be a little easier for you to tend to details today." She picked up her cane and turned to Mama. "Have you decided what you're gonna do about it?"

Mama turned away and straightened the blanket on her cot. "I ain't thought it through. I guess the first thing is to call the mine and see if there's any death insurance. If not, I don't know what I'll do." She turned back to Mammaw. "What did you do, Mother?"

"I was lucky. Your daddy spent time in the military and became a member of the Lodge. If not for them to depend on, we wouldn't a made it. Y'all woulda ended up in the orphanage."

"The only thing Vernon joined was the VFW when they met up to drink and play poker. He never did a blasted thing smart."

"Orphanage?" Coreen's heart jumped in her chest as she stared at Mammaw and then Mama. "You mean you might send me to an orphanage?" Her voice cracked.

"Mercy sakes, no, Coreen." Mammaw patted Coreen on the arm. "You ain't going to no orphanage. I'll make sure of it. None of my family's going nowhere. The good Lord will provide a way. You wait and see, both of you. You're both strong and you will survive this." She put her hands on her hips and dipped her chin.

Coreen hoped she could trust her.

"No house, no husband, no job … Yeah, looks like I'm doing great. Come on, Mother, let's get out there so you can take your medicine and have some breakfast. I think I smell bacon cooking."

"It always tastes better when somebody else cooks it for you—and then cleans up."

"Bacon? Yummy." But even bacon couldn't distract Coreen's thoughts completely. What would they do without any money? Seemed she jumped from one awful life to another one.

"After you go to the bathroom, you eat something before you go see that dog, you hear me? There might not be none left if you wait."

"Yes, ma'am." At the overwhelming aroma of bacon, her stomach growled in anticipation. She bolted out the door, through a buzzing mass of disheveled families, making sure not to run into anybody along the way, and burst into the bathroom, only to find a girl about her age standing at the sink, washing her hands.

Coreen gasped. "Sorry. I didn't know nobody was in here. I'll wait outside."

"I'm almost done. Come on in." The girl spoke with a slight drawl, softer and prettier than Coreen's own. "I guess I should have locked the door."

As Coreen waited for the girl to leave, she studied her intently. Her long, straight dark-brown hair glistened with strands of gold as the sunlight from the window bounced around the small room. Her dress looked store-bought, and her shoes matched the dress. She noticed the bright-pink polish on her fingernails. This girl definitely did not come from the mining camp. Coreen tried to straighten out the wrinkles in her new dress and hid her gnawed nails behind her back.

"You know, you're wearing my sister's dress."

"What?" Coreen looked down at the dress and then at the girl. "No, I got it from … the … room down there. I didn't steal it."

"No, no. I meant it used to be my sister's dress. She outgrew it and my mom brought it to the clothes closet, since none of my sister's clothes fit me."

"I see."

"Actually, I think it looks better on you than it did on her."

"Thanks." Coreen smiled at the girl. Not sure what to say, she clasped her hands and glanced around the room.

"I'm Betty Anne." She hesitated, then blurted out, "My mom's helping fix your breakfast this morning. Lord knows why—she's a terrible cook. But she's always trying to do things for other people and make herself look good." She stopped talking and took a deep breath. Then smiled.

"I'm Coreen. We got flooded yesterday. And … and my daddy … drowned in the river." Coreen fingered the ruffles on her dress.

"How awful." Betty Anne blinked and frowned.

Coreen swallowed hard.

"Are you all alone now?"

"No." Coreen shook her head. "Mama's here—and Mammaw. But our house is gone—and everything in it. That's why I'm wearing your sister's dress." She spread out the skirt and grinned. What a dumb thing to do. The skirt dropped back into place.

"Well, it's not her dress anymore, it's yours. My mom's gonna wonder where in the world I've gotten to. I'm supposed to be helping her in the kitchen now. Maybe I'll see you again later. Bye, Coreen." Betty Anne waved as she opened the door.

"Bye, Betty Anne." Coreen waved back.

"And don't forget to lock the door," Betty Anne said with a giggle as she rushed out to the kitchen.

* * *

The line at the kitchen window, long and slow as mothers dragged screaming, hungry children through, took too long. Coreen's stomach complained loudly. As she watched the kitchen workers, happily going about the task of preparing the food and serving it to the people with smiles and kind words, she saw Betty

Anne carrying oversized cans of peaches to a lady with dark hair who must be her mother. Catching Betty Anne's attention, Coreen waved and smiled.

"Hi, Betty Anne. I remembered to lock the door." As soon as she spoke the words, she felt silly.

"Good." Betty Anne gave her the "okay" sign.

Her mother whispered loud enough for Coreen to hear, "Who's the girl, Betty Anne?"

Coreen pretended not to listen to them talking as she slowly moved toward the bacon.

"Coreen. Her dad died in the flood yesterday."

Coreen picked at the food to delay moving along, but glanced at the pair a couple of times.

"I heard about him. How in the world do you know her?"

"I met her in the restroom."

Just as Coreen glanced at them again, Betty Anne's mother stared at her. With warm cheeks, Coreen looked down at her tray like she didn't notice. But she did notice the peaches she dripped on the table.

"I see she's wearing your sister's old dress, and it fits her perfectly. Do you think I should bring her more of Farrah's old clothes?"

"Probably. They lost everything in the flood. Even their house."

"I'll go through Farrah's things tonight and see what I can find." Betty Anne's mother waved the spoon in the air and dripped peach juice down her arm.

Coreen tried not to giggle. Especially since she planned to give her more beautiful clothes.

"I imagine she's not wearing any shoes either. Here, Betty Anne, help me carry these peaches over to the window." She grabbed a towel and wiped the peach juice off her arm. "Think you can find out what size shoes she wears?"

Coreen hurried to the end of the line before Betty Anne and her mother could approach. Would she really bring her more clothes? Beautiful new clothes. How wonderful it would be. She sighed as she pictured herself in dresses like city girls wear. Like the girls in her books must wear. Normal girls.

She settled at a table by herself, keeping an eye out for Mama and Mammaw as she crammed the first slice of bacon into her mouth, barely taking time to swallow. Glorious. The second slice joined a bite of eggs and some grits. This food tasted so much better than the bowl of soggy cereal she usually ate. Then she bit into the most fabulous yeast roll she'd ever eaten. She stopped and breathed in the amazing fragrance. With her eyes closed and sighs between bites, she savored every chew. Although still hungry, she put aside a portion of her breakfast into her napkin for Patches. When her plate was empty as it could be without licking it, she carried the tray to the area marked "Tray Return" and turned to head outside.

Betty Anne popped out of the kitchen door. "Hello again, Coreen. Where're you going in such a rush?"

Coreen glanced over her shoulder and whispered. "I'm taking some breakfast to my dog, Patches."

"Dog? You have a dog here?"

"Yep, he's at the pastor's house."

"May I come with you?"

Coreen's mouth dropped open, but she snapped it shut quickly. "Sure. If you want to."

"Wait a minute. I'd better tell my mom first so she can find me if she needs me."

Betty Anne disappeared into the kitchen and returned a moment later with a plate heaped with bacon, sausage, and eggs. "Okay, let's go. I brought some extra food for your dog."

"Patches'll love meeting you."

The girls threw open the back door and ran across the churchyard to the pastor's house. Rays of sunshine forced their way through weak spots in the fog.

Coreen shaded her eyes. "The sun's so bright I can't hardly see where I'm going."

Patches greeted them by dancing on his hind legs and yelping with glee.

"I'm so glad to see you too. Get down, boy, so we can get in the gate." Coreen giggled as she danced around in a circle and held the food up higher. "Wait a minute, wait a minute. I'll give you your breakfast if you'll stop jumping on me." Coreen laughed as Patches took turns jumping on the girls to reach the source of the smells.

Patches jumped on Betty Anne's legs and she stumbled back. "Help! Your dog's going to knock me down."

"He's hungry. If you put the plate down on the ground, he'll stop jumping on you."

The girls placed their gifts on the grass and he attacked, practically inhaling the food.

Betty Anne laughed and clapped her hands as they watched. "He's so funny. I've never seen a dog eat like that before. What kind is he, anyway?"

"He's a Mountain Feist, a squirrel-hunting dog. My daddy takes him hunting." Coreen suddenly stopped. "I mean, Daddy used to take him hunting. I guess Patches won't be going no more." Coreen bit her bottom lip and tears glazed over her eyes. "Poor little guy. He loves chasing them squirrels more than anything in life." Her heart ached more about Patches not getting to hunt than it did about Daddy dying.

"Is it okay to pet him?"

"Sure. Let's sit down on the steps here. It'll be easier for you since he's kinda short and the grass is still wet. Come on, Patches."

The dog bounded over to the girls and smothered each with grateful doggy kisses. One big swipe covered Betty Anne's face.

"Yuck, he licked my mouth. Get him off!"

"Those are kisses. Don't your dog give you kisses?"

"I don't have a dog. My parents think they're too much trouble. Of course, if my sister wanted a dog, I'm sure she would have gotten one."

"Don't you like your sister?"

Betty Anne crossed her arms across her chest and leaned forward. "She's too perfect—and my parents think I should be perfect too." Her head shook from side to side, followed by a sigh. "She looks perfect, not like me. My parents think I should be skinny like she is. And she makes perfect grades and has perfect friends." She grumbled, "Everybody *loves* her."

"I always wanted a sister. I thought it'd be fun to have somebody to spend time with and talk about stuff." Coreen scratched Patches' ears.

"Well, believe me, that's not how it is. I wish I'd been an only child—maybe my parents wouldn't think I'm such a failure then." She sucked in her bottom lip and lowered her head.

"You ain't a failure. I think you're really nice and beautiful, and I like you a lot. And so what if you ain't perfect. Nobody is. I sure ain't perfect. Actually, I'm about as far from perfect as you can get." Coreen stuck her hands on her hips and nodded.

"Coreen, I think you're wonderful." She smiled.

"No, I ain't—at least that's what my parents always tell me. I'll never amount to much of nothing. Guess I'll always live in a mining camp and be a nobody."

Betty Anne leaned over and gave Patches a scratch. "What's it like to live in the mining camp?"

"Wha' ya mean?"

"What was your house like? What TV shows do you like? Do you take bubble baths? Do you have any hobbies?"

Coreen wrinkled her brow and answered the first question. The rest didn't have answers. "Well, our house had four rooms."

"Only four? What were they?"

"A living room with a pot-bellied stove in the middle, a dining room—that's where I slept—a kitchen, and Mama and Daddy's room."

Betty Anne held up a finger. "And the bathroom."

"We didn't have no bathroom." She chuckled. Imagine a bathroom in their house. "We used an outhouse. There weren't no water either."

Betty Anne opened her mouth and her eyes got big. "How'd you take a bath?"

She lifted her shoulders. "We pumped water, heated it on the coal stove, and poured it into a big metal tub in the kitchen."

Betty Anne cocked her head. "I don't think I could live without an indoor bathroom—and bubble baths. I love bubble baths."

"I never really thought about it. You got what ya got. What kinda house you live in?"

"I live in a yellow brick house in Mt. Pleasant. It has two stories—three if you count the basement. I don't like the basement. It's really creepy down there. But I like my room. It's pink and I have a ruffled purple bedspread and curtains. I spend a lot of time in there—mostly to stay away from my sister. I have my own bathroom—where I take lots of bubble baths—and a big closet for my clothes and stuff."

"Wow." It would be glorious to live in a house with a bathroom—let alone her own private bedroom with its own bathroom.

"What are your mama and daddy like, Betty Anne?"

"I guess they're okay. My dad's rarely home. He's manager of the Bank of Mt. Pleasant and works all the time."

"What's a manager?"

"He's the boss."

"What about your mom?"

"She spends her days doing things for other people."

"Wha'd she do for 'em? Clean houses or something?"

"Heavens, no." Betty Anne reared back and laughed out loud. "She mostly throws big parties to raise money for different causes like cancer, education, hunger, and church stuff. She'll probably throw a big party to raise money for the people who lost their homes in the flood—like you."

"It's really a nice thing for her to do. She sounds like a great mama."

Betty Anne pulled the neck of her shirt to her mouth and looked at the sky. "I guess so. I wish she cared as much for me as she does everybody else." With a smack to her thighs, she leaned forward. "What TV shows do you watch?"

"TV shows? I ain't never watched a TV. I did see one at the hardware store once."

"You don't have a TV? What do you do for fun?"

What did she do for fun? She sucked her lips in and put her fist under her chin. Fun things weren't a regular part of her life. "I swing on the front porch and read books mostly." Her hand moved to her head and she tapped her fingers on her hair. "I write songs. I want to sing at the Grand Ole Opry someday and get out of this place." She hung her head. Who was she to think she could sing at the Grand Ole Opry? "I play with Patches a lot."

Patches, hearing his name, raised his head and looked at Coreen, anticipating playtime. When no one stood up, he lowered his head again, and the girls continued to caress his fur.

"How old are you, Coreen?"

"I'm twelve." No, she wasn't. "Silly me. I'm not twelve. I'm thirteen."

"How could you forget a thing like that?"

Coreen looked down at her bare toes, wiggling in the drying grass. How could she forget? Especially after what her daddy promised. "My birthday was yesterday."

"What an awful day for a special birthday." Betty Anne patted Coreen's hand.

"Yeah, and what's even worse … nobody remembered." Nobody but Daddy. "Nobody wished me a happy birthday either … nobody gave me a present or even baked me a cake …"

Betty Anne threw her arms around Coreen. "I'm so sorry. I'm sure they didn't hurt you on purpose. Nobody could hurt you—you're too sweet."

The words acted like a key to a locked room filled with secret pain. When the door opened, nothing could stop the flood of tears and sobs. She couldn't stop crying if she tried. Like when the flood waters overflowed the riverbanks.

Betty Anne's hands loosened. Coreen tried to stop crying but couldn't. Then Betty Anne squeezed her even tighter and held on until the tears ran out.

Coreen sniffed and wiped her face on the inside of her skirt tail. She stared at the grass. "Sorry I cried."

"Coreen, it's okay to cry. Look what you've been through. I cry all the time, and nothing so awful ever happened to me."

"Yesterday wasn't the worst day of my life though. Almost all the days are my worst."

"What do you mean?"

Coreen wiped more tears off her cheeks and sighed from what felt like her toes. "My daddy weren't a nice man. He hurt us a lot."

"Oh." Betty Anne blinked her eyes and put her hand over her lips.

Coreen wanted to tell her new friend the deep dark secret she held hidden. If she didn't tell somebody, she thought she might explode. As she opened her mouth to speak, the beep of a car horn and a yodeling voice caused Patches to leap from the porch steps and run, barking, toward the gate.

"Betty Anne! Yoo-hoo, we have to get to your piano lesson. Hurry up." Betty Anne's mom waved her over.

"I forgot I have my piano lesson today. I've got to go, Coreen. I'll talk to you later, okay?"

"Yeah. And thanks for being my friend today." Coreen looked up at her, only managing a crooked partial smile. The secret would stay a secret for now.

Betty Anne leaned down to give Coreen one last hug. "Happy birthday, teenager." She smiled and rushed across the yard. At the gate, she patted the dog one last time. "Bye, Patches."

After the excitement died down, Patches returned to the steps and sat down beside his friend. Coreen held him close and kissed his head. "I got some news, boy. Daddy died yesterday. That means you ain't going hunting no more. Sorry."

Coreen glanced around the green yard and then at the cotton-ball clouds drifting across a blue sky. Nothing. She didn't feel nothing.

"I know I oughta be sad, Patches ... but I don't feel nothing at all. I do feel a little bad I prayed and wanted him dead. What if it's all my fault? I ain't sad he's gone, but I feel bad that I don't feel bad. Ain't I an awful person?"

Patches whined, gave a little soft bark, and took one paw and laid it on Coreen's lap. As she leaned down to him, Patches gave her a big doggy kiss. Coreen smiled and held her friend under the chest and rubbed her cheek against his fur, breathing in the doggy aroma, warmed by the sun, as if he wore an expensive perfume.

"I wonder what'll happen to us now, little Patches."

Chapter 10

Sarah paced behind the pastor's desk. Her heart thumped so loudly she could hear it in her ears. She stared at the phone, reached out for it, and then stopped midair. She whirled away and glanced at the bookcases lining the office. So many books—books of different sizes and colors. All about stupid religion. Among the books were photographs, crosses, and a gold-trimmed diploma from the School of Divinity.

She emptied her lungs with a long blast of air and turned back to the desk. The phone sat there like a beacon of doom, taunting her. Next to the phone rested a stack of books, jagged strips of paper peeking out from the pages.

"You're being stupid, Sarah. Get it over with," she said out loud to nobody and reached out her hand. The hand stopped before reaching the phone, suspended. She raised her eyes and stared straight ahead at a large picture on the wall. A ship being tossed around in a storm. The sailors fought to control the sails as torrential rains pelted them and huge waves crashed over the sides of the boat. The fear on the sailors' faces made her throat tighten. She read from the bottom of the picture, *Cast your burdens on the Lord and He will protect you.*

Sarah turned away with a snarl. God never protected her from anything, and He sure wouldn't help her now. The only one she could trust to save her was herself.

She grabbed the phone and dialed the number.

"Hello, Shell residence."

Sarah inhaled deeply. "Della, it's Sarah."

"What the hell are you calling about? I'm watching my show," snapped Della, the demon mother-in-law.

"I'm sorry to intrude on your life ... but I got some bad news."

"It better be bad with you a calling me right in the middle of the most exciting scene in weeks. Well ... what is it?"

Sarah's heart hammered in her chest and her body tingled. "Della, the flood totally destroyed our house and—"

"Well, don't expect me to invite you to come live with us. I ain't got enough room for you and your snotty-nosed brat. So put that idea right out of your head."

Her voice became almost a whisper. Her eyelids closed to block out the world. "That ain't why I'm calling, Della. Please ... listen." She clinched her teeth.

"You sure got the nerve telling me to shut up, you tramp."

Sarah gathered all her strength and whispered calmly, "Della, Vernon's dead."

"What'd you say?"

"I said, Vernon ... is dead."

Della screamed. Sarah winced and held the phone away from her ear.

"What happened? You killed my baby!" Shouts and wails erupted over the phone.

"No, I didn't kill him." Thoughts of throttling her mother-in-law entered her mind though. "They think he got caught up in the flood waters on his way home from the mine and drowned."

The other end of the line erupted. "God above, not my baby. Otis, my baby's dead. She's done killed him to death."

Sarah gently pressed the receiver with her finger, silencing the outburst. A sense of cold numbness overwhelmed her. The room went dark. She closed her eyes and wanted to disappear from this life of hell, a life with no hope of ever being happy or protected.

When she opened her eyes, the picture loomed in front of her again. She couldn't take her eyes off it. She noticed something she didn't see before. In the corner, above the darkest clouds, a bright spot, a tiny dot with a ray of light, spread down through the clouds.

She lifted her finger from the button and dialed Red Diamond Mines. "Hello, Edith. It's Sarah Shell."

"Honey, I'm so sorry about Vernon. I don't know how you're surviving. I mean, losing your house and your husband in one day and all. I think I'd go crazy. Is your mama okay, honey? And Coreen, bless her little heart, losing her daddy and all. I bet this is awful for her."

Did Edith ever take a breath? Sarah leaned on the desk and waited.

"What ya gonna do? I can't imagine. But I'm rambling on here, honey. Now, I'm sure you called for a reason. How can I help you? Although, I can't think of a thing I could do to help you at all. Bless your heart."

Sarah's head ached. She wanted to throw the phone across the room and run screaming. Instead, she took in a deep breath and calmed her internal storm. "Edith, I gotta ask a question, okay? I need to know if his file shows whether he got any insurance at all. I know y'all keep a list of them things—in case."

Edith quieted. "Well, I don't know. Let me check to make sure. Hold on a minute, hon. I'll be right back."

After what seemed an eternity, Edith spoke softly into the phone. "Sweetie, I'm afraid there ain't a thing in his file about no insurance plan."

"You mean there ain't nothing listed for his burial either?" Sarah's throat tightened and her ears rang.

"I'm afraid not, honey. I … I don't know what to tell you. I ain't got no good news for you at all today. I'm sorry, Sarah, I really am. We always tell our men they need to have something to protect their families. But—"

"It's okay, Edith. Ain't your fault. Thanks for looking." Sarah lowered the phone to its cradle and stared at the painting. For a moment, she saw herself in the waters, washed over by waves and sea monsters circling her.

"What do I do now?" Tears welled up, ready to rush like waves.

Sarah blew out a couple of breaths, wiped her eyes, and put on the composure of self-control as if it were an old dress. She could only count on herself, and that's exactly what she planned to do.

She opened the door to the office and found Pastor Turlington standing directly in front of her. With a yelp, she jumped backward.

"I'm sorry, Sarah. I didn't mean to startle you."

Sarah managed a smile. "It's okay. I ain't hurt or nothing."

"I'm sorry for your loss, and if there's anything—anything at all—I can do to make this a little easier for you, please let me know."

"Thank you, Pastor. I appreciate your offer, but I'm fine. And thank you for all you've done for my family."

"Could I offer you a ride over to the funeral home? It would be no trouble at all."

"No, no. I think I could do with the walk, if you don't mind."

"Of course. I understand."

* * *

Coreen hummed as she walked down the darkened hallway in the back of the church. She approached a door with a sign that read "Pastor's Study" and heard a voice through the open door.

"Ed, I know this is a lot to ask, but it's a special situation. This poor family has lost everything. They don't have a single penny."

Coreen stood still and tried not to make a sound.

"Yes, I know the fund is generally used for church family … but Ed, remember what the Bible says about taking care of widows and orphans … It's our responsibility. What do you think the Lord would say if we didn't do what we could? Uh-huh."

Mama's a widow now. Would be nice for somebody to take care of her. Coreen put her ear closer to the door.

"The Lord will bless you, Ed. It's a wonderful thing you're doing. Thank you. Yeah ... I'll call the funeral home and let them know. She's on her way there right now. Bless you. Good-bye. I'll see you Sunday."

Funeral home? Did somebody else die? Coreen heard a click and then Pastor Bob's voice again.

"Hello, Mr. Prescott, this is Pastor Bob Turlington ... Fine, thank you. And you? Good. There's a young woman coming to see you in a few minutes, and I need to give you some information. The church is going to pay for the funeral for her deceased husband—just a modest package ... Yes, we need to keep it reasonable. It's for Vernon Shell. Her name is Sarah Shell."

Coreen gasped and threw her hand over her mouth.

"Don't tell her who paid for it. Tell her ... anonymous, or something like that ... Yes, that will do. Fine. Just make sure you don't mention the church, okay? Thank you. Ed Scott will cut you the check as soon as we know the total amount due ... Thank you. Good-bye."

Coreen leaned against the wall and wondered how much a funeral cost. She hadn't thought about having to pay to bury him. What had Mama planned to do? They didn't have any money. Her stomach ached. She hadn't thought about money when she wanted him dead.

But Mama wouldn't have to worry about it now. She smiled and the hallway seemed brighter. Some things could go right when she thought they'd all gone wrong. Even things that were her fault.

Pastor Bob flew out of his office and nearly crashed into her. "Coreen! I'm sorry, I ... Did you hear what I said?" He scrunched his eyebrows.

Coreen winced. Caught. "Yeah."

He put his hands on her arms. "I'm going to ask you to do me a great big favor. Please don't tell your mom what you know, okay? I think she'd be happier not knowing."

She screwed up her mouth for a moment and nodded her head. "I think you're probably right. I promise to keep my mouth zipped, no matter how hard it is."

He smiled and patted her on the shoulder. "Thanks. Now, I have to tell Loretta. I'll see you later."

Chapter 11

Estelle wriggled in the metal chair as she sat alone at a table. Her hip burned from sitting too long. How she missed her La-Z-Boy. You never know how good you got it till it's gone. So true.

A smartly dressed lady with lovely silver hair smiled and walked up to her table. "Hello, I'm Imogene Morgan, a member of the church here. I wanted to introduce myself and see if there's anything I can help you with."

"I'm Estelle Kincaid." She started to offer her hand but stopped and opted for a nod of her head instead. "Don't reckon there's a thing I need right now." Estelle lowered her chin and her voice. "Well, 'cept maybe a softer seat. I got a bad hip, and this here metal chair's downright torture."

Imogene gently touched Estelle's shoulder. "I bet you're in awful pain. Those chairs are hard on my old bones, and I don't have a hip problem. Let me see what I can do for ya. I'll be right back, okay?"

Imogene crossed the room and approached the pastor. They talked for a moment and then the pastor smiled and trotted to the back of the room and up the stairs as Imogene came back to the table. "There. Bob's gonna find the perfect thing for you."

"You're a darling." Estelle reached out and touched her arm. "He's done so much for us already. I hate to ask him for more. But my poor old body ain't doing so good with all this abuse I been putting it through. Every bone in my body's complaining, along with every muscle and joint—and I don't blame 'em."

"I know this has got to be awful for you. Did you get water in your house?"

"'Fraid so. I watched the river cover it up."

Imogene leaned toward her and shook her head. "Did you get anything out in time?"

"Some family photos." Estelle whispered, "I didn't even get me no clean step-ins. Ain't it awful?" She hid a chuckle behind her hand.

"You poor dear. I can take care of that problem. You tell me your size, and I'll bring you some myself."

"I can't let you do that."

"No problem at all." Imogene smiled and crossed her arms. "You see, I own

Morgan's Department Store over in Mt. Pleasant, and I can do anything I want to."

The two ladies chuckled together as Bob arrived, breathing heavily, with one of the fancy throne-like chairs from the sanctuary. "Now, how's this for service?"

Estelle placed one hand on her cheek. "It shore 'nuf looks comfy—and heavy. You're a sweetheart, Bob."

"Aw, shucks, ma'am," Bob teased as he arranged the chair. He held onto Estelle's arm as she struggled to get up from the metal chair and take her place on the throne.

"This is heavenly. Bless your pea-pickin' heart." Estelle laughed. "I feel like I'm a queen."

"There's more. I'll be right back with a stool for your royal feet."

"You're even more than a sweetheart." Estelle chuckled even though she couldn't help but feel a tad guilty for putting him out.

As Bob ran out the back door of the church, Imogene filled a tray with coffee, condiments, and a few cookies. She carried it to Estelle's table and set it down. "How would you like to have a nice hot cup of coffee with me?"

"I think it'd hit the spot."

"Good. I've got a few minutes to take a break while the next pots of water come to a boil. I can't believe how much we've gone through already. Thankfully, somebody's supposed to bring some bottled water later today."

Estelle sipped her coffee carefully. It was good—and hot. "You heard anything about how the river's doing?"

"I heard this morning it finally crested and started to drop. There's been a lot of damage. Do you have family here in town?"

"Yeah, I do. They're here too. My daughter and her girl lost their house too. We also lost my son-in-law."

Imogene threw one hand across her chest. "What happened?"

"They think he drove home from work and got caught up in the water on the road. Reckon he couldn't get out and it overtook him."

"How devastating for your family—to lose a loved one like that." Imogene reached over and patted Estelle's hand gently, a tear gathering in her eye.

"Thank you, but they'll fare fine—probably a far bit better than before." Estelle leaned in and whispered, "He weren't a man of character, if you know what I mean." A demon's what he was. She wrinkled her nose. "Didn't treat 'em like ladies—at all."

"Well, Estelle, the good Lord takes care of them what can't take care of themselves."

Estelle stared into her coffee. Sometimes the taking care part ran a long and painful path. "Reckon life ain't meant to be easy though. Even when the good Lord rescues us, we got to bear the scars."

"Hopefully, the scars will fade with time." Imogene patted Estelle's hand. "Lord willing."

Chapter 12

Sarah pushed open the heavy green door of the church and stepped out into bright sunshine. Her newly acquired sandals from the clothes closet clacked on the stones as she made her way down the steps and onto the sidewalk. The scenery gave no indication of the depth of devastation a mere couple of miles in the other direction. She couldn't think of one good moment in her old house. Would her memories always choke her and keep her from being happy?

A slight breeze tousled her hair. She slowed her pace, hoping to find a solution for the funeral. Vernon still held a grip on her life, even in death. How she wished she could walk away and let somebody else worry about how to bury him. Thoughts of burning him in a coal furnace gave her more pleasure than she knew she ought to have. *Guilt.* She shook her head. Why should she feel guilty about the death of the man who destroyed her life? Wasn't this what she wanted all along?

A car horn honked in the street and jarred her out of her reverie. She walked over to the window of Disney's Five and Dime and stared at the displays of mannequins wearing summer dresses, sparkling jewelry, and pumps. The next window sported household wares with a new couch and side tables, lamps, a rug, and knickknacks.

Her heart ached to be normal.

Then she passed Morgan's Fine Clothing, a place she could never afford. Her pace picked up a bit as she passed Mt. Pleasant Music Store and then Saylor's Drugs. At the corner, Sarah turned left and walked one more block, to the only funeral home in town.

The last place she saw Daddy.

At the double doors, she paused to settle in her mind what she would say to the mortician. The cheapest service possible, with burial in the Shell family graveyard, would help. As to how she planned to pay for it, she figured she could plead mercy and ask to make payments, extremely small payments, over time. If her plan didn't work, she would have to come up with a different one.

Cremation seemed a proper alternative. Besides, if hell exists, he'd burn anyway. She might as well give him a head start.

Sarah took a deep breath, raised her chin high, and entered.

A tall man dressed in a dark suit approached her immediately. He seemed well matched for his job, since he gave the impression of an emaciated corpse himself. He stood, hands clasped in front of him. His expression combined sadness and joviality. In a soft voice he asked, "How may I be of assistance, miss?"

Caught off-guard, Sarah stuttered, "Uh … I'm here … because …" She forced herself to get control of her tongue. "You've got my husband." When his eyebrows arched, she continued, "I need your services for my husband. He passed yesterday. I'm Sarah Shell. Wife of Vernon Shell."

"Of course, Mrs. Shell. I've been expecting you. Please, join me in my office so we can discuss this in private."

Sarah couldn't help but wonder who they needed privacy from since there was no one else around—except maybe the dead people. She glanced around the room to make sure that if there were such things as spirits, Vernon wasn't one of them.

The mortician led her into an overly decorated office with massive furniture and poufy curtains. Large vases of fake flowers filled the room. Interesting, considering the entire building reeked of fresh ones.

"Please, have a seat here." He pointed to a tapestry-covered chair that looked like a stuffed pincushion. He sat behind his desk in a chair that seemed to swallow him up. "Do you have an idea of the type of service you would prefer? I have a brochure here with information on all of our packages. We want to make sure the day leaves a sweet memory in your heart, and we will do everything in our power to make you happy. I also have a brochure with our choices in caskets. We have some lovely ones—and if you would like to look at them, some are available to see. I'm sure you want your loved one to spend eternity in a quality resting place."

Sarah's head spun. Her stomach churned. He kept talking, but she couldn't hear a word he said. *Stop it, Sarah. Tell him what you need. Do it.* "I'm sorry, Mr. …" She shook her head. "What's your name?"

"Pardon me. I didn't tell you, did I?" He tittered. "My name is Wilbur Prescott."

"Mr. Prescott. I'm afraid I got … some problems. You see, my husband didn't leave no insurance policy and we lost our house in the flood—and the car. So, I ain't got much. Actually, Mr. Prescott, I ain't got nothing at all. I don't know what to do. I need to get the cheapest burial you got and then pay you for it as I can. I mean, I don't have no job … but I'm planning to get one soon as I can … so I can pay you back. Is it possible? I don't know what else to do." As an afterthought she blurted, "Or we could burn him."

Her chin dropped as she realized how stupid she sounded. And desperate. She slumped into the pincushion chair. Sheer determination held her together. She bit her lip and stared at a vase of ugly orange tulips.

Mr. Prescott lowered his gaze to his desk. Apparently he didn't want to look at the woman making a fool of herself in front of him. She wrapped her fingers around the chair's carved arms until her knuckles turned white.

Mr. Prescott opened a folder, removed a slip of paper, and placed it on the desk. He interlaced his fingers and smiled at her. "I have some good news for you. I have the order for your husband right here, and it is stamped PAID IN FULL. So you don't have to worry about a thing. It's all taken care of."

Sarah wrinkled her brow and shook her head. "What? I don't know what you're talking about. Are you sure you're not looking at somebody else's order? 'Cause ... I didn't order that. I couldn't have. Please, check it again."

"No, right there. It says Vernon Shell. See?" Mr. Prescott, with a little twinkle in his brown eyes, handed her the piece of paper and pointed at the PAID IN FULL on the bottom.

"But, Mr. Prescott, if it's real, who paid for it?" It couldn't be Vernon's parents. Ain't no way they would let her off the hook. She sat up straight and crossed her arms. "It weren't paid by Otis Shell, was it?"

"No, no. That name's nowhere in the file."

"But ... I don't understand." She held up her hands, out of ideas.

"Mrs. Shell." He leaned forward and smiled. "Sarah, apparently an angel unaware has taken care of all this for you. Accept it—and consider yourself blessed. Now, my dear lady, I do have a couple questions for you. Who will be presiding over the service, and where will it be held?"

Sarah stared at nothing. "I ... don't know. Vernon weren't a churchgoer, and we really don't know nobody."

"How about the pastor over at the church where you're staying right now? Bob speaks well on behalf of those without a church affiliation. You can have the service here in our chapel instead of the church."

"I'll ask him and let you know."

"Of course, my dear. Here, let me give you one of my business cards."

Sarah dropped the card, a copy of the order, and a couple of brochures—for a future time—into her pocketbook. After verifying a few details and setting up the times for the viewing and the funeral, she shook Mr. Prescott's surprisingly strong hand and journeyed back to the church.

As soon as she stepped outside, the day took on a totally different hue. She breathed in the mountain air and watched the leaves dance in the summer breeze. As she walked down Main Street, she caught her reflection in the window as lively music flowed from the music store and surrounded her. The Sarah in the reflection smiled. Her pocketbook swung to and fro as her heels clacked on the sidewalk. The tune from the store danced in her mind. She hummed it all the way back to the church.

Chapter 13

Sarah approached her mother, seated in her thronelike chair and chatting with a lady she didn't know. "Mother, you sure look comfy."

"Ain't it wonderful? Bob brought it down for me and even went over to his house to round up a stool for my poor old feet. It's sure more comfortable than that flimsy old chair I's sitting on earlier. 'Course, I got Imogene to thank for getting it all."

Sarah smiled and nodded to her mother's friend. Mother's eyes got big and blinked at her. Did she think she couldn't be nice to people?

"I'm Imogene Morgan. I've been having a lovely chat with your mother here. I want to tell you how sorry I am for your loss."

"Thank you. I'm Sarah." She offered her hand and the lady shook it. Sarah smiled again and turned to her mother. "I really need to talk to you about a few things when you have time."

"Don't mind me. I need to get over and open up the store. I enjoyed chatting with you, Estelle." Imogene stood and turned to Sarah. "I'm glad to meet you too, Sarah. See ya both later." She waved good-bye.

As Imogene left, Mother directed her to sit down and reached over to pat her hand. "Well, Sarah, how'd things go? You're acting like it went fairly well."

Sarah sighed as she leaned in to Mother. "I talked to the mine this morning and found out Vernon didn't have no insurance at all. I can't believe it. What was he thinking?"

"That man never did have a lick of sense. Wha'ya gonna do? Maybe they shoulda let the river keep him. It would've took care of the problem."

"I thought the same thing. Why should it have to be my problem?" Sarah waved her hand across her face. "But that'd be too easy, I guess." She flopped back in the chair and blew out some air. "I'm realizing when he was alive, at least I had me a place to live and food to eat."

"I guess everything has an upside. What ya gonna do about the funeral? How in the world you gonna pay for it? I got a little bit of money saved up."

Sarah held up her hands, trying to get her mother to stop talking. "Mother, if you'd hush, I'll tell ya. I don't need no money. When I got to the funeral home, they told me somebody already paid for it."

"What? Already paid for it?" Mother put her hands over her mouth and blinked. "Who?"

Sarah screwed up her mouth. "I don't know. He said there ain't no record of it, but I think he lied to me. I think somebody paid it and told him not to tell me."

"Who in the world could it be?"

"I ain't got no clue." Sarah threw her hands up. "I don't know nobody who's got money they can throw away on a ne'er-do-well like Vernon."

"Do you know when it's gonna be?"

"Yeah, the viewing's tomorrow at ten o'clock and the funeral's at eleven."

"That's pretty quick."

Sarah leaned back in her chair. "Thank goodness. I want this over with. I dread being there with his parents though. Especially Della, the mother-in-law from hell."

"I can't believe them snakes haven't bit 'em both dead from all their meanness." Mother smacked the table with her hand. "You tough it out through this funeral, and you won't never have to see 'em no more. Right?"

Heat on the back of Sarah's neck brought out perspiration. A little longer. Could she survive a scene with Della? She smacked the table too. Yes. Yes, she would survive it. "Right. If I can keep my mouth shut."

"For your sake and Coreen's, you'd better."

Before Mother went off on telling her what a rotten mother she was, Sarah rose from her chair. "I got a lot to do." She took a few steps and turned. "I realized something. What am I gonna wear? I can't wear this." She looked down at the soft green dress she found in the clothes closet.

"It's all taken care of. Imogene's gonna take us shopping."

"Shopping? What you mean?" She stuck her hands on her hips. "I ain't got no money to buy nothing."

"We don't need no money." Mother held out her hands and grinned. "Imogene owns Morgan's Fine Clothing, and she said she can do anything she wants—and she wants to make sure we got something decent to wear to the funeral. Ain't that the berries? She'll take us over there at five o'clock today, right after the store closes, so we can have the place all to ourself."

Sarah blew out a puff of air. She wanted to say no to the offer, but she didn't have any other choice. "Okay, I give in. I guess we're going shopping."

"Shopping?" Coreen bounced up to the table in time to hear the news. "Are we going to a commissary? What we gonna get?" She danced around, clapping her hands and making a scene.

"Calm down, Coreen. We're gonna get something to wear to the funeral. That's all. We need something dark and solid—not like the dress you're wearing."

Coreen's face drooped and her lips pooched. "Shucks, I thought it was gonna be something fun." She looked at her mammaw for support. "Wow. I like your chair, Mammaw."

"It's pretty comfy, girl. Where you been all morning?"

"My new friend, Betty Anne, and me took some breakfast to Patches and then we sat and talked a while. She's real nice. I like her."

Sarah knew Coreen would make a fool of herself. No rich city girl could be friends with a mining-camp nobody. She'd find out soon enough. She started to say so, but she glanced at her mother and saw her eyes boring a hole through her. Like her mother could read her mind. She stopped and then looked at Coreen. "I'm glad you've found a friend, Coreen. Make sure you don't make a nuisance of yourself, you hear?"

"I won't, Mama." Coreen rolled her eyes.

"I almost forgot, Sarah. The Red Cross is coming this afternoon to talk to everybody about ways they can help us. They're bringing a nurse to give everybody a tetanus shot because of all the germs in the water."

"I hate shots." Coreen hugged both arms and looked like she would cry.

Why couldn't the child just calm down and deal with it? She shook her head. Maybe she reacted the same way about Della-the-mother-in-law-from-hell. And the problem of paying for the funeral. Her shoulders relaxed. "Coreen, looks like lunch is ready. Go get Mammaw's plate. I got things to do."

"Lunch? Hot diggity."

Sarah grinned as she headed to Pastor Bob's office.

* * *

Hungry people walked to the window, corralling their children along the way. Coreen, although still distracted by the thought of having to get a shot, followed her nose to the glorious smell of homemade yeast rolls. Those rolls must be the best things she'd ever eaten in her whole life. Living solely on those rolls crossed her mind, until she saw the fried chicken. Then she saw the mashed potatoes.

After filling plates for Mammaw and herself, she headed to the table. The Doepels were sitting at her table. She stopped short and nearly toppled a glass. The Doepels were the bullies in the camp. Daddy had threatened to shoot their oldest son, Clyde, if he ever laid hands on Coreen. She looked down at her food and pretended they weren't at the table.

"I's sorry to hear about Vernon, Estelle. How's Sarah holding up?" Dirt stained the edges of Brenda Sue's scrawny fingernails. They must not know about soap. She could use a brush for her hair too.

"Making do."

Jimmy muttered, "Yeah, guess this is one of them things even duct tape can't fix." He guffawed and slapped his knee at his own joke.

Coreen snarled and stuffed a roll into her mouth. He must be as dirty on the inside as on the outside. She looked at her plate to keep from staring at the coal dust trapped in every wrinkle and crevasse. Especially his nose. She glanced at Mammaw and scooted her chair a bit closer. Clyde and Willard, his brother, sat across from each other at the end of the table. Their hair stuck up all over like a frayed rope. From the looks of them, they hadn't had a bath in a couple of months. They stunk too.

Mammaw's eyes narrowed like a snake's as she said, "Have you found a new place yet?"

"Yeah, they's a couple of places up at LeHigh. We's going up there this afternoon to check 'em out. How 'bout y'all? Found anything yet?"

"No, not yet. Not much of a chance with all the arrangements and such."

Jimmy stuffed his mouth full of food and tried to talk around it. "Well, I wouldn't worry 'bout it none. I reckon you'll find something." He swallowed, drank the whole glass of iced tea, and belched so loudly everybody in the room could hear him. "'Course, you can't move into a mining camp now Vernon's dead. Not unless Sarah wants to climb into the mine with us boys. I'm sure she could find a miner to take Vernon's place real quick." Jimmy's laugh made Coreen shudder. If only he'd choke on his chicken leg.

Coreen watched Mammaw stare at her fork as she stabbed at her food, moving it around on the plate.

The chatter quieted down as they avoided eye contact with the Doepels and concentrated on their forks. Even Jimmy kept quiet as he stuffed mashed potatoes into his mouth.

Coreen wouldn't miss the Doepels at all. Nope, not a bit.

Chapter 14

Sarah stood in front of the door to the pastor's study. She pulled back her shoulders and tapped. After a few seconds, the door opened. "Hello, Sarah."

Bob had a strange expression she couldn't figure out. His eyes blinked and his mouth hung open. Had she interrupted something? Maybe she should leave. He chuckled and looked at his feet. "Come on in. You need the phone?"

"I's hoping to ask you about something. Is it a bad time?"

"No." He stared a few seconds, smiled, and opened his door. "Come in. Have a seat."

Sarah watched him walk to his chair and sit.

He tapped his fingers on the desk and then crossed his arms. He looked like a child who had stolen a cookie. "I hope you and your family are finding what you need here. I wish we could provide better accommodations for your mother. It must be difficult for her."

"We're doing fine ... considering. I appreciate all you done for us."

Bob kept fiddling with a pen on his desk. Sarah thought he looked like Coreen when she did something she shouldn't do and got caught. Why was he acting so funny? Did he hear about what Vernon did to her fourteen years ago—or some other gossip? Maybe Della called him.

"My mother's a tough lady, but this has been hard on her. She's real thankful for the soft chair you brought down for her. It's helped a lot." Sarah wanted to make him feel appreciated before she asked for her big favor.

"I'm glad I could help."

Sarah shifted in the chair. *Get on with it, girl.* "Bob, I need your help with something."

He reached up and scratched the back of his neck. "Of course. What do you need?"

"Well, Vernon and I didn't know no preachers. His family's all holy rollers, and he kinda got turned off to the whole church thing and ..."

"Of course, I understand."

"Well, you probably don't really, but it don't matter. The problem is ... I need somebody to say a few words for his funeral, and since he weren't a church-going man, I guess ..."

"I do understand, Sarah. You need someone who can say a few words for somebody who isn't expected to be in heaven right now. Right?"

Sarah smiled as her body melted into her chair. "Yeah, you hit it right on the nail head."

"No problem. I've done more of those than you'd probably imagine. I have something appropriate."

"Thanks. I ain't had much practice at doing a funeral. I went to my daddy's over twenty years ago."

"I imagine you were a very little girl."

Sarah smiled again, the stress flowing from her body. "Thanks ... for agreeing to do the funeral—and for the compliment."

"You're welcome. I wondered if you need to call any family members and let them know. If you do, feel free to use the phone."

"I have two brothers, but they're in the service and on a ship somewhere. My sister, Shirley, lives in Cincinnati. I might call her later. I don't want her to think she has to drive down here in this mess. But thank you."

"If there's anything else I can do to help, please understand nothing gives me more pleasure than to be helpful."

"I ain't never known nobody like you and Loretta before. You're ... special."

Bob smiled and leaned back in his chair. He seemed a lot more relaxed than when she first got there. What made him nervous, anyway? She couldn't imagine.

Sarah walked to the door and turned back. "There's one thing I meant to ask. D'ya think it'd be okay to pick out something from the clothes closet for Vernon? Otherwise we'll have a closed casket so nobody can see him." A chuckle let loose and Sarah slapped a hand across her mouth. What would Bob think of her laughing about her naked husband in a casket? Then she looked at Bob. He clamped his hand across his mouth too. Their eyes met and they both spluttered a bit.

Bob cleared his throat, his eyes still twinkling. "No problem. Help yourself."

Sarah didn't dare say anything. A giggle deep in the pit of her stomach fought to get out. She held up her Hand in a good-bye gesture and left. She practically ran through the darkened hall and into the clothes closet. When she closed the door behind her, the giggle finally escaped. So much of her stress seemed to ride along on the back of it.

Alone. It felt good to be by herself for once. She saw a chair in the corner between some racks and snuggled into it like a stuffed animal left behind by a child. She needed to think. She needed a place to live. She needed a job to pay for the place. How could she find a job when she didn't know how to do anything?

The funeral popped into her head and buzzed around. She tried to block it out, but thoughts of his mother stomped in and caused a ruckus. No doubt Della would cause one at the funeral tomorrow with all the people watching. She raised her brows. Maybe nobody would show up. After all, Vernon hadn't been rich in the friend department.

Sarah covered her face with her hands. She wanted it all to be over and done. Energy drained from her, leaving her tired and weary. Why did everything have to go wrong? Thanks to Vernon, not one thing had gone right since that one day. The day she didn't ask for and took no part in making happen. If only she could go back fourteen years ago and use the knife to run him through.

Sarah lowered her hands and stared at the racks of men's clothes. She might as well get this over with.

The metal chair creaked as she stood and walked over to the jeans. Her hand stopped before grabbing a pair. She turned to the rack with dress pants, suits, and dress shirts. That giggle came back.

"Vernon would be furious if I put him in a suit."

She hesitated, bit her bottom lip, and giggled as she reached for the suits. A navy pin-striped suit and a pink shirt jumped right out at her. He would explode if he knew about the pink shirt. She snatched a bright paisley tie to finish the look. Tears trickled down her cheeks as she laughed. She hadn't had such fun in years. A pair of socks would be enough. No sense wasting a good pair of shoes since they'd be hidden under the lid.

She wiped away the tears as she placed the clothes on a hanger and admired them. At the last minute, she remembered to get a belt for him and slid it through the belt loops.

With her face under control, she walked over to her mother while a Red Cross representative stood up front talking to the group. "Mother, I'm taking clothes to the funeral home for Vernon. I'll be back in a bit."

Coreen pinched her sleeve. "Mama, you can't leave now. You gotta get your shot."

"I'll get it when I get back. I gotta go now."

"Can I come with you to help?"

Sarah saw the sly grin on Coreen's face and knew what she was up to. "No. You stay here with Mammaw and get your shot."

"I hate shots. Besides, guess who's giving 'em to us. It's ole Nurse Boggs. She hates children."

"It'll be over with soon. Try to go first so you don't have to worry about it so much. Then you can watch everybody else get theirs."

"Okay. Thanks, Mama." Finally, a big smile lit up her face.

"Sarah, go ahead and do what you gotta do. My, my, what a nice-looking outfit." Mother cocked her head and looked closer at the pink shirt. "Are you sure Vernon would have approved?"

Sarah looked at her mother and smiled. "I'm sure all right."

As Sarah turned and walked away, her mother chuckled behind her.

Chapter 15

When the Red Cross lady finally stopped talking about what could and couldn't be done for the flood victims, she told everyone to line up for their shots. Coreen ran to the front of the line, but Pastor Bob got there first.

"You beat me to the front of the line, Pastor." She put one hand on her hip.

"Sorry, Coreen, you can go first."

"Eh, eh, eh, Robert. You get up there and take your shot like a man," Loretta teased as she walked up behind them.

"What's the matter? You chicken?" Coreen laughed.

"No, not at all." His brow furrowed as he cocked his head down at Coreen. "Hey, what is this anyway? Aren't you afraid of getting shots?"

"'Course I am, I mean, we're getting it from Nurse Boggs." Coreen leaned toward him and whispered, "She's downright mean. I know. She's shot me before—and it really hurt!"

"Thanks a lot, Coreen. You're really making me feel better about this."

Nurse Boggs barked an order. "Who's first? Get up here."

Pastor Bob held his breath as he towered over the petite woman with the needle. Nurse Boggs looked up to him and frowned. "Sir, unless you want me to give this to you in your buttocks, you're gonna have to get down here on my level."

Coreen laughed. When Nurse Boggs glared at her, she slapped a hand over her mouth. Big mistake. Her heart thumped. Bob bent down, turned his head toward Coreen, and squeezed his eyes shut. She resisted the urge to laugh again.

"Next."

Bob opened his eyes and stood. "See, easy. No pain at all."

Loretta whispered, "You know it's a sin to lie, don't you?"

"I tried to make a bad situation easier. I think, this time, it was justified."

Coreen crept to the desk, smiled, and said, "Hello, Nurse Boggs. Nice to see ya again."

Without saying a word, the nurse stabbed her arm.

"Ouch!"

Coreen gently patted her wound as she wandered a safe distance away from the nurse, observing the children in line as they got stabbed. Some squeezed their eyes shut so tightly their faces got all smooshed up. Some turned their heads. A few required being held down as they squawled. The younger ones who screamed and cried made tears bubble in her eyes. A hug would have made it a lot easier on them.

Someone behind her said her mother's name. She thought she recognized the voices and peeked around. Yep, the Doepel boys, talking to a boy she didn't know. She pretended not to hear but crept a few steps closer.

"I heared she wooed him when he come home from Nam and threw herself at him. When she got in the family way, they made him marry her."

"Yeah, it's no wonder he was such a drunk. She made his life miserable."

"Guess it's why he cheated on her too. You can't love somebody they force you to marry. I kinda feel sorry for the guy."

"I heard she wanted to marry him for his money." The boy laughed an ugly laugh. "Guess she was disappointed when he stayed here and went to the mines."

"Yeah, and Coreen. No matter when he married her mother, she's still a bastard child." Their laughter echoed inside her head.

Her insides heated up like a stoked fire, with hot embers ready to belch. She whirled to confront the bullies with a death stare. She spat flames at them. "How dare you spread lies about us. I hope you burn in hell."

The brothers sneered at her as they walked up to her and laughed in her face. "Well, I guess we'll see you and your sorry parents there." Clyde poked her chest with his dirty finger and backed her against the wall.

Her mouth filled with bile. They were just like her daddy. If only she could hurt them as much as they had hurt her. But she felt powerless—again.

Clyde poked her again and laughed in her face. Fire surged within her, building up steam, until she growled and shoved Clyde off her, knocking him into his brother. She spun and ran out the backdoor of the church.

* * *

Shirley Kincaid-Lamont exploded into the basement of the church like a miner's searchlight on a mission. Surely they would be here. As she approached the rows of tables, she smiled and quickened her steps. "Look at you sitting there on your throne."

Mumsie jerked her head up at her, eyes and mouth wide open. "Shirley! What are you doing here?"

Shirley gave her mother a great big bear hug. "Well, you refused to answer your phone. I had to drive down and make sure you didn't drown."

"I'm so glad to see you."

"I'm glad to see you too. Are you okay?"

"At least I'm alive. How'd you find us?"

"Well, I stopped at the first gas-station-slash-moonshine-market and asked where everybody was, and they told me where to try. 'Course, this would be the fifth place I looked. You have to make it hard on me, don't ya?" Shirley's laughter echoed in the room. "Where's Sarah and Coreen? And Vernon. Guess he's having to behave in a church." She chuckled as she looked around for them.

"Vernon ain't here." Mumsie took her hand.

"Where is he?" Her mother's face sagged, and Shirley's chest fluttered. "What's wrong? Mumsie?"

"Vernon's dead, honey. Dead."

Shirley dropped into the chair next to her mother. Her informer didn't know about Vernon. "You've got to be kidding. Why didn't you call me?"

"We don't have a phone, Shirley. Besides, we just haven't had a chance to think about it yet. Sarah's been busy taking care of details too."

"Poor Sarah." If only Sarah had called and let her help. "How did he die, Mumsie?"

"They think he tried to cross some water and got stuck. Found him in his car."

"Drowned?" It relieved her that Sarah hadn't done him in. Although it would be justified.

"I guess you don't know about the houses either, do you?"

"Did they get water?"

"It's more like water got them. They's both gone. We watched the river completely swallow 'em up." Mumsie dropped her head. Her chin trembled.

Tears puddled in Shirley's eyes. "Mumsie ..." Shirley threw her arms around her mother's neck and patted her back. "I'm sorry. Mercy me. I'd no idea it was that bad. Bless your heart."

"It's okay. We'll be fine. As long as you don't smother me to death with that Chanel Number Five you're wearing."

Shirley released her grasp. "Sorry. I wasn't trying to kill you. Tell me, where you gonna live?" Shirley held up her hand. "Wait, I know. You can come up to Cincy and live with us. We'd love to have you. It wouldn't be no trouble at all. What'ya say?"

"Shirley, honey, I can't. It's really sweet of you to offer, but this is my home—even if I don't have a house right now." Mumsie smiled the smile Shirley loved to see. Even if it wrinkled a bit around the edges now, it warmed her insides. "I'm too old to change. Besides, Sarah and Coreen need me now. She don't have no job, and what if she can't find one? Vernon didn't leave them a dadburn penny." She smacked the table with a fist. "Not even insurance. Besides, you got your family to take care of, and you shore don't need an old woman to deal with."

Shirley rested her face on her hand and forced out a breath. "I figured that's what you'd say. You're stubborn as a mule. But remember the offer stands—any time you're willing to lower your standards. Y'hear?" She wrinkled her brow. Funny how she felt more like the mother sometimes.

"You're a wonderful daughter, and I appreciate your offer."

Shirley gave her a kiss on the cheek, leaving an impression in bright red. "I marked ya." She giggled as she dug into her purse to retrieve a tissue and wipe the red from Mumsie's face. "Now, where's Sarah? I think I need to talk to her."

"She took clothes over to the funeral home for Vernon." Mumsie chuckled as she leaned over and said, "You ain't gonna believe what she picked out for him—from some clothes they had here at this church. A suit and tie."

Shirley laughed. "Vernon would have died—well, if he hadn't already."

"But the best part is she picked out a pink shirt for him." Mumsie shook with giggles.

Shirley exploded too. "A pink shirt?"

Several people turned toward them. Mumsie smacked Shirley's arm. "Shhh. Hush, girl. Everybody in the place is staring at us."

Shirley whispered, "Vernon will be rolling in his grave." When they finally calmed down, she asked, "Where's Coreen?"

Mumsie glanced across the room. "Well, she went over there to get a tetanus shot, but I guess she's got hers already. She's probably outside playing or with her dog next door at the preacher's house."

"At the preacher's house? What's her dog doing at the preacher's house?"

"Well, we couldn't bring him in here, so they offered to keep him."

Shirley stood up and unstuck her pants from her thighs. Metal chairs. "I guess I should go find her then. I got a little birthday present for her."

Mumsie slumped back in her chair and clicked her tongue. "I plumb forgot. Poor child. Nobody even wished her a happy birthday. Bless her heart."

"I'd better go find her and fix it right now." Shirley gave her mother another hug. "If Sarah gets back before I do, don't tell her I'm here, okay? I want to surprise her."

"Mum's the word."

Chapter 16

Coreen exploded out the basement door and ran across the yard to her best friend. Patches, seeing her coming, ran to the gate, jumping up and down on it like a doggie ballet dancer.

The latch on the gate slammed shut behind her. The dog continued his dance around her feet and barked softly in welcome. As she leaned down to pet him and ruffle his ears, she told him all about her latest catastrophe.

A yellow ball lay on the crispy grass. Coreen pulled back her foot and kicked as if it was the Doepels, sending it whirling across the yard.

"Ouch." Her bare toes now regretted the kick. Patches thought it was a game and ran to retrieve the ball, dropping it at her still-throbbing toes.

"I reckon this means you wanna fetch." Coreen slammed the ball across the yard. Patches retrieved it. They continued the game until she forgot about the Doepels. "I'm tired. Let's sit down and rest a bit."

Even though the afternoon sun shone on the edge of the porch, she sat on the top step, being careful to pull her dress down far enough to protect the back of her legs from the scorching concrete. As Coreen caressed Patches' head and back, she sang some of her songs.

Patches jumped up and barked. When someone opened the gate to enter the yard, Coreen's heart leapt and a smile stretched her face.

"Aunt Shirley! I'm so glad to see you." Coreen scampered to her aunt and flung her arms around her neck with such force, the two did a little two-step across the yard. She laughed as Aunt Shirley's red curls bounced around her head. Patches joined the frivolity and ran circles around their legs, almost tripping them.

"Coreen, honey, I'm glad to see you too—but you're gonna knock me off my feet."

"Sorry. I'm excited you're here. It's been awful. It's been the worst days of my life—and that's saying a lot." Coreen still clung to her aunt, head buried in her ample bosom.

Aunt Shirley stroked her hair. "I know you've had a really tough time of it, but everything's gonna be okay. Come on, sweetie. Let's go over here and sit down a minute. It's hot out here."

The two made their way to the shade of the porch and took a seat on the metal glider. It wiggled and rocked beneath them as they plopped onto its floral cushions.

"Whew. Much better. Hello there, Patches." Aunt Shirley leaned down and patted the still-dancing dog on the head. Now acknowledged, the feist plodded over and lapped up the entire bowl of water. Then he jumped onto the seat beside Coreen, causing the glider to wiggle again.

"Coreen, you've got to tell me all about what happened."

"It's been awful." Coreen told Aunt Shirley every detail from the time she saw the river water coming till DeWayne rescued them.

"I'm proud of you being such a strong girl." Aunt Shirley twirled her finger around Coreen's ponytail.

"I did what needed to be done. I'm just glad we got out of there in time." She lowered her gaze. Her heart squeezed tight in her chest and tears collected in her eyes.

"How you feeling about what happened to your daddy?"

Coreen sighed and picked at a scab on her arm. She worked her bottom lip between her teeth. Should she should tell the truth? Aunt Shirley would understand. "You know how he ..."

"Yeah, I know."

Coreen picked at a fingernail. "I know he was my daddy and all ... but ... he hated us so much that almost every night he come home and beat up on one of us—or both of us. I thought he might kill us." Coreen's chin quivered. Should she tell her the rest? Would Aunt Shirley think she was awful? "I think his dying is my fault." Her chin dropped to her chest.

"None of this is your fault, sweetheart." Aunt Shirley wrapped her arms around Coreen and drew her close.

Coreen drew back. "You don't understand. The day he died, I prayed God would kill him and send him to ... you know ... *hell.*" She whispered the bad word.

Aunt Shirley wrapped her arms around Coreen again. "You can't make God do anything He hasn't already decided to do. Your daddy's demons made him that way, not anything you or your mama did. You're a wonderful, special girl who's loved dearly."

"Shore don't feel that way." Her uncelebrated thirteenth birthday for instance.

"I know. Sometimes it doesn't ... even for me."

"You? How could you feel like you're not loved? You're the greatest person I know." Coreen slipped her arms around Shirley's waist and hugged her. "You've always been my favorite."

"And you're my favorite too." Aunt Shirley kissed her head. "Always remember, ya hear?" Shirley pulled back from the hug and cocked her head at Coreen. "Are you feeling a tad like you're glad this all happened?"

The storm brewing in Coreen's body erupted. She couldn't hold it back. "I'm sorry. I got tired of all the beating and—and all the other things he done." The words the Doepels said haunted her. Did they lie? Shirley would know. She needed to know. "D'ya know why he hated us?"

"He was a miserable little man who didn't know how to love anybody."

"I wish I could be happy. Sometimes ..." Coreen swallowed hard. The words fought to get out. "I wish I drowned in the river."

Aunt Shirley rocked Coreen gently as she stroked her hair and mumbled, "Oh, honey. My precious girl."

Patches raised his head, whined, and put his paw on Coreen's leg.

"I need to blow my nose."

"Wait a minute." Aunt Shirley searched in her purse and pulled out a tissue. "I think I may need one too."

"Thanks." She blew her nose with gusto and wiped away any remaining tears.

"Coreen, you're gonna survive this. I got faith in you."

"I wish I did. I just want to leave here. These mountains is a prison. I mean ... well, look at 'em." Coreen pointed with both hands to the enormity of the mountains on all sides. Green walls everywhere. "It's like we're in a bowl of mountains and we can't get out. We're stuck—like a bird in a trash can. We flutter our wings like crazy and hop around ... but we can't fly straight up, so we're stuck in the bottom—till we die. I feel like I'm gonna have to spend the rest of my life stuck here with ... nothing." Coreen flopped back into the glider and covered her face. Why wouldn't the mountains let her go?

"I do know how you feel, sweetie. I grew up here too, remember?" Aunt Shirley sat still. Her voice was quiet and gentle. "I got out. But getting out doesn't solve your problems." The sharpness in her tone made Coreen look at her. "You need to figure out how to find some joy, no matter how miserable you are."

"How am I gonna do that?" Coreen crossed her arms.

"When things get a little crazy—"

Coreen rolled her eyes. "You mean like right now?"

Aunt Shirley smiled. "Yeah, like right now. You need to calm yourself down, quiet your heart, and listen."

"Listen to what?" Coreen wrinkled up her face.

"Listen for a whisper. Now, it can be hard to hear, but you just keep on listening for it."

"What's this whisper gonna tell me?"

"It'll give you a whisper of hope."

"Hope? For what?" Coreen didn't believe in whispers. The only ones she'd ever heard were mean ones.

"Hope is a promise that good things can happen, even when there's bad stuff all around you."

Coreen wasn't sure at all what her aunt meant, but she could at least give it a try. But how would she know if she did it right? "How do I make myself be quiet enough to hear it?"

"You tell yourself to be quiet. And you keep saying it until you don't hear the bad stuff talking to you anymore. Then you can hear the whisper." Aunt Shirley yelped and threw her hands up.

Coreen and Patches both jumped.

"I almost forgot. I brought you something."

Coreen clasped her hands together as her aunt dug around in her huge pocketbook. Gifts were a pleasure she rarely received.

Aunt Shirley plucked out a small box wrapped in pink paper, tied with a sparkly silver bow.

"Happy birthday, Coreen."

"Wow." Tears puddled in the corners of Coreen's eyes as she stared at the box.

"Well, ain't you gonna open it, birthday girl?"

She smiled, then ripped the sparkly bow and paper off, tossing it toward Patches, who sniffed it out and began chewing on the remnants. Inside was a square pink velvet box. Coreen stroked it, closed her eyes, and gently rubbed the softness of it against her cheek. She took her time, enjoying the magic right before opening a rare gift. Holding the box in front of her, she raised the hinged lid to reveal a small gold heart with a tiny diamond suspended in the center.

A breath caught in her throat. "It's beautiful. It's the most beautiful thing I ever seen in my life. Thank you, Aunt Shirley." Her chin quivered.

Her aunt's red lips stretched. "Now you take good care of this. It's real gold—and a genuine diamond in the middle. You're thirteen now, and I thought it high time for you to have something real to wear around your precious neck."

"Real gold? Real diamond? You're the best aunt in the whole world." She threw her arms around Aunt Shirley's neck, still holding the box in one hand and watching the diamond sparkle in the sunshine. She felt sparkly on the inside too.

"Can I put it on now?"

"'Course. Here, let me help." Aunt Shirley fastened it as Coreen held her waist-length ponytail out of the way. The chain tickled as it fell into place. When she tucked her chin, she could see the heart. She moved it between her fingers as the diamond caught the light and sparkled.

She'd never felt special before. A sound felt close to her ear. A voice? She listened carefully, but nothing. She gasped. Could it have been a whisper ... of hope?

Chapter 17

"Mother, I'm back."

Estelle turned to find her daughter staring down at her, grinning. The funeral home seemed to be good for Sarah's mood. "How'd it go?"

"You shoulda seen the undertaker's face when he saw the shirt. I didn't move a muscle." Sarah plopped down on a metal chair.

"Lordy, what a hoot. Now, you best be prepared when they see him at the funeral. It's likely to cause a ruckus, for sure."

"Let it. I really don't care what nobody thinks, especially Della the Demon. I'm gonna do what I want to do, and nobody's gonna order me around no more."

"Well, you've certainly loosened up a bit." Estelle watched her daughter sit straight in the chair with her chin held high. About time she showed some spunk. "Good for you. I'm proud of you."

"Where's Coreen? It's almost five o'clock and we're supposed to go to Morgan's, ain't we?"

"She went outside after her shot. You'd best get yours before we go. Looks like the line's getting down to the end now. Probably won't be here when we get back."

"You get yours?"

Estelle lifted her left sleeve and pointed to an invisible spot. "Yep, got it right here. Didn't hurt a bit. I don't know what Coreen worried about."

Sarah mumbled, "She's a kid. Supposed to worry about things like shots, I reckon."

Estelle watched her daughter walk away. Shots weren't all Coreen had to worry about. Not all Sarah worried about either. She leaned her forehead into her hand and sighed deep down inside. Hard times ain't easy to survive. Sometimes, though, they's necessary to get where one needs to be.

Coreen skipped toward the table. Shirley followed several steps behind. "Mumsie, this child's gonna kill me. Don't she know how to walk like a normal person?" Shirley pounded her ample chest and plopped into a folding chair, gasping for air.

Coreen giggled. "I can't walk as slow as you. Look what Aunt Shirley gave me for my birthday, Mammaw." She flicked it back and forth in her fingers so it would sparkle. "Ain't it beautiful? It's real gold and a real, live diamond too."

"Just gorgeous. Now you be careful with it. You wouldn't want to lose it now, would you?"

"I'll protect it with my life." Coreen sparkled as much as her new necklace. "Is Mama back yet?" She looked around the room.

"Yep, she is. She went over to get her shot."

Coreen clapped her hands together, and her grin widened even more as she scurried to the line. "I gotta see this."

Estelle smiled at Shirley. "Mighty sweet of you to bring such a fancy present for Coreen. You didn't spend too much money, did you?"

Shirley rolled her eyes and sighed. "No more than I could afford. Besides, that dear little girl needs to have somebody show her some love and attention. Lord knows, she don't get none at home."

"Sarah's lived a rough life, Shirley. She ain't been allowed to show no emotions."

"It doesn't mean Coreen should have to suffer from it. She desperately needs to know she matters to somebody."

"Are you assuming things you don't know for sure?" Estelle propped her elbow on the table.

"No, I ain't. And I ain't basing it on personal experience only. You shoulda heard what that sweet child told me. She wished it'd been her that died in the river."

Estelle shook her head. Not Coreen. "I can't believe she'd say that."

"She told me herself, just a few minutes ago. She's miserable. She even thinks she's responsible for him dying." Shirley turned to her mother and took her hands in hers. "Somebody's gonna have to pay some attention to her or she's gonna be in trouble. She's a teenager now and them hormones is gonna rage something fierce. She's gonna find affection somewhere and it might be in the wrong places." Shirley dropped her head and heaved a sigh. "You'd better keep an eye on her—in case Sarah ... don't." She stared directly into her mother's eyes and pounced on every word. "We all know what can happen now, don't we?"

Estelle stared back into her daughter's eyes. She remembered all too well what happens when you want attention.

A squeal from Sarah broke the trance as she stopped short, gasped, and then smiled. "Shirley, what in the world you doing here?" The sisters embraced.

"What? You think I'd let you have all this fun without me?"

"Hello, ladies. Are we ready to go?" Imogene joined the group.

"Where we going?" Shirley chimed in.

Estelle introduced them. "Imogene's generously offered to take us to her store to shop for the funeral."

"How sweet. Well, let's get shopping."

* * *

As Imogene opened the door, a bell chimed. Row after row of lights flipped on and revealed an overwhelming array of racks filled with clothes Sarah could never afford. Seeing all these beautiful things made her heart twitch a little. She wanted to touch them.

"I ain't never seen such beautiful stuff. Where do I start?" Coreen squealed.

Imogene softly chuckled. "I think you should start in the girls' section, which is in the far right corner."

Sarah grabbed Coreen's arm. "Remember, we're looking for something dark." She watched Coreen skip across the store. "I reckon I'd better help her. No telling what she'll pick out."

"Please, let me help her, Sarah," Imogene offered. "It's fun to shop with young girls. You can help your mother."

"If you're sure you don't mind." Sarah puckered her forehead. "Let me know if you need help with her."

"She'll be fine. Don't worry. Now, you look to your heart's content. The dressing rooms are on the left wall over there when you need them."

Sarah saw her mother checking out the price tags on a few garments. "Finding anything, Mother?"

"Well, honey, there's a few—but they're too expensive. I ain't never paid this much for a dress in my life."

"Probably 'cause you ain't never bought a dress in your whole life. Everything you ever wore you made right on your old Singer." Sarah slid hangers across the bar.

"I just remembered." Estelle gave a painful sigh and lowered her head.

"What's wrong?"

"I remembered I ain't got my Singer no more. How am I gonna have any clothes to wear?"

Sarah's machine was gone too. So were her clothes. She reached up to squeeze her forehead. A headache pounded. So many problems. Today she would concentrate on getting past the funeral. Tomorrow she'd think about her new life and all the new problems. If only she could be happy about her new freedom and not have to worry.

But what about her mother?

Mother slid a couple of hangers across the rack. She seemed to be in a lot more pain and sagged more than usual. How would her mother survive on her own? Where would she live now?

Where would any of them live?

Sarah knew she would have to find work, but she didn't know what she could do. She took in a breath and mentally wiped the worries out of her mind for now. "Don't worry about new clothes, Mother. There's always a way."

The little bell chimed on the front door.

"I'm here. Where are y'all? Mumsie? Sarah?"

"Back here, Shirley. Come help Mother shop so I can find something for me, will you?"

"I'm on my way. Look at this pretty blouse." Shirley stopped and fingered a couple of items in the women's section.

"Shirley."

"I'm coming, I'm coming."

* * *

Coreen stood at a rack, sliding the hangers one at a time and stopping at the colorful dresses.

Imogene joined her. "Ah, I see you found the girls' section. See anything you like?"

"Lots. But I don't think Mama would agree. She wants me to get something dark, and I don't want nothing dark. I want something with happy colors." She'd had enough dark stuff in her life. And green stuff. She slid a dark-green dress right on by.

"I can certainly understand. Unfortunately, this time we have to do what's expected instead of what gives pleasure."

"I'm kinda used to it." Coreen slid more hangers.

"Coreen, how about this one? It's navy blue, but it has a little happy red trim on it. It could work."

"It ain't bad at all. Is there a place I can try it on?"

"The dressing rooms are all the way over there against the wall. Why don't we find a couple of things so you can try them all on at once?"

That made sense. "I love looking at all these dresses. My mama always made mine for me until I got old enough to reach the pedal myself." Coreen giggled as she whispered, "Well, except for my undies and socks."

Imogene spoke quietly. "Do you know where you're gonna live yet?"

"No, I ain't heard them talking about it at all." She pulled a dress off the rack.

"Ooh, this one's pretty, ain't it?"

"Yes, but not dark." Imogene smiled. "Has your mom talked about what she's gonna do about a job?"

Coreen wrinkled her forehead. She hadn't thought about that. "No. I guess she'll have to find one though, won't she?"

"Yes, I'm afraid so, dear. Do you know if she has any skills for working?"

Coreen stopped sliding hangers. Aside from cooking and cleaning, she couldn't think of a thing her mama could do. "I don't think so. I know she ain't never worked at a job before. Daddy wouldn't let her."

"Here's a lovely dress. Want to try it on?"

Coreen shrugged her shoulders and took the dress. "That makes four. Is it enough to try?"

"I believe so. If they don't work, we'll keep looking."

* * *

Sarah looked up from a rack. Nearby, her mother struggled to shop with one hand and hold herself upright with a cane in the other. Her sister had disappeared from sight. "Shirley? Shirley, where are you? Mother needs help."

Shirley popped her head of curls over a nearby rack. "Right here. I'm coming, Mumsie."

"Look at them arms loaded down. Lord-a-mercy, Shirl, what you doing with all them clothes?" Sarah glared at her sister.

"I'm shopping too, of course. I don't always find pretty stuff in my size." Shirley squeezed through the racks and hung her clothes on a rack outside the dressing rooms, then turned to her mother. "Let me take those for you, Mumsie."

Coreen waved under the dressing room door. "Mammaw, don't come in this one. I'm in here trying on my dresses, okay?"

Sarah fingered a black suit with a discreet ruffle around the collar of the jacket. She saw the price tag and couldn't bring herself to remove it from the rack. It was beautiful. Classy. And too rich for her.

"A beautiful suit, isn't it?" Imogene cooed. "Go ahead and try it. I think you would look beautiful in it."

"It's—too expensive. I couldn't expect you—"

"I made the offer without any restrictions, Sarah. Besides, I paid a lot less for it than the ticket says."

"Okay, I'll at least try it on. We'll see."

Sarah saved the suit for last and dressed with her back to the mirror. She turned around. It fit her perfectly. She fingered the ruffle and smoothed the skirt.

Imogene had made it clear she should consider it, but would she consider her greedy?

"Sarah, you about ready?"

Her mother sounded tired. "I'll be right out." Sarah changed back into her clothes closet dress and looked at each of the outfits. It had to be the suit. She squeezed her eyes shut, opened them, and took the suit.

Imogene smiled and hung the suit on a rack beside the counter. "Now, is there anything else anyone needs?"

Sarah hesitated, then spoke. "I hate to sound greedy, but if you have some, I could use bobby pins or clips to curl my hair. I hate for it to look a mess for the funeral." With such a beautiful suit, her hair should be respectable too.

"You're in luck. I have some in the stock room. Would you like to accompany me back there?"

In the large back room, Imogene walked over to a sigogglin stack of bins that looked like they might come crashing down at any minute. "Ah, found them."

Sarah joined her and took the box of pins. "Thank you. I've missed curling my hair. It looks awful."

"Honey, you look fine. I don't see a thing wrong with your hair. I'm sure you'll be glad to finally get to bathe properly though. It's been awful having to do a little basin bath with the bottled water. I'm glad they gave us the go-ahead to take a proper bath again."

Sarah didn't admit taking a basin bath was normal for her. "The church has been real nice to us … but I miss being at home. It weren't much, but you have a sense of comfort in what you know."

"I understand completely. Sarah …" Imogene placed clasped fingers to her chin. Then she smiled. "I've been considering something for a while now. I'm getting too old to unpack all these boxes I get almost daily for the store. You can see how they're piling up back here. And then there's all the seasonal stuff I need to organize. Not to mention what should go to the burn box."

Sarah had noticed boxes of all sizes lined the walls. Why would Imogene tell her about them though?

"I've been hoping to find the right person to hire. Part time's all I can afford right now, but I need somebody young who can unload the boxes and put all the tickets on the merchandise and then put it out on the floor for me. Especially now, after the flood. Business will pick up since so many lost everything. And I wondered … are you looking for a job? You can think about it—and let me know when you decide."

Sarah shouted for joy on the inside. "I don't have to think about it. I'd love to work here, if you think I can do the job. I ain't never worked before. Not since

I's thirteen. But I'm a hard worker."

"I'm certain you are." Imogene grinned. "I'm thrilled. Now, I can't pay much, but it's as good as anybody else around here could offer. As for when you can start, that's totally up to you. I know you're going through some things right now that require your full attention, so don't feel rushed. I don't want to cause more burdens for you."

"I appreciate what you've done for my family and me. I ain't never known nobody kind and giving. Besides, the thought of getting to open all these boxes is exciting. It'll be like Christmas every day. And I'll get to see it all first."

Sarah's face glowed warm. One more problem solved.

Chapter 18

Estelle heaved a sigh as Imogene pulled up to the church entrance and popped the trunk of her Caddy. Thank goodness for a backdoor with no stairs. The shopping trip had drained her, and she had to buck herself up to face the short walk into the church. Grunting, she struggled out of the car and clung to the door to steady herself.

Shirley pulled into the spot next to them and helped Sarah and Coreen gather the bags to carry inside. If only they could take the air-conditioning from the car inside too. The basement wasn't terribly hot, but a heavy blanket of moisture made it harder to breathe. She wouldn't have noticed the heat at all if they hadn't spent the past couple of hours in air-conditioning. Spoiled already.

Sarah paused long enough to say, "Thank you, Imogene, for all you've done for us. We wouldn't have nothing to wear without you. I'd give you a hug—if I could reach you around all these bags."

Estelle raised her eyebrows. Maybe change was possible.

"Happy to help. Besides, I think Shirley made up for anything you've got in your bags." Imogene's laugh sounded like a dove cooing.

Estelle smiled.

As Imogene drove away, Estelle crept down the walkway, her cane clacking on the concrete as she held on to the rail. "Whew. I'll be glad when I ain't got to make this trip no more. The back door's easier than the front though." She stopped and leaned on the rail, exhausted from the pain. "I wouldn't make it up and down them stairs without a couple of strong handsome young men to carry me." She chuckled.

"For goodness sake." Sarah shook her head.

Estelle paused for another breather. Sarah stayed with her as Coreen and Shirley went on to the church. Tomorrow would be hard on them. She hadn't said anything, but her body struggled more than usual.

"Feels hotter out here after being in that air-conditioning, don't it?" Estelle lightly touched the metal handrail as it burned her fingers.

"Yep. Take your time, Mother. No need to hurry."

Estelle didn't mention how much more painful her hip had become. Enough to worry about without bringing it up. Besides, what could anybody do about it? She had to be at the funeral. She took a few more steps. Almost there.

How she dreaded Vernon's crazy family. Maybe it wouldn't be as bad as she expected. Or maybe they wouldn't show up. She knew better. They'd show up to cause trouble for Sarah. Nasty vermin. She'd like to whop 'em upside the head with one of their stupid tambourines and throw 'em into a pit of rattlesnakes. Think they're so religious. Never acted religious toward Sarah—or Coreen. Judgmental against everybody but their perfect son. Perfect demon. She squinted and grabbed the rail again, not considering how hot it was.

"Mother, d'ya need some help?"

Estelle looked up at her. Sarah's brows were drawn together and her eyes glistened. Guess she didn't need to tell her how much she hurt.

"Mammaw, Mama, you ready to come inside? It's time for supper." Coreen rushed over to them.

Sarah handed her bags to Coreen. "We'll be right there. Take these inside and hang them up so they don't get all wrinkled."

"Okay, Mama. The food smells real good, Mammaw. Chicken and dumplings."

"I'm moving as fast as I can."

* * *

Coreen ran to the line, happy to see there weren't many people in front of her. As she loaded her plate, she heard a familiar voice behind her.

"Coreen. I wondered where you were."

Coreen smiled. "Hi, Betty Anne. Miss Imogene took us to her store to get something to wear to Daddy's funeral. We got dark stuff though, nothing pretty and colorful." She rolled her eyes.

"At least you got to go shopping."

"Yeah, I had fun. I ain't never been shopping for clothes before. I could get used to it." Coreen's tray weighed heavy with food. "I gotta put this down before I drop it. Wanna come with me?"

"Sure. I haven't met your family yet."

They sat across from Mammaw, who asked, "Who's your friend, Coreen?"

"This is Betty Anne." She pointed as she introduced her family. "This is Mammaw, there's Mama, and beside you is Aunt Shirley. She drove down from Cincinnati today to check up on us." Coreen leaned over to whisper in Betty Anne's ear. "She's my favorite relative—and look what she brought me for my birthday." She held the heart in her fingers and wiggled it a tad to make it sparkle in the light.

"How lovely."

"It's real gold and a real diamond too."

Mama arched her eyebrow and glared at Aunt Shirley. Was Mama mad she didn't get a gift too?

"What?" Shirley raised her eyebrows. "I brought her a birthday present."

Mama stabbed a dumpling and popped it into her mouth. What had Coreen done wrong now? She picked up her yeast roll, breathed it in, and sighed as she took the first bite.

After she emptied the plate, she stuck out her tummy and patted it. "I'm stuffed. Look."

Betty Anne frowned. "I can't believe how much you can put in that little stomach of yours, Coreen. I can't eat anywhere near so much—and look at me."

"I think it's her energy. She burns it all off." Aunt Shirley pointed her fork at Coreen. "And it ain't fair." She pushed her chair back. "I'm gonna see if they have something a little bit sweet over there."

Betty Anne nodded. "They do. I ate before you got here, and there's some blackberry cobbler—and boy is it good."

Aunt Shirley waddled over to the counter. She came back with four heaping bowls of cobbler with a scoop of vanilla ice cream on top of each. Everyone dug in. Coreen drooled as she scooped the warm cobbler and melting ice cream into her eager mouth.

When she scraped the last morsel from her bowl, Mammaw asked Shirley, "Where you staying tonight?"

"With my friend, Kathy Strunk. She lives up on the mountain, so the water didn't get near her. I probably should get going soon so I can find my way up there before it's too dark. Definitely wouldn't want to get lost on the mountain."

"I'd feel a lot better if you got there before dark too. Otherwise, I'll be worrying something fierce."

"Mumsie, you always worry. That's why I never tell you nothing."

Mammaw let out a *hmph* as Aunt Shirley continued, "By the way, how long are y'all gonna be here at the church?"

"Good question. We ain't got a clue. I don't know how we're gonna afford nothing. I get Social Security, but Sarah won't get nothing yet."

"I forgot to tell you." Mama actually smiled. "I got a job. Imogene hired me."

Aunt Shirley squealed. "How wonderful, sis. Exactly what are you gonna do there?"

"I get to open up all the new merchandise, tag it, and put it out in the showroom. It's only part-time, but at least I'll be able to make some money. I think it's something I can do. It even sounds like fun."

Mammaw smiled at Mama and patted her arm. "I'm really happy for you, honey. You know, I wondered about something. I got a little money from your dad—and now you'll have a little. Maybe the smart thing would be to find a place for the three of us and we could share the expenses."

Mama rubbed her cheek and seemed to ponder the idea. Coreen liked the idea of living with Mammaw. Would Mama?

"It's a good idea. 'Course, if we can find a place cheap enough …"

Betty Anne, sitting quietly as the family talked, started wiggling in her chair like she needed to go to the bathroom. She turned to Coreen and whispered, a little too loudly, "You're not gonna have to worry about it much longer."

Coreen saw a sparkle in her eyes. "What'ya mean?"

Mama looked at Betty Anne and wrinkled her forehead. "Yeah, Betty Anne, what'ya mean?"

Betty Anne gasped, jumped up from her chair, and said, "I think I hear my mom calling me." She ran to the kitchen.

"Coreen, d'ya know what she's talking about?" Mama asked.

"Ain't got a clue."

"Sounds interesting now, don't it?" Aunt Shirley stared off toward the kitchen. "Now, Sarah, tell me all about the funeral."

Coreen bored with funeral talk. She followed Betty Anne into the kitchen. "What'd you mean about us not having—"

Betty Anne twirled around, wide-eyed, and placed a finger over her lips. "Shhhh! Not here. Let's go outside." She grabbed Coreen by the arm and dragged her out the back door and to a bench near the trees.

"Why'd you drag me out here? What's going on?"

Betty Anne leaned toward her and whispered, "My mom told me to keep quiet about something she's trying to do. I can't tell you anything more—or she'll kill me."

"Kill you? Wow, it must be amazing then." What would warrant killing?

The summer sun settled behind the mountains for the day, and darkness crept around them. Fireflies sparkled golden green and katydids sang.

Golden moonlight glistened in Betty Anne's shiny hair. If only her hair would glisten like that. Coreen fingered the heart around her neck. The diamond sparkled. "Diamonds even sparkle in moonlight."

Betty Anne smiled. "You sparkle in the moonlight too."

"That's the nicest thing anybody ever said to me." She reached over and took Betty Anne's hand. If only she believed it.

One day until the funeral, with a casket and a dead daddy. And it was her fault. How could she sparkle like a diamond when she felt like a lump of coal?

Chapter 19

Morning came much too quickly for Sarah. She dreaded today. She sat on the side of the cot and attempted to clear the fog from her brain. After a moment, she rose, made her way to her sleeping daughter, and gave her a little nudge. "Coreen, Coreen, you need to wake up now."

She moaned and rolled over on her other side. "Already? I'm still tired."

"We gotta get ready. Come on, get up."

"Okay, Mama, I'm coming." Coreen sat up with her eyes still closed and rubbed them vigorously. "Yum, I smell breakfast."

Sarah smiled and shook her head. "You're gonna end up as big as Shirley."

"So what if I do? Besides, you say I'm skinny as a rail. So I reckon I ain't gotta worry about it no how." Coreen jumped up and left, slamming the door.

Sarah's mother jolted awake. "What's wrong?"

"Nothing, Mother. Coreen slammed the door. We might as well get going. You wanna get cleaned up first or eat your breakfast?"

Mother squirmed to upright herself, groaning slightly. Sarah steadied herself and pulled her mother up from the cot.

"Thanks, honey. I'll be glad when I have a real bed again. I guess it'd be best to eat and take my medicine first. Give the stiffness a chance to work its way out before I get cleaned up. Wears me out."

"I wish you didn't have to go through all this." Sarah gathered up their clothes for the day. "I wish I didn't have to go through it." *Except it means he's dead.*

"Sarah, this is a part of life. We gotta do things we don't want to do because it's the right thing."

Seemed to Sarah the right thing was only right for somebody else. Never right for her. A wave of emptiness washed over her.

"Sarah? You ready?"

Sarah snapped out of her fog and looked at her mother standing with her cane by the door. She seemed to have aged ten years in the past two days. She leaned over her cane farther than before. Her dress, needing laundering after two days and nights, hung from her body in wrinkles that matched her face. Shocks of white hair strayed from the pin curls on her head. Sarah thought her mother looked exactly the way she herself felt.

She forced a smile. "Ready as I'll ever be."

* * *

Sarah, her mother, and Coreen, having bathed as thoroughly as possible with their limited resources, and dressed in their new clothes, stood in front of the mirrors in the dressing room. Coreen fiddled with the oversized collar and smiled at herself in the mirror. "We look purdy, even if we are dressed in dark colors."

"Prettier than frog fuzz. Sarah, your suit looks beautiful on you." Her mother touched the ruffle around the collar and picked a string off the sleeve.

Sarah heaved a sigh. The closer time got to the funeral, the more she wished she could run away and hide. "Let's get this over with."

"Don't worry. You'll do fine." Her mother patted her on her shoulder as they made their way out the door and toward the exit.

Shirley waited for them inside the backdoor. "Well, don't y'all look gorgeous. Are you ready to go? I saw the limo outside when I got here. I guess I can ride over with y'all and not take my car. Okay?"

"Limousine? We're riding in a limousine? Hot diggity."

Sarah's stomach twisted like a fresh plug of chewing tobacco. Maybe breakfast wasn't such a good idea after all. Bright morning sun blinded her as they approached the shiny black car. A tall, lanky young boy stood waiting, dressed in a loose-hanging black suit. He opened the front passenger door and took Mother's arm. "Would you like to sit shotgun up front with me, Miss Kincaid? I think it might be a tad easier fer ya to get in and out that way."

"Thank you. I think you're right."

He assisted her as she climbed into the front seat and then went to the back to open the door for Sarah and the remaining passengers. "Here ya go, ladies. Climb right in."

"Wow, look at this thing, Mama. It's beautiful. I wanna sit on one of these little seats, okay?"

"Just get in." Leave it to Coreen to turn a funeral into a game.

The driver closed the door and made his way to the driver's seat. "I'll get this conditioned air going in a sec, ladies. Whew, it's a hot one out here today."

The car pulled up to the the funeral home's entrance. Her insides quivered. She took a few deep breaths.

The driver hopped out and opened their doors. He escorted Mother to the building and held the door for them. Sarah tried to hide a smile. Nobody ever treated her like a lady before. A little odd, but it left a satisfying taste in her mouth.

"I'll be right here when you ladies is ready to go home—err—well, to the church building, that is."

A blast of frigid air washed over them as they entered, and Coreen said, "Man, it's cold in here. I think they could freeze ice cream."

"Coreen, please. Try really hard to be quiet today, okay?" Sarah wagged her finger. "This is a serious day, and we need to show some respect." To the people who come, if not Vernon.

"Yes, ma'am. Sorry. I didn't mean being cold was a bad thing. I kinda like it. I guess they have to have it this cold because of all the dead bodies and all."

Sarah gave her daughter the evil eye.

"Sorry. Being quiet now." Coreen zipped her lips.

Mr. Prescott glided into the room like a haint and spoke softly, causing Sarah to startle. "Ah, Mrs. Shell, you're here. And this is your family?"

"Yes," Sarah whispered in return. "This is my mother, Estelle Kincaid, my daughter, Coreen, and my sister, Shirley Lamont."

"Shirley Kincaid-hyphen-Lamont. Glad to meet you, Mr. Prescott," she said a bit too loudly and reached out to shake his hand, a bit too vigorously.

Coreen leaned to her aunt and whispered, "Mama wants us to be quiet, Aunt Shirley."

Shirley glanced over her shoulder at her sister and whispered almost as loudly as before, "Sorry."

Mr. Prescott directed the group to the viewing room and opened the double doors, revealing a dimly lit room with electric candles placed around the perimeter. All eyes went directly to the front where a dark-colored coffin sat, with one section opened, gushing in plush white satin. A few floral displays sat on pedestals, filling the room with the heavy sweet aroma of fresh flowers. Sarah felt nauseated and turned away. To her dismay, recorded organ music played. She hated organ music.

In his nasally twang, Mr. Prescott said quietly, "I'll keep the doors closed to give the family privacy until the guests arrive. If there's anything you need, please let me know."

Sarah considered asking him to turn off the organ music, but realized it was part of the process and she might as well ignore it. "Thank you, Mr. Prescott."

He glided out of the room backward, closed the doors, and left them alone with the coffin. Sarah stood, transfixed, waiting. Her family waited too.

"Mama?" Coreen eventually whispered. "What are we supposed to do?"

Sarah didn't know. She turned to her mother. "Mother, what do we do now?"

"This is the viewing. We view. I really need to sit down soon—so I'll go first, if it's okay."

* * *

Estelle hobbled to the coffin, the sound of her cane muffled by the thick shag carpet, and peered inside. She didn't know what she expected to see—but it seemed a surprise. Maybe because of the peaceful look on his face—or the suit and pink shirt? Her hip burned with pain and her leg tingled. Even in this icebox of a room, she perspired. She leaned heavily on her cane for support.

Estelle stared at his dead face. Funny thing about life—and death. She never thought she'd see him lying here. The bad ones seemed to outlive the good ones. Not this time. She smiled—Lord forgive her for thinking it—but it blessed her. Blessed them all. The misery he brought on the family.

She rubbed her throbbing hip. His fault too. Just because she tried to protect her girls. Pain shot through her hip, just like the day he rammed that poker through it. She grabbed the coffin as her leg buckled. At least his drunkenness made him miss his intended mark—her heart.

He finally got what he deserved—eternity in hell. Estelle sighed and turned to her family. They stood staring at her like a herd of sheep. She shook her head.

"I'm gonna sit. Who's next?" She crossed to the closest chair, dropped into it with a grunt, and ignored the box of tissues on the table next to her.

* * *

Shirley patted Sarah on the shoulder. "I'll let you and Coreen do your thing. I'll help Mumsie to her chair. She's looking a bit peaked."

Sarah nodded, but stood in place and stared at the casket. Her feet wouldn't walk. She put her hand on her daughter's shoulder and nudged her. "Go ahead, Coreen."

"Mama?" Coreen screwed up her face. "I can't walk up there by myself. Please go with me?"

Nausea swept through Sarah's body. Her head buzzed. Why does this have to be so hard? She looked at her daughter's face and then glanced toward the casket. It had to be done.

She raised her shoulders, pointed her chin, and took Coreen's trembling hand. "Come on. Let's get this over with."

They crept to the coffin, getting barely close enough to peek in and see his face. Coreen leaned closer. "It looks like he's asleep and he's gonna wake up any minute—and yell at us for staring at him."

"He ain't asleep, Coreen. He's dead. He ain't never gonna yell nothing at us again."

"I wanted him to love me." Coreen swiped away a tear. "I tried so hard to be perfect for him. But he didn't care." She sniffed. "Daddies are supposed to love their kids, ain't they?" She walked up to the casket and looked inside. "When I look at him now, I sure don't feel no love."

"If all you give's hate, then you can't expect to get nothing but hate right back. It ain't your fault." Sarah walked to the casket and stared at the dead face. Nope. Nothing but hate.

Coreen took her hand. "I love you, Mama, and all I ever wanted was for *you* to love me too." Coreen threw her arms around her mother and sobbed.

Sarah gasped. Whether an impulse or a need, Sarah wrapped her arms around her daughter and held her close. A tear trickled down her cheek. A tear for the wasted years of hate. After a moment, Sarah wiped the tear away. "We need to get ready in case somebody shows up."

The two released each other and turned around. Mother and Shirley sat sniffling and dabbing their eyes with tissues.

Sarah gaped. "What in the world are you two blubbering about?"

"I ... I think I may be allergic to all them flowers. They're making my eyes water." Shirley grabbed another tissue and blew her nose.

"It's so cold in here, it's making my nose run." Mother honked into her tissue.

The double doors squeaked open and Mr. Prescott announced in his whispery voice, "Mrs. Shell, are you ready?"

Sarah took a deep breath that rattled her body. "Let's get this over with."

Mother plucked some tissues from the box next to her. "Here, you and Coreen need to stuff a tissue in your pockets. You don't have a pocket, do ya? Stuff it in your brassiere."

"Mother, I ain't gonna need a tissue."

"Here, take it. In case. You never know when it might come in handy."

Sarah figured it would be easier to take the tissue than to quibble. She and Coreen took seats with her mother and Shirley and waited. The room seemed to spin inside her head. Like she wasn't really there.

As well-wishers entered, Coreen asked, "Mama, what are we s'posed to do now?"

"I never did this before either. I guess we let 'em look and thank 'em for coming."

Mother shifted in her chair. "Remember to be calm and quiet—and pleasant. I stress the quiet part."

"Yes, ma'am." Coreen sighed.

Shirley kept wiggling on her chair. "Lordy, I'm starting to dread this now. Sarah, I don't see them yet. Maybe they won't show."

"Life ain't never that simple. I'm sure they'll be here. Della wouldn't miss an opportunity to wail in public."

The turnout surprised her. She knew a few—a couple of former neighbors from the camp and a few from the church. She assumed the rest were there out of curiosity.

She caught herself smiling as she greeted the church people and thanked them for coming. To her delight, the wadded-up tissue she grasped prevented her from having to shake hands. If only it stopped people from hugging her.

* * *

Coreen wandered around the room, looking at each of the flower arrangements, sniffing each flower, and reading the tags. The pink ones smelled good. Spicy. *Our Sympathy, Your Friends at New Hope Baptist Church.* How nice.

She wrinkled her nose at a large display in the shape of a horseshoe because they were plain old white and stank. The card read, *We'll miss you down there, Red Diamond Mines.* She approved of the little miner's cap on the card.

An oversized vase with lilies, white mums, and small blue flowers sat on a table. She sniffed each one. Then she searched for the card. Attached to the bow, a cute little yellow telephone and a streamer with the words "Jesus called."

Why would Jesus call her daddy? He sure ain't going to heaven. *I guess he called to tell him where he's going.* She caught herself as she giggled, slapped her hand over her mouth, and looked around to make sure nobody heard her.

Two people caught her eye. An older man, wearing bib overalls and a cap, dragged a girl about her age up to the front. Tears shone on her face. Looked like the man was hurting her arm. She watched them closely as he pushed the girl right up to the casket and told her to look inside. Who were they, anyway?

She clearly heard what the man said. "You look at him, girl. That's what happens to devils. They go to hell."

The girl yanked her arm away and ran crying through the room and out the door. The man went after her, stomping his feet and pumping his arms. Coreen frowned at him. He looked all whiskery. Coal dust blotched his face and hands. Would he hurt the girl like Daddy used to hurt her? Chills broke out on her neck. She didn't like him at all.

He stormed out the door and nearly ran into Betty Anne and her mother.

She joined them as they stepped aside. "Hi, Betty Anne. Hi, Mrs. Wilhoit.

I'm whispering because my family told me to."

"How are you doing, dear?" Mrs. Wilhoit stroked her arm.

"Okay. I'll sure be glad when it's over though." Coreen peered out the door. "Did that man hurt you?"

Betty Anne answered. "Not me. He seemed upset though."

"He sure was. He had a girl with him and she ran out crying."

"Who is he?" Betty Anne moved closer to Coreen.

"Ain't got a clue. Never seen neither of them before."

Mrs. Wilhoit patted Coreen's arm. "I should speak to your mother before things get started. You two keep it down, okay?"

Must be a mother thing to tell children to be quiet.

Betty Anne stared at the coffin, her lips pursed and hands clasped. "Is your dad in there?"

Coreen leaned in close to whisper. "Yeah, it's kinda creepy, ain't it? I never seen nobody dead before."

"Me either. Is it scary?"

"No, not really. Looks like he's asleep. D'ya wanna look?"

"I guess. If you'll come with me." Betty Anne grabbed Coreen's arm. "I don't think I could do it by myself."

"Me neither. You ready?"

The two girls joined hands and slowly made their way to the casket. They got close enough to see him if they raised up on their toes.

Betty Anne wrinkled her nose and bit her lip. "Eww, it's a little yuck to see somebody … dead. Your dad looks like an interesting man. My dad wouldn't be caught dead in a pink shirt." She gasped and her eyes got big. Coreen almost giggled. "I meant …"

"It's okay. Neither would Daddy. 'Cept it's exactly what happened. Mama put it on him as a sorta payback thing for being mean. I think it's funny."

Betty Anne glanced across the room at Coreen's mama and grinned. "I think I like your mom."

Chapter 20

An ear-splitting wail reverberated throughout the outer hallway and into the viewing room. Sarah closed her eyes and stiffened. She recognized the voice. Determined she could not handle her mother-in-law, she turned to her mother and sister, hoping they could offer a solution. Instead, she stared into two faces frozen in fear.

"Mother?" Sarah's voice trembled.

Sarah's mother took her hand and smacked it a couple of times. "Don't let her get to you. She's gonna try." She made a fist and shook it in Sarah's face. "Stand your ground, you hear me?"

Della Shell entered the room, clinging to her husband with one arm, a handkerchief near her mouth, allowing full volume to escape. She wore black—to the ground. A floppy hat with a veil hid part of her face. Otis walked stoically beside her.

"My baby. My poor, sweet baby." Della's voice resembled a donkey's bray as she ran to the casket, threw herself on it, and wailed some more.

Sarah turned away. Everyone else watched the drama as Della hugged the coffin and wailed some more.

Shirley whispered, "I swear, if she starts babbling in tongues again, I'll drag her outta here myself."

Sarah smacked her.

Mother rocked back and forth, mumbling, "Lord-a-mercy, Lord-a-mercy."

Coreen dragged Betty Anne over to where Sarah stood.

"Who is *she*?" Betty Anne asked.

"She's my crazy grandmother."

"Wow."

The atmosphere in the room changed from shock to discomfort as Della continued to wail and kiss Vernon's dead face repeatedly. For Sarah, who tried to be invisible, the room seemed filled with dense fog. If only it could hide her from the embarrassment. A scream jolted her.

"What have you done to my baby, you witch?" Della's floppy black hat bounced. "Did you put them clothes on him? How dare you!" Della crossed the room toward Sarah, crouched, her face unrecognizable with fury, her finger wagging, and her voice shrill like a banshee. "You put a pink shirt on my boy. You evil demon, you. God's gonna strike you dead, you hussy."

Sarah, backed up against a chair, had nowhere to go. She wiped the spittle off her face with the back of her hand. Enough. She stood up straight. No more.

"You ruined my precious boy's life by tempting him into sin, and now you're gonna rot in hell for killing him. I know it was you. You killed him, you tramp. You Jezebel. You ... sinner."

How dare Della call her the sinner after what her son did. She drew back her hand and made a fist. Just as she swung, Shirley pushed between them and knocked Sarah backward. She fell into a chair.

Stunned, Sarah watched as Shirley loomed over Della, fists drawn, and forced her back. Her voice shook the room. "Enough. You either shut your trap and say you're sorry to my sister or you get yourself outta here."

Della straightened her hat and snarled. "Who d'ya think you are, you uppity fat pig?" Her face flamed red. "He's my baby. She don't deserve to be in his presence—her and her ... bastard child."

The entire room became deathly silent as everyone locked on the scene.

Shirley's face flushed beet red. Her fists tightened even more.

Sarah jumped up and tugged at her before there could be a knock-down drag-out fight right in the middle of the funeral. "Shirley, she ain't worth it. Stop!"

"Let me go, Sarah." Shirley's dead cold voice sounded like the hiss of a rattlesnake. She shook Sarah off.

Della's face drained of color. She stumbled backward and stopped making noise.

"I promise you, Della, if you ever try to hurt my sister again, it'll be the last thing you ever do. D'ya hear me?" Shirley stuck her fist close enough to Della's face to feel her breath.

Della gulped and whimpered, "Otis, help me. She's gonna kill me."

Otis scooted across the shag carpet and put one arm around his wife. With a slight stutter, he whined, "You stay away from her, you ... you monster."

"What ya gonna do about it, Otis? You gonna hit me? You wanna hit a woman—like your son always did? Or is it your wife who has the balls in your family?"

Otis shook, his eyes wide. He turned and ran behind his wife. Della bared her teeth at Shirley, but didn't move any closer.

Shirley cackled. "Does she hit you, Otis? Is that where Vernon learned it?"

Otis peered around his wife's hat. "The Lord will strike you down, you heathen."

"Why don't you take your venomous wife and slither back into the holler where you belong?" Shirley stormed over to Otis and Della with fists ready.

"Stop it, stop it. Please. I can't take this no more." Sarah ran through the crowd, leaving shreds of tissue in her wake.

As she reached the back, DeWayne opened the doors and caught her in his arms. She struggled and pleaded through sobs, "Let me go. Please."

He opened his arms and took a step back. She bolted from the room.

Chapter 21

Sarah ran through the lobby and down a hallway. She had no idea where it led, as long as it took her away from Della and all those people. When she saw the door marked "Ladies," she went inside and turned the lock. Finally, alone. She couldn't think, so she sat on the toilet lid, lifted her knees to her chest, wrapped her arms around them, and cried.

After what seemed like a moment and yet an eternity, someone tapped on the door. She considered telling them to go away until she heard Mr. Prescott's gentle voice.

"Mrs. Shell? Sarah. Are you all right?"

"No."

"I hate to intrude, but we've got a little problem. The mother of the deceased brought her pastor and insists he do the service. We need you in there to straighten things out."

Would this never end? She grabbed a wad of toilet paper, wiped her eyes, and blew her nose. She looked into the mirror. The makeup was a waste. At least now she looked like a grieving widow. "I'm coming."

Mr. Prescott allowed her to go first back down the hall. She noticed he left a bit of space between them. Perhaps he worried he might get caught up in the next catfight. With her stomach in knots, she flung open the door and marched inside. Hot embers smoldered inside her head and her hands fisted as she stomped to the front of the room.

DeWayne rushed up to her and smiled. "Sarah, you don't have to worry about it. We've got it all worked out. Bob's gonna do the funeral, just as planned. No problem." He lightly touched Sarah's arms, below her shoulders.

She relaxed.

"We agreed to allow Preacher Randall to do the graveside service at the Shell Cemetery. Is that okay with you?"

She stayed quiet for a minute while she thought. "Della has to shut up until the funeral here's over?"

"That's right."

"And then she can take him to his burial?"

"If that's what you want." He moved his hands down her arms to take her hands.

Chill bumps rose. She could barely breathe. Why did he affect her this way? In the silence of the room, all she heard was the beating of her own heart. And the blasted organ music. She looked into DeWayne's eyes and said, "Thank you. Can we get this over with now?"

"You bet. I'll take you to your seat and let Bob know he can start."

"You're staying here, ain't you?" She wondered if she wanted him there more to fend off trouble from Della or because she still felt his touch on her arms.

"I'll be right behind you."

* * *

Bob's talk ended quickly. Sarah thought it just right. When he led the prayer, she eagerly said amen at the end. The only thing left to endure remained the people walking by to say kind words and leave. This would be interesting considering what had happened earlier.

Surprisingly, it didn't bother her. She'd used up all her caring. Almost over. Just a couple of details to arrange.

Sarah turned around to DeWayne. "D'ya have some free time tomorrow?"

"I reckon. What'ya need?"

"We need to go by the houses and see if there's anything we can save from the mess. That is, if the houses are still there."

"Sure. No problem. Shirley coming?"

"I ain't asked, but I reckon she will."

"Then I'll bring Steve to help her go through your mom's house. If we go early, we can beat the hottest part of the day."

"Sounds good." Sarah made a good effort at a smile. "See you tomorrow morning then. DeWayne, thanks for helping today."

"Anytime you need me, Sarah." He smiled into her eyes.

She felt a bit wobbly in her stomach. "I—I need to see Mr. Prescott. Bye." She acted like a silly schoolgirl.

Mr. Prescott didn't run when he saw her coming. Sarah offered her hand. "Thank you for all you did today. I'm sorry for such a mess."

"It wasn't your fault, Mrs. Shell. Besides, you wouldn't believe some of the goings-on we have at funerals. This one was mild. Nothing broken and no bloodshed."

"Is our limo already in line for the procession?"

"Yes, it is."

"Can we go ahead and leave now?"

"You don't want to attend the burial?"

"Absolutely not. We're done. She can have him now."

"I understand completely. I'll have Jim Bob pull out of the line and meet you out front. You can slip out when you're ready." Mr. Prescott's smile spread across his face.

"Thanks."

Sarah rushed up to her family and whispered, "We need to go now to the limo."

Shirley cocked her head. "What? But they haven't taken Vernon out to the hearse yet."

"Exactly. Let's go home."

"Well, praise the Lord." Shirley snapped the band of her bra. "I can't wait to get out of these new clothes."

Sarah stopped at the door and turned back to the room as Mr. Prescott closed the lid on Vernon. She scanned the room and stopped at DeWayne. Her heart skipped a beat.

Chapter 22

Shirley climbed into the back of the limo and melted into the seat. Good thing her kids weren't here to see her today. And Richie. She hadn't exhibited God's love to anybody. She did, however, exhibit a fierce love for her family. Should she be ashamed or proud?

Sarah huddled against the window, her hands on her head and leaning forward until her elbows rested on her knees. Exhaustion? No, despair. Shirley knew exactly what they both needed.

Diversion.

"Sarah, when we get back, let's change into comfortable clothes. I want you to come with me for a ride."

Sarah kept her head in her hands and shook without looking up. Shirley tightened her lips. "I'm your big sister and I ain't taking no for an answer."

Sarah lifted her head. "I don't wanna go nowhere. I wanna disappear."

"And do what? Pout? Feel sorry for yourself? Get depressed? You need some stress relief, and that's exactly what you're gonna get."

They pulled into the parking lot and quietly walked to the church. Shirley wondered how many people already knew what happened at the funeral. She guessed they all did. From the diverted glances, she guessed right. News traveled fast in a tiny mountain community.

After they changed, Shirley guided Sarah to the door. She moaned but walked out to the car and got in.

Shirley got into the driver's seat. "Whew, it's hot in here. Let's open up these windows and let some of the heat out. I'll turn the A/C on."

Shirley turned the key and blasted hot air in their faces until the air-conditioning finally kicked in and offered blessed relief. They pulled out of the lot and drove to the main road. After they passed the city limits, Shirley turned onto a crooked road and headed up the side of the mountain. They were both silent as the road became shady under the canopy of trees, with cliffs rising up on one side and a drop-off on the other leading down to a fast-moving creek. The car struggled as they climbed higher, hugging hairpin curves. After what seemed an eternity, Shirley flipped her left turn signal and slowed to make her turn onto a gravel road.

"Where you taking me? I didn't think there was anything up here but trees—and maybe a panther."

"Or a moonshine still?" Shirley chuckled.

"She's gonna get me shot. Or drunk." Sarah allowed a quick chuckle to escape for the first time today. "Actually, right now getting drunk don't sound bad."

Shirley didn't dare take her eyes off the trail as they snaked their way through the ancient forest. The tires crackled on loose gravel. She tried to clear her mind of the day's activities. Losing her temper surprised her. Chills came over her as she remembered how close she got to clocking Della. But she had asked for it. Sarah had come so close to attacking Della, she had to stop her. The one time Sarah fought back should not be in front of everybody—at a funeral.

She glanced at her sister holding on to the door handle. "I want to apologize for losing it today. I know I didn't help matters at all."

"Shirl, I wish I could've said them things myself."

Shirley chuckled. "You came close to clobbering her. I guess it was all worth it to get Della to shut up for a minute. I thought she's gonna have a heart attack."

"You made her whimper. It was kinda fun." Sarah smiled and turned to stare out the car window. "But she said some things I don't want to deal with—and in front of the world."

"D'ya think Coreen knew what she's talking about?"

"I don't know. I keep thinking of her as a child—but I weren't much older than her."

Shirley crept through the gravel, one eye on the side of the road with a sheer drop into the valley below. As she approached a blind hairpin curve, she blew her car horn to warn any oncoming vehicles. There were none. They continued the ascent, surrounded by trees with wild grapevines clinging to them, rich with clusters of grapes.

"I'd roll down my window, but it's too hot." Sarah held open the top of her shirt and leaned toward the cool air. "I'll sure be glad when cooler weather comes. This has been the worst summer I remember."

"Especially without any air-conditioning. I don't know how y'all stand it."

"You're spoiled," Sarah told her, but with a smile.

"Thanks a lot."

"Well, you are. You can't deny it."

"I could." Shirley lifted her chin. "But I guess you're right. Look at the kudzu over there. It's all over the place up here."

"Yeah, Mother says it hides the ugly." Sarah stared out the window. "I sure wish kudzu could hide all the ugly in my life."

"It's better to get rid of it. Dig it up or burn it instead of just hide it. Then the beautiful hiding underneath can grow."

"Where d'ya think there's any beauty in my life?" Sarah's chin quivered and her voice cracked.

"How about your wonderful child? You're lucky to have her. But you treat her like a disease."

"No, I don't," Sarah snapped, fire in her eyes.

"Yes, you do. And d'ya know what she said to me before we left? She asked me to tell you she loves you."

Sarah lowered her head till her chin rested on her chest. "I don't know why."

"And you know what I wanna know? I wanna know if you've ever—ever—said them words to her. Actually, I wonder if you ever said them words to anybody."

Sarah sniffed and turned her head away. Shirley watched the blur of greens and browns as she drove. The sisters sat in silence until Shirley pulled the car off the road into a cleared spot on the right side, against the mountain, and screeched to a halt. A cloud of dust surrounded them. On the drop-off side of the trail, loggers had cleared acres of forested land nearly fifty years before as electricity came into the mountains. The opening provided a clear view of the mountain range beyond. Shirley put the car in park and turned off the engine. After rummaging through her purse for a tissue, she offered one to her sister, who had already sniffled a couple of times. Sarah accepted, blew her nose, and wiped her eyes.

"We're here. Come on."

Sarah followed Shirley gingerly across the chunky gravel. The quartz chips and sandstone beneath their feet sparkled in the sunlight like diamonds. Shirley led her to the edge of the mountain. The glory of Appalachia stretched out across the horizon in layers of mountains that faded into haze in the distance.

Old-growth trees framed their view. Birdsongs echoed in the woods. Somewhere nearby, a spring trickled down the side of a hill. Jar flies and June bugs joined the symphony. A squirrel added his chatter to the song as he chased another squirrel away from his cache of nuts and jumped from limb to limb. The moist air carried a blend of fragrances—wildflowers, dirt, foliage, and moss—creating a perfume that wafted to Shirley's very soul. The garden of Eden must have been a lot like Appalachia.

Shirley took a deep breath and released it. "Isn't it glorious here?"

Sarah raised her eyes and looked out at the misty blue mountains rising up in front of her. "Yeah, it is. How in the world did you find this place?"

"Richie brought me here when we's dating. Romantic, ain't it? Sometimes

I borrowed his car and came up here when life got really tough on me—which happened most of the time. I came here a lot. It took me away from all the painful stuff after Daddy died. We barely survived. I thought for sure Mumsie would have to send us away. Coming here reminded me how small our troubles really were." Shirley dabbed at a tear.

"You know, you look at these here mountains and you think how awful that they destroyed all them beautiful trees. Or you look at it and think if they didn't tear down them trees, we'd never have been able to see the beauty of the mountains over yonder." Shirley walked closer to the edge. "When I come up here, I realize we gotta go through some chopping down too, so we can see the beautiful stuff hidden behind it."

Sarah twisted her hair and held it off her neck. "Shirley, I know you're trying to help ... but I can't see nothing beautiful in my life right now." She turned away. "Except that he's dead. I've been through too much pain—more than you could ever know. And now, here I am all alone."

"I know you've been through more than anybody ought to have to go through. I know what he did to you—well, some of it. I know it wasn't your fault too. But this is your chance to start over. You get to make the choices now. And you need to start with Coreen. She's almost the age you were when it all happened. Don't let it happen to her." Did she waste her breath telling her sister what to do? She had to try. "You need to tell her the truth so she can be prepared and not go through what you did."

Hugging herself, Sarah whimpered, "I can't. I can't talk about it. It still hurts too much. And nobody believed me when I told them the truth."

Sarah leaned over, her face contorted.

Shirley bit her bottom lip. She had to say what must be said. "You *have* to tell her. You owe it to her. None of this was her fault. Don't punish her for being a victim like you. I know he abused both of you." Shirley grabbed her sister's elbows. "Did you ever think he would do to her what he did to you? Did ya?"

Sarah crumpled to the gravel and threw her hands into the stones. In a gruff voice, she said, "Of course I wondered. I saw the way he looked at her sometimes. But she's his child. How could he? And what could I have done to stop him if he did?"

Shirley ached. Tears welled up. *Lord, only you can heal this.*

"We were both helpless, Shirley. I wanted him dead." Sarah growled. "You wouldn't believe how many nights I dreamed of taking one of them hunting rifles of his and shooting him dead in his sleep." She sat up, her voice a whisper. "It's my fault. I wanted him dead—and now he is." She covered her face with her hands and rocked back and forth.

Listening to her sister's sorrowful whimpers nearly ripped her heart out. Shirley hugged Sarah. "Honey, it ain't your fault. You didn't kill him. His own evil did him in. God's the one who took his life from him, not you."

Sarah turned abruptly to her sister, fire in her eyes. "God? Where was God when I was a helpless young girl who needed protecting from an evil man? Where was God when a child was conceived and I was forced to marry that demon?" Her voice became a moan. "Where was God when he beat me so bad I nearly lost the child and was never able to have any more? Where was God when we were both humiliated and forced to be his slaves?" She shook Shirley's arms. "Where was he? Can you tell me that?"

"I'm sorry, Sarah. I can't fix it for you. I can't give you any answers you're gonna accept. You need to work it out for yourself. But one thing I know—you've got a beautiful, sweet, talented little girl who loves you, in spite of everything. I think your responsibility to her is to learn how to love her in return."

"I do ... love ... her," she whispered.

Shirley inhaled. "Have you ever told her?"

Sarah pulled herself up and dusted the limestone off her dress. She walked to the edge of the cliff. "I don't need to tell her. She knows."

Shirley shook her head. "Just how d'ya reckon she knows?"

"The same way we knew Mother loved us. She took care of us, fed us, made our clothes, and she never said it. We knew."

Shirley looked at her sister and blinked. Dumfounded. "And how's that been working for you, squirt? I know how it worked for me. I go to a therapist every week trying to convince myself I'm worth being loved. Why d'ya think I'm so overweight? It's because nothing says 'I love you' like chocolate cake and french fries and fried chicken and ice cream ..." Shirley broke into sobs.

"Okay, okay, Shirl, I get it." Sarah turned and stared at the mountain behind the car. "Are we gonna go home before Mother sends out the rescue squad and DeWayne Mayhall to find us?"

"I brought you up here to get away from everything for a while and to think about what you're gonna do with the rest of your life. Didn't work so good, did it?" Shirley dabbed at her tears. She needed to focus. Ask the right questions. "Have you thought about what you're going to do now that you're free to be yourself?"

"Free to be myself?" Sarah wrinkled her forehead. "I don't even know who I am. I've always been who *he* thought I should be."

"You're gonna have to figure that out on your own now. But I can get you started." Shirley took Sarah's hands and smiled at her. "You, Sarah, are a young, beautiful woman with a family who *loves* you. Start there. Make some choices all by yourself—without anybody telling you what to do. You'll figure out who you are." Shirley shook Sarah's shoulders. "Don't let him have any more power over you. Bury it all with him and be done with it."

Sarah dug her toe into the sparkling gravel and then linked arms with Shirley. They gazed across the valley at the seemingly never-ending mountains. Dark clouds gathered in the distance and advanced slowly toward them. A blue mist appeared and obscured the farthest mountain and then the one in front of it.

"Shirley, I think rain's coming right at us."

"We don't wanna get stuck up here in a downpour. This road could get slick. Let's get in the car."

Shirley carefully turned the car around and headed back down.

"Be careful, Shirl. I sure don't wanna take the quick way off this mountain."

"I'm not gonna go off the mountain. Sit back and enjoy the ride."

Now was not the best time to talk to Sarah about the rest of her plan. A plop of rain hit the windshield and then another. Soon they were in a driving downpour. The dust from the mountain road mixed with the rain created a soupy mess on the windshield of the car. Sarah's fingers wrapped around the dash.

Shirley laughed. "That mud's making me hungry."

"What? How in the world is a muddy windshield making you hungry?"

"It looks like chocolate—and chocolate makes me hungry, of course."

"Shirl, you're hopeless. But you know, I could really go for one of them chili dogs at Ray's Drive-In 'bout now. I ain't ate nothing since breakfast."

"Me neither, and Ray's chili dogs are the best in the world. Of course, I also love their Doolies." She licked her lips, thinking of soft vanilla ice cream smothered with chocolate syrup and topped off with whipped cream and a cherry. "I ain't eat one of them since ... well, I guess since the last time I came home for a visit." Shirley filled the car with laughter. "Sarah, we still have some time before supper. Let's stop."

"It's too expensive."

"Nonsense. It's my treat."

"You don't have to."

"Yes, I do. I'm starving to death and I can't eat unless you do."

They laughed as they pulled into Ray's, under a wavy fiberglass shelter painted a faded red and blue, and placed their orders in response to the twangy voice from the menu board speaker.

Rain pelted the parking lot and cascaded off the fiberglass above them. Shirley turned to Sarah. "Have you considered what kind of job you'd like to do?"

Sarah sighed. "I don't know. I'm glad I can work at Morgan's. But I can't work part-time for the rest of my life. I need a real job. I want to do more than just exist."

"Then get a real job."

"How? I don't even have a high school diploma."

"Get one."

"What?" Sarah shook her head. "You expect me to go back to school at my age? I can see it now, walking to school every day with Coreen. Mother and daughter."

Shirley chuckled. "Honey, they have special programs for adults to get their diplomas. Then you could even go to college or some other school and learn a trade."

"What kind of trade? I don't even know if there's anything I can do. Or want to do. Besides, they don't have nothing around here." Sarah's shoulders dropped.

Shirley jumped as someone tapped on the fogged-up car window. She rolled down the window and passed the food to Sarah. When the girl left, they dug into their treats, moaning with delight.

A thought nagged at Shirley. *Is this from you, Lord?* Crinkling the hot dog wrapper, she reached for her Doolie. Should she ask Sarah? Could it work? The spoon paused. "Come home with me to Cincinnati long enough to get educated. Maybe then you could figure out what you'd like to do."

Sarah swallowed a bite of hot dog. "I can't do that. I ain't got no money and Mother needs me. She's gone downhill since the flood."

"Coreen could watch after her for a while. You wouldn't be gone long." Would this work? Is it asking too much for Coreen to stay behind when she wants to leave so desperately? *Work it out, Lord.* "It's your one big chance. Besides, you're a widow and a single mom now and can get your education for free."

"I don't know."

"Well, you dwell on it a bit. And talk to Coreen. See how she feels about it. Then let me know what you decide." She plopped another spoonful into her mouth.

Sarah looked up at her with the naughty sparkle in her eye she remembered from childhood. "Shirl? If I decide to do it, would you teach me to drive?"

"Drive? Oh, girl, that's how you repay a kindness? Send me to the hospital with heart failure?"

They both laughed. Shirley savored the last bit of her Doolie. Driving. If that's what it took, it was worth the sacrifice. *Work it out, Lord.*

Chapter 23

As Estelle and Coreen crossed the common room in the church basement, the lively chatter died. Heads lowered and gazes averted. Estelle brushed off the chill, held her head a little higher, and made her way to their room. She noticed Coreen's scrunched shoulders. She looked like a scared rabbit. Even though Coreen may not know the meaning behind what happened, she was fully aware of the negative vibes.

The two closed the door to their sanctuary and sat on folding chairs. Coreen broke the silence. "Mammaw, d'ya need me to get you anything?"

"No, honey, I'm fine for now. I think I'd like to sit here a spell till I'm ready to go out there."

The muscle on one side of Coreen's mouth tightened, exaggerating her dimple. "I know what you mean. Guess they all heard about what happened, huh?"

"People talk, honey. They always talk, even when they don't know what they's talking about." Estelle twiddled her thumbs, watching as they chased each other around and around.

Coreen fidgeted on her chair, sighing occasionally. Her foot jiggled. "Mammaw?"

"Yeah?"

"I want to ask you a question." Her fidgeting spread to her knees and fingers.

Estelle looked up and stopped her twiddling. "What is it, child?"

"Grandmother Della said some things I didn't understand. What's a bastard child?"

Estelle's heart jumped. The one question she didn't want to deal with right now. Her stomach felt a bit queasy. "She's being mean. It don't mean nothing at all. Don't you worry about it none."

"But she ain't the only one said that word about me."

Estelle wrinkled up her brows. "What? Who else said it?"

"I heard the Doepels talking about it when they didn't know I's there."

"Ornery people." She clicked her tongue. "They try to cause trouble. Don't listen to 'em. You hear me?"

"Yeah, I hear you. But I still don't know what it means."

"It ain't something a child needs to worry about." Estelle clamped her jaw tight, determined the conversation now ended.

"I ain't a child, Mammaw. I'm thirteen now—a teenager. I'm almost growed up. Besides, how am I ever gonna learn stuff if nobody'll tell me what it means?"

"Don't rush it, Coreen. Stay a child as long as you can. Growing up ain't all it's cracked up to be." Estelle's heart ached as she looked into her granddaughter's eyes. "It can be a pretty sad world out there."

"And you don't think I already live in a sad world?" Tears bubbled up in Coreen's eyes. "I really need to know."

Estelle shifted in her chair. She ran her hand across her chin. "Coreen, I know he was mean and said awful things. He beat on you too. I know. It coulda been a lot worse. But now he's gone, and none of the other stuff matters no more."

"Yes, it does. It all matters, 'cause I can't get it to go away." She made fists and slammed them on her thighs. Her eyes reddened as tears gathered in the corners. "Mama still don't love me, and he still haints me in my dreams and blames me for everything that's wrong. And maybe it is my fault—'cause I prayed he'd die. I wanted it. And it happened." She jumped up from her chair and paced. She stopped in front of Estelle and dropped to her knees. "I'm an evil person what don't deserve nobody loving me. I should be dead too."

Tears poured down Coreen's cheeks like the rains. Her face splotched with red.

Estelle barely recognized her. She desperately wished she knew what to say. "Coreen, it ain't your fault—"

"You don't understand. Neither does Mama. Nobody knows and nobody cares." Coreen stood and whirled around, flung open the door until it slammed against the wall, and ran bawling from the room.

Estelle buried her face in her helpless empty hands and sobbed her prayers to God. He would tell her what to do.

"Mrs. Kincaid? Are you okay?"

Estelle looked up to see Betty Anne, tears in her eyes, standing in the doorway. "Yes, dear, as okay as can be expected, I guess." She sniffed and wiped her cheeks with the backs of her hands.

"Is Coreen ... okay? I kinda saw her leave."

"She's having a real bad day, honey." Her words came out a whisper.

"Yeah, I guess so." Betty Anne heaved her shoulders. "Do you think I should go find her?"

"She could probably use a friend right now. I reckon it's a good idea."

"Okay." Betty Anne turned to leave, stopped, and turned back. "I don't really know what to say to her."

The girl's kind heart touched Estelle. "I reckon when there ain't words to say, sometimes just listening's all ya need to do."

"Thanks. I guess I can do that. Do you need anything before I go?"

"I'm gonna sit here a spell, but thank you for asking."

Betty Anne gave her an awkward smile and backed out of the room, gently pulling the door closed.

Estelle shook her head. "Hmph." Her advice to Betty Anne answered her own prayer. Instead of trying to do something to fix everything, maybe she needed to just sit and listen.

Wouldn't be easy.

Chapter 24

A tap sounded on the door. Estelle opened her eyes and answered with a weak, "Yes?"

The door opened slowly to the sound of glasses clanging together. "Mrs. Kincaid?"

Estelle looked up at a refined young woman she remembered seeing at the funeral. "I thought you might like to join me for a glass of lemonade. May I come in?"

Estelle preferred solitude, but the lemonade did look really good. "Of course. A glass of lemonade would rightly hit the spot." She took the offered glass and swallowed a big gulp, followed by a longer one. "I didn't realize how thirsty I was. Thank you."

"You're welcome. I'm Mary Anne Wilhoit, Betty Anne's mom. Do you mind if I join you for a minute?"

"Sure. Have a seat." Estelle motioned to a metal chair. "It ain't too comfortable, but you're welcome to join me—and I'm just Estelle. You ain't from around here, are ya?"

Mary Anne smiled. "No, I'm originally from Connecticut. I met my husband in college, and we moved here almost seventeen years ago."

"Coreen's become attached to your daughter. She's a sweet girl. I'm sure you're really proud of her."

Mary Anne ran a hand around the moisture that collected on her glass. "I'm proud of her. But I don't think she realizes it. Teenagers can be moody."

"I know what ya mean. I lived through four of 'em—and now we have Coreen."

Silence lingered between them for a moment. Each took a few sips of lemonade. Estelle nearly gave up on any conversation when Mary Anne twisted in her chair.

"Estelle, I came in here because I need to talk to you."

Estelle placed her glass on a small table and steeled herself for nosy questions.

"I know you and your family lost your homes and belongings in the flood. My husband is Jim Wilhoit, the president of the Bank of Mt. Pleasant, and he has an associate … actually he's more than an associate. He's a good friend. They play golf together all the time."

Estelle wrinkled her nose and stared at the woman. She sure meandered a lot.

Mary Anne chuckled and took a deep breath. "I'm not saying this very well. Let me try again. My husband's friend is Maurice Cooke. He owns, of all things, a monument company. You know, where they make grave markers and headstones. Well, his business is growing so he opened a new office in Knoxville. Recently, he decided to move over there to get it up and growing. So he needs someone to take over the daily operations here."

She paused to take a breath, so Estelle spoke up. "Mary Anne, dear, I'm confused about why you're telling me this."

"The thing is that Maurice lived in the business here—it's a house—and he displayed the gravestones in a side yard for people to view and place orders and such. Sounds a bit macabre when you talk about it like that, doesn't it?" She flicked her short hair away from her ear.

"I still don't understand."

"He needs someone to live in the house and take orders for the stones here— and I'll call them stones because it sounds more civilized—send him the orders, and then let the people know when they're going to be placed in the cemetery."

"Live in the house?"

"Yes. And this is the exciting part. It's a three-bedroom house with one and a half bathrooms. Also, since he lived in the house himself until recently, it's pretty much completely furnished—except for beds."

"How much would this house cost to live in?" Estelle readied for a big disappointment.

"Absolutely nothing. That would be your salary for taking orders and sending them to him. It also includes all utilities."

Estelle's eyes grew wide and darted back and forth with realization. "You did say it wouldn't cost us anything—anything at all—except for being there to take orders?"

"Exactly."

A smile stretched across Estelle's face. "And you did say bathrooms, didn't you?"

Mary Anne leaned forward and laughed. "Running water in the kitchen and the bathrooms. And the house has a lovely front porch, a little sun porch in the back, and a fenced yard for Patches." She waved her hands as she described everything.

"Mercy, it sounds perfect. I mean, I'd always be there because I ain't able to go nowhere no way." She patted her lips. "I got a couple of questions—like how will I know how to do the job? And where's it at? Sarah's gonna be working over at Morgan's and Coreen'll have to go to school somewheres."

"Maurice will arrange a time to come over and teach you how to do things. It would probably be a good idea to include Sarah and Coreen in case they need to help you out. The location is convenient to anything in Mt. Pleasant. It's a small town, less than a mile to get anywhere. Sarah can easily walk to Morgan's and Coreen can walk to school. It's Betty Anne's school too, and is close to the library and the park. There's lots for her to do in town."

"One more question, dear." Estelle leaned over to her and spoke secretively. "When can we move in?"

The two burst into laughter and joined hands like old friends.

Chapter 25

Coreen stumbled across the common room, her vision blurred by tears. She felt the stares from every person in the room. She didn't care. Let them. People always whispered behind her back. She flung open the backdoor and ran. Her feet barely touched the ground as she crossed the church yard, threw open the gate, and dropped to the ground. She threw her arms around Patches and buried her face in the dog's fur.

"Why won't nobody understand? Why don't I matter to anybody? I'm so sick of being treated like I'm a bug that needs to be squashed." Patches wriggled out of her tight grasp. "I'm sorry, boy. I didn't mean to hurt you. You're my only family member that ever truly loved me." Patches came to her and curled up in her lap. "I've tried so hard to make them love me. I obey them. I work really hard and do my chores when I'm supposed to. I don't sass or talk back. It doesn't help at all. They yell at me and tell me how stupid I am. Daddy beat me so hard I thought he might kill me. Mama hit me too." Coreen gently stroked Patches.

"It's like she hit me 'cause she couldn't hit him. Hate. I hate him too. There. I said it. It's true. I got so much hate built up in me that I wanted to kill Daddy myself." Coreen blew out all the air in her lungs and gasped for air. Could she have killed him?

"I hate men. I don't never want to get married. Men are mean and no good. I'll just live with you, Patches." The horrible things Daddy did played out in her mind. Why would a woman want to be married? Money? Well, she refused to depend on a man for money. She'd earn it herself. If she was smart enough. And talented enough. She chewed on her lip.

Maybe they were right about her though. If so, what would she do then?

Death. The idea never left her mind. Never again would she be beaten or hated by a man. Darkness filled her up. If only the God who killed her daddy would kill her—or else make her dreams of a happy life come true.

No. He wouldn't do that. She pulled her knees up to her chest.

God must hate her too. Her heart ached that even God considered her unworthy of love. She lay facedown in the grass and cried, cried until she couldn't cry any more.

A rattling sigh ended the tears. Coreen raised up, sucked in lungs full of humid air, and wiped at her eyes and nose. Patches raised his head, wriggled himself free, and wandered over to Betty Anne.

Coreen cocked her head. "How long you been sitting there?"

"A while."

"Why didn't ya say nothing to me?"

"I sat here with you while you cried."

Coreen glanced at her new friend, bewildered and touched in a funny sort of way. Nobody ever treated her with such kindness before. "Thanks."

Betty Anne leaned forward and ran her fingers through the hot grass as if she were massaging the earth beneath. Patches whimpered and squeezed himself under her arms. She switched her attention to massaging the dog's head.

Coreen plucked blades of grass and tossed them away from her. "D'ya ever wish you could leave everything—and everybody—and go somewhere where you don't know nobody at all and live all by yourself?"

"Sometimes, I guess. Why? You want to go somewhere else?"

"I dream about going to Nashville to the Grand Ole Opry and singing my songs. The whole crowd would clap their hands for me and tell me how good I am. They'd all want to be my friend, including all the famous people like Loretta Lynn."

"Well, maybe it'll happen. I don't see why not."

"Have you been there?"

"No, not Nashville. I've been to a few other places though."

"Like where?"

Patches curled up in Betty Anne's lap as she continued to run her fingers through the dog's fur. "We went to Florida a few times and rented a house on the beach."

"I ain't never seen no beach. I read about it in books. Is it as beautiful as they say? Did you swim in the ocean?"

"Yeah. It was fun."

Coreen stared up at the mountains surrounding her. Family fun? Her shoulders drooped forward as the day's events chased around in her head like a swarm of angry bees. She glanced at Betty Anne, sitting quietly beside her staring up at the same mountains. If only she had a family like Betty Anne.

"Betty Anne ... since you know so much stuff ... maybe you can tell me something."

"I don't think I'm as smart as you think I am—but I'll try."

"You are smart too. Heck, you know things I ain't never even heard of before. How'd you learn it all anyways?"

Betty Anne moved closer to Coreen and crossed her legs in front of her. Patches climbed on. "Umm, mostly on TV. I've learned a lot there. Don't you watch ... Oh, I forgot. You didn't have a TV."

"Nope."

Betty Anne giggled and smiled, showing her perfect white teeth. "Don't you worry. I think you'll be learning all about TVs real soon."

Coreen wrinkled her brow as she saw the twinkle in Betty Anne's eyes. "Here ya go again with secret stuff. I'm tired of secrets. What'ya mean?"

"Didn't you have a question you wanted to ask me?"

"Yeah, I forgot." She sighed, lifting her shoulders to bring in fresh air. "There's something important I really need to know. I tried asking Mammaw, but she wouldn't tell me. She still thinks I'm a baby or something and won't talk to me about things at all."

"Is that why you left her crying earlier?"

"You saw that, huh? Yeah. Part of it." She stared at the grass again.

"What do you want to know?"

Coreen sighed and reached out to knead Patches' ear. "Ya remember when Grandmother Della screamed her head off today at the funeral home?"

"Some of it." Betty Anne lowered her eyes.

"Well, I need to know what she meant when she said bastard child."

"Oh."

"D'ya know what it means?"

"Well ... I ... uh ..."

Coreen begged. "Please, tell me."

Betty Anne squeezed her bottom lip between her fingers. "I think it's a bad word. She probably said it to hurt your mom. It may not mean anything at all ... But ... I think it means a child who's born ... you know, like before the parents get married. But it can't be, can it? Weren't your parents married when you were born?"

Coreen felt a combination of confusion, disgust, and relief. "I don't know. I weren't there when I's born. I mean, I weren't old enough to know what's going on. But they're married. I'm sure. My last name's Shell, ain't it?"

"Hmm, I suppose it could mean you were almost there when they got married." Betty Anne straightened up and opened her eyes wide. "Do you know when their anniversary is?"

"I don't know the year. I never seen a marriage license or nothing. You mean, my mama coulda been—you know, with me—before they got married?" Her face screwed up like she'd bitten into a persimmon before first frost.

She stared at a mountain. Would her mama have—could she have—done *that* before ... She shook her head. Hard enough to imagine her mother and father caring enough for each other to have her in the first place. But then, women apparently didn't much have a choice in such matters. Like her daddy's promise? Her stomach churned. She might throw up.

Coreen dropped her head into her hands, leaned on her knees, and said, "My brain's hurting thinking about all this stuff. Let's forget it."

"Good idea." Betty Anne let out a huge breath, lay back on the grass, and looked up at the clouds. An open invitation to Patches, who rushed to smother her face in kisses, and caused her to wriggle and burst into a cascade of giggles. "Patches, stop it. You're getting me all wet in dog slobbers."

When Betty Anne sat back up to avoid more licking, Coreen asked, "I got one more question. What's a hussy?"

"It's what they call a woman who's always running around with boys and trying to get them to kiss her and stuff." Betty Anne wrinkled her brow. "Why?"

"That's what Grandmother Della called Mama." Coreen snarled.

Betty Anne waved her hand. "Nah, sounds crazy to me. Your mom is quiet-like and ... normal. I think your grandmother's wacko. Sorry."

"She sure is. She ain't never been nice to me either. I think she hates us both."

"Don't let her upset you. She's nuts." Betty Anne took Coreen's wrists. "She doesn't matter. I think you're great."

Smiling up at her, Coreen said, "I think you're great too."

"Girls? Betty Anne, Coreen?"

Patches jumped up and down and barked at the approaching figure. Betty Anne stood and dusted herself off as her mother approached the gate.

"I thought you'd be over here. You girls need to get inside. They're getting ready to serve dinner."

"Supper!" Coreen jumped up from the grass. "I sure don't want to miss supper. I'm starved. I ain't eat a thing since breakfast. Come on, Betty Anne."

The girls slipped out the gate just as a flash of lightning lit the sky. A raindrop plopped on Coreen's head. Seemed like life was just one storm after another. Thunder rumbled.

Coreen tucked her chin. The storm inside her head scared her more than the one raging around her.

Chapter 26

The crackle of thunder made Estelle jump. Raindrops spat against the casement windows and slid down. Rain. Again. The natural light dimmed in the room until she could barely see. It mirrored how she felt right now—in a dark place where she couldn't see a way out.

The new house and job gave encouragement to her situation, but it didn't take care of the deeper darkness in her family's life. Would there ever be an end to their storm? If only she could make things right. Every time she tried to fix things though, she made a bigger mess. She reckoned she needed to sit back and let them try to work it out.

Lightning flashed. Time to do something positive instead of dwelling on things she couldn't fix. The chair squeaked as she struggled up, grabbed her cane, and hobbled over to the wall. She flipped the light switch and looked around the room. She needed to occupy her fingers.

Changing out of her new clothes would mean walking through all those people outside. It could wait a while longer. She heaved a sigh and glanced around the room. Her pocketbook rested on a shelf nearby. A good time to go through the papers she stuffed inside before leaving the house. She retrieved the bag, dragged her chair in front of the cot, and settled into it. She dumped the contents onto the cot.

The everyday items went back into her pocketbook. Then she separated papers from photos. She hoped she got all the important stuff. One official envelope contained birth certificates for each of her children. Another made her pause.

Sarah and Vernon's marriage certificate.

Sarah hadn't wanted it. She told Estelle to keep it, since the marriage was her idea and not Sarah's. Did she do the wrong thing? What else could she have done? She dropped the envelope on top of the stack.

Each faded image reminded her of happier days. Tears threatened to flow. She paused as she picked up one sepia photo of her young family while Jack still lived. The tears let go. One fell onto the photo. She dabbed the tear away with the skirt of her dress. They looked so happy.

She caressed each person in the photo, as if touching them made their happiness real again. "How I miss you. My sweet, sweet Jack. How I wish you were still here with me—with all of us. If you'd been here, none of this awful stuff would have happened to Sarah. You would have protected her. You wouldn't have let Vernon get away with what he did to her. Things would be so different. I did my best. I really tried. But I failed her. I failed our baby. I'm sorry, Jack."

Estelle wiped away the remnants of tears on her wrinkled cheeks and gently placed the photo on top of the stack. *I love you, my precious Jack. It won't be long till I'll be with ya again.*

She continued to go through the photos until she came to one of a young Sarah, surrounded by her sister, Shirley, and her brothers, Larry and John Jr. They all smiled as Sarah blew out the candles on a cake—thirteen candles. John Jr., dressed in his navy whites, looked all growed up at only nineteen. The last happy picture taken of Sarah—so full of hope and innocence.

A knock sounded on the door. Estelle dropped the photo back onto the pile. "Come in."

The door opened a few inches. "Miss Estelle? It's DeWayne. Can I talk to ya a minute?"

"'Course ya can. Come on in."

DeWayne, dressed in his sheriff's uniform, jingled from the gear around his waist as he entered the room and closed the door.

"Here, have a seat so I don't have to look up at ya, okay?"

"Sure thing." He dragged a chair around and settled himself, clanging loudly against the metal. He removed his sheriff's hat and exposed closely cropped red hair.

"Looks like you got a little wet there. Reckon it's still raining, ain't it?"

"Yeah, not too bad. 'Spect it'll stop soon. Don't seem to have the heart in it from earlier this week, thank goodness." He tapped his hat, causing a spray of raindrops. "Uh, Miss Estelle, I wanted to check up on y'all. Everybody okay? I's a bit worried 'bout Sarah. I didn't see her out there."

Estelle searched DeWayne's face, which twitched a little. "I don't know. Shirley took her someplace. I 'spect she's trying to calm her down."

"I'm sorry y'all went through that. Della ain't an easy bird to handle. Apple don't fall far from the tree now, does it?"

Estelle nodded. "I guess you're right there. At least Sarah shouldn't have to deal with her no more after today."

"Yeah." DeWayne smacked the hat a bit harder.

Estelle wrinkled her eyebrows and stared at DeWayne. He looked troubled. "Is there something else you need to say?"

He looked into her eyes and screwed up his mouth. "Yeah. Guess I do. I probably should tell Sarah first, but ... you need to know too, and she ain't here."

"What is it? Something wrong?" A stone seemed to be lodged in the pit of her stomach.

"It's about Vernon. He didn't drown in the flood."

"What ya mean?" The stone felt like a boulder now. If Vernon wasn't dead after all, he would hunt down Sarah and Coreen and the misery would continue. But it couldn't be possible. They all saw him in the casket today. She shook her head.

"Well ... he didn't *drown* at all. You see ..."

Estelle watched DeWayne fidget with his hat and tear up his face like he was about to confess to his mama about something awful. She reached out and put her hand on his. "Honey, tell me what it is. Ain't no need to suffer so."

He took a deep breath and looked right at her. "I'm sorry, Miss Estelle. Truth is, Vernon didn't drown in his car. Somebody shot him."

"Shot?" Estelle visibly relaxed. "You mean somebody shot him—or did he shoot his self?"

"Homicide. Murder. Somebody shot him dead."

"D'ya know who done it?"

"Not yet. We're investigating. Maybe you can help. D'ya know anybody who'd want to shoot him?"

She slapped her knee and turned her head with a click of her tongue. "Child, who didn't want to kill him? I don't reckon nobody liked him in the whole county. And maybe the next one over too."

"Yeah, I kinda figured. But no one person stands out to you?"

"You mean like my daughter? Or me?"

"No. I know y'all didn't do it. You didn't have no way to get out where it happened."

"Well, thank goodness." She didn't tell him how much she wanted to shoot Vernon. "Where'd it happen?"

"Off a little path not too far from the mine. I ain't got no idea why he was down there. But it was close to the river. That's why we thought he drowned at first. The water was up over the front end of the car."

"Lands a mercy. Who'd a thought. I hate to say it, but I almost hope you don't figure out who done it. Can't help but think he—or she—shouldn't be punished for taking care of an evil varmint."

The door to the room burst open as Coreen and Betty Anne entered, laughing. "Oops. Sorry, Mammaw. I didn't know you had company. Hi, Sheriff Mayhall."

"Howdy-do, ladies."

DeWayne hefted himself and his gear off the chair and moved to the door. "Well, I'll see you ladies later. I'm gonna look for Sarah."

"Mammaw, it's time for supper. Are Mama and Aunt Shirley back?"

"Not yet, honey. They'll be back soon. Can you help me up, Coreen? I been sitting in this dadburn chair too long."

"Shore, we'll help you up." Coreen pulled on Estelle's arm while Betty Anne attempted to help with the other. Time with her friend sure had changed Coreen's attitude.

The girls escorted Estelle to her comfortable chair. Sideward glances followed her. To her surprise, a few of the women she knew made the effort to approach her and smile, offering a pleasant greeting in passing. By the time she arrived at the chair, she had relaxed.

"I'll get your supper for you, Mammaw. Be right back." Coreen patted her shoulder and then made her way with Betty Anne to the counter.

Estelle allowed her eyes to wander around the room. The numbers were way down. Apparently several folks either returned to their homes or found a new place to live. Her heart skipped a beat as she thought about her news, good and bad. She searched the room, hoping to find Sarah and Shirley. They still weren't there.

"Hello, Estelle. You okay?" Imogene Morgan asked, subdued.

"Yeah, fine as possible, I reckon."

"I saw you frowning and wondered if something else …"

Estelle leaned forward and whispered, "Them rowdy children almost knocked the tray of food out of a poor old man's hands."

Imogene looked in the direction of the still-running children. "It's a bit difficult when children are confined indoors and the parents are distracted. It'll be better for them when they find a place to live. I'm sure this hasn't been easy for anybody."

"You got that right. 'Course, I'm glad the church could help us. But I admit, I'll be glad to be home again. You know what I mean?"

Imogene sat across from Estelle. "I sure do. Although I love being with my grandbabies, I'm plumb wore out. It'll be nice to get back to my house too. Have you and the girls got any leads yet?"

Estelle sat upright and grinned. "I certainly have. I'm so excited. Mary Anne Wilhoit told me about a house in Mt. Pleasant available. It's actually a business for tombstones."

"Mr. Cooke's company?"

"Yep, it is. And the great thing is, it's a job for me to take care of it while he's

136

in Knoxville. I get paid with free rent and utilities."

"Estelle, how wonderful." Imogene clapped her hands together. "I'm excited for you. How the Lord blesses. When do you get to move in?"

As Estelle started to answer, Coreen appeared with a tray of food. "Move in where, Mammaw? Why didn't you tell me?" She plopped the tray down with such force the food danced on the plate and the glass of tea sloshed over the side. Then she stared at her grandmother with pursed lips, hands on her hips.

"Be careful, Coreen. I just this minute found out. Besides, I's hoping to tell you and your mama at the same time. Now, you keep your little mouth quiet and don't spoil it, ya hear?"

Coreen rolled her eyes. "Yeah, yeah, I know. Be quiet, Coreen. Don't say nothing, Coreen. Story of my life. Where we moving—and when?"

Estelle patted her granddaughter on the arm and whispered, "It's a house in Mt. Pleasant and we're moving in day after tomorrow."

"Hot diggity. That's great, ain't it, Betty Anne?"

"Yeah, it is." Betty Anne smiled coyly.

"Wait a minute." Coreen glared. "You already knowed about it, didn't you?"

"Uh-huh."

"Is that what the big secret was?"

Betty Anne smiled bigger.

Coreen huffed.

Estelle said, "Honey, go get your dinner before it's all gone. This shore looks good. The one thing I'm gonna miss like crazy is the great cooks in this church."

"Me too, Mammaw. Miss Cora makes the best yeast rolls in the world. And Miss Gloria cooks everything dee-licious."

"How'd you know their names?" Estelle crossed her arms.

"Mammaw, don't you know you always have to be nice to the cook?" Coreen giggled as she and Betty Anne locked arms and rushed to the dinner line.

"Mercy, that girl." Estelle laughed.

"We do have wonderful cooks here—and wonderful people. I'm going to miss all the new folks I've met this week though." Imogene patted Estelle's arm and smiled.

Estelle finished chewing and swallowed. "Me too. The church's been real good to us. Y'all got a sweet preacher too—and his wife. Such a precious couple." She gazed around the room. Lots of empty seats. "Looks like the crowd's a little lighter today."

"I believe so. A few went back to their own homes. I understand the flood destroyed the whole lower camp of Dodge. Some of the families found a place at another camp, and HUD put a couple of families into trailers."

Estelle stopped eating long enough to snarl her face. "Ooh, I'd hate to have to live in a trailer. For one thing, I don't think I could make it up the steps to the door. I also heard they's like an oven in the summer and go up like a dry brush fire if you ain't careful."

Imogene nodded. "I guess it's better than nothing."

"Yeah, better than nothing."

"What's better than nothing, Mammaw?" Coreen asked as she and Betty Anne took the seats next to Imogene.

"Girl, you are plain ole nosey."

"Gee, Mammaw, how'm I supposed to learn stuff if I don't ask?"

Imogene cooed, "I think she's got ya, there, Estelle."

Coreen smiled smugly and looked at her grandmother, expecting an answer.

Estelle stabbed a green bean and held it up. "They's times, little Coreen, when it's best not to know too much. Knowing can be worse than not knowing—you remember that."

"I can't win. But I can keep secrets."

Estelle looked closely at Coreen. What secrets could she be carrying around? She remembered when another young girl carried a secret. A secret that destroyed her life. *Lord, please don't let Coreen's secrets ruin her.*

What had Vernon done to warrant killing? Guess he had some secrets too. At least one secret nasty enough to lead to his final comeuppance.

Chapter 27

Shirley pulled into the parking lot of the church. "It's still raining a little. Guess we're gonna get wet."

"Yep, reckon so. Or … we could sit here in the air-conditioning till it stops." Sarah didn't relish rushing herself into a room with all those people. Gossip surely got around blaming her for Vernon's life—and death. Wouldn't be easy to keep her mouth shut. But secrets needed to be kept.

Nobody's business but hers.

Besides, they wouldn't believe her anyway. People wanted to believe the worst, whether it's true or not.

Shirley giggled. "I don't think I have enough gas in the car."

The rain slacked off, but Sarah stayed put.

After a couple of minutes, Shirley stared out the windshield. "You know, you're gonna have to go in there eventually. Who knows, it might not be as bad as you think. At least you know Della won't be there."

"I'm getting myself ready for it. Hope Mother managed okay."

"'Course she did. She's a tough ole bird. She ain't gonna let anything get to her."

"Yeah, she's tough all right. Sometimes I wish she didn't expect me to be as tough as her."

"I know. She never did understand how I felt about nothing either. But she took care of us even when things were really hard for her. Guess she figures if she can do it, so can we."

"Yeah." Sarah watched the collected raindrops roll down the windshield and gradually make their way haphazardly to the bottom.

"Before we go in, I got something I brought for y'all." Shirley reached for her bag and rummaged around inside. She retrieved a wrinkled pink envelope and held it in both hands like a treasured heirloom. "My friends at church heard about what happened to y'all and they got together. This is a gift from them to you and Mumsie to help you get back on your feet."

As Shirley held out the envelope, Sarah stopped it with her hand. "No, wait. What is it?"

"Well, look inside and you'll know."

"But ... Shirley ... I ..."

"Sarah, it's okay. There's some really nice people out there who care about you—even if they've never met you."

Sarah twisted in the passenger seat, her legs ripping loose from the damp leather seat like removing a Band-Aid from a wound. She cringed. Nobody had ever treated her kindly before. Now it seemed everybody wanted to help her. She wiggled in the seat. Her stomach twisted. With a moan, she faced her sister.

Shirley patiently sat with the envelope extended. Finally, Sarah blew out the air in her lungs and flopped her hands in her lap, squeezed her eyes closed, and opened them again. The envelope was still there. She hesitantly took it and stared. Her heart thumped. The car filled with fog as she opened the flap on the envelope enough to see a collection of twenty-, ten-, five-, and one-dollar bills inside.

"Shirley ... It's too much. I can't take this." She shoved the envelope back.

"Hon, you're gonna need help getting started. Consider this a blessing and let it go. How were you planning to get new clothes and food after you found a place to live? I know Miss Morgan offered you a job, but you won't get a paycheck for a while yet. And it won't be much when you do. Y'all need this."

Sarah felt the hot dog and Doolie from Ray's battling with each other in her stomach. She knew the money would come in handy, but she didn't want to be beholden to strangers. From her sister's steel-eyed expression, she knew she was beaten on the issue. "It ain't like I don't appreciate it. It's ... well ..."

"I know, sweetie." She cupped Sarah's face with her hands. "You're not used to anybody being nice to ya, and it's gonna take getting used to."

Sarah smiled at her sister. "Guess so. Please tell your friends I said thank you. I didn't know how I's gonna make it. You know, it's kinda funny. Here I am in one of the most awful times of my life—one of them, mind you—and yet it's one of the best times of my life. I don't get it."

"Sometimes it takes an awful thing to happen for us to have the courage to grab hold of the good things."

"I still don't right understand it, but I reckon I'm gonna have to be settled with whatever comes. I got one more question for ya." Sarah pointed her finger at her sister and squinted.

"What?" Shirley asked wide-eyed, as if being falsely accused.

"How'd your friends know about the flood taking our house, when you said you didn't know what happened till you got here?"

"Well ..." Shirley said in her singsong twang. "I wanted to give you the chance to tell me everything. I didn't have all the details."

"You're awful. You know it, don't ya?"

"I don't know." Shirley jutted out her chin. "But I do know I love ya, sis. I know that for sure."

Sarah reached out and threw her arms around Shirley in a tight squeeze. Shirley gasped. Her sister let go and pulled back to her side of the seat. Her eyes glistened as she stared at the envelope in her hand and smiled. Shirley smiled back.

"I love you too, Shirl."

Shirley gasped again. And then the tears came.

Chapter 28

Coreen carried the bags of clothes Betty Anne's mother brought her into the dressing room, found a stall, and pulled the curtain shut to give her total privacy as she tried them on. Uneasily, she peered out from behind the curtain to make sure no one was around. She wished the door would lock. Taking the first bag, she turned it upside down and dumped it on the floor. Picking up the first item, she ran her fingers over it, smelled the clean scent, and smiled. After removing her dirty funeral dress, she quickly replaced it with one from the bags. Then, to see how it looked, she pulled back the curtain slightly and stood in front of a mirror on the wall.

She squealed with delight. She looked like a princess. Head held high, she threw back her shoulders. The girl smiling back from the mirror deserved respect.

She took her time, went through each piece, tried it on, and admired herself in the mirror. Finally, she reached the bottom of the second pile and decided to wear the pink shorts and matching patterned shirt. A new person, born in the mirror, picked up the dress she wore earlier in the day and hung it next to the ruffled floral dress from the clothes closet. Beside the new clothes hung the faded and threadbare dress from her old life.

A scowl replaced the smile. Hot blood rushed through her body.

Coreen reached up and yanked the dress off the hanger with a growl. As the hanger danced violently on the rod, she balled up the dress, walked across the room, lifted the metal lid off the trash can, and propelled the dress into the black abyss of debris. With a deep sigh, she slammed the lid onto the can.

The smile returned.

* * *

Shirley squeezed Sarah's arm as they opened the back door and entered the common hall. "I feel you resisting me, Sarah. Come on."

"I'm resisting because you're squeezing my arm off. You're hurting me. Cut it out." Sarah tried to break loose from her grasp, but like when they were kids, Shirley was too strong. She did the only thing she could think of—a dead stop.

"I'm okay, Shirley. You don't have to force me into the room. I'm gonna have a bruise on my arm." She glared at her sister. "A bruise like Vernon always give me."

"Sis, I didn't mean to hurt you. I wanted you to be brave and not hightail it out of here. I'll let go as long as you're sure you can do this."

Sarah breathed in deeply, her stomach still twisted in knots. How wonderful it would be to turn and run and never deal with any of this again. But it wouldn't solve anything. She decided to face it and demand respect.

"Shirl, I'm shore. Now get off me."

"Fine. Let's go." Shirley gestured for her to lead the way.

Sarah raised her chin and walked toward *their* table. Every eye in the room seemed to burn a hole in her back. Sweat dripped down her neck. The sick feeling returned. She willed herself to take the next step and then the next.

When they got to the table, Estelle's throne sat empty. Sarah raised her eyes and stared directly into all the eyes staring at her and judging her. She would make them look away. She would be the strong one.

Imogene Morgan approached with a smile. "Hello, ladies. I'm glad to see you made it back safely." She took Sarah's hand and spoke softly while looking into her eyes. "I hope you're doing okay, Sarah."

"I'm doing all right, Imogene. Sorry you were a part of it all."

"Don't worry about me, dear. I work with the public, remember. I know how people can be."

"D'ya happen to know where my family is?" Sarah glanced around the room again.

"Yes, I do. Your mom visited the little girl's room, and Coreen's trying on the clothes Betty Anne and her mother brought her. Are you ladies hungry? I believe they still have food in there."

Sarah smiled and rubbed her stomach. "No, thank you. Shirley and I stopped by the drive-in during the rain and ate."

Shirley popped into the conversation. "Well, speak for yourself. I think I'm gonna go up there and check it out."

"Shirley, where d'ya put it?" Sarah asked as her sister bounced toward the kitchen.

"I put it in my mouth, dear sister, in—my—mouth." Shirley giggled as she pointed to her lips and continued walking.

Mother, wearing her old dress, approached. "Sarah, you're back."

"Yep. But I thought Shirley was gonna kill me out there."

"Kill you? Where you been?"

"Come over here and sit down and I'll tell you all about it, Mother." She took her arm and assisted her to her chair.

As they got settled, with Imogene joining them, her mother gave an exaggerated smile. With her arms crossed, she tapped a rhythm on her upper arms. "Before you tell me anything, I got something to tell you first."

Shirley joined the group with a plate piled high with chicken fried steak, mashed potatoes, and slices of fresh garden tomatoes, accompanied by a dish of banana pudding.

"Shirley, I'm glad you're here. You need to hear the news too."

"News? What news?" Shirley mumbled around the first bite already stuffed into her mouth. "Mmmm, this is good."

"I got good news and not so good news. I reckon you're gonna want the good news first."

"I can't handle much more bad news. Reckon you better start with the good." Sarah reared back in her chair and ran her fingers through her hair, twisting it into a bun.

"Okay. The first good news is we got a house to live in."

"What? Where? How much is it gonna cost?" Shirley and Sarah shouted over top of each other.

"Hold on. I'll tell you." Sarah leaned forward as her mother told them about the new house, the job, and all the details. "I been thinking about our old houses. You know there might be some things in there we could still use. Maybe you could ask DeWayne to take you up there tomorrow to see. I'm afraid if you wait much longer, the looters might beat you to it."

Sarah's stomach did a flip-flop when her mother mentioned DeWayne. She pushed the reaction aside. "I already thought of it, Mother. DeWayne's gonna pick us up in the morning. Shirley, can you go?"

"'Course I'll go." Shirley tried to talk around a mouthful of food. "I can work on Mumsie's house and you two can work on yours."

"It's settled." Sarah squinted her eyes. "Now, Mother, what's the bad news?"

Her mother's deep frown made Sarah's neck tingle. It looked like more bad news.

"What's the bad news?"

"DeWayne come by while ago looking for you."

Her mother's downtrodden voice made her feel cold all over. Did somebody else die? Or did Della find another way to torture her? "It ain't Della, is it? She causing more trouble? I swear, if she tries to—"

"No, it ain't Della. It's something else."

"What? What is it, Mother?" Sarah pleaded for her mother to get it over with. She didn't know if she could handle one more thing, but she needed to know.

"Honey, Vernon didn't drown in the flood. He was shot dead."

Shirley choked on her banana pudding and spluttered it all over the table. Imogene chirped like a frightened bird. Sarah felt the blood drain from her entire body. The room seemed to go silent. Her head buzzed. Shot? Murdered?

The room turned black.

* * *

Coreen bounded up to the table carrying the two large bags in time to hear Mammaw say her daddy didn't drown. Somebody shot him dead. The bags dropped to the floor with a *pop* that sounded like a gunshot. The room whirled around her. She might throw up.

"Coreen, go to the kitchen and get a cold rag for your mama. She's passed out colder than kraut. Coreen! Go." Mammaw's sharp voice snapped her out of her shock.

She turned and ran to the kitchen, grabbed a towel from the counter, and poured water over it. When she got back to the table, her mama lay flat on the floor. Shirley grabbed the rag and laid it across Mama's neck. Coreen wrung her hands. After a minute, Shirley turned it over and put it on her forehead. A crowd huddled around the still figure, talking to her and smacking her hands and cheeks. Coreen felt dizzy. Would she hit the floor next? After what seemed forever, Mama moaned and started to move.

"Sarah, you okay, honey? Sarah?" Tears gathered in Mammaw's eyes.

"Sis, time to wake up now."

"Mama, you all right?" Coreen tried to get to her, but the crowd of people wouldn't let her pass.

Mammaw grabbed Coreen's arm as her mama sat up. "She'll be fine. There's been a bit too much excitement today. Why don't you take your new clothes over to the room and put them away for now? Your mama will be fine in a minute."

"But Mammaw, I don't wanna leave her."

"It's okay." Mammaw nodded and spoke softly. "Go ahead and take them clothes now. She needs a bit of quiet. Go on, honey."

"But …" Coreen growled in anguish. *Go away, Coreen. Leave us alone, Coreen.* She snarled with as much disrespect as she could muster. "Yes, ma'am."

"Go on, take 'em now."

Coreen snatched the bags and stormed across the room. Always the same. *We don't want you, Coreen. I hate you, Coreen.* Hot tears rolled down her cheeks.

She stopped at the door to their room and looked back at the table. Mama sat up now and held the rag on her face all by herself. Miss Imogene and a few other people were all clustered around the table. The table where she should be.

Why did they always push her away? Coreen entered the room and searched for an appropriate spot to stash the bags so her mother wouldn't gripe at her later. Should she should go back to her mama anyway? Or sit all alone? She didn't think she could handle anymore pushing away today. She stood in the middle of the room, doing nothing.

Sunlight filtered into the room through the narrow window. The storm must be over.

Daddy was shot. Which meant somebody murdered him. But who? And why? So many questions.

A thought popped into her head. Maybe they wouldn't figure out who done it. Maybe they should just be glad and let it go.

A stack of photos on Mammaw's cot caught her attention. She picked up the picture on top. Four young people stood around a birthday cake with candles glowing. She tried to count the candles, but the photo was too blurry. Turning it over, she read the names of the people in the photo—Shirley, Sarah, Junior, and Larry. Sarah's 13th birthday—followed by a date. She smiled at the younger version of her mama and Shirley. Then she frowned at the date only a year before she was born.

"Mama was thirteen ..." She counted twice on her fingers. "Fifteen months before I's born? Now I know Miss Hickey said it takes a baby nine months to be born. That means Mama was ... about thirteen and a half when she ... uh ... got me. Thirteen and a half? That can't be. I must've counted wrong."

Coreen counted again and got the same result. Her head whirled. Girls didn't get married when they're only thirteen.

She picked up the stack of papers and carefully looked at each one. One envelope addressed to Estelle Kincaid showed promise. Her fingers tingled as she removed a document, opened it up, and read the certificate of marriage for Vernon D. Shell and Sarah E. Kincaid. The date was six months before she was born. She stared at the paper, expecting the numbers to change but they didn't. Her knees nearly gave out.

"I'm a bastard child."

Her body melted onto the cot as she tried to figure what it meant. Shame shrouded her like the shell around a rotten egg.

Did everybody know but her? Did everybody whisper about her all her life?

She filled with a mixture of wanting to run away and hide—or stomp her feet and tell all those mean people she didn't do anything wrong and to leave her alone.

Tears dripped from her cheeks and left splotches on her new blouse. Spots. Imperfections.

She could dress up in beautiful new clothes, but she was still Coreen Shell, bastard daughter of Vernon and Sarah Shell. No wonder her parents hated her. She was a mistake. A sin. The reason for her mama's beatings and terrible life. Coreen would never have happiness either. She didn't deserve it.

Chapter 29

Estelle rested her chin in the cup of her hand. Shirley had taken Sarah off somewhere to revive her from her unexpected news. Murder. Never expected something like this in her own family. Seemed no matter how many good things happen, there's always something to put a kink in it.

A familiar laugh caught her attention. She raised her head.

Doug Adkins pumped his arms to propel himself through the room, a combination of a hillbilly Burl Ives and Santa Claus with his rotund gut and graying facial hair. His cheeks flushed as he smiled and nodded to each person he passed. He made a point of giving a hearty hug to every woman over fifty—or thereabouts.

He approached Estelle and threw his arms around her in a tight squeeze and then topped it off with a big smooch on her cheek. "Hey there, beautiful. How ya doing today?"

Estelle giggled and her cheeks warmed. "I'm doing better now, handsome. What ya doing here, Doug? You a member of this church?"

"I sure am. I came over here tonight to get y'all in a good mood. I bet you're going stir-crazy sitting around here all day."

Estelle touched his arm. "Did your brother and his family make it out of the camp in time? I wondered about them, since they ain't here."

"Yeah, they made it. They been staying with us. I'm sure glad to see you here. Heard about Vernon. Sarah and Coreen okay?"

"Surviving. Things are looking up."

"Good. Now, are you ready to do some singing?"

Estelle clapped her hands together. "You're gonna sing for us?"

"I shore am. Think I can rustle up a few folks to join me? Where's Coreen?" He scanned the room. "I'll get her to sing with me. You know, she's got a voice like a songbird in spring. I been working with her over at the Dodge Camp School and I'm mighty impressed—and it takes a lot to impress me." Doug's laugh filled the room and sounded like a *ho-ho-ho*.

"I ain't sure where she went. She's probably eating. Or playing with that dog of hers."

He took a few steps toward the piano in the front of the room. "Well, if you see her, send her up to me."

Doug sat at the ancient upright piano, worn and stained with years of use, and began to play a lively Southern Gospel tune. The tinny and slightly out-of-tune ramblings across the keyboard soon gained the attention of most of the adults and practically all the children. As he sang, a few people joined in. Some made a beeline to their cots and retrieved well-worn cases holding beloved instruments salvaged from the rising floodwaters. They might not have a change of clothes, but they had saved their prized possessions.

One by one the instruments joined in—banjo, guitar, fiddle, mandolin, dulcimer, and even a tambourine. Even JT, the reason Estelle survived her escape from the camp, came forward and pulled a Jew's harp from his pocket and joined the song. Thankfully, he had emptied his mouth of the "backer" first.

Sarah and Shirley slipped in and sat with Estelle. The men played and some of them sang as they worked through their common repertoire of gospel and bluegrass. Even the children quieted down, moved to the music, clapped their hands, or twirled around on the slate floor. Around the room, the faces took on a glow of hopeful smiles. Shirley energetically sang along. Even Sarah sang, too softly to hear.

* * *

The music drew Coreen out of her sanctuary of depression with an irresistible power. She must seek it out, become a part of it.

Her salvation. Her escape.

She stood, walked to the door, and opened it a crack. Life came back into her body. Her heart beat to the rhythm as she stepped into the dining area.

When the song ended, Doug looked up and smiled. "Well, there you are, Miss Co-reen. Come sang with us."

Coreen's heart fluttered as she drew near to the group. Nothing else mattered except the music. She sang loud and clear. Passionately. A smile took the place of tears. Her heart lifted with the freedom of music. Energy flowed through her body. She was alive. Each of the instruments took a turn to shine in their own way as the makeshift band moved from one song to the next. Coreen forgot everything except music.

As the song ended, Doug turned to Coreen with a smile. "It's your turn, girl. How about 'Song of Hope'? You know that one, don't ya?" He winked at her.

A jolt of fear poked her in the stomach, but she answered. "Yeah, guess I do, since I wrote it."

Doug danced his fingers up and down the keyboard. Some of the men joined in as they figured out the direction of the melody. Coreen fingered the gold heart hanging around her neck as she waited. She took a deep breath, tried to ignore the rocks in her belly and her wobbly knees, opened her mouth, and sang strong and clear.

I breathed my first breath
Of sweet mountain air
Deep in a holler
'Neath two mountains there.

Daddy's a miner
My mama stays home
Tends to the children
And prays he'll come home.

Life ain't so easy
We struggle each day
Oh, things is real hard
But we've found a way.

When things get real bad
My mama will sing
A song in the night
To keep us hoping.

Oh, song of my hope
I'll sing you again
Bring me sweet promise
And help me again.

When Coreen finished, she heard a whoop. A glance across the room showed Shirley on her feet, clapping wildly. Her cheeks warmed and she rolled her eyes. Aunt Shirley. She would applaud even if she was awful.

She glanced around the room. Other people clapped too. Not just Aunt Shirley. Some even whooped. Coreen's cheeks warmed. She smiled and lowered her head slightly. What fun.

Doug stopped clapping and said to Coreen, "Now let's do 'Above the Fog.' Okay, girlie-girl?" Doug turned to the audience. "Y'all, this special young lady don't only sing prettier than any angels I know, she also writes her own songs. This one here's called 'Above the Fog.'"

Coreen took a deep breath of positive air as the crowd quieted and Mr. Adkins played. Her body hummed with excitement as she sang.

> *The clouds get heavy with our sadness*
> *And lay down on the mountains each night.*
> *They cover our sorrows with dense fog*
> *That soothes us and helps us to fight.*
>
> *Beneath the thick fog of the morning*
> *A bird sings his song in the darkness*
> *To wake up everyone still sleeping*
> *With a promise of sunshine's caress.*
>
> *Above the fog, the sun still shines,*
> *Beneath the mist the mountains stand.*
> *Don't matter none how dark your life seems,*
> *Because the fog is in God's hand.*

* * *

Tears pooled in Shirley's eyes as Coreen sang. Her heart burned inside her chest with pride. The precious girl's talent amazed her. She sounded like an angel. At least what Shirley thought an angel sounded like. She never realized Coreen could sing so beautifully and wondered if Sarah knew it before now.

She glanced beside her to question her sister but found an empty chair. She wrinkled her brow and scanned the hall in time to see the door to their room shut. She pushed back her chair and scooted behind the group, trying not to be noticed. At the door to the room, she sucked in a deep breath. Sarah found it necessary to leave the room instead of showing pride. The idea that perhaps it was jealousy tickled at Shirley's thoughts. Should she stick her nose into this?

She didn't have a choice.

She sighed and gently knocked on the door.

"Who is it?"

As the crowd expressed their support for the girl they whispered about only a while ago, Shirley opened the door. "It's me. Can I come in?"

"Do I have a choice?"

"No, not really. What's up?" She gently closed the door behind her.

"Nothing. Why d'ya think something's up?"

Soft light filtered into the room from the fading sky outside, casting shadows into the corners. Sarah sat cross-legged on her cot.

"Maybe it has to do with the fact you left the room while your daughter sang. Singing beautifully, I might add."

"What's wrong with it? I felt like leaving, that's all." Sarah clasped her fingers, unclasped them, and then rubbed them together repeatedly.

"Are you jealous of your daughter?"

"Don't be silly. Why in the world would I be jealous of a twelve-year-old child?"

Shirley squinted her eyes. "She's thirteen, not twelve. And you are jealous. Why?"

Sarah pounded her fists on her knees. "Maybe it has something to do with the fact she has what I never got a chance to have."

"What you talking about?"

"I dreamed too. I reckon you forgot I used to sing. I wanted desperately to get out of this place and be famous. I never wanted to be stuck here with a child I never wanted. A husband I hated."

Sarah's pouting did not impress Shirley. But she did understand broken dreams. Sarah exhibited more than regret. She was angry. There were no tears in Sarah's eyes this time.

"She ruined my dreams. She and Vernon destroyed my life. I hate Vernon for what he did to me, and I can't help but see him in her face." Sarah jumped up from the cot and paced the room, pounding her head with her fists.

Shirley grabbed Sarah's wrists and pulled her hands from her head. "Sarah, I'm sorry you hate what you have. I truly am. But you're gonna have to stop dwelling on the one thing you can't change. You've got to stop letting it have control over you." She lifted Sarah's chin. "You're free now. Take back your life. Stop punishing Coreen for what Vernon did to you."

Sarah turned away from her.

She spun her sister back around and pleaded until her head ached. "Build a new life ... a life you can love ... a Sarah you can love ... and a Coreen you can love."

"Love? I *hate* my life. I hate everything about it. I wish Coreen had died when Vernon beat me and tried to kill her."

Shirley gasped. Sarah had never had so much venom in her voice before. "You don't mean that. You're upset right now."

"Please leave me alone." Sarah pounced on every word. "Go on, get out!"

"But Sarah—"

"Go away!"

The sun sank close to the mountain, plunging the room in semi-darkness. Apparently, the sun had set on Sarah's heart too.

There was nothing she could do for her sister now. She must allow her to find answers on her own. She turned away and opened the door to leave. On the other side of the door stood an ashen, trembling Coreen.

"Coreen. No. Honey, I'm sorry." Shirley reached out to Coreen, but she took a couple of steps backward, stared at the floor for an instant, and shot off through the rows of cots toward the back of the room and up the stairs.

Shirley whirled around and stuck her hands on her hips. "Well, good job, Sarah. Coreen heard every word you said. I hope you're proud of yourself."

Shirley huffed out of the room and back to her mother. She dropped her chin. She blamed herself for this whole mess. Why hadn't she stayed out of it? If she'd kept quiet, Coreen would never have heard those words—words that probably destroyed the heart of a precious child who deserved a mother who loved her.

* * *

Coreen bounded up the stairs and out the front doors of the church. After a couple of steps, she stopped. Her head felt full of marshmallow cream and her ears buzzed like a nest of yellow jackets.

After a moment, she trudged down the steps like in a fog and ended up on the edge of the road. Cars whizzed past. The sun hid just below the ridge of the mountains and shot rays of brilliant crimson, gold, and purple into the leftover clouds from the brief rain. Billows of mist rose up from the hollers as moisture from the soggy earth mixed with summer heat. She saw the beauty of her surroundings but was numb to its effect.

She was as close to dead as she could get and still breathe. Maybe she should take one more step. At just the right moment. She closed her eyes.

No. Coreen opened her eyes. Her hand rested on the gate to the pastor's house. How did she get here? Patches whined and jumped up and down in anticipation. She flipped up the latch on the gate and entered, letting it slam shut behind her.

Patches danced. Coreen leaned down and smoothed the dog's ears with her hands. "Not now, Patches. I ain't in the mood. Let's sit down for a while and I'll rub your tummy, okay?"

Coreen plodded onto the porch, collapsed into the glider, and made it sway wildly. Patches waited until it stopped moving and jumped up beside her and lay down.

As the dog rolled over on his back, Coreen took her fingers and swirled them around and around on his pink tummy.

Coreen's throat burned deep into her gut. Her mama wished she had died. She hated her that much. Worthless. Nothing in life is worth fighting for if your own mama hates you and wants you dead.

She had tried to be good enough to love, but she failed. Why was she born in the first place? If only she had died. Then she wouldn't have to know what it's like to be hated by both parents. *I hate my life. I hate this place. I hate me too. I'm so tired of it all.* Coreen heaved sobs.

Patches whined and pawed at her arm. Coreen ignored him and let loose the anguish in her heart. She felt like an inner tube slashed by a big knife. All the air flowed out until it laid flat and dead on the ground, useless to everybody.

A movement made her gasp. Loretta stepped out of the dark doorway, sat down beside her, and wrapped her arms around her. She held Coreen tightly as they rocked together. Coreen whimpered as tears raced down her cheeks.

Loretta whispered as she caressed Coreen's hair. "Shhh. It's okay, honey. It's going to be okay. I'm here for you."

The two sat in silence on the glider, stared into the darkened yard, and watched the lightning bugs twinkle. The mountains totally hid the sun to the west and a barely visible half-moon peeked between the clouds. They sat in silence as the yard grew darker like someone lowered the wick of an oil lamp. Crickets sang their welcome to nightfall.

In the cloak of darkness, Coreen spoke. "Miss Loretta, do your mama and daddy love you?"

Loretta whispered, "Yes, they do."

Coreen sniffed and wiped away a stray tear. "I wish I could stop crying."

"It's okay to cry, honey. It can be a healing balm."

"What's a balm?"

"It's like a salve or medicine to heal a hurt."

"I guess I do feel a little better after I cry. But I seem to cry all the time. Sometimes I think by the time I'm eighteen, I'll be all cried out—and then what'll I do?"

"Maybe you should find more things to laugh and be happy about."

Coreen cocked her head. "What difference would that make?"

"Laughter cancels out the tears, especially if you laugh so hard you cry. It gives you twice as many tears for later."

Coreen turned her head to Loretta. "Miss Loretta, you're joshing me."

Loretta chuckled softly. "Sort of. But it does make sense. The more time we spend thinking about the happy things in our lives or making happy things happen, then the more time we don't spend thinking about all the not-so-happy stuff."

"I never thought about that." Coreen tapped her chin with her finger. "You know, Mama usually don't cry at all. She's ... quiet. 'Cept of course today."

Loretta turned to Coreen. "Honey, have you ever thought maybe your mom's all cried out?"

Coreen wrinkled her brow. "You think so?" She pinched her lip between her fingers. "It's kinda sad, ain't it?"

"Maybe she needs laughter in her life too."

Her heart softened. "Maybe she does, if only she wanted to."

Loretta squeezed her shoulder. "Be patient. I think eventually she'll decide it's what she's wanted all along."

"I hope so. You know I'm really gonna miss you when we move into our new house day after tomorrow."

Smiling her special smile, Loretta said, "I'm going to miss you too. Of course, you know where I am and you're always welcome to visit."

"Thanks. You might see me again—real soon."

"I loved your singing tonight. You have a lovely voice." Loretta made the word *lovely* sound soft and cuddly.

Coreen lowered her chin. "Thanks. I love to sing. I love to sing more than anything in the whole world—even more than eating, and I love eating."

"Then let your singing be your happy thoughts. You can have it with you wherever you go and whenever you need it."

"I guess you're right."

"You know, Coreen, your life's changing quite a bit right now. Your old life is gone. Of course, there are parts that'll still be with you—like your mom and the things going on with her. But you've been given a wonderful opportunity to grow. You're making new friends and you'll be starting a new school soon. I hope you take advantage of all the things you can learn. If you do, you can make your dreams come true."

"It's really scary thinking about it. I don't know much about the world at all, and I don't even know how to act around people. I try to watch Betty Anne and learn stuff from her. But I feel so dumb."

"You're starting right. Watch people, listen to them when they talk. But Coreen, I want to make sure you understand one thing." Loretta cupped her chin. "You may be changing some things about your life to help you meet your dreams, but make sure you don't change who *you* are. Be yourself." She smiled a sad smile. "Every person won't like you—it's the way it is. It's the same with me too."

"You're the nicest and sweetest and smartest person I ever knowed."

Loretta's smile shone in the dark. "Don't ever lose the part of you that cares about other people—even when they act like they don't care about you. Sometimes it's just a lie they're telling themselves. Be patient."

They sat quietly for a while. Coreen thought about the things Loretta said. Could Mama change, even if she didn't want to? Her mama would never love her. But maybe she could try to give her some moments of happiness. Maybe it could help.

Maybe she should tell her secret. Would that help her forget her own bad stuff?

Coreen petted Patches, asleep beside her on the glider. The lightning bugs flashed near the edge of the porch. "Can I tell you something secret?"

"Of course you can."

A tickle jumped in Coreen's throat and she doodled on Patches' tummy with one finger. "Before my daddy died, he did something awful."

Loretta stared into the backyard. "What did he do, Coreen?"

She dropped her head and whispered, "He touched me in places a daddy shouldn't touch."

Loretta didn't say anything. Maybe Coreen should have kept her mouth shut too. What if Loretta thought she was dirty now?

"I am so sorry, Coreen." After a moment, Loretta asked, "Did he only use his hands—or more?"

Coreen whispered, without looking at Loretta, "He ... kissed me ... on the mouth."

"When did he do this?"

"The day before the flood. The day before my birthday. He ..." She lowered her head. "He said he was going to teach me how to be a woman when I turned thirteen."

Loretta gasped. "Does your mom know?"

Coreen sat upright and begged, "No! Please don't tell her."

Patches bolted awake and yipped.

"It's okay, honey." Loretta patted Coreen's hands. "Don't worry. I'm not going to say *anything*. To *anybody*."

Coreen looked at Loretta. Her eyes sparkled in the moonlight. Could she trust her? She squeezed Loretta's hands and pleaded. "You gotta promise. Please?" The thought of anyone else knowing her secret made her want to disappear from the earth. What he did made her dirty. What she knew he planned to do was even worse. Dirtier than the river that chased them up the mountain. Even dirtier than the stinky outhouse. If anybody knew … she couldn't survive it.

"I promise. I won't tell anyone. You can trust me."

Coreen relaxed and slumped back into the glider. "Thank you. Nobody else in the whole world knows about this."

Loretta wrapped her arm around Coreen's shoulders. She relaxed with Loretta's touch.

Coreen pondered telling her the rest. Loretta felt safe—and caring. And telling secrets made them lighter. "I found out something else today."

"What?"

"I found out I'm a bastard child."

"What do you mean? Where did you hear that word?" Loretta leaned forward.

"My other grandmother said it. I asked somebody what it meant. Then I found my mama and daddy's marriage license. They got married six months before I's born. It means they wasn't married when they … you know …"

"Coreen, do you know about how babies are … made?"

Coreen's cheeks got hot and she stared at the floor of the porch. "Yeah. I heard Janice and Lawanna talking about it. They went to my school. They's always talking about boys … and stuff. So I know all about it. I guess it's why I was skeered about—"

"Do you know how old your mom was when you were born?"

"Yeah, I saw a photo of her thirteenth birthday, fifteen months before I was borned. So she was fourteen."

Loretta covered her mouth with one hand and seemed to stare out at the lightning bugs, but her eyes were closed.

"Miss Loretta, you okay?"

As the moon broke through the clouds and cast its light on their faces, Loretta smiled her special smile. "Yes, dear. I'm fine—and so are you. There's always hope. Like the song you sang tonight."

"Above the fog, the sun still shines?"

Loretta added, "And beneath the mist, the mountains still stand. Don't forget, dear girl, the fog is in God's hands."

Chapter 30

Coreen opened her eyes to a room still dim from the early morning fog. She looked across the room to make sure her mother and grandmother were still asleep and slid off her cot. The tiles felt cool as she tiptoed to the door. Quiet as possible, she turned the handle and opened the door, stepped outside, and gently closed it behind her. She flung her arms above her in a stretch as she lifted herself up on her toes, yawned, and then rubbed her eyes. Voices and soft banging of pans in the kitchen made her hurry. The kitchen hummed with activity as she entered.

"Good morning, Miss Cora. Good morning, Miss Gloria."

Cora, dressed in a brightly patterned apron making a sorry attempt to protect her girth, turned and said in her deep Southern drawl, "Well, good morning there, missy. What you doing up so early?"

Coreen smiled. "Well, Miss Cora, I'm gonna move to my new house tomorrow."

"Fine. Fine indeed."

"I wondered if I could watch you make them wonderful yeast rolls before I go so maybe I can make some myself—and teach my mammaw too. They's the most delicious things I ever ate in my whole life."

Cora's laugh filled the kitchen. "Well, ain't you the sweetest thing. Why, shore you can come in and help me make 'em—but only iffin you warsh them hands real good with lots a soap first."

"Okay, be right back."

Coreen practically slid out of the kitchen and into the restroom. She took the time to make use of the facilities first and then washed her hands twice for good measure. Back in the kitchen, she joined Cora at the oversized table.

"Okay, I'm back—with clean hands." She held them up for inspection. "What do I do first?"

Cora grabbed an apron from a rack on the wall with her chocolate-colored hand and handed it to Coreen. "First, you put on this here apron so's you don't mess up that pretty little outfit you're a wearing. Then we get the flour ..."

* * *

Estelle listened for signs of movement in the room. She glanced over to Coreen's empty cot. Then she looked to Sarah's cot. She assumed she still slept soundly since she hadn't moved. Estelle needed to get up, but she couldn't get out of bed without assistance. She thought how nice it would be when she didn't have to depend on help to get to the bathroom.

For a few moments, she lay there pondering the new house. Indoor plumbing. Mercy. She wondered how many of her possessions from the old house were gone. Funny how she missed that house. She had a lot of memories there. Guess that's what she missed. But how could she grieve over those lost items when the good Lord blessed her with a new home? *Sorry, Lord, for seeming so ungrateful.* A comfortable bed and chair was all she needed.

Sarah still didn't move. Urgency forced Estelle to act. "Sarah? Sarah, you awake yet?"

Sarah stirred on the cot. "What is it, Mother?"

"Were you awake?"

"I am now."

"I'm sorry. I can't climb up from this cot on my own."

Yawning loudly and squeezing the back of her neck with one hand, Sarah twisted herself sideways on the cot and stood. "Come on, Mother. Twist your legs around. Now grab my arm. Pull."

The two ladies struggled a tad, but Estelle finally managed to get off the cot and stand up. A little out of breath and not able to stand upright yet, Estelle stretched from side to side, trying to minimize the pain and stiffness in her body. "I'll be glad when we get into our new house. Won't you? We're gonna be starting a whole new life."

Sarah's face stayed expressionless as she turned to her mother. "I thought you needed to go to the bathroom."

Estelle grabbed her cane and slowly shuffled the few feet to the door, opened it, and left in silence. She hoped, above all else, her family would heal in this new house.

* * *

Coreen and the rest of the family ate breakfast in silence. Even Aunt Shirley kept quiet. Seemed like nobody wanted to risk another fight. She didn't even bother to tell them she helped make the rolls this morning.

Mama stood up with her tray and announced, "Coreen, you need to put your old clothes on before DeWayne gets here."

"But I can't put on my old clothes." She leaned away slightly, hoping she wouldn't get smacked or yelled at.

Mama's eyes looked like they would burst into flames. "Why not?"

Coreen looked down. "'Cause I threw 'em away."

"Why in Sam Hill did you throw 'em away? Are you too good for the stuff I made ya now?"

Aunt Shirley stood up and carried her tray around the table. "It's not a problem. I got a solution for her and me. I certainly don't want to get river mud on my clothes. Come on, Coreen, let's take our trays up and get something a little worn from the clothes closet."

Mama whirled around and clomped over to the window with her tray.

"Mumsie, you finished with your tray yet? If you are, I'll take it back for you."

"I think I'd like to finish eating first, if you don't mind. I'll find somebody to take it for me after y'all leave."

Coreen wanted to giggle, but she kept quiet by stuffing the last roll between her teeth.

* * *

Coreen slid across the backseat and crashed into Aunt Shirley as DeWayne swerved around water-filled gouges in the road and fallen trees. He pulled up as close as he could to the houses. The mud and silt completely hid the grass.

Coreen felt a pang in her heart when she saw their houses, swept off their foundations and tilted catawampus. It seemed a couple of big trees kept their house from floating on down the river. Their house had held back Mammaw's. Sad looking. The gray boards were now brownish-black. Mud coated the windows.

DeWayne got out of the car and opened the back door for Coreen and her aunt. Mama got out herself and stood looking at the house with her hands on her hips.

One of the deputies pulled in beside them, and DeWayne went over to get some waders and shovels out of the truck. Both men donned their waders and shoveled a narrow path through any wet mud so they could get to the houses.

DeWayne leaned on his shovel. "I'll go in and help Sarah and Coreen. Steve here'll go with you, Shirley. Remember to be careful. Ain't no telling what's in the mud. It's gonna be slick in there too. I got some trash bags for the stuff you can salvage. If you need to, you can bring any trash out here and dump it. I figure they'll be leveling this place since the houses ain't worth fixing. Remember, whatever you leave here will probably be gone through by somebody. You know how people can be. So if you don't want prying eyes, don't leave it."

DeWayne held onto a front porch support as he pulled Mama and Coreen up. The heat of the sun had already sucked some of the moisture out of the mud on the porch and made it easier to maneuver the incline to where the screen door once hung. They entered and stood in silence, staring. The mud and silt inside covered everything with a thick sludge of brown slime. The furniture, dislodged and knocked over, now lay heaped together on the lower side of the house.

Coreen pinched her nose. "Pee-yew, it stinks in here."

DeWayne replied, "Well, it's got dirty river water, dead fish, garbage, and the outhouses in it ... and it's all been cooked in the summer sun. So yeah, it stinks to high heaven."

"Whoa." Coreen took a step and slid across the floor.

"Remember what I said, little girl. It's slick."

"Shore 'nuf. I can't believe this stuff came from the river. It shore did made a mess. Look, Mama, the couch is all squishy and it's on the other side of the room."

DeWayne readied his shovel. "I'll try to get some of this mud out of the way so we can get around a little better. You girls watch out for broken glass and stuff."

Mama struggled to climb up toward the bedroom. "I'm gonna go to my room and see what's still there. Coreen, you go to the kitchen and see if you can find any dishes that ain't broke—or pots and pans."

"Yes, ma'am. Whee ... this is kinda fun." Coreen slid toward the kitchen in the rain boots she found in the clothes closet.

* * *

Sarah leaned on the bedroom door frame, partially reclining, and looked around the room. The walls were the color of faded newspaper. The quilt her mother made for her lay wadded in the floor and stained with a mixture of coal dust, oil, and mud. She struggled through the muck to get to the dresser and pulled the metal rings to open a drawer. It wouldn't budge. She tried each drawer only to find they were all swollen shut. Remembering a hammer on the shelf in the closet, she pulled herself across the floor, with the aid of the bed and a dresser, to the closet. The door wouldn't open. After several grunts and jerks on the doorknob, it finally gave way, flew open, and released about two feet of river water. The water hit Sarah with such force it knocked her down into the silt and she slid against the wall.

From the other room DeWayne yelled, "You okay in there?"

"Yeah, they's water in the closet and it knocked me down. I'm okay."

"Need any help?"

"No. I'm fine. Slimy, but fine."

With feet flailing, thankfully DeWayne didn't see her attempts to get back to the closet. He would have laughed at her. She wasn't in the mood for humiliation.

The clothes hanging inside were stained with brown blotches and stinking. She figured they would never come clean, but she knew she might need them anyway. She didn't have anything else to wear, unlike Coreen. She found the hammer and turned away from the closet.

Cautiously moving back to the dresser, she lifted the hammer into the air and whacked the drawer front with all her might. It felt good. She whacked it again and again and again—until she panted and her muscles throbbed.

DeWayne appeared at the door. "Well, I reckon you killed it."

Sarah looked at the dresser, lying in pieces in the mud and at the hammer in her hand. Then she looked at DeWayne. Her mouth formed a smile. A giggle came. DeWayne responded with a laugh of his own. Suddenly, they were laughing so hard they bent over.

Tears rolled down Sarah's cheeks.

* * *

Shirley grabbed hold of Steve's hands as he struggled valiantly to pull her up onto the porch. "Mercy, you got some big, strong muscles in them arms of yours, Stevie boy." After some heaving, and a few grunts from Steve, she threw her right leg onto the porch and then rolled the rest of her body onto it. "Look at me. I ain't even stepped inside and I'm already covered in mud." She saw Steve hiding a smile behind his fist. "I see you smiling, Mr. Stevie."

"Sorry, ma'am. It's … You have such a good sense of humor, that's all."

"Yeah, right. I can see I'm gonna have to watch you."

The two held their hands out to balance themselves. "I don't mind telling ya I ain't looking forward to this. We've got our work cut out for us, Stevie, my boy."

"Yes, ma'am."

Shirley put her hands on her hips and almost fell. "We're gonna get along fine if you stop calling me ma'am. Deal?"

"Yes, ma … I mean yes, Shirley. If you agree to call me Steve."

"Deal." They shook hands. "Now let's get cracking."

Steve used his shoulder and hip to force the door open. Shirley followed him inside. The complete devastation made them stand still and stare.

"Look at this place." Mud coated everything. Furniture had slid to the low side of the house and bunched up against the wall. The pot-bellied stove had broken loose and rolled into the dining table, smashing it into pieces. Broken whatty-knotties peeked out of the mud like a haphazard mosaic. "I can't believe how much damage a little water can do. It's all ruined. I don't see how there could possibly be a single thing worth keeping, do you?"

"Well, uh … Shirley … I'm here to help you make sure. It's all we can do."

Tears clouded her eyes as she worked her way through the house, room by room, and wondered where she should start. A rock churned in her gut. Memories of her life in this house popped into her head like grease popping from a hot pan of fried chicken. Funny how she only remembered the good stuff now it's all gone.

"Poor Mumsie. I'm glad she can't see this. It'd break her heart to have to throw this stuff out herself. You know, she didn't have much, but I guess that's what made it special." Shirley leaned down and pulled a vase of plastic flowers out of the muck. It dripped of the brown silt that coated what used to be lavender flowers. "Bless her heart. She's been through too much to have to go through this now."

Steve stopped shoveling for a moment and leaned sideways on the shovel. "It is sad. It's like losing your whole life in a blink of your eye."

"Well, honey, let's see how much of my dear mom's life we can salvage."

"Yes, ma … Shirley."

"You almost got yourself in trouble, didn't you?" Shirley giggled.

Steve responded with a boyish grin. They worked their way through the house, finding a few undamaged items needing some hot sudsy water to clean them up. Treasured quilts, made with talented fingers out of scraps, were stained and smelly. Unwilling to give up on them, Shirley gently stuffed the heirlooms into a trash bag. She'd heard, if laid on the ground at night, the morning dew would take the stink out of a quilt. Worth a try. She also retrieved a couple of rag rugs from a closet, and she smiled as she uncovered a dark blue glass bottle of Evening in Paris perfume with its stopper intact. Mumsie told her daddy gave it to her on their first anniversary. She only wore it on special occasions.

She fingered the bottle gingerly. "Who knows, maybe she'll have another special occasion someday soon."

She stuck the bottle of perfume into her pants pocket for protection and gave it a gentle pat.

* * *

"Mama, do ya want me to throw out the flour and stuff and save the canisters or do I throw it all out?" Coreen yelled through the house.

Sarah hollered back. "Throw out the food and keep the canisters."

Coreen held the canister of brown flour and turned up her nose as she looked around for a place to put it. "Mama, where do I put all the dead food? On the floor?"

"No, Coreen. Toss it out the door or through the window. Try to keep it away from where we'll have to walk."

"Okay."

The path to the door angled uphill and made her slip around, so she opted for the window. Since it refused to budge when she tried to force the swollen wood frames, she picked up a skillet and squeezed her eyes shut as she turned her face away from the glass. When she whacked the window, glass shards sprayed onto the muddy ground outside with a loud crash. She hit the window repeatedly to remove all the glass.

At a loud thump behind her, she turned in time to see DeWayne hit the floor and slide into the kitchen. Coreen stood over him with the skillet in one hand and the canister in the other.

"You okay, DeWayne?" She couldn't hide her smirk.

He looked up at her and grinned. "I planned to ask you the same question. What ya doing in here?"

"Mama said to throw the food out the window, so I ... opened the window." Coreen grinned.

DeWayne picked himself up and grabbed hold of the cook stove. "Well, you did a good job of it."

"Thanks." Coreen whirled around in the mud and put down the pan, opened the canister and shook it out the window until the flour caught the breeze and created a muddy cloud as it traveled across the back of the house. "This is fun."

* * *

Shirley used a screwdriver she found in the closet and jammed it into the thin line around the drawer of the dresser. After much grunting and a broken nail, she finally pried off the front and started to remove the contents. The large drawer held lingerie, sleepwear, and nylons. Feeling a bit like she intruded upon something personal and private, she hesitantly removed each item and inspected it for damage. In the back of the drawer, her hand hit something hard and cool. Reaching in with both hands, she pulled out an alabaster box engraved with roses. Shirley's brow wrinkled as she stared at the box she never remembered seeing before. Curiosity won out and she lifted the lid.

There wasn't much there. A vintage necklace with purple stones, probably amethysts. A handful of Dodge Mining Camp scrip in one-dollar coins. A pair of earrings that matched the necklace.

In the bottom of the box a lavender ribbon secured a stack of letters. Even though the envelopes were stained and some of the ink smeared, she could read "My Beloved" on each one—except the one on the bottom of the stack. Addressed to Mrs. John Kincaid, it held the inscription of Dodge Mining in the top left corner. A couple of tears dripped down her muddy cheeks. She returned the items to the box, replaced the lid, and hugged it.

* * *

Coreen finished bagging up all she could salvage in the kitchen and made her way to the dining room. The mud oozed around her boots as she removed a chair from her cot and dragged the buffet around so she could open the doors on the front. With grunts and tugs, one door relented and sent her flying backward onto the waterlogged mattress.

"Eww, this is disgusting. I'm totally soaked in muddy yuck." This adventure had lost its fun now.

Going back to the buffet, she stuck her hand inside cautiously, half expecting a fish or snake to be inside. Only the special tablecloth from her great-grandmother, some fabric purchased at the dime store to be made into new dresses for the school year, and a couple of patterns occupied the space. She put the tablecloth into a bag and left the rest.

Coreen turned to the door on the other side. Using a bit more caution, she yanked on it until it finally opened. Her personal hideaway for all things precious. She clamped her teeth onto her bottom lip and leaned over to peer into the dark recess. Smelly water oozed out into her hands, along with a book, still wet and stained with silt.

"It's ruined." What would she tell the lady at the Bookmobile? Two more books slid out, in basically the same condition. She held them close and caressed them, like a pet that just died. With a raspy sigh, she laid them on the floor.

Then with a gasp she wailed, "My songs! I bet they're ruined too." Coreen dropped to her knees and reached far back where she kept them secreted. The stack of papers now stuck together, with the words faded and bleeding onto each other. She refused to throw them away. Maybe she could read them well enough to rewrite them on new paper.

Losing her songs would be like losing a part of herself.

* * *

Shirley pushed her curls out of her face, leaving a mousse of mud on the red strands. "Man, I'm beat. How you doing in there, Steve?"

"I'm getting as many of these dishes as I can. There's a lot of 'em broken. Ouch. Dang!"

"What's the matter?" Shirley trudged into the kitchen to find Steve holding shards of a green plate in his hand. Blood dripped from his hand into the mud on the floor.

"I cut myself on this here plate. I'm okay though."

"You better get it cleaned up quick. Who knows what horrible germs are in this stuff."

"I'll get a wipe out of the crime scene pack in my truck when we leave."

Shirley chuckled. "It does sorta look like a crime scene in here now, don't it? I hate all those canned vegetables are broken." Mason jars, laboriously canned by Mumsie, spewed tomatoes, green beans, beets, and pickles all over the floor. What would she eat this winter? "I think I'm about finished with the rest of the house. Not too much could be salvaged at all. I'm sure glad she grabbed her photos before she left because the family Bible's a mess. Guess I'll take it to her anyway. You 'bout done there?"

"Yeah, I think this is about it. I'll start carrying it out to the truck for you."

"Okay, I'll drag these bags as far as I can get 'em. At least we're going downhill to get outside." Shirley dwelled on a good hot shower. She looked down at her arms and legs, coated in silt. River mud. Who knew what was in this stuff—or how long it took to get the smell out of skin and hair? Shirley's laugh echoed throughout the house. To think, some people paid big bucks to be covered in mud.

* * *

Sarah stared at the chifforobe lying catawampus on the floor. Vernon's private domain. He had forbidden her to touch it. She knew where he kept the key—on a nail he'd hammered into the top of the door-facing. She searched the room for something stable to stand on and found a small stool. Hoping she would be able to reach high enough—and hoping the key hadn't washed away—she climbed up and stretched to the top. Her fingers blindly felt around until they touched the nail. Something moved. The key.

The stool rocked precariously as she jumped down, crossed to the wardrobe, and stuck the key in the hole and turned. Open. There were no handles on the doors, so she dug her gnawed fingernails underneath until the right door moved enough to grasp. Her hands trembled as she pulled the door until it fell open. Inside, she found a collection of rifles, shotguns, ammunition, and three heavy handguns. There were also two broken jars of what smelled like white lightning.

The second door wouldn't open. Sarah searched the inside wall for a hook release. She found it, unlatched the door and lifted it open. This side held more promise. On a shelf, she found a stack of disgusting magazines. She refused to even touch them. Another shelf held more ammunition in smaller boxes. She assumed it fit the handguns. A mystery where he got all the guns. And why. A person didn't hunt with pistols.

She grabbed the tarnished ring on the front of a drawer and pulled it open slowly. Because of the angle of the cabinet, a few things fell out of the drawer and into the dark recesses behind it. Sarah laid the box down, dug the items out of the space, and put them back into the drawer. She closed the right door and sat on it to go through the items.

Touching his things, even though he was dead and buried, brought back the sense of doom she experienced every time he pulled up in front of the house. She took a deep breath, told herself to get over it, and reached into the box.

Sarah removed an old train engineer's pocket watch, a set of gold cufflinks, a gold lighter, and a diamond-and-ruby brooch. At least they looked like real gold, rubies, and diamonds. Where did they come from? They couldn't be his. A spark of remembrance caused the blood to drain from her face.

The room spun. Her head floated above her body. She picked up the watch and knew before she looked what the inscription said. With a click of the button, the lid popped open to reveal *Love forever on our wedding day —Estelle*. She closed the watch with a sharp click. A surge of freezing cold blood coursed through her body. Bile churned in her stomach. Her disgust for him intensified.

Water and silt sloshed as she grabbed the drawer and wildly searched the remaining contents. A money clip caught her attention first. It held a lot of money in its grasp, too much money. She pulled out the limp bills and counted them. Two thousand, three hundred and sixty dollars. Intense burning hatred built up inside her throat like gasoline waiting to be lit by a match.

She rammed her hand back into the box, fingers sifting through the silt and dampness. Something metallic chinked across the box. Sarah placed her fingers across one side of the box, then tipped it over enough to drain the water and some of the silt. Several scrip coins lay at the bottom, stamped Dodge Mining Company. Vernon never worked for Dodge. But her daddy had. She wondered where he got them.

Mixed in with the scrip, a couple of cufflinks slid into the corner of the box. They were engraved with the initials JK. *John Kincaid.* The room spun again. If somebody hadn't beaten her to it, she believed today she could have killed him herself.

Sarah wiped out the box with the bedspread and replaced each item in the drawer. The man who stole her innocence, her life, her future—also stole her past. Today she would have had the courage to take one of his guns and blast his head off. So what if she ended up in jail the rest of her life? Her life already felt like being in jail. At least she would have some dignity.

The room stopped spinning. It filled with bright light where there used to be nothing but darkness. The light seemed to spread into Sarah's mind and entire body like melting lard in a hot skillet. She was more lucid than ever before.

"I didn't have to do it myself. Somebody did it for me." Laughter echoed off the gray walls until DeWayne stuck his head into the room.

"Sarah, you okay? I thought I heard you—"

"I'm finer than I've ever been in my life. Today I realized what a lucky woman I am."

DeWayne wrinkled his bushy red brows. "Okay. Good to hear. I think."

"I found some guns and stuff in here. I guess you need to take 'em so you can test them and make sure they wasn't used to kill him."

"Sarah, I know they wasn't the ones."

"But you need to test 'em anyways, don't you? So you can say they wasn't the ones? I got a couple of things here and then I'm ready. Are you and Coreen about done?"

DeWayne slid across the room to the chifforobe and checked each of the guns, unloading their bullets or shells. "Yeah, I think we've done about as much as we can. I'll get these and anything else you bagged up. What ya want me to do with the guns?"

"You mean after you check 'em?" She looked up at him with a smile. "If they still work, you can have them."

"Are you sure, Sarah? You may want to hang on to these."

Sarah looked at the muddy guns. "You know, DeWayne, anything I would ever need them guns for is already dead. You take 'em."

"I'm shore glad you won't ever need 'em. I'll take these to the Jeep." DeWayne checked each gun to see if it was loaded before stacking it on the chifforobe door. He reached into a dark corner. "Did you see this, Sarah? There's another box in here behind the rifles."

"No, I didn't." What secret would this one hold? Sarah took the box and tried the lid. "It seems to be locked."

"I don't see the key nowhere. Maybe it's in here hidden away. You never know what he mighta stashed in here."

Metal and old, with rust in spots. Probably a snuff box. Except snuff boxes didn't have locks.

"I didn't find the key. Sure you don't want one of the guns to shoot it off?" He grinned at her.

Sarah grinned back. "Very funny. I'll take it home. It probably ain't nothing important. But you never know. I got a couple of things to take out to the trash pile, then I'll join you outside."

"What about the other box in your hands?"

Sarah tapped the sides of the drawer and smiled. "This is going home with me too—and back to where it belongs."

He shrugged his shoulders and slid across the floor while balancing the weapons.

Sarah took her time crossing through the sludge and stopped in the living room to yell at Coreen. "You 'bout done in there, girl? I want to get out of here."

"I'm putting the last of it in a bag. Be right there."

The sunshine blinded Sarah as she stepped out onto the porch, put down the drawer and box, and then hopped off the edge. Taking the boxes, she walked to the police car, opened the door, and placed her treasures on the floorboard. The screen door slammed as Coreen dragged a heavy bag through it and across the porch. DeWayne trotted over to help her.

"You're squeaking, DeWayne."

"Thanks a lot, munchkin. I can't wait to get these things off. I think I have more mud inside the waders than I do on the outside."

"DeWayne. There's something I been meaning to say to you."

"What's that, munchkin?"

Coreen rolled her eyes at him. "Munchkin. I ain't no kid no more. I'm a growed-up teenager. I think it's time you started using my name, Co-reen. Got it?"

"Yes, ma'am. I apologize. From now on, it's Co-reen. Now let's get this stuff loaded up, sweet Co-reen."

Sarah smiled as DeWayne's rubber-covered legs smacked together. There were some good men. At least one or two. Her daddy had been a good man too. She looked at the house one last time. It was over. She would never see this house again.

And she would never see Vernon again.

Debris from the house rose like a miniature mountain at the end of the porch. Sarah twirled the thin band of gold on her left hand with her right thumb and forefinger. The remnants of her life—the mud-soaked mattress she shared with Vernon, broken dishes, the stained chair where she read her books and dreamed of another life. Useless tokens of nothing worthwhile lay heaped in a muddy grave. A life, in shades of brown piled before her, begged for pity, or regret, or some sense of importance or meaning.

But she felt nothing.

The gold band on her finger worked loose and fell into her other hand. The lonely whistle of an approaching coal train sounded farther down the line. Sarah held up the ring, flung it into the pile of trash, and turned her back on the house.

The mud and silt in the front yard had dried into the jagged pattern of aging skin—cracked and broken. One solitary dandelion broke through its grave and shouted to the world its new life with glowing yellow petals. Sarah hummed her way to the car.

Chapter 31

A cloud of dust stirred around the car as DeWayne pulled into the rear parking lot of the church. Sarah peeled herself off the plastic bag and slid out of the car.

Her sister climbed out and stuck her arms out like a clay figure. "I think we ought to hose ourselves off before we track all this inside the church."

Sarah pulled her shirt away from her body and sniffed it. "I agree. They don't need this where they serve food."

As they gathered up the items they brought back, DeWayne blurted, "You need any help carrying your stuff? I'd be glad to help."

"I think we got this." Sarah smiled at him as she held the boxes away from the mud.

"Need any help hosing off?"

Shirley laughed. "I think you'd better let us deal with the bathing."

"I didn't mean …" He picked at the muck clinging to his hands. His face flushed redder than his hair.

Sarah stifled a guffaw.

"You embarrassed him, Aunt Shirley. Look at his face." Coreen laughed.

"Shame on y'all. He worked so hard today and you're making fun." Sarah chuckled and caught his eye. "Sorry, DeWayne. Thanks for helping us today. You're a good friend and I appreciate it."

DeWayne's face reddened again when Sarah smiled at him, and he lowered his gaze to the box she held. His brows furrowed. He whispered, "You do know your ring's not on your finger, right, Sarah?"

She looked at her finger. One corner of her mouth rose ever so slightly as she looked him in the eye. "Yep … I know." She smiled at him again, then turned and sashayed down the sidewalk.

* * *

Laughter echoed through the backyard of the church as Coreen, Mama, and Shirley took turns hosing each other off. They managed to remove most of the mud from their feet, legs, hands, and arms. Their hair and clothes dripped. After squeezing out as much water as possible, they sat in the sun to dry off so as not to drip all over the church.

Coreen lay in a dry spot on the grass and stared up at the thin clouds as they floated past. A good day. Why did she think that? Seeing everything ruined wasn't good. Neither was all the stuff they threw away. Then she smiled at the clouds. The laughter. The first time she ever heard her mama laugh like that. And then the second time. Yeah, it was a good day.

It didn't take long in the afternoon heat until the three dried off enough to go inside and get cleaned up.

Coreen slid her treasures under her cot as her mama put two boxes on a bookcase. What did those boxes hold? She'd never seen them before.

Coreen picked through her new clothes, careful not to get mud on anything, and chose a mint-green outfit and some undies. She hid the undies inside her clothes so no one would accidentally see them. "I'm sure glad we can use the water again. I can't wait to get into hot soapy water." Coreen opened the door to their room.

Shirley grabbed up the clean clothes she retrieved from her car as she headed to the shower as well. "I agree with Coreen. I want to wash this stink off me. Wonder if all this mud's made my skin any softer."

Sarah gathered her toiletries. "It probably sucked the moisture right out, and we'll have skin like the ground at the camp. Did you see it all cracked and gray looking?"

"Thanks a lot. I do something nice for Mumsie, and I get the life sucked out of me. Let's get them hot showers, little sis, we're stinking up a storm. Shoo-ee."

* * *

Estelle and Miss Cora sat at a table, stringing green beans from a bushel basket. Each deftly grabbed a handful of beans, snapped the pointed end and pulled the string down to the other, snapped it off, and pulled the string back to the front. Then they snapped the beans into bite-sized pieces and dropped them into an oversized aluminum dishpan. The strings dropped onto the lap of their aprons, to be discarded later. The proof of your expertise at snapping beans was how many snapped beans you could hold in one hand before needing to drop them into the pan. It wasn't a competition but a badge of honor. Estelle conceded she was in good company with her companion.

Sarah, Shirley, and Coreen joined them at the table, fresh from their showers. "You girls shore look better than when you ran by here the first time. Get all squeaky clean?" Estelle asked.

Shirley spoke up. "I never knew how glorious a little hot water and soap could be. I feel like I could squeak now."

"Me too—and I shore 'nuf smell a lot better than I did." Coreen gave Estelle a big hug.

"Well, you do smell good. What'd you do, take a bath in flowers?"

Coreen's laughter filled the room. "No, Mammaw. But I did rub yummy lotion all over me so I wouldn't be dried out like an old prune."

Shirley put her hands on her hips and sucked in her lips. "Are you saying I look like an old prune, young'un?"

Giggling and holding her hand on her stomach, Coreen said, "No, Aunt Shirley. But I can get lotion for you if you want it."

Estelle smiled. Apparently, the girls were in a much better place than when they left. She couldn't figure what did it, but she welcomed it.

Sarah sat next to her mother and grabbed a handful of the beans and began stringing them. "Well, Mother, we tried to salvage a few things. Shirley and one of the deputies—"

"Steve." Shirley interjected as she grabbed a handful of beans from the basket and sat.

"It's gonna take scrubbing to clean the mud off everything. We'll see."

Estelle noticed Shirley's stringing hadn't improved over the years. She snapped at a much slower speed than the rest of the ladies and seemed to need her tongue stuck out one side of her mouth to be able to snap the beans. Poor Shirley never showed much interest in cooking, just in eating.

Coreen grabbed her second double scoop of beans from the basket. She turned to Cora. "Hi, Miss Cora. This is my mama, Sarah, and that's my Aunt Shirley. I guess you met Mammaw."

Estelle stopped mid snap. "I'm sorry I didn't introduce you, Cora. How d'ya know Coreen already?"

"Miss Cora taught me how to make those wonderful yeast rolls she's been making for us every day."

Shirley pulled her tongue in long enough to say, "Really?"

Cora's deep laugh resonated as her face glowed. "And you folks is in for a real treat. She did a fine job. She's a hard worker."

Sarah stared at her beans. "Yeah, she's a hard worker. She helped quite a bit today at the house."

Estelle's hand froze. She glanced at Coreen and saw her face flush as she raised a trembling hand to grab hold of the gold heart hanging around her neck. Mercy sakes alive.

Estelle went back to snapping. "Loretta said there'll be an eighteen-wheeler at the A&P grocery store tomorrow morning with all kinds of stuff—like clothes and household items." Estelle grabbed another handful of beans. "Might be worth getting there early and see what they got. Wish I could go. I really need some clothes."

"Sarah, I can pick you and Coreen up and take you over there. Seven thirty sound okay?" Shirley stopped stringing and rubbed her fingers as if they were hurting.

Estelle chuckled, knowing she just finished her first handful.

"Sounds good—if I can wake up in time."

Cora spoke up. "Honey, I'll be here cooking breakfast. How 'bout I knock on your door 'bout seven?"

"Thank you, Cora. I'd appreciate it." Sarah dropped her snapped beans into the dishpan. "Mother, could you hand me some more beans?"

"I have some more news too. The Red Cross came by. We have a voucher for Simpson's Furniture Store. We can get beds and whatever chairs we'll need. The store will know what applies."

Estelle moved the strings from her apron to the string pan. "Coreen, could you empty these strings in the trash for us? We're running out of room."

Coreen added her strings to the pan and hopped up. "Shore, Mammaw." She breathed in and smiled. "I love the smell of fresh-broke green beans."

Estelle turned to Sarah. "Mary Anne dropped by. She can take us to the house tomorrow right after lunch. We need to get all our stuff packed up and ready to go before she gets here."

Coreen returned with an empty pan and grabbed another handful of beans.

Sarah said, "Soon as we get done with these beans, I'll pack up my little bit of stuff. Coreen, you go ahead and get your stuff ready now. You got more than we do. They's a couple plastic bags laying in there. Stuff your things in one of them—if they all fit—and put 'em aside and out of the way till tomorrow."

"Okay, Mama." She finished stringing her beans, added them to the pan, and poked along to the room, humming.

Estelle smiled. How in the world could a child so damaged be so wonderful?

Sarah stopped breaking her beans for a minute. "Mother, when we get done here, I need to talk to you about something."

"Okay. You can't tell me now?"

Focusing on the beans again, Sarah said, "Not now. I ... I gotta *show* you something."

Shirley leaned forward onto the table and placed her chin on entwined fingers. "I need to talk to you about something too, Mumsie."

Estelle stop snapping a bean in mid action. What now? Every time things looked encouraging, she got smacked in the face with some reality.

Chapter 32

The door to the room creaked as Estelle entered. She looked at her daughters' faces. Shirley grinned, her eyes sparkling. Sarah's frown and downcast eyes suggested an opposite demeaner. *What's in Sarah's craw now?*

Coreen looked up at them as she scooted a stuffed black trash bag into the corner of the room. "Are they out of the way enough, Mama?"

Sarah glanced toward the corner. "Go outside and let your hair dry."

Coreen pooched out her lips. "I'll go see Patches. *He'll* want to see me." She marched out of the room and slammed the door.

Shirley helped Estelle to a chair. "Is it okay if I go first? Then I'll leave you two alone to talk."

Estelle's heart fluttered. "Okay with you, Sarah?"

"Sure. Shirl, you want me to wait outside?"

"No, you can stay."

Shirley opened the bag she held in her hand, reached inside, and pulled out the blue glass bottle. "Guess I'll start with this. I thought you'd like to have it, Mumsie dear. I found it in the house today."

"My perfume." She lunged for the mud-encrusted bottle and held it to her chest as a tear readied itself in the corner of her eye. She removed the stopper and took a deep whiff. Almost felt like Jack stood there in the room with her when she smelled it. What wonderful memories. "May be a simple thing, but it's really special to me. Thank you, Shirley."

"I knew you'd really want it. I'm glad the stopper didn't come loose." Shirley reached back into the bag and gently pulled out the alabaster box and handed it to her. "I also found this."

Silent, Estelle placed the perfume bottle on the table next to her and reached for the box with trembling fingers. She ran her wrinkled fingers over the carved flowers on the lid. The gift he gave her on their wedding day. She smiled as she remembered when she opened the box the first time and found a letter inside. Jack rarely said what he felt, so he wrote her letters. A declaration of his love.

She opened the box and laid the lid on the table. Something wasn't right. She moved the items around, searching. Where were they? Her pulse quickened and she breathed faster. She looked up at Shirley.

"Is that all you found in the box?"

Shirley glanced inside and raised her brows. "Yes, Mumsie. Why?"

"There should be a watch—and cufflinks—and a money clip ..."

Sarah walked to the bookcase, picked up a box, and handed it to Estelle. "I think this might be what you're looking for."

Estelle put the alabaster box on the table and took the box from Sarah, her mind racing and confused as she peered inside. She fingered the cufflinks, watch, and money clip. "Where did you find these? I ain't never seen this box."

Sarah sighed long and loud, like a death rasp. "I found 'em locked in a drawer in Vernon's chifforobe."

Estelle and Shirley blurted together, "What?"

"They was locked in Vernon's chifforobe." Sarah slammed her hand against the wall.

"Now wait a minute." Shirley put one hand on her hip and pointed at the box with the other. "Are you saying demon Vernon—Lord, forgive me for saying that word in your house." Shirley gazed heavenward. "He stole from our mother? From her bedroom?" Shirley threw up her arms and whirled around. "Dear Lord in heaven. He stole it from her underwear drawer." Shirley paced the room, stomping on the tile floor and huffing like a bull. "I can't believe he stuck his filthy hand in your underwear. That man *was* a demon, and he's right where he belongs—in hell."

Estelle removed each item from the box with two fingers. Vernon had dirtied them. One by one, she dropped them back into the alabaster box. As she picked up the money clip, she asked Sarah, "Did ya count the money?"

"Yeah. Two thousand, three hundred and sixty dollars."

She tossed it into the box with a sigh of disgust. "Well, I wonder what he wasted my life savings on—probably women and booze. I saved it for my burial and any hospital bills."

A prayer of forgiveness for the emotions racing through her soul would come later. Right now her righteous indignation made her want revenge. But revenge couldn't come because he died already. A quick death. He deserved to be tortured first.

She took the empty drawer and looked at it. Then she flung it across the room and smashed it against the block wall with a bang as she dropped her face into her hands. Her head buzzed. She might pass out. Would she ever get past Vernon's evil? Would any of them?

Shirley wrapped her arms around Estelle's shoulders.

Sarah dropped to her knees and whispered, "I'm sorry, Mama."

"Well, we knew he weren't no good. This shouldn't surprise any of us. My things are back where they belong—'cept for my money. But we'll survive. We always have before and now's no different. Thank the good Lord he's dead and gone." Did she believe it? At least she had to say it. "We can't let him hurt any of us anymore. We gotta let it go."

Sarah jumped up from the floor and paced the tiny room. She flailed her hands. "But Mother, I can't let it go. I can't forget what he's done to me. I shore as hell ain't about to forgive him. And now, to see what he did to you ..."

Estelle figured if he had been in the room, Sarah would rip him into shreds right now. She expected her to pick up a chair and throw it against the wall. "You don't have to forgive him, Sarah. Just turn your back on him. Don't let him keep hurting you by letting him get to you. It pains me how he hurt you."

"It makes me mad as Hades he lied to me about what happened. I'm sorry I believed him when he said he loved you. I'm sorry I pushed you into marrying him." Estelle smacked the cot. "I just wish you'd spoken up and told me the whole story. If only—"

"Only what, Mother? D'ya really think you would have changed your mind? You were so desperate not to have a bastard child in the family that you would've accepted anything to make it legitimate. No matter what I said."

"No, I wouldn't."

"Yes. You would." Sarah glared at Estelle with venom in her eyes.

Estelle shuddered. Such hatred. "He stole your life. But, Sarah, he stole you from me too. Not just these things and my health." Her voice broke. "Please don't let him keep on stealing from us. You're gonna have to choose."

Sarah stood still, her chin lowered. "I understand, Mother, but it ain't easy."

"Nothing's easy, Sarah. Nobody ever said it would be. But when you overcome, it shore feels sweet." Estelle pressed her hands against her face and slid them around to the back of her head—like the action could wipe away Vernon for good. "I got overcoming to do too. You ain't alone. He crippled me for life. I thank the good Lord for directing that poker into my hip instead of my heart, but it's still a hard thing to forgive." She raised her eyes to Sarah. "He crippled you and Coreen too, in a different kind of way. I reckon most people have something in their lives that cripples 'em. If they let it."

Hate festered so deep inside her, she wondered if it could ever be rooted out. Did Sarah feel the same? And Coreen? Had she been expecting God to get rid of it—while she held the shovel? Maybe they needed to pick up pitch forks instead, and loosen some of the roots that had wrapped around their souls. One root at a time.

"Sarah? Maybe the way we can stop him is by removing his power over us one thing at a time."

Sarah's voice sounded gravelly. "How d'ya think we can do that?"

"Let's not ask his permission anymore."

Chapter 33

Coreen led the way into the church. Thankfully, they left all the bags of stuff they found at the A&P truck in Shirley's car. Lunch. She breathed in with her shoulders and closed her eyes. "Ahhhh, yeast rolls. They make the day worthwhile."

Shirley giggled behind her. "Sweet girl, I'm gonna miss you. You delight my day."

"I'm gonna miss you too, Aunt Shirley. You're the greatest." Coreen fingered the heart around her neck. "You make me feel loved."

"Well, you are loved."

Coreen linked arms with Aunt Shirley and tried to skip to the food. Her aunt couldn't skip and slowed her down.

Plates overflowing, they joined Mammaw at the table. "Hi, Mammaw. Look what we're having today—baloney salad sandwiches on Bunny bread. And of course, those wonderful yeast rolls. Yummy."

"Baloney salad? I ain't had none since last Christmas. Is it as good as mine?"

"Nobody could make it as good as you do." She took a bite of her sandwich. Good thing Mammaw asked if it tasted as good before she'd bit into it. She wouldn't want to hurt her feelings by telling the truth. "Mama's bringing yours."

Shirley crunched on a chip. "We got quite a few things for you this morning. I hope you like 'em. I'm glad for that measuring tape I had. It helped a whole lot in choosing clothes the right size."

"Hello, ladies." Loretta smiled her special smile as she approached the table.

They responded with greetings between bites. Coreen made sure she swallowed first. Mammaw said, "Have a sit down, Loretta dear."

She slipped into an empty chair. "I guess you're excited to get moved today. Is Mary Anne taking you to the house?"

Mama slid Mammaw's tray in front of her and sat. "She oughta be here any minute. Soon as we finish eating, me and Coreen gotta carry our stuff outside to pack into Shirley's car. If it'll fit."

Shirley laughed. "Yeah. It's already stuffed with the things we got this morning from the truck at A&P. But I don't think there's that much here to move—except for maybe Coreen's clothes." Shirley giggled and wrinkled her nose at Coreen.

Coreen scrunched her nose back. "Aunt Shirley, for heaven's sake, I ain't got that much. Just a coupla bags of clothes. And a few other little things—like my papers and bathroom stuff." Shirley cocked her head and opened her eyes wide at Coreen. "Okay, so I got more than Mama and Mammaw."

The ladies chuckled as Loretta asked, "And how are you planning to get Patches to the house?"

Coreen stopped mid bite as her heart seemed to stop pumping. "I plumb forgot about getting Patches there. Mama, what do I do?"

Her mama shook her head. "That dog. I knew it'd be a problem. We shoulda left it at the house."

Tears threatened to flow. Her heart squeezed tight. She whispered, "Mama, please. Patches is my best friend in the whole world. I love him. Don't say things like that. I couldn't live without him."

"For goodness sakes, calm down. We'll get him there somehow. You can walk him if nothing else. It ain't far."

Coreen sniffed. "Okay." She stopped moving. "But I don't know how to get there, Mama."

"You will after we go to the house. You can come back for him later—if it's okay with Loretta."

"Certainly. Take all the time you need. He's no problem at all. In fact, we've really enjoyed having him with us. I think we've almost decided we need to find a dog of our own."

"Great, Miss Loretta. You'd love having a dog. They're wonderful friends—and really good listeners too." Coreen nodded so hard it made her dizzy.

Loretta chuckled and her eyes sparkled. "Yes, I've noticed. I've had more than one conversation with him."

Betty Anne scampered up to the table and stood beside Coreen. "Hi. You about ready to go to your house? Mom's ready when you are."

Coreen wiped her mouth with a napkin and stacked her empty dishes on the tray. "I'm ready. I just have to take my tray back."

"Don't forget about the rest of us, Coreen." Mama turned to Betty Anne. "I'm ready too. I'll take our trays and then we'll carry our stuff out. Is your mom parked in the back?"

"Yes. She's as close to the door as she could get, Mrs. Shell."

"Mother, you sit here for a few minutes till we get the cars loaded up. You don't need to sit out there in the heat and suffocate. Let's get crackin', Coreen."

* * *

Estelle stayed with Loretta as the girls trotted off to gather up their belongings.

Loretta asked, "Are you happy about the move?"

With a sigh that seemed to come from her toes, Estelle responded. "Excited … anxious … nervous … and, yes, happy. My life's gonna totally change now. I gotta make changes with it. Change ain't easy for nobody—let alone an old woman. You know, as hard as being here's been on my old body, I really enjoyed it. Been wonderful having all these sweet folks around me all the time. I done more conversing this week than in the past ten years. I miss … people. Gets lonesome by yourself."

Estelle noticed tears collecting in the corners of Loretta's eyes. "I have truly enjoyed having you here. Being a preacher's wife can be lonely too. It's hard to make friends when we have to take on the role of a secret keeper. We must hold things in confidence that … we wish we could share." Loretta looked away, and Estelle suspected Loretta hid more than a few secrets inside. Safe secrets. "But when we're bound by a promise, we have to trust God to take care of it for us. Otherwise, trust is lost. Everyone needs someone they can trust completely."

The two reached out and clasped each other's hands. Loretta didn't seem to want to let go and stared deeply into Estelle's eyes, like she wanted to say something important. Did Loretta have a secret in her confidence that troubled her? Whose secret could it be? She was right about one thing—God could handle secrets. And Loretta could be trusted to honor her promise to keep them secret.

Loretta smiled. "I'm going to miss you. You've really … inspired me. You're welcome here any time, I hope you know. You're also welcome in my home."

"You're such a sweetheart. I appreciate it. Only, I can't get around so good. I'd love to come here to hear your sweet husband preach the Word. I ain't been able to go to church in years—since my hip … since the … accident." The time wasn't right to talk about that. Another secret. "But if you get a little lonesome, you come over and visit me. I'll shore 'nuf be right there."

"Thank you, Estelle. I'll take you up on it. I promise."

Shirley huffed up to the table with a red face. "Mom, are you ready? As soon as I catch my breath"—Shirley leaned on the table and gasped in air a few times—"I'll help you out to the car."

"It's been a pleasure meeting you, Shirley." Loretta reached out a hand.

Shirley wiped her hand on her shirt before she reciprocated. "I'm really happy to have met you too, Loretta. You're a darlin'."

Loretta took the hand and held it in both hers. "Thank you. Are you going back home tonight?"

185

"Yeah, I'll be heading out when we get everything unloaded. I've missed my babies so much. Of course, I've missed my Richie too. You take care now. I'll be praying for you and your little church here."

"Thank you, Shirley. We always appreciate the prayers."

"Well, Mumsie, let me help you out of your throne there, and we'll head to your new house."

"I'm gonna miss this throne of mine." Estelle patted Loretta's arm. "You make sure you tell your sweet hubby thank you for all he did for us."

"I certainly will. He'll be sad he missed seeing you off."

Estelle took hold of Shirley's arm and grabbed her cane. They took a few steps, and she looked back at Loretta in time to see her wipe tears from her cheeks. She took a deep breath as a few tears dribbled down her own face. Her heart ached. Not because she'd lost a good friend, but because of something else—a nagging queasiness in her gut wouldn't go away. When life seemed to be going right, how come she couldn't shake the feeling trouble still cast a shadow on them all?

Chapter 34

Coreen stared out the car window at a pinkish-orange brick house with white trim that made her squint in the noonday sun. Bushes neatly spread beneath a porch. The yard had the greenest grass she'd ever seen. Beside the house, a fenced area looked like a graveyard with monuments lined up in rows. Was she dreaming?

"Is this our house?"

Betty Anne clapped her hands together. "Yes. Do you like it?"

"It's the most beautiful house I ever seen. It's … big—and brick. Not old gray boards."

Mary Anne turned around and smiled at her. "Well, are you ready to go inside?"

Coreen whispered, "I sure am."

Mary Anne turned off the engine and opened her door as Shirley pulled in beside her.

* * *

Estelle's stomach tied in knots. Such beautiful houses on this street. What would hers look like?

Shirley pulled onto the parking pad beside Mary Anne. "Here we are, Mom. Now ain't this lovely? Moving above your station, now aren't you?" Shirley chuckled as she turned off the engine and opened her car door.

"Heavens above. Look at it." Estelle smacked her hands in front of her. Tears welled up. "I never thought I'd ever—ever—live in a house like this. There's a ramp up to the front porch. And look at them pretty bushes all around. I hope they's some flowers come spring." She flung open her door and grabbed her cane and pocketbook. "It's beautiful. Let's get inside."

For a brief moment, she forgot about her body's inability to leap from the car and run up the ramp to her new life. As soon as she twisted in the seat, she got a reminder it would be a slow walk to her new front door.

"I'll be right there to help you, Mumsie. Let me carry your pocketbook.

Sarah, you coming?"

Estelle turned and watched Sarah gather some of the bags filled with their belongings. She saw a light in Sarah's eyes for the first time in years.

"Sarah, let's go see our new house. Okay?"

"I'm coming, Mother." Sarah bumped the car door shut with her hip and joined Estelle as they progressed up the ramp and onto the porch to join the rest.

Mary Anne presented the key to Estelle, who inserted it into the lock and turned. As the door opened, the coolness of the house enveloped them and drew them inside. They flowed into the front room like a happy brook.

Estelle wrinkled her brow. "It sure is cool in here. How can that be?"

Mary Anne closed the door behind them. "That's because of the air-conditioning."

Coreen yelled, "You mean our house is air-conditioned? I've done gone to heaven."

Everyone laughed. Sarah shook her head at Coreen. Estelle thought she might cry. No more steamy nights when sleep refused to come. No more sweating in the kitchen to cook a meal.

Shirley set down some bags. "Guess Mary Anne will have to show you how to adjust the temperature. It might get too cold for you after living without it for so long."

Mary Anne walked to the front of the group. "It's in the hallway. I'll show you where it is and how to operate it as we progress. We'll start here, in the dining room and office. Mr. Cooke left some of the furniture here. The cabinet by the wall has materials for the business. The dining suite is for doing paperwork with clients—when you're not using it to eat your meals."

Estelle fought back a lump in her throat as she realized the dining suite was exactly like the one she grew up with in her parents' home in Tennessee. She couldn't explain it, but even though she'd barely walked in the door, she knew she belonged here. Her gaze took in the rest of the room. Creamy beige paint covered the walls and dark-walnut stain on the quarter-round and baseboards made the room seem elegant. The windows sported pale-green drapes. The room appeared rather bare and without adornment. It had a masculine feel, and her thoughts immediately began to dwell on ways to soften the look.

"Through this archway is the living room. Right now there's not much furniture in here—a couch and one small chair. I understand you received vouchers for furniture, didn't you?"

Estelle spoke up. "Yes, we did. I guess Sarah'll have to do our shopping. Right, Sarah?"

The couch met with her approval, but the chair would never do. The hard seat would be painful, for sure. Hopefully, Sarah would find an easy chair for her like the one she used to have.

"I planned to when we figure out what we need, Mother. We need to make a list as we look around."

"I can drive you over there if you want." Shirley finally put her two cents' worth into the conversation.

"Maybe you can drop me off on your way back to Cincy. I don't want to hold you up. Besides, I have a few more errands to run after I go to the furniture store."

Shirley smiled and heaved her shoulders. "I'll drop you off and go home from there."

"If we go through this door, there's a hallway—where the thermostat is located. On the left is the kitchen, and on the right are the two bedrooms and the bathroom."

"Bathroom? One of the best rooms in the house." Coreen clasped her hands together. "But wait." She sucked in one side of her lip. "You said two bedrooms. I thought they's three."

"Your room is upstairs."

"Upstairs? We got an upstairs?" Coreen jumped up and down. "I ain't never seen a house with no upstairs before. Where is it?"

Betty Anne giggled. "You're funny. The stairs are in the living room. Come on, I'll show you."

The two girls giggled as they danced back through the hall, across the living room, and to the door leading upstairs. The thumping of feet traveled up with them. Estelle smiled after them. To be young and so full of life. Quiet again, Mary Anne showed them the air-conditioning controls and then continued the tour.

"Here's the front bedroom. I guess you'll want this one, Estelle, since it will be closer to the monuments and you can hear clients better when they arrive."

They followed Mary Anne into the room with pale-green wallpaper covered in trees and small blue birds. The painted white woodwork in this room made it bright and cheerful. Two windows faced the front porch, and one window faced the lot with the monuments and a small gravel parking area. Estelle walked into the empty room. There were built-in drawers and cabinets on one wall and a closet on another.

A pretty, bright room sure made a difference on your emotions. This room made her happy merely being in it. Made her feel alive. She chortled. "Well, looks like I'm gonna need a bed and a little table to put a lamp on. Sarah, let's look at yours now."

The group streamed out of the room and to the other end of the hall into Sarah's room. It seemed to be the same as the front room—but a mirror image. The walls had pink wallpaper crowded with white trellises covered in climbing red roses.

Mary Anne said, "Sarah, if you want to change the walls, feel free."

"Thank you, Mary Anne. I think I can live with it—at least for a while. It shore is a might different from what I been used to." Sarah slowly turned to see the whole room. "It's a happy room. The only thing I need to add is a bed—and a table and lamp like Mother's."

She turned the glass doorknob on the closet and peered inside. "This closet's a lot bigger than I thought. It even has shelves on each end. And it has the same happy paper. This'll do fine." Sarah closed the door with a smile. If only she had clothes to put inside. "Okay, I'd like to see that bathroom. How about you, Mother?"

"I can't wait. I'm excited I won't have to traipse down a path and sit with the spiders no more. This is heaven on earth." Estelle squeezed Sarah's arm and gave her a pat on the back. She must be dreaming and any minute would wake up and be back in the dreary little camp house. Sad that it took destruction and death to have a better life.

"Look at this, Sarah. There's the toilet—and a sink. It has a cabinet with room to put our toothbrushes and stuff on top and store away things underneath. And a little closet to put towels in—were you able to get towels this morning?"

"Yes."

Estelle kept going. "Look, a shower. Mercy me. I can walk into it and close the door. I won't be having to clean up out of a washtub no more. And look at them walls—such a pretty shade of lavender."

Sarah and Shirley giggled.

Estelle glanced at them. "What? Lavender's my favorite color. This house sure has almost every color of the rainbow in it, don't it? Mercy sakes, this is the best day of my life. I thank the good Lord for taking such good care of me." Tears ran a jagged path down Estelle's wrinkled face. "Look at me. Mercy, mercy. Can you believe I'm so emotional about an indoor bathroom?" Estelle laughed.

"Can I get a piece of toilet paper, Mumsie? I think I need to blow my nose. Must be dusty in here." Shirley ripped off a few sheets and vigorously blew.

Sarah walked out the door. "How about a tour of the kitchen now, Mary Anne?"

"Right this way, ladies."

She led them through another archway into a roomy kitchen. Estelle walked over to the double-bowled sink and tried the faucets. Then she looked out the three windows over the sink and counter into the fenced backyard beyond. What a beautiful view. She ran her hand over the countertops and pulled back the red-and-white checked curtains covering the shelving below. She leaned heavily on her cane as she stood at the electric cook stove. Then she limped to the refrigerator and opened the door. Completely empty.

"Well, Sarah, I guess we're gonna have to get groceries. Not a dadblamed thing in here." She cackled.

"I'd planned on it, Mother. Don't worry. At least there's a table and chairs in here. And lots of storage space."

"Why, you two will have this place whipped into shape before you know it. Next time I come down to visit, maybe I can bring a few things to add to your décor too. I almost forgot about all them bags of stuff we collected from the houses." Shirley looked under the sink. "You need some cleaners too. Sorry I won't be here to help you clean 'em up."

"I bet you're sorry." Sarah poked her sister in the arm.

"What's over there—the back door?" Estelle limped toward it. The intense pain made her sweat, but she refused to stop until she saw everything.

Mary Anne moved closer and took hold of her arm. "This is the door to the sunroom. Here, let me show you."

A white cotton curtain, matching the rest of the windows in the kitchen, hung on the door's window. Mary Anne opened the door, revealing a small room walled by windows. Another door with a glass panel led to the backyard.

"Well, will you look at this. What a pretty room. I could grow all kinds of flowers and some herbs in here too. Did you see this, Sarah? Won't this be a great place to sit in the sun and soak in them rays? And to hang the shucky beans to dry too."

"When it's not too hot or too cold outside, Mother. Do them windows open up?" Sarah walked over to a window and tested it, releasing the latch and lifting it to the top.

"Well, I guess they do. It'll certainly make it nice on warmer days." Estelle struggled to talk now and felt her body weaken. The pain from her hip shot down her leg.

Shirley walked over and took hold of her mother's arm. "Mumsie, I think it's high time you rested a spell. Sarah, we need a glass so Mumsie can have a drink of water. You got one this morning when we's at the Red Cross, didn't you?"

"Yeah, they're in your trunk. Give me the key and I'll go out and get the rest of the stuff out of the car. Mother, why don't you sit a spell in the living room while I get the rest of the stuff?"

"I ain't gonna fight it. I shore 'nuf could use a little rest." Her body seemed to be filled with sand. She fought to lift her feet as Shirley guided her to the only chair in the living room. Her muscles relaxed as she sat with a deep sigh. It would be much better with her La-Z-Boy recliner to put her feet up, but this would do for now.

It warmed Estelle's heart when her daughters noticed her pain and took care of her. She wished she could be the one taking care of them though. Blasted Vernon.

Mary Anne followed Sarah to the door. "I'll go with you. I have a few bags in my car too."

Chapter 35

Coreen burst into her new room with Betty Anne close behind. "Wow. This is great. 'Cepting it don't have no bed yet. But look at this fluffy white rug on the floor."

She kicked off her new flip-flops from the Red Cross truck, flinging them across the room, then walked in circles, scrunching the rug between her toes. It felt better than fresh spring grass. Then she ran across the room and looked out the window.

"Betty Anne, I can see the tombstones from here. Eww, it's kinda spooky."

"Coreen, there aren't any dead bodies out there, you know." She giggled.

"I know. It's the thought of tombstones in your yard. I guess I'll get used to it. There's built-in cabinets up here for all my stuff."

The drawers squeaked and complained as Coreen opened each one and looked inside. Then she turned to inspect the rest of the room. The walls were covered in delicate yellow wallpaper with pink rosebuds splattered all over.

"I love the wallpaper. Yellow's my favorite color. Besides pink. It's bright and happy. Not at all like the walls in my old house. Is that the closet over there?" She ran across the room and grabbed the glass doorknob. "Did you see this doorknob? It looks like a diamond."

Betty Anne joined Coreen as she opened the door to the closet and stepped inside. A string dangled from the ceiling. "Look, my closet has a light in it. It won't be all dark and scary inside."

"Are you gonna be afraid to stay in your room all alone?"

"No. I think I'm gonna like it—a lot. I ain't never had a place all my own before. The room's big and has lights in it. What's the door over there?"

"It's a storage room. It may be a little creepy at first, but it has a light in it too. I looked in it when I came with my mom. There's all kinds of interesting old stuff in there. Maybe you can find a table for your room. Let's look." Betty Anne bounced over to the door and opened it. Coreen followed her at a distance. A blast of hot air made the girls take a step back and gasp. The light from the only window cast shadows around the room.

"It's really hot in there. And scary. I ain't sure about this, Betty Anne."

"It'll be okay as soon as I find the light switch. Here it is."

The two crept into the room. Coreen held onto Betty Anne's arm, shivering even though it was hotter than the old kitchen when her mama fired up the coal stove to cook supper. The walls were bare, and the room smelled like the camp school after being locked up all summer. Furniture, boxes, suitcases, and trunks were scattered around the room. Cobwebs made Coreen sputter as she wiped them away with her hand.

"Yuck, spider webs. I don't like this place. Makes me think a haint's gonna jump out and grab me."

"Silly. Ghosts can't grab you. They're spirits of dead people and don't have any real bodies. Of course, I'm not sure if there's really ghosts at all. The only one I know about is the Holy Ghost and it doesn't hurt anybody."

"Well, I ain't taking no chances. I think we should go." Coreen puckered her lips.

"Look at this trunk over here. Let's see what's in it." Betty Anne dropped onto the floor in front of the trunk. A thick layer of dust lay on the top like a blanket of felt. She swiped it and the cobwebs away and then worked on opening the latches, rusty with age. The first latch popped open.

"Maybe you shouldn't open it." Coreen's voice trembled. She told herself not to be silly and haints weren't going to pop out of the trunk. Then she wondered if Mr. Cooke would be upset if he knew they were looking at his stuff. Betty Anne opened the second latch, and the lid creaked as she lifted it.

"Well, there aren't any haints in here, but there's a lot of interesting stuff. Come and look."

"No, I don't want to see it." Coreen stood in the same spot but leaned forward enough to peer into the trunk.

"What a beautiful umbrella. It looks like it's lace." Betty Anne pulled it out and started to open it, but Coreen stopped her.

"Don't open an umbrella in the house, silly. It'll bring bad luck. Lord knows I don't need no more bad luck."

"Okay, okay. But there's a lot more in here." Betty Anne replaced it and rummaged through the trunk.

Coreen couldn't resist seeing. She sat down with Betty Anne and they went through things one at a time. Much of it didn't interest them, like baby clothes, blankets, and toys. But a book caught her attention right away. The front said "Diary." Inside, somebody wrote the name Angela Cooke. Pages of writing filled up most of it. Coreen decided it could provide some reading time until she could borrow some books from the library. If they would let her have any since the last ones were ruined in the flood.

"Here are pictures of the Cookes. Here's Mr. Cooke and his wife. She died in a car wreck, I think. And here's their daughter, Angela. She was our age when she killed herself. Nobody knew why. I think she died about five years ago."

Coreen took the photo and stared into the girl's eyes. She wondered why a girl her age would be so unhappy that she would kill herself. And then she remembered how much she wanted to die a few days ago. Could it be Angela lived the same kind of life she did?

"I wonder why she did it?" Coreen wiped dust from the image.

"I don't know. I heard my mom and dad talking about it once, and they said somebody hurt her really bad right before it happened."

Did Mr. Cooke beat up on Angela like Daddy did her? "That's awful. And then her mama died too?" Did he also hurt her mama?

"Yeah. A car wreck, I think. I could ask my mom. But I think she died a year after Angela."

"I don't think I wanna do this no more. It's too sad."

"I know what you mean, Coreen."

The girls returned the contents, except the diary, to the trunk and closed it. Coreen flipped off the light and they closed the door. As she put the diary on a shelf, she noticed another door.

"Another room. It ain't scary, is it?"

"You'll like this. Go ahead, look." Betty Anne smiled.

Coreen closed one eye and cocked her head at her friend. "Are you sure?"

"Yep, I'm sure. Go ahead."

Cautiously, Coreen slinked up to the door and turned the glass knob. The door creaked as it opened. She hesitated, took a deep breath, and opened it the rest of the way.

"It's a bathroom! I got a bathroom in my own room? I don't gotta run downstairs when I gotta go?" Coreen jumped up and down, giggling.

Betty Anne, caught up in the excitement, jumped with her. The two locked hands, laughing. After their little happy dance, Coreen went inside to take a better look. A tiny room, not much bigger than the closet, sported the same yellow wallpaper. She flipped on the light switch to reveal a pink toilet and washbowl. Above the sink hung an oval mirror flanked by lights with frosted glass shades. A small table fit snugly on the far wall.

"It doesn't have a bathtub. You'll still have to go downstairs for that. But, hey, you have a toilet and a sink all to yourself."

"I'm so excited I could die." Coreen danced around her room and collapsed like a snow angel onto the plush rug.

Betty Anne flopped down on the floor beside her, still giggling. "You're funny, Coreen. It sure doesn't take much to make you happy."

"I guess. But you gotta remember a few days ago I didn't have nothing at all to make me happy. But now ... I got so much more than I ever figured I'd have in my whole life."

Betty Anne whispered, "Your being happy makes me feel guilty."

Coreen turned to her and stared for a moment. "Why?"

Betty Anne lay completely still on the rug for a moment. She sighed and said to the ceiling, "Because I have so much and I feel like I don't have anything. But you have a little bit and you feel like you have so much."

"What in the world are you talking about?"

She rolled on her side and faced Coreen. "I live in a really big house. My dad makes lots of money—and I do mean lots. My folks can buy me anything I want. Sometimes I think it's to get me to leave them alone so they can do what they want to do."

"You mean you're rich?" Coreen studied Betty Anne carefully to see if there were any detectable oddities about rich people.

"Yeah, I guess."

"I ain't never met nobody rich before. What's it like being able to buy anything you want in the whole world?"

"I guess I like getting things. But it gets boring after a while."

"Boring? What kinds of things do you buy that you think's boring?"

Betty Anne rolled over to her tummy and plucked at the fibers in the rug. "I like clothes ... and stuff for my room. I buy music to listen to. I spend a lot of time in my room all alone watching TV or reading books."

"What don't you already have?"

She plucked at the rug so long Coreen reckoned she wasn't going to answer. Finally, she sighed. "It's kind of funny, but the one thing I really want is something you can't even buy with money."

Coreen rolled over to face her friend. "What can't you buy?"

A tear rolled across Betty Anne's face and dripped onto the rug. "I want my parents to think I'm special ... like my sister. I want to see them smile when I walk into the room. I want them to spend time with me and hold me in their arms, look me right in the eyes and tell me they love me—more than their money."

Coreen used a finger to wipe the tear from Betty Anne's cheek. "I understand. I always wanted my daddy to love me the way a daddy's supposed to love his daughter, not yell at me and beat up on me till I wanted to die. And I wish my mama didn't hate me so much. I want her to love me and think I'm good for something. I think she blames me for all the bad stuff my daddy did to her, but it don't make no sense." A tear slid down Coreen's cheek and dripped onto the rug.

Betty Anne leaned over and wiped the tear from Coreen's face. They smiled to each other. Both girls flopped onto their backs and stared at the ceiling.

"Betty Anne?"

"Yeah?"

"D'ya like living here—in Mt. Pleasant, I mean?"

"I guess it's okay. How about you?"

"This house is really nice and all. I mean, I never reckoned I'd ever have my own room—let alone a room with its own indoor bathroom. It's more than I ever dreamed. But ... there's something inside me like a block of coal. It feels like I can't breathe, and if I don't get out of this town I'm gonna die."

"Maybe you can go away to college and get a job in a big city like Lexington."

"College? I can't go to college." Coreen smacked the rug with her hands.

"Why not? All you have to do is get good grades."

"I like school. It's like my brain wants to know more and more. I read all the time. When I'm not singing or writing a new song, that is. The problem is the more I read, the more I feel like I don't know much. Not like you. You know all kinds of stuff I never even heard about before. You're *really* smart."

"No, I'm not. I hate school. I have to work like crazy to pass the tests. What I know is because I've seen it—not because I learned it. Why wouldn't you go to college if you like school?"

"I ain't got no money, silly."

"I didn't think about that."

The girls stared at the ceiling in silence for a few minutes.

"Betty Anne, d'ya like going to church?"

"Yes. Bob and Loretta make it fun. We do lots of fun stuff. Kids our age, I mean. We go camping, take hikes in the mountains, have parties where we play all kinds of games, and we even went horseback riding once. We always have fun. Bob tells really good scary stories around the campfire too."

"I like them. Especially Loretta. She's good to talk to." Coreen didn't mention how she kept secrets.

The two girls lay quietly on the floor. A train whistle blew in the distance. A car horn blasted nearby. The engine of a heavy truck revved as it hit a bump in the street and bounced its load.

"Betty Anne?"

She giggled softly as she turned to Coreen. "Another question?"

"D'ya believe there's a God?"

"Of course I do. Don't you?"

"I don't know. I mean ... The missionaries come to my school and told us about Him, and I don't think they'd lie about it. But … well … my life's been pretty miserable up till now, and I don't see how the God they talked about could let my life be so awful." Coreen ran her fingers through the rug. "Mammaw reads her Bible and prays sometimes. But Mama and Daddy only talked about him when they was yelling at somebody—and they didn't sound respectful." Coreen flopped back down on the rug, her arms outstretched. "I just don't know."

"Maybe you should talk to Bob or Loretta about it."

"Maybe I will. Some day."

Coreen remembered her prayer. She guessed a real God would be pretty mad at her for praying such a mean prayer. She didn't want to go where bad people go. Even though her new life seemed wonderful right now, would God, if He existed, punish her? The thought that she could end up with Daddy again, for all eternity, made her body sting with electricity. Heavy fog expanded inside her like yeast in dough.

Something on the ceiling distracted her. "I think I'm seeing things. I swear I see stars on the ceiling."

"I think I can see 'em too."

"Why do I have stars on my ceiling?"

"Maybe they're stickers. They might glow in the dark." Betty Anne turned to Coreen. "I guess you'll find out tonight."

Air-conditioning. Stars on her ceiling. Her own room. Coreen wasn't the poor coal-camp girl anymore. Or was she? Can you really change who you are by how you live?

Coreen fingered the gold heart around her neck.

Footsteps clomped on the stairs. Coreen and Betty Anne turned their heads to watch the door open. "Hi, Aunt Shirley."

Panting and with her hand on her chest, Aunt Shirley said, "Well, hello girls. What in the world are ya'll doing on the floor?"

"Relaxing." Coreen picked herself up and threw her arms around her aunt. "Isn't this a great room, Aunt Shirley? It's all mine." She ran around the room, showing her aunt all the details.

When Coreen finished her tour, Aunt Shirley said, "Girls, I came up here to get you. Your Mama wants you to go with her to pick out the furniture and get some supplies, Coreen. After I drop you off, I'm gonna head back to Cincinnati to Richie and the kids."

Coreen's smile drooped. "I'm gonna miss you, Aunt Shirley. I wish you could stay."

"Well, it's better than the other day. You wanted to go home with me."

Coreen smiled and glanced at Betty Anne. "I guess my life's gotten a little better the last few days. But I'm still gonna miss you."

"And I'm gonna miss you too. You're my favorite, you know."

Taking the gold heart in her fingers, she looked at her aunt. "Yeah, I know. And you're my favorite too."

The two embraced until Aunt Shirley said, "I can't breathe. You're squeezing the air out of me."

Coreen chuckled. "I love you."

"I love you too, precious girl."

Would her mama ever be able to say those words to her and mean them? If only she could learn how to love from Aunt Shirley. But to do that, they'd have to spend more time together. How could they do that?

"Now, come on, you two. People's a waiting for us."

Chapter 36

Coreen waved good-bye to Betty Anne from the back seat of Aunt Shirley's car. "Mama, d'ya think Mammaw'll be okay by herself?"

The car lurched as Aunt Shirley hit the gas and pulled into traffic.

"I reckon we should all be more concerned about us being okay the way your aunt drives," Mama said.

"What? I needed to step on it to get out before somebody hits me."

Coreen settled back as her mama dug her fingers into the dash in front. Big trees hung over the street on both sides, offering shade. Then they turned onto a street with buildings all standing next to each other. One building, a light-yellowish brick, displayed a sign out front that read "Mt. Pleasant Library."

"The library!" She screamed so loudly Aunt Shirley hit the brakes and her mama grabbed hold of the dash.

"Coreen, are you trying to get us killed?" Mama jerked her head around.

"Sorry, Mama. I got excited when I saw how close we live to the library. I can walk over here anytime I want to get more books. If it's okay with you, that is."

"Use your brain. You almost made your aunt kill us."

"I didn't nearly kill us. I was being cautious."

Aunt Shirley made one more turn and pulled into the gravel lot next to Simpson's Furniture Store. "Here we are. D'ya want me to come in with you?"

"You need to get on the road, Shirl." Mama opened her door. "Thanks for being here when we needed you. Don't forget to tell your friends I said thanks too. Come on, Coreen, we got work to do." Just as her mama started to get out, she reached across the front seat and hugged Aunt Shirley. "I'll call you when I decide"—she glanced at Coreen—"about the other thing we discussed."

"Okay, girl. You take care—and be smart." Aunt Shirley smiled at Mama.

Coreen leaned over the seat and stretched her arms around her aunt's neck. "I love you, Aunt Shirley. Thank you for my birthday present—and everything."

Aunt Shirley reached back with her hand to pat her arm and planted a kiss on her cheek. "I love you too, kid. I expect to get a letter from you soon about your new school. Now don't you forget them whispers of hope, okay?"

"Hurry up, Coreen."

"I'm coming, Mama. I won't forget. Bye, Aunt Shirley." Coreen climbed out of the car to join her mama in the parking lot.

The two waved as Shirley left in a puff of dust from the loose gravel, turned right, and disappeared from sight. Both sighed heavily and coughed as the dust caught up with them.

* * *

Estelle scanned the room, taking in the details, claiming each as her own. Blessed but still empty, the kind of empty furniture can't fill. Not just her, but Sarah and Coreen too. Could this new life they'd been given fill that emptiness? They had survived the past, but they needed to find a way to move past it and thrive.

Vernon deserved killing, but she trembled when she thought about whether they would catch the one who did it. Maybe it would be best if they never caught him—or her. If only it could be resolved and forgotten.

"Enough." Estelle raised her hands in the air and shouted to the empty house. No use dwelling on negative stuff when there's a lot to do. Best get up from the uncomfortable chair and tackle her first job—look through the papers Mr. Cooke left behind.

As she reached out to grab her cane, loud knocks sounded from the front door and made her jump. Calming herself, she moved forward on the chair enough to stand up. Before she could get to a standing position, the door creaked open.

"Hello. Estelle? Sarah? You have visitors. Can we come in?" Loretta's voice drifted in.

Turning toward the door, Estelle stretched her lips wide in a smile. "Of course you can."

"Don't get up. We'll come to you." Loretta led the group of Bob, Mary Anne, Betty Anne, Imogene, and Cora as they filled up the living room, their arms overflowing with pokes and baskets.

"I'm as happy as a bullfrog in spring to see you. What's in your arms?"

Mary Anne said, "We're having a housewarming party. We'll take all this to the kitchen and put it away, if that's okay. You just sit there and we'll take care of it for you. Is Sarah here?"

"Not right now. She and Coreen went to get our new furniture and a few supplies. They should be back 'fore long."

Bob came back from the kitchen, minus the pokes. "I've also got another surprise in the car. It's Patches. I think I'd better hurry and get him out of there before he mistakes the carpet for grass."

Estelle giggled. "I reckon you're right. You'd better get him out quick. The backyard's all fenced in, so you can put him there."

Cora peeked her head into the room. "Estelle, this basket has some dinner for you girls. I'll put it on the kitchen table for you."

"I won't have to starve tonight. Bless your heart. You don't know how much I'm gonna miss your cooking, Cora."

"Thank you, kindly." She spread a smile across her face and disappeared into the kitchen again.

Estelle sat back in her chair. Her face ached from smiling. And to think, she'd been sitting there feeling sorry for herself. The Lord surely blessed.

Chapter 37

The afternoon sun radiated in waves of heat off the sidewalk. Coreen attempted to keep up with her mother as they passed the post office, Greyhound bus station, and Smith's Drug Store. They stepped between two parked cars, checked for oncoming traffic, and crossed the one-lane street to the dime store. As she pulled open one of the double doors, the cool air from inside the store enveloped her, making the perspiration tickle her skin.

"It shore feels good in here, don't it, Mama?"

"Here. Hold on to these."

Coreen wrapped her arms around some pads of paper and pencils and then followed her mama to steps that led down to the lower level. They squeezed between other shoppers and bins of towels and bathroom accessories until they found the bed linens.

"Look for full sheets, Coreen. They should be around here." They both rummaged through the shelves.

"Hello, ladies. Can I help you find something?"

Coreen popped up with a gasp and dropped the items she held in her arms. She then chased them under the bins and shelves. After retrieving them, she looked up at a withered and skinny woman frowning down at her.

Mama frowned back at the lady and snapped, "I need full-sized sheets. Where are they?"

"They're right over here." She swished over to the shelf and leaned over to check the labels. "We have a few colors. There's white, of course. We also have pink, yellow, and blue."

"I want yellow." Coreen realized she should have said it a little softer.

Mama chose two sets of white and paused slightly before pulling out a set of yellow sheets. She plopped them into Coreen's already loaded arms and said, "Happy birthday."

Coreen's jaw dropped open, and she spilled the pads of paper and pencils again.

The sales lady frowned but picked them up for her. "Let me take that to the counter for you."

"Thanks, ma'am. And thanks, Mama." Coreen spread her mouth in a big smile. Could this day get any better?

At the register, her mama pulled out a wrinkled envelope and removed enough money to pay for the items. Where'd she get that money? She didn't dare ask. Instead, she grabbed the bag and headed to the front door and then out onto the sidewalk.

The flip-flops smacked the bottoms of her feet as she followed her mother like a baby duckling through town. The place between her big toe and the next toe hurt. The heat of the sun, combined with the heavy load of purchases she carried, caused her to sweat in all the places touching the plastic bag. She tried to adjust the slippery load and didn't see her mother come to a dead stop directly in front of her. She smashed into her and dropped the bag onto her aching toes.

"What's wrong with you, girl?" Mama frowned at her. "Watch where you're going. You pert near knocked me over."

"Sorry, Mama." Would there ever come a day when she could do things right?

"Well ... be more careful."

Coreen lifted her eyebrows. That was easier than usual. She left a bit more space between them as Mama opened the door to the next storefront.

"Ain't this Cousin Gracie's beauty shop? Why we coming here?" Coreen bunched up her nose and lips. She'd only been here once when Daddy stopped to pick up something for Grandma Della. As she entered, pungent odors of chemicals mixed with powdery fake floral scents attacked her nose. She held her breath but realized she couldn't hold it long enough to escape the horrible smells. She compromised by holding her nose and breathing through her mouth.

An air conditioner rattled violently above the door to the shop. A blue-haired woman sat in a chair in front of a row of mirrors, completely covered below the neck with an animal print drape as Gracie juggled a comb, a pair of pointy silver scissors, and a spray bottle of water.

Gracie looked up as they entered and smiled. "As I live and breathe. If it ain't Sarah. I never thought I'd ever see you in here."

"Hi, Gracie. Yeah, it's me."

Gracie continued working on the older woman's hair; silver-blue curls littered the floor around them. Gracie's hair drew Coreen's attention though. She thought it looked like a brand-new copper scouring pad, the ones she used to clean iron skillets after Sunday fried chicken.

"It's high time. I gotta say I'm as surprised as the groundhog when he sees his shadow." She turned back to the blue-haired lady. "Hon, I want to say how sorry I am about—well, you know. Hang in there. You'll be fine." Gracie looked up at

Mama and smiled. "Are you here for a shampoo and set, Sarah?"

Gracie spoke in the garbled twang of a deep holler. Coreen hated having to listen to her because she sounded like she put a bunch of marbles in her mouth and talked around them. Most of the sound seemed to come from her nose, not her mouth. Working hard at listening usually gave her a headache. She had been relieved when Gracie's husband died in a mining accident and she had to move out of the camp. She'd always spent a lot of time hanging out on their front porch—and talking. She liked to talk.

"Have you got time to ... cut our hair?"

"Cut *our* hair?" Coreen reached up and grabbed her ponytail and hugged it to her heart. Nobody was going to cut off her ponytail.

"Cut your hair? Sarah, honey, you almost made me snip a bit too much off Mrs. Howard's do. Don't worry, Mrs. Howard, I didn't snip a thing didn't need snipping."

"I think it's time for a change, and there ain't nobody to stop me no more." Mama looked in the mirror and pulled her hair into a tight wad on her head.

No way would Coreen get hers cut off. She loved her long hair—except for washing it and brushing it. That hurt. And drying it in the winter took a long time. She looked at her mother's long curly hair. Why would she ever cut it?

"I think it's a wonderful idea, Sarah. I am simply itching to get my scissors on them locks. What'd you have in mind?"

Mama studied her hair in the mirror, adjusting the length of it by gathering it in a bunch. "I'd like something easy to take care of and ... short."

"Gracious be. Not what I expected. You do need a do that's more ... stylish though. It'll perk you right up." She trimmed some more blue hair and turned to Coreen. "What about you, Miss Coreen?"

"I like my hair the way it is." She frowned and stroked her hair as if it was a puppy.

"It needs a little trimming up. Get rid of them split ends. We could make you a bit more stylish too."

"No, not short," Coreen almost shouted. Her hands trembled.

Gracie snorted. "It ain't got to be short, honey. How about going through them books over yonder on the table and see if you can find a do that floats your boat."

Coreen walked over to the table scattered with books and magazines. She dropped the bag of purchases onto the floor and wiped the moisture from her hands onto her shorts. Choosing several of the magazines, she wiggled herself into a worn and wobbly wicker chair with a limp floral cushion and thumbed through the pages. Since the only magazines she'd ever seen were Weekly Readers at school, the photographs of women dressed in unusual clothing with their hair in strange styles and colors fascinated her. She oohed as she took in page after page of sequins, rhinestones, and fur-accented outfits on models with lips brighter than a vine-ripened tomato. Her heart jumped as she wondered if the jewels adorning their ears, necks, and hands were real. Longing for beautiful things made her reach up and touch the gold heart around her neck.

"Sarah, honey, I'll be with you girls when I finish Mrs. Howard. Bless her heart. I got to get her ready for a funeral. She lost her sweet little granddaughter yesterday."

"How awful. How old was she?" Mama sat in another of the wicker chairs.

The elder blue-haired lady sniffed and pulled one hand from under the leopard print cape to dab at her eyes with a tissue. "She was only thirteen years old. It's such a sad thing. I don't know what's going on with these kids to do such a terrible thing."

Coreen put down the magazine and stared at the floor. "I'm thirteen too. What happened to her?"

"Coreen." Mama smacked her arm and gave her an evil stare.

"It's okay, honey child. My baby killed herself. I don't understand why." Mrs. Howard burst into tears.

Gracie handed her another tissue and patted her on the shoulder. "There, there, honey. It's awful, but you'll be okay. Time heals."

Coreen's heart ached for the lady. And the girl. Coreen looked down at the magazine in her hands. She didn't remember picking it up or seeing a single picture as she flipped the pages.

Gracie announced to the world, "You're finished, Miss Howard. And you look purdy as a picture."

"Thank you, Gracie. You always do a wonderful job." Her voice trembled still.

Gracie took a soft brush and dusted tiny blue hairs from her neck and shoulders. As the old woman struggled to get out of the vinyl chair, she reminded Coreen of Mammaw. The lady pressed her hair to test the hairspray holding each blue hair in place. Coreen figured it wouldn't move for at least a week. They all waited in silence until the bell clanged and the door shut.

* * *

Gracie clapped her hands together and turned to Sarah. "Bless her heart. What a shame."

"Did the girl really kill herself? Anybody know why?" Sarah put down her magazine. No matter how much she hated her life, Sarah knew she would never have killed herself. Blowing his head off? Maybe. But not herself. It would have given Vernon too much pleasure.

"According to the paper today, it was definitely suicide. Here, look for yourself. There's even a picture of her. Pretty little thing."

Gracie opened up the newspaper and held it out for them to see. The black-and-white image of a smiling face, sparkling eyes, and blonde curls filled a quarter of the front page.

Coreen popped up. "Hey, I seen her before."

"Where would you have seen her? You ain't been nowheres." Sarah shook her head.

"I know I seen her, Mama. I can't remember when though. Or where." She sat back down on the wicker chair and tapped her chin. Her brows furrowed.

Gracie turned to Mama and clapped her hands together. "Well, are you ready? I'm as tickled as frog fuzz to get my hands on your hair."

Sarah stood. Butterflies flitted inside her stomach. Her decision. Not his. She sucked in some air. "I'm ready."

"Have a seat while I sweep up this hair." Gracie swept the blue hairs into a pile next to the wall. She shook out the leopard drape and covered Sarah with it. Lowering the chair back until her neck rested on the curve in the basin, Gracie tested the temperature of the water, squirted shampoo into her hand, and worked it into a rich lather. Sarah's shoulders relaxed and her eyes closed as Gracie's fingers worked their magic. Heaven.

Over too soon, Gracie wrapped a towel around her hair and raised her back up. "What ya want, missy?" she asked as she ran her fingers through the long waves.

Sarah stared into the mirror. Vernon insisted she keep her hair long and curled for him. But it's her life now. She pointed her chin at the Sarah in the mirror. "I want it all cut off."

Coreen gasped. A magazine hit the floor.

"How much *all* d'ya want cut, hon?"

"Gracie, I want just enough left to still look like a girl."

The Gracie in the mirror cocked her head. "Are you shore? I mean, after I make that first cut, it's too late to change your mind."

"I know, Gracie. I'm sure." She grinned.

"You ain't gonna be mad at me after I snip it off, are you?"

"No. Now do it."

Gracie put her hand to her cheek. "Mercy, mercy. You better not cry." Gracie took a deep breath, let it out in a burst, and readied her scissors.

Sarah glanced at Coreen. She sat with her mouth open and her hands across her chest. Sarah chuckled. "Why's everybody so worried?"

Only Gracie responded. "I'm shore glad he ain't still alive. He'd skin me. After he skinned you."

Gracie combed through the thick hair and gathered it in one hand at the back. She looked heavenward and raised her scissors. Sarah's heart pounded in her chest. Her decision. Her life.

One big snip and hair lay on the floor, dead. Chills raced up and down Sarah's body.

"It's done." Gracie exhaled and grabbed onto the back of the chair. "I'll put some shape and style into what's left." She chuckled. "I bet your head feels a bit lighter now. Are you okay?"

Sarah stared into the mirror, a grin stretching across her face. "I feel great. My whole life feels lighter now."

"I'm glad. I thought I's gonna pass out cold there for a minute." She laughed again. "Whoo-ee. How exciting."

Sarah watched as Gracie shaped and trimmed up her hair. She giggled as it sprang into curls. No more weight to drag it down. Just like her.

"I'm glad y'all found a new place to live. Where'd you stay after the flood?"

"We stayed at New Hope Church. It proved a little hard on Mother, but we managed. Nice folks."

"I felt awful for you at the funeral. I tell you what—Della's a piece a work. I don't know how in the world Otis puts up with her." Gracie measured with her comb to make sure both sides were even. "Can't believe their church ain't kicked her out of there. She's more venomous than them snakes of theirs, for shore." She lifted Sarah's chin and looked at her this way and that. "You know, the rest of the folks at that church is as sweet as they can be. I think Della's a bit tetched in the head. Guess that's where Vernon got his. She learnt him how to be a rotter too."

Sarah shifted in the chair to see better. "I'm sorry I didn't get to talk to you much at the funeral, Gracie. I kinda left in a hurry."

"Honey, I seed you. I can shore see why. I think I woulda needed another funeral right then and there. Believe me, I'm glad I'm related to the other side of his family and not Della's." Gracie spun Sarah around in the chair and Coreen giggled. "Well, how d'ya like your haircut, hon?"

Sarah ran her fingers through the curls and looked at herself in the mirror. She looked—and felt—younger.

"I love it."

"I think you look beautiful, Mama."

Gracie unsnapped the drape and shook it out. Sarah stood and leaned into the mirror as she fluffed out the hair that now sprang into curls. She smiled as she sashayed back to the wicker chair.

* * *

Coreen bit the side of her lip as she curled her ponytail into a spiral and held it tightly in her hands. Gracie swept up the black remnants of Mama's hair littering the floor. The pile heaped taller than the blue one. Coreen whirled the chair around and stared at herself in the mirror. Her knees went weak. She took a deep breath and released it slowly.

Gracie approached with the drape and flung it around her.

"I don't want mine cut off like Mama's. I want a teeny little bit cut. I like having my ponytail and making a bun on top of my head."

Gracie chuckled. "Okay, I won't cut it off, baby doll. How 'bout I trim off them dead ends and make it look a little neater? I could thin it out a tad too. And how 'bout bangs? I think they'd look good on your face."

Coreen scrunched her face. She took a wisp of hair and held it to her forehead. Betty Anne's bangs looked really nice. "I reckon bangs would be okay. As long as they ain't too short."

"Alrighty. Not too short. Now, let me give you a little shampoo here."

Gracie yanked on the blue ribbon tied into a knot around her ponytail. Coreen winced. Gracie lowered her to the sink.

She giggled as Gracie sprayed water on her hair. "The water feels good. Ooh, scrubbing my head feels even better." Her eyes glazed over. She'd never had a real shampoo before. Mama always scrubbed her head so hard it hurt. She regretted when the rinsing began. Gracie squeezed the excess water from her hair and grabbed a towel from the stack.

"You got so much hair I might have to use two towels, girl. Let's set you back up now and I can get started."

As Gracie picked up a fresh comb and her scissors, Coreen reminded her with a wag of her finger, "Not too short."

"Yes, ma'am. Now you keep real still so I don't accidentally cut something I shouldn't."

"I won't budge a smidge," Coreen assured her as she froze her body and clenched her jaw.

A few snips later, Gracie said, "Now don't you look beautiful? It ain't too short, is it?"

"No … I reckon it's okay." Coreen reached up and grieved for the two inches now laying dead on the floor encircling her chair.

"Now, you hold real still while I cut your bangs." Gracie ran her scissors across her forehead, trimming the hair even with her brow.

"It tickles." Coreen wrinkled her nose as stray hairs slid down her face and onto the drape on their way to the floor.

"Don't move yet. You don't want me to get 'em crooked. There. Now let me look at 'em. Open up your eyes."

Coreen took her hands and dusted stray hairs off her face before opening her eyes. She spun the chair around to see herself in the mirror. "Wow, I look different, don't I? What'ya think, Mama?"

Sarah looked up from a magazine. "Well, you don't look as scraggly as you did."

"I think you look lovely. It makes you look a lot more growed up." Gracie smiled at the mirror image.

Coreen stared more intently into the mirror. "I think you're right. I do look growed up."

Sarah tossed the magazine onto the table and stood up. "Thanks, Gracie. How much do I owe you?"

"I enjoyed this. You ain't gotta pay me nothing."

"I got money. I want to pay."

"You shore, hon? I mean, with all you've got happening. I didn't think … you …"

"I got a job. And Mother's got a job too."

"Well, I'll be. Where you gonna work?"

"Morgan's. Mother's working for the monument company. He's letting us live in the house there too."

"Now ain't that dandy. I'm glad things is looking up for y'all. I know it ain't been easy for you. Never has been. Even if he was my cousin, I knowed Vernon were a rotter." She leaned over and whispered loud enough for Coreen to hear, "I'd a called him something else but Coreen's here."

"How much is it? And tell me the truth."

Coreen picked up a few strands of her hair from the floor and stuffed them into her pocket. Then she walked over to the pile of hair on the floor and retrieved a few long strands of her mother's hair. After stuffing it in her other pocket, she leaned back down and grabbed a wad of the blue hairs and added those to her collection.

"Come on, Coreen. We still got things to do. Don't forget the bag." Mama took another look in the mirror and fingered her curls. She smiled at her reflection.

"Coming. Bye-bye, Gracie."

The little bell clanged as they left the chemical coolness of the shop and stepped back out into the humid heat.

Coreen's toes ached as they rounded the corner of Main Street and entered the A&P grocery store. Inside the entrance, Coreen paused. Holding the bag in one hand, she struggled to lift her left foot and remove the flip-flop without toppling over.

"Ouch. I got a blister." She sucked air between her teeth.

"Come on, Coreen. We need to hurry and get this done before they show up with the furniture."

Coreen stuck her flip-flops into the bag. As she splatted down the aisle behind Mama and the buggy, she sighed at the coolness of the tiles on her feet.

Mama flitted all over the store, up one aisle and down the other, dropping things into the buggy. The longer they shopped, the hungrier Coreen became. Must be time for dinner.

As they stood in line at the register, Coreen picked up a newspaper. She stared and stared at the photo. Where had she seen that girl?

Chapter 38

Almost home. Coreen couldn't wait to drop the pokes and rest her sore feet. Sweat dripped down her back, and the new bangs clung to her forehead as she followed Mama in silence. She wondered how her mother could stay dry with two bags clasped in each hand and a new broom wobbling under her right armpit.

Seeing her house gave her renewed energy to walk a little faster. They crossed the crispy grass, and as they reached the front door, it flung open.

Pastor Bob stood in the doorway. "Welcome back. Here, let me help you with those bags."

"Hi, Pastor Bob. What you doing here?" Coreen chirped.

"Well, right now I'm helping you bring in all this stuff. Here, let me take those, Sarah." Bob took the bags and waddled like a mule with packed saddlebags to the kitchen. Coreen giggled as he turned sideways to squeeze through the archway.

Betty Anne popped around the doorway with a smile. "Guess who's here."

Coreen squealed. "Betty Anne."

"Patches is in the backyard too."

Coreen gasped. "Let's see how he likes his new home."

As Coreen started to follow Betty Anne, Mama grabbed her arm and made her flinch.

"Help get the stuff put away before you even think about running out there to that dog."

"Yes, ma'am." Coreen rubbed the sore spot on her arm. She shrugged to Betty Anne and followed her mother.

Mary Anne turned to get another poke and stopped short. "Sarah. Your hair. I love it."

"I think it really suits you." Loretta smiled and nodded.

Mama fingered her curls. "Thanks."

"I got my hair cut too." Coreen held her hands to the side of her head in ta-dah fashion.

"It looks really nice, Coreen. Except it's dripping wet." Betty Anne laughed.

"It's really hot out there—and my arms were full of pokes."

The kitchen looked like a beehive with everybody zooming around putting things away. "D'ya really need me in here, Mama?"

Her mama glanced around and motioned to Coreen. "Go on."

"Thanks. Come on, Betty Anne."

The girls dashed to the front door and opened it. Two young men in jeans and dirty T-shirts stood outside. The girls stopped short, eyeing them uneasily. "Who are you?"

"We're here with a delivery from Simpsons Furniture Store. Is this the Kincaid house?"

"It shore is. Just a minute."

Coreen found her mama just as Mammaw said, "Sarah! Where's your hair?"

"The furniture's here."

* * *

The delivery men maneuvered the new chair through the front door. Estelle watched them carry it into the living room and stop in front of her.

"Where you want us to put it, ma'am?"

"How purdy. It's robin's egg blue." She clapped her hands together. "Can you boys put it over there by the window?" They moved the old chair out of the way and hefted the new one into place. "You shore 'nuf are strong young men. Turn it a little bit this way and I can see the TV too." She directed them, inch by inch, until it was just right. "Perfect. Now let me try it out."

Estelle plopped her behind into the chair with a great sigh. "It rocks too. How d'ya get the feet to go up?" The man showed her the handle and her feet shot up in the air. She giggled and patted the arms of the chair.

"Hope you enjoy it, ma'am. We'd better get the rest of the stuff. Is it where you want it?"

"It's perfect, young man. I could fall asleep."

They left as the group from the kitchen entered the room laughing. Mary Anne said, "Estelle, dear, we got the groceries put away in the kitchen. I hope you can find it all when we leave."

"Thank y'all for helping put things away. You've been a blessing. Ain't my new chair purdy?"

"Looks really comfortable too." Bob gave her chair a once-over.

Estelle tilted her head. "You ain't coveting my new chair, are ya?"

Bob chuckled. He stepped aside as Sarah led the boys through the throng and told them where to take the mattress as she waited in the hall.

Estelle patted the arms of her chair and called out, "My chair's beautiful, Sarah. Thank you."

Sarah stepped into the living room. "Glad you like it, Mother."

"I love your haircut too. Makes you look—brighter."

Loretta entered the room. "I agree. You do look brighter."

Sarah turned to the group as they joined them in the living room. "Sorry I left y'all to the job in the kitchen."

Loretta chuckled as she turned to Sarah and then Estelle. "I hope you still appreciate it when you try to find things in there. You may have to do a bit of rearranging."

Estelle rocked. "I'm sure you did just fine."

"Since tomorrow's Sunday"—Bob glanced at his wife—"I'd better get home and do more work on my sermon. This week has completely messed up my schedule. But I have to say, it was worth every minute."

"I'd better get home too." Mary Anne patted Sarah on the arm and then gave Estelle a big hug. "If I can locate my daughter. I saw the girls leave the backyard a while ago, and who knows where they are now."

Sarah pointed. "I saw them over by the monuments when I came in last time."

"Mercy." Mary Anne put one hand on her hip. "Leave it to a couple of teenage girls to be attracted to tombstones."

The group made an opening as the delivery men entered with another mattress. The women watched as the men crossed the room and disappeared down the hall.

Estelle verbalized what every woman thought. "They sure do have big muscles."

The women giggled. Bob raised his eyebrows and gave them a pastoral frown of judgment. "Well, I know what I should be preaching on tomorrow. Loretta, are you ready to go home now, or are you planning to wait for the next pass-through?"

Loretta's cheeks turned a soft pink. "I suppose it would be a good time to retreat. Enjoy your new home, Estelle and Sarah. If you need us for *anything*, please call."

Bob and Loretta took turns hugging Estelle as she sat in her new chair, then said their good-byes to the rest of the group. Imogene took a seat on the couch as Estelle relaxed into her new chair and fought to keep her eyes open. Wouldn't take much to doze off.

* * *

Coreen plopped down on the grass in front of an oversized pink marble headstone. "This feels kinda weird, don't it?"

Betty Anne joined her. "At least there's no real bodies here. When I die, I want a tombstone like this one. It's pretty—and pink."

The girls giggled as they lay side by side in front of the monument and crossed their arms over their chests. Coreen reached into the grass beside her, plucked a dandelion. The girls giggled even louder. A bumblebee buzzed past them as it flew a haphazard path around the girls. She reached up and rubbed the gold heart and thought about what Shirley said. Whispers of hope. Yes, Betty Anne was another one, just for her.

"There you are. I've been looking all over for you two." Mary Anne stared down at the girls. "What in the world are you doing?"

The girls giggled, glanced at each other sideways, and said in unison, "Nothing."

"We need to get home, my girl. Daddy expects dinner."

The girls stood up and dusted themselves off. Coreen put the dandelion on top of the pink marble and smelled her fingers. She wrinkled her nose. Dandelions stunk.

Betty Anne waved at Coreen. "Later, Coreen. Tomorrow's Sunday and we have church. Maybe you could come with me."

Coreen pinched her bottom lip. "I don't know. I'd have to ask Mama, and I think she wants me to do a lot of work tomorrow."

"Okay. Maybe next week."

"Yeah, maybe next week. I'll ask her about it."

"Well, see you." Betty Anne waved.

"Bye." Coreen waved back.

Coreen watched as they walked across the yard. Her heart seemed to drop into her aching toes. She didn't want to laugh anymore, or even smile. If she didn't go to church, would she ever see Betty Anne again?

But she didn't know if she believed in God. Why go to church if you don't believe?

She wondered if she and Betty Anne could be real friends anyway since they came from such different places. She stared at the ground as she wriggled her blistered toes in the grass, then looked up to see Betty Anne running back to where she stood.

"I'm going to miss you, Coreen."

"I'm gonna miss you too." The two girls hugged. A whisper.

"Betty Anne. Come on, honey. Let's get going."

The girls smiled as they let go of each other, and Betty Anne ran across the yard to her mother. Coreen sighed. She wondered how a girl like Betty Anne could really like a nobody like her.

She swung her arms as she slinked to the gate behind the house, entered the yard, and sat down on the back steps. Patches joined her, smothered her in kisses, and wallowed on her lap. Coreen smiled as she caressed her oldest best friend. "I love you, Patches. It's good to know no matter who I am, you love me." She leaned down and hugged Patches close.

The trees, bushes, and flowers in the new backyard cast inviting shadows. A tire swing hung from the big oak tree. Running her fingers through Patches' warm fur, she sang her happy songs.

Chapter 39

Coreen entered the bathroom and closed the door behind her. She slid the barrel lock into place and shut out the rest of the world. The old clawfoot tub, not quite white on the inside and painted a darker shade of lavender on its underbelly, stood like a royal carriage waiting for her to indulge. She adjusted the handles until the perfect temperature of water rushed out of the faucet. How wonderful to never pump water and carry it inside ever again.

She climbed into the warm water. Every muscle in her body relaxed—except for the ones between her blistered toes. She sank down into the water until only her nose and eyes were above the water line.

Baths were one of the best things in the world.

After several minutes of trying to float in the water and turning over on her stomach and pretending to swim, she lay still. Her life had changed so much. Just like that. Last week, who would have guessed she would be taking a real bath, living in an air-conditioned house, and having her own bedroom.

She bit her bottom lip. And who would have guessed Daddy would be murdered?

Coreen sighed as she lay back in the water and sang "Song of Hope." She sang the last verse twice.

Oh, song of my hope
I'll sing you again
Bring me sweet promise
And help me again.

She stopped singing. She reckoned Mama didn't pray Daddy'd come home like in the song. Seemed they both wanted him dead and gone. But who killed him—and why?

Maybe he had a fight. He enjoyed hitting people.

Coreen stared at nothing. Her body sank into the water like a lump of coal. She brought her arms up into the air and dropped them onto the water, causing it to splash. "I ain't gonna think about him no more. I'm gonna think of happy stuff."

She filled her mind with thoughts of her new bed, her own room, Patches, a bathroom, air-conditioning, and a new friend. The room filled with happy songs as she took the bar of soap and scrubbed away all the dirt.

Coreen dipped her hair into the water to get it all wet, including her new bangs, and took the bar of soap and rubbed it into her hair. She massaged out the sweat, debris, the leftover remnants of her haircut, and tried to copy the way Gracie washed her hair. Not the same. Sucking in a huge breath, she dipped into the water, swished her head and used her fingers to rinse away the soap. Humming replaced the singing while she dunked under the water. She came up for air and dipped one more time.

Coreen climbed out of the now cool, dirty water. She grabbed her towel and wrapped it around her. The water still in the tub, she leaned over and pulled the plug attached to the faucet by a long beaded chain. The water swirled as it went down the hole and disappeared. So much easier than carting the tub of dirty water to the backyard to empty. Leftover dirt stained the walls of the tub. She used her washcloth to scrub the offending ring. After a quick rinse of the tub and washcloth, she smiled.

Coreen dressed in her pajamas, combed through her wet hair, and smiled at herself in the mirror as she fluffed her bangs. She dabbed up the water she splashed onto the floor and hung the towel and her washcloth on the side of the tub to dry. She slid open the bolt on the door and considered how wonderful to be able to lock out the rest of the world. She floated down the hall to the living room.

"I'm all clean," she announced to Mama and Mammaw, her arms outstretched.

Her mother did not look up from her romance novel. "I hope you didn't leave a mess in there."

Coreen stood tall and squared off her shoulders. "No, Mama, I didn't. I cleaned it up. Every drop."

Sarah looked up from her book. "I bet. You never do nothing right."

"I'm gonna go to my room now. Good night, Mama." Silence. She turned to her grandmother. "Good night, Mammaw. I love you."

"Good night, sweet girl. You enjoy your new bed now."

"I will." She rushed over to give her a hug and a kiss on the cheek.

When she glanced at her mother, Sarah had returned to her fantasy world as the TV played out the perfect American family in front of her. Coreen turned and trudged up the wooden steps to her private world above. Not everything in her life had changed for the better.

* * *

Soon as Coreen disappeared, Estelle hissed her reprimand. "Why you got to treat her mean?"

Not taking her eyes off the book, Sarah answered, "What are you talking about?"

"Why you gotta be so daggone mean? Why can't you say something nice every now and then?"

"Maybe I didn't have nothing nice to say. Or maybe I was busy reading."

"Well, I think it's high time you looked for something nice to say to her. She don't deserve being treated worse than a dog."

Sarah turned down the corner of her book and hit the couch with it, making a loud thump. "Mother, I don't want to talk about it. Why can't you mind your own business and leave me alone? Living in the same house don't mean you got the right to tell me what to do. I'm through with people trying to bully me around. It's my life."

Estelle leaned back in her chair. Her eyes blinked as if a strong wind blasted her in the face. Why couldn't her daughter see that she just wanted to help? "Sarah, I know you been through a lot. I ain't trying to upset you. I'm really trying to help." She leaned forward slightly. Her face softened as a tear welled up in one eye.

Sarah spat her words. "You mean like you helped when you made me marry a monster?"

"Honey, there weren't no choice at the time. What else could you do but marry him? The whole town woulda known. You woulda been humiliated."

"Well, it really worked, didn't it?" Sarah crossed her arms, wrapped her hands around them, and rocked forward and back. "You didn't do it for me. You did it for yourself—so's you wouldn't be humiliated at that church of yours."

"That ain't true and you know it. I did it 'cause I loved you."

"Loved me? Loved … me? Nobody's ever loved me."

"'Course they have and they do. I love you, your brothers and sister love you, and your daughter loves you."

"My daughter? She's his daughter, not mine. I never wanted her. She's a burden I have to wear around my neck to remind me how horrible my life is."

Estelle placed her hand on her chest and lowered her chin. She whispered, "I'm sorry. I didn't know what else to do."

Would Sarah ever understand? Would she hold it against her the rest of her life? And against Coreen—and God? Or … maybe Sarah hated the whole universe simply because things didn't go her way. She raised her head and looked at her daughter. "What d'ya suppose I shoulda done?"

Sarah stopped rocking, paused a few seconds, and turned to her mother. "You shoulda killed him."

Estelle's blood ran like slushy ice in her veins. Sarah's voice sounded like molten metal and Estelle knew she meant it. "You know I couldn't kill him."

"Why? You let him kill me. You nag me about how I treat her, but look what you did to me." Sarah's face flushed. Her eyes grew wide. "I still ain't free from him now, even if he is dead. I don't think I'll ever be free." She grabbed her hair between her fingers. "Sure, I cut my hair off, picked out my own furniture, and tonight I won't have to share a bed with him or take his beatings. But I ain't really free because I still got her." Sarah flung her arm toward the stairs. "I'm still stuck in a life I never wanted and I didn't deserve. I dreamed big dreams to get out of this horrible place. He stole it all from me. And now it's too late."

"Sarah …"

Picking up her book and opening it to the dog-eared page, Sarah droned, "I don't want to talk about it no more. Nothing you say's gonna change it. So just shut up about it."

Estelle's heart burned like it had been shredded. She bit her tongue to keep from saying anymore. The laughter from the family depicted on the television screen bounced off the walls of the room, mocking the silence. When her heart slowed to a more normal rate, Estelle leaned over and released the lever to lower her feet, wiggled herself to the edge of her new chair, and grasped the arms to heave herself up. She grabbed her cane and took a couple of steps. "I'm going to bed now. I'm weary."

Sarah mumbled, "D'ya need help?"

"No. I'm quite capable of getting myself to bed, thank you." Estelle suspected her words sounded a bit snippy and regretted saying them as she shuffled across the room.

At the doorway to the hall, she turned around. "Sarah. Please. Do whatever it takes to get rid of his poison in your life while there's still time."

* * *

Sarah lifted her head from the invisible words on the page to watch her mother leave. Why did she feel guilty when she spoke the truth? Nobody understood her pain. Nobody ever listened to her when she tried to explain what happened. They assumed it was her fault. They figured she made her bed and now deserved to lie in it. But they didn't understand then, and they probably wouldn't understand now. The truth became a secret only because they wouldn't listen to her, not because she didn't try to tell them.

Laughter filled the room. Fake laughter. She looked up at the television and snarled. She put down her book again and turned the TV off so it wouldn't remind her of what she would never have. The screen faded to black. Sarah stared into the blackness until her eyes focused on her reflection in the glass.

Blackness.

* * *

Coreen picked up the journal she and Betty Anne found in the trunk and hopped on top of her bed. She wanted to know what this dead girl named Angela Cooke wrote before she killed herself.

Angela wrote about school friends, classes she hated, and how her parents didn't understand her. Coreen skimmed over several pages until she read the words "Red Diamond Mine." Finally, she and Angela shared something in common.

Angela wrote that her father lost his job at a store that closed and decided to work the mines until he could get something better. Apparently, she and her mother hated his new job because of the danger and because of all the coal dust he brought home. Coreen could relate to the coal dust too.

Angela's grandmother in Corbin was sick and close to death. Since the grandmother wouldn't come to Mt. Pleasant and be with them, Angela's mother drove to Corbin to care for her and take her to doctor appointments. Angela needed to be in school and her parents didn't think she should be at home alone, so the school bus dropped her off at the mine office until her daddy's shift ended. She stayed with Edith and did her homework or helped out in the office.

The stories Angela told about the office seemed like fun. Coreen wished she could do something like that. Angela went to the mine more often as her grandmother got worse.

Then Angela wrote about a creepy old guy who kept coming into the office to talk with her. She referred to him as "COG." Coreen gasped and then giggled. COG—must mean Creepy Old Guy. She wrote that he made her skin crawl and she tried to avoid him when she could.

Coreen read every word now. She wanted to know who this creepy guy could be. Maybe he worked with Daddy. He could even be the one who killed him. She wanted to find a clue, like Miss Marple in the Agatha Christie books she read.

May 12—It's a little warmer today. Grandma's getting worser. Mama went to Corbin again. It's probably wrong to say it, but I hope Grandma dies soon so I don't have to come here to Red Diamond no more. COG spends more time here after his shift. He scares me. He grabbed my arm last time and wouldn't let me go. Thank goodness, Miss Edith came in and ran him out. I hate going there. I'm trying to come up with a plan to hide from him. Now that it's getting warmer, I might be able to.

May 13—Mama's still in Corbin. That means I went to Red Diamond again. Yesterday, when I saw COG coming, I ran out the back door and hid in the storage shed. I figured I'd have to stay there all night, but COG gave up and left. Miss Edith came looking for me and told me he left. She said I should tell my daddy, but I can't. There ain't nothing else we can do. Mama's gotta be with Grandma.

May 17—COG sneaked up on me today. He backed me up against the wall and put his dirty hands on my hair. His breath smelled worse than an outhouse. I thought I'd vomit from being scared. He told me I was a pretty little thing and that he needed to teach me how to be a woman. I screamed and kicked him in the leg and ran into the office and locked the door. I don't want to go there no more. But there ain't nothing I can do.

June 3—Grandma died last night. A day too late to save my life. What can I do? I want to die.

Coreen turned the page. Blank. She read June 3 again and her heart turned to stone. Did whatever happened to Angela make her kill herself? Tears dripped from Coreen's eyes. *How sad. How very, very sad.*

Something gnawed at her. Something familiar. What could it be? She stared at the last page, then closed the book and put it on her bedside table.

She regretted reading the book. Made her feel like a beanbag doll without any beans. Lifeless and empty.

Chapter 40

Holding the open romance book in her hand, Sarah stared at the blank screen of the television. She shook off the spell and looked around the room. A chill colder than the temperature of the air-conditioned house made her shiver.

Enough.

She put down the book, stood up, and flipped off the light. Was it sadness or fatigue that numbed her heart? She walked down the hallway to her room and flipped on the light. Her own private sanctuary. Never again would she have to share herself with a disgusting, grimy, coal-dust-infested monster. She wouldn't have to smell his stale smoke and liquor breath. And he would never lay a hand on her again.

If only the memories would go away. His being gone hadn't solved all her problems. Like Coreen. No matter how hard she tried, she couldn't change the way she felt about *her* daughter. She didn't want to hate her—or blame her for everything. Sarah pressed the heels of her hands into her forehead until it hurt. How stupid to blame everyone else for what Vernon did to her.

She changed into her nightgown. After turning on the lamp by her bed, she closed and locked the door, then flipped off the overhead light and retreated to her bed by the lamp's glow. Pulling back the blanket, she sat on the side of the bed.

She'd treated her mother so badly. Easy to blame her for everything wrong in her life. Maybe she blamed her too much though. What if she really had tried to do what was best and failed out of caring, not spite? She still failed though. The evil of one man destroyed them all. Vernon might have finally got his comeuppance, but the score would never be even.

Sarah's shoulders relaxed as she absently ran her fingers across the new sheets and then the pillow. *My bed. My room.* Safe.

There must be a way to get on with life. Maybe Shirley was right about going to Cincinnati and getting some training. A whole new life might be what she needed to rid herself of Vernon for good.

Sarah switched off the lamp and pulled up the blanket. Her body sighed into the mattress. The darkness shrouded her in fear of the unknown. A thought kept popping into her head—whispers of hope. Where had she heard those words, and why did they keep popping into her head?

Sarah rolled over onto her side and curled up. A train whistle faded as she drifted into sleep and dreamed.

A young girl, with the blush of youth on her cheeks, pulled back her hair and tied it with a blue ribbon before entering the back door of her client's house. She retrieved the cleaning supplies from a pantry off the kitchen and started her work. As she scrubbed the counters and then the stove, she sang to the empty house. Her clients both worked during the day. The girl sang joyously to distract her from the boring tasks.

"Well, who are you?"

The girl gasped at the unrecognized voice. She twirled around to face it. The handsome roughness of a young man several years her senior made her cheeks heat. She lowered her head. "I'm Sarah. Sarah Kincaid. Who are you?"

A self-confident smile spread across his face as his eyes studied her. "I'm Vernon Shell. This is my house."

"Oh?" She wrinkled her brow. "I didn't know nobody else lived here 'cept Mr. and Miz Shell."

Chuckling, he leaned against the archway. "I'm the son."

"I see." Sarah's cheeks warmed again.

"I just got back from Nam. Yep, I'm an army man." He strutted as he approached her.

Slinking back against the stove, Sarah's heart raced from a mixture of attraction and fear. Vernon lifted her chin. "You're a pretty little thing. Makes an army man hungry."

The edge of the stove dug into Sarah's back. He reached behind her head, untied the blue ribbon, and dropped it on the floor. He pressed his body against hers as he ran his fingers through her black curls that hung to below her shoulders. Vernon leaned down and kissed the girl. The rancid odor on his breath nauseated her. The room spun. She knew it was wrong, and yet it also excited her. Her first kiss. She tried to pull away, but his strong hands refused to release her from his grasp.

"I think I should show you what a fine army man I am, pretty little Sarah."

As he dragged her out of the kitchen and into the nearest bedroom, Sarah fought to get away. She didn't know what he planned to do to her, but she knew it was wrong. She pulled against his grasp and hit him with her fists.

"No. Please don't hurt me. Let me go. Please," she begged.

He threw her onto the bed and climbed on top of her. "I'm gonna make a woman outta you."

She sobbed. Her mind became a blur of confusion, pain, and embarrassment as he stripped away her childish innocence and left her view of life forever tainted.

"No!" Sarah shot up in her bed and screamed into the darkness. She covered her face with her hands and sobbed with total abandon for the first time since that day.

* * *

Coreen yawned so widely she thought her lips would split. She stretched her arms as far as they would go and then clasped her hands behind her head.

Time to get to sleep.

Yawning again, she stood up, stared at the door to the attic, and decided to check the lock one more time. Still latched. Safe enough to go to bed.

After flipping on the lamp on her bedside table, she looked back at the attic door. Hoping nothing but a few spiders were inside, she turned off the overhead light and jumped onto the bed and under the blanket, instead of on top of it like she used to do. Having a cooler house made her toes a bit too cool, so she reached under the blanket to rub them, making sure not to touch the blisters.

The lamp cast a gentle glow. Coreen looked at it and then the attic door. She pulled her arm from under the blanket and reached out to turn off the lamp, paused in midair, and stuck her arm back under the covers.

Not tonight.

Although her body begged for sleep, her mind would not be still. Her week replayed in vignettes before her closed eyes. The movie slowed as she thought about her father in his casket in his pink shirt. Sadness gnawed at her. But didn't she want him dead? His meanness made her hate him, but he was her daddy. For some reason she missed him too. Crazy. Why would she be sad, especially after the last time she saw him?

The memory of that last day appeared on the movie screen of her mind. She tried to block it out, but it kept playing.

Daddy sneaked up behind her in the kitchen as she cleaned the countertop. She gasped and spun around, waiting for him to smack her or scream at her for something she'd done wrong. Instead, he smiled a jagged yellow-brown smile and got right up next to her. The smell of stale tobacco and whiskey made her want to puke. She tried to run.

But he blocked her path.

Then he reached up and pulled the blue ribbon from her hair. His coal-tinged fingers draped her hair over the front of her shoulders. He ran his fingers through the strands, poking his fingers through it until they lingered on her breasts. He smiled his sickening smile again, making her shiver. Her body burned when he touched her. She wanted to flee but couldn't move.

His breathing got louder and faster. Coreen thought she might pass out with fear. She tried to move away from him, but he grabbed her shoulders and pressed against her. Then he leaned down and kissed her on her lips so hard it hurt. She thought she would suffocate. She wanted to scream, but fear made her mute.

When he finally stopped, he rubbed his rough hand across her cheek. "You're shore getting to be a pretty little thing. On your birthday, tomorrow, I'll teach you how to be a woman."

The back door slammed shut. He backed up a bit.

Mama with a bucket of water. She set it down on the table with a thud and walked into the living room. She had a funny expression on her face when she looked at Daddy and then Coreen. "Here's your lunch bucket." Her voice sounded gravely as she handed it to Daddy.

Mama didn't see what happened—but her face. Did she suspect? If somebody hadn't beat her to it, would she have done anything to protect Coreen?

She burrowed her head in the pillow and cried.

Evil. Completely evil. She knew what he planned to do. She'd heard the girls talk about such things. And she knew it was wrong. Bad wrong. But who killed him? And why? She wanted to know the truth.

Coreen bounced onto her side, smacked the pillow with her hand, and curled herself into a ball. With a sharp sigh, she reached out from the covers and turned off the lamp.

Light filtered into the room from outside, casting shadows. A car passed the house, hitting a bump as the engine hummed. Crickets sang their mating calls in the woods behind the house. In the distance, the lonely music of a coal train whistle joined the symphony, accompanied by the percussive squeaks of metal wheels against rails. Coreen caressed the gold heart to the beat of the train's wheels. She joined the song and hummed a lullaby. The music faded out as sweet sleep took its place and tiny stars sparkled on the ceiling above.

Chapter 41

Morning sunlight filtered through the sheer curtains, sending golden rays throughout the living room. Sarah sat on the couch as her mother rocked in the new chair and laughed at cartoons on the television. How quickly her mother had adapted to her new life.

On Sarah's lap sat the metal box she brought home from Vernon's wardrobe. Determined to get it open, she tried using a bobby pin. When it didn't work, she retrieved a knife from the kitchen and stabbed it into the keyhole.

"What are you doing? Be careful or you'll cut yourself right open."

"I'm trying to get this stupid box open."

"Ain't ya got a key?"

Sarah stared at her. "If I had a key, why would I be using a knife?" The cartoons were affecting her mother's brain already.

"Where'd it come from?"

She knew she wouldn't have any peace until she told her. "We found it in Vernon's chifforobe. I want to know what he's got hidden in here." If only he had squirreled away all the money he didn't spend on her.

"Why don't you try a screwdriver or something?"

"Because I don't think we got no screwdriver."

"Well, I know there's a hammer under the kitchen sink. How about trying that?"

"Mother."

"Just a suggestion. It's better than bleeding all over the house."

Sarah growled as she took the box and the knife to the kitchen, got the hammer, and pounded on the box. Finally, the lid bent enough for the lock to pop open. She looked inside. A Polaroid camera and several snapshots lay among a collection of hair ribbons. She frowned. Why in the world would Vernon hide a locked box of hair ribbons and a camera? He never took pictures that she knew about.

Except one. A long time ago.

She pulled one of the photos out of the box and looked at it. A young girl, around Coreen's age. Did he have another child? Sarah flipped through some of the photos and realized they were all different girls about the same age. She didn't recognize any of them.

She put the photos down and reached for the mass of hair ribbons. Why would a man have a box full of hair ribbons? One ribbon caught her attention. She picked it up and ran it through her fingers. An embroidered daisy. One on each end of the ribbon. The ribbon she had embroidered. Bile rose to her throat.

She picked up the photos again. Her fingers trembled as she went through them one by one. And then, there it was. Memories swarmed around her like buzzards as she held the picture he had taken after he killed her soul.

Coreen clomped down the stairs and rushed into the kitchen. Sarah quickly stuffed the photo into her pocket.

"Hi, Mama. I'm hungry. What'ya doing?"

"What? I'm ..." She picked up the photos. "D'ya know any of these girls?" Sarah handed them to Coreen.

"Not her. Or her. Or ... wait a minute ... I've seen this one before."

"Where? School?"

"No. I can't remember ... Wait, I know. Me and Betty Anne looked at some pictures in the attic, and I think it's the girl in some of them pictures."

"Are you sure?" Why would a picture in Vernon's secret box be of a girl in Mr. Cooke's attic?

"I'll go up and get it." Coreen ran up the stairs as Sarah looked through the rest of the photos. She didn't recognize any of the girls. At the bottom of the stack, the last three looked like they weren't from Mt. Pleasant. They looked foreign, like photos her brother John sent home from Vietnam.

Why would Vernon have pictures of young girls in Vietnam? Then she remembered—he served in the army in Saigon for a while. A sick feeling grew inside her stomach. Maybe she hadn't been the first ... or the last.

Coreen practically jumped down the stairs coming back and slid into the kitchen with a photo and a small book in her hand. "Here, Mama. It's her, ain't it?"

They compared the two girls. The only difference seemed to be the expressions on their faces. The girl in Vernon's picture looked like she'd been crying. Sarah looked through the pictures again and realized all the girls bore similar expressions—like the picture of her. Terror. Sadness. Disgust.

"D'ya know what her name is?" Sarah turned to Coreen.

"Yeah. It's Angela Cooke, Mr. Cooke's daughter. This is her diary."

"Daughter? I didn't know he had a child."

"He used to. Betty Anne said she killed herself. And her mama died a year later in a car wreck."

Sarah's head spun. None of this made sense. At least it didn't make sense unless …

"Coreen, d'ya recognize anybody else in here?" She handed back the stack of photographs. "Look real close."

Coreen looked through each one carefully. She stopped about halfway through. "I know I've seen this girl. But where?" She tapped the photo against her head. "Wait a minute! I know who it is. It's the girl what come to the funeral."

"Come to the funeral? Are you positive?" Why would that girl come to the funeral? Sarah's head spun. It didn't make sense—especially if he'd done what she thought.

"Yeah, remember I told you about her? She and some man in overalls come to the funeral. He held on to her arm and dragged her up to Daddy's casket and made her look inside. She cried up a storm, but he made her look." Coreen wrinkled her mouth. "Then he told her, 'This is what happens to a devil,' or something like that." Coreen looked at the photo again. "Anyway, the girl started bawling and skedaddled out of there like a flash. He stormed right after her." The color drained from her face.

"Coreen. Is something wrong?"

Coreen blinked her eyes. She slowly turned her head to look at Sarah. "Mama, I just realized something." She held up the photo of the girl from the funeral. "This is the same girl what killed herself the other day."

"Wait. What? You mean the girl that come to your daddy's funeral is the same girl what killed herself?"

Coreen nodded.

Sarah squeezed her forehead. No. How can this be? She squeezed her eyes shut and went over everything in her head. Vernon, the girls, the photos, the suicides. What had happened to her … This is what happens to a devil … Isn't that what Coreen said the man told the girl?

"Sarah, Coreen? Is something wrong?"

Sarah opened her eyes. Her mother held on to the door frame as her gaze shifted between them.

"What's wrong?" Her mother pleaded.

Sarah shook her head and threw a glance at her daughter. She didn't want to tell her mother now. Not with Coreen in the room. Coreen stood silent, her face still pale. Their eyes locked. Sarah squinted. Did she suspect … But how could she? Silence enveloped Sarah as the world slowed down.

She turned to her mother. "Vernon was eviler than we ever imagined. And he ain't the only one who died." Sarah gathered the photos, diary, and ribbons and

233

stuffed them into her pocket book. "I gotta see DeWayne." The door slammed behind her.

* * *

Sarah ran down Laurel Street and crossed to Chestnut and then to Main Street. The sun beat down, causing perspiration to pop out on her upper lip. Thoughts and questions chased each other in her head. At Gracie's Beauty Shop, she stopped and caught her breath. The bell clanged as she opened the door and entered the noisy coolness.

Gracie looked up from a head partially covered in pink and green rods and frowned.

Removing a pink rod from her mouth, she said. "Well, I'm surprised to see you so soon. Your haircut okay?"

"Yes, it's fine. I happened to pass by and wanted to ask you a question."

"Alrighty."

"When we's in here the other day, you's working on a woman whose granddaughter just died. I thought I recognized her, but couldn't remember her name. I've been thinking on it ever since and it's driving me crazy." Better to lie than explain.

Gracie shook her head and clicked her tongue. "Yeah, her only grandbaby. They buried her today, I reckon. She's Miss Howard, Agnes Howard."

"Agnes Howard? Don't know why I thought I knew her. Her name don't sound familiar at all. Was it her son's daughter? I forgot if an accident took her— or something else."

"Yeah, her son Laman's girl. But it weren't no accident, honey." Gracie leaned toward Sarah and whispered. "Poor child up and killed herself."

Gracie picked up a square of white tissue and rolled another section of hair. "Nobody ain't saying why for, but they's been whispers she was in the family way. Mercy, teenagers these days. You gotta watch 'em like hawks."

Sarah's knees grew weak. She knew all too well what the girl went through. There were more questions though, and she needed to pull herself together and ask them. "Is Laman a miner?"

"Yeah, I reckon he works the Red Diamond. He probably knew Vernon."

Sarah's heart dropped to her feet, but she forced herself to smile at Gracie. "Thanks for setting me straight. Still don't know why I thought I knowed her. Best let you get back to work now. I got a few errands to run. Later, Gracie."

Gracie waved a pink curler in the air as Sarah opened the door and stepped outside. The weight of the heat laid itself back on her shoulders. But the weight of what she now knew to be true weighed even heavier. She wanted to do the right thing, but her heart sent mixed messages about what *right* meant.

* * *

"Can I help you, ma'am?"

"What?" Sarah looked up and realized she stood inside the sheriff's office. A man who looked like a child sat at the desk in front of her.

"Can I help you?" His beige-and-brown uniform looked brand-new, as did the shiny star on his pocket.

"Is Sheriff Mayhall here?"

"And you are?"

"Sarah Shell."

"I'll see if he's available." He sauntered across the room, rapped on a door, and opened it about six inches.

The door flung open and DeWayne crossed to her. "I didn't expect you. You checking up on the case—I mean, on Vernon?" A grin stretched across his face. "You cut your hair."

Sarah reached up and fingered the curls. "Yeah."

DeWayne nodded. "You look lovely."

She glanced around the dingy room. A mishmash of chairs lined one wall. "I gotta tell you something—in private."

DeWayne arched one eyebrow. "We can talk in my office. Want a Coke?"

"Got a root beer instead? I used to love root beer when we was kids. Remember?" She half smiled.

"Yep. Josh, bring a couple of root beers to my office."

DeWayne led her to a chair in front of the desk and sat in the one beside it. The deputy brought the drinks and closed the door as he left.

After a swig, DeWayne put his bottle on the desk. "What do you want to tell me?"

Condensation dripped down the bottle and plopped on her hand. She met DeWayne's eyes. Those gentle eyes. "I need to tell you something that might help you find Vernon's killer."

"Really?"

"The problem is, I ain't certain I want 'em to get caught."

He furrowed his brow and leaned forward. "Sarah, why would you say that?"

"'Cause I can understand why he done it." Sarah took a sip of the root beer. The bottle trembled in her grasp. She set it on the desk. "I ain't never told nobody this before."

DeWayne's duty belt smacked against the chair arms as he wiggled in his chair. "Something to do with his death?"

"Sorta. Just let me tell you, okay?"

"Okay."

"There weren't never no emotional attachment between us—well, 'cept for hate. Nothing about our marriage gave pleasure. The only reason he married me was to keep himself out of jail."

"Jail? Sarah, what are you talking about?" He scratched the red stubble on his chin.

"When I turned thirteen, and you and the boys went to war, Mother made me clean houses to help feed us. One of them houses belonged to the Shells." Sarah took a deep breath. She stared at her root beer as drops of moisture slid down the bottle and onto the desk. "One day I went there to clean and found Vernon there. I never seen him before. He'd just come back from the army. He'd been drinking, as usual, and he backed me into the stove and wouldn't let me go." Her chin trembled and tears gathered in the corners of her eyes. "I screamed and fought as hard as I could, but he was too strong."

DeWayne nearly came out of his chair.

Sarah flinched.

He made a sound between a whimper and a growl. "Sarah. I thought—"

"When Mother figured out I was gonna have a baby, and by who, she went to the sheriff. After talking to the Shells, they all decided the proper thing to do was get married. More than likely, the Shells decided to protect Vernon. Nobody asked me what I wanted. And nobody listened to me when I tried to tell 'em what *really* happened." Sarah gulped back the sobs.

DeWayne took her hands. Moisture gathered in his eyes. "I'm sorry I didn't protect you, Sarah. I wish I hadn't left you." He leaned toward her, and tears dripped down his cheeks like the moisture on the root beer.

Sarah wanted to touch the tears. Touch him. "Nobody knew it would happen. And then it was too late. What could you have done, anyways?"

DeWayne dropped to his knees in front of her, still holding her hands. "I could have been the one to marry you."

Her head buzzed. Blood raced through her body so fast she nearly passed out. "DeWayne … don't be silly. People woulda thought—"

"It wouldn't matter. I would have done it anyway. I would have protected you."

Sarah stood and took a few steps away. "No sense talking about it now. It's over and done with. And now Vernon's dead." If only. No sense dreaming about what could have been.

DeWayne stood up. He grabbed his root beer and downed half the bottle. "Sarah, I still don't understand how this has anything to do with him being murdered."

"They's more to it. Me and Coreen figured it out." Sarah unlatched her pocketbook and pulled out a photo. "Coreen and her little friend found this in our attic. It's Mr. Cooke's thirteen-year-old daughter, Angela. She killed herself about five years ago. Rumor has it she was in the family way." Sarah pulled the book out of her bag. "Her diary. Coreen read it."

DeWayne took it and opened the book. "I still don't understand what this has to do with anything."

"At the end of the diary she talks about a man she calls 'Creepy Old Guy' at the Red Diamond and how he ruined her life and she wanted to die."

"But ..." He wrinkled his brow.

"DeWayne, you remember the locked box we took out of Vernon's chifforobe?"

"Yeah."

"Well, they's a camera, hair ribbons, and a bunch of pictures in it. Pictures of girls about thirteen years old. One of them photos was of this girl, Angela."

"What?" DeWayne cocked his head and scrunched his face. "Are you saying you think he did to her what he did to you?"

"I'm saying we ain't the only ones. Coreen recognized another girl in them photos. The thing is, that girl came to the funeral with her daddy—and a few hours later she killed herself."

DeWayne paced the room. "You mean the Howard girl?"

"Yeah. I knowed he was evil, but I never imagined ... Gracie at the Beauty Shop told me they's rumors she was in the family way too."

The room seemed to close in around her. The air became thick and hard to breathe. She struggled about whether she should tell him the rest. It wouldn't make any difference now. Vernon could never destroy another girl.

Poor Mr. Howard. If only she'd spoken up about what Vernon did to her fourteen years ago, made somebody listen to her, maybe none of this would have happened to these girls. Maybe they wouldn't have died.

She reached into her pocket and pulled out the photo she hid from Coreen. With a deep sigh, she held it out to DeWayne. "I found this in the box too."

He took it. His eyes narrowed, his face flushed. "It's you. Sarah—"

She held out the stack of photos. "All the girls in these pictures must be victims. They's also three girls who look like they's from Vietnam. He might've started all this over there. I'm wondering what happened to the rest of these girls." Her voice broke. "Are they dead too?" she whispered. "Or do they just wish it?"

DeWayne flopped into the chair and scrubbed his face with his hands. "It also means Vernon's murderer is probably one angry daddy."

Chapter 42

Cartoons blasted from the television as Mammaw rocked in her chair. Every so often she chuckled. Coreen found it difficult to concentrate on her new library book. With a deep sigh, she turned down the corner and stretched out her legs from her end of the couch, making sure she didn't kick Mama, who curled up on the other end reading a new romance.

"Mama? D'ya think Mr. Howard's the one what killed Daddy?" Coreen waited for a reply. None came. "Mama. Please. Can we talk about it?"

"Coreen, I'm trying to read. Besides, it ain't nothing a child needs to know about."

"I ain't a child no more. Besides, I helped figure it all out, so I think I deserve to know what's going on."

Mama rested her book across her lap and looked up. "There's some things it ain't proper for a girl to know. Besides, DeWayne ain't told me nothing else about it. I reckon he's gonna talk to Mr. Howard. I reckon he's gonna talk to a lot of people. We gotta be patient and wait till he's ready to tell us something. Now d'ya think you could let me read my book in peace?"

"Sorry, Mama. I's curious." Patience refused to come easy for Coreen. Questions raced through her head like the cartoon characters. One thing she knew for sure—Mama figured it out before DeWayne did. A smile of pride lit up her face. "Mama?"

"Coreen, what'd I say?"

"Sorry." All she ever said to Mama was *sorry*. "I wanted to tell you I think you're pretty smart."

"What?"

"You're smart. I mean, you figured out about all them girls and who probably shot Daddy. You even knew how to get clues like Miss Marple does in them Agatha Christie books I read. You'd make a really good detective."

"Detective? I ain't even finished high school. I can't be no detective."

"Shore you can. If you want to."

Mammaw grabbed her cane and struggled to get up from her chair. "I'm gonna take a break from these here cartoons and get a few onions and peppers cut up for supper. I might even slice a 'mater and cuke too. You two can detect whatever you want." She hobbled into the kitchen.

"Mama?"

Her mama glared at her again.

"Sorry. Just … I've been thinking about something."

After putting down the book, Sarah crossed her arms. "I know you won't hush until you tell me, so get on with it."

Coreen pulled her shoulders back. "I been thinking about you needing a job you'd enjoy and that would pay more than at Morgan's. And I thought, maybe … you could go to school. I still think you'd make a real good detective—if that's what you wanted." She sucked in a breath.

Her mama cocked her head. "And have you come up with a way to do that? Like how to pay for it and where to go?"

"Yes, I have." She nodded. "Betty Anne's mom said you could get a scholarship since you're a widow and a single mother now. And about where—I thought I might know how you could do that too." She waited to see if her mama called her crazy.

"Go on."

"Aunt Shirley tried to get Mammaw to come stay with her. So I thought maybe she would let you stay with her long enough to go to school." She frowned when her mama grinned a crooked grin at her.

"What about you and your mammaw?"

Coreen sat up straight. "I'm getting growed up now. I could help Mammaw while you's gone. I know how to cook and clean, and I could run all her errands for her." She nodded. "We'd do fine. Till you got back, that is."

Mama chuckled. "I planned to talk to you and your mammaw about this very thing. I figured you'd accuse me of deserting you."

Coreen dropped her jaw, then giggled. Not crazy. Not stupid. "Mama, that's great. So you gonna do it?"

Loud banging at the front door caused Coreen to jump. "Who in the world's trying to tear the door down? You think it might be a customer?"

"Go check on it. If it is, let your mammaw know."

Coreen hopped up from the couch, padded to the front door, and opened it, expecting a stranger. Instead, she found Mr. Howard towering over her and a shotgun aimed at her face. Her legs turned to jelly. The room spun around her.

"Where's your mama?" He backed her into the dining room, the gun still aimed at her face. His beard looked longer and scruffier than before. His hair stuck out around his head like a bird's nest ripped apart. The blood pounded through Coreen's body.

"Coreen?" A weak voice she barely recognized came from the living room.

"You. Get in there with your mama. Go on." He poked her with the barrel.

"What d'ya want? Why are you here?" Mama backed into the corner of the couch and pulled her legs up.

"I'm here for you, Mrs. Vernon Shell." His speech slurred. "I'm here to show you what happens to people who butt their noses into things they oughta leave alone. You got the sheriff looking for me."

"I'm sorry. I didn't mean no harm—"

"No harm? You're the one who caused my baby to die. It's all your fault. You shoulda kept that fool of a husband home and happy instead of letting him come after my little girl." He cocked the gun. "It's your fault."

Coreen's brain filled with a flurry—like a field of dandelions lost their seeds all at once and floated around in her head. She couldn't think.

Mama paled. Mr. Howard looked like a big bear ready to devour.

Right when her life seemed to be getting better, she was going to die. Coreen dived onto the couch beside her mama and hugged her tight enough that she could whisper in her ear, "Do something, Mama."

They locked eyes for a few seconds. "Laman, I know you're upset about what Vernon did. I didn't know nothing about it till yesterday. I wish I could've stopped him. I really do. But I promise you, he was evil to me too."

He moved closer and aimed the shotgun at her heart. "You're alive though, ain't ya?"

"It's according to how you look at it. She weren't the only one he done this to. He done it to me too. When I's thirteen, he raped me when I went to clean his folks' house."

Coreen's heart stopped. The dandelion seeds spun inside her head.

"When we found out I was in the family way, they made me marry him— the very one who did such an awful thing to a precious young girl. It didn't stop there. He hurt me every day for thirteen years. I hated him for it—hated him a little more every day and wanted him dead."

Coreen snuggled into her.

"But I didn't have the courage to do it myself."

Coreen stared up at her. No wonder Mama hated her. No wonder she hated everything.

"I don't care about your sad little story. All I care about's my precious girl's gone and now the sheriff's gonna kill me too, and it's all because of your family." Tears drained down his face and his nose dripped.

"Let my daughter go. It ain't got nothing to do with her. She was his victim too." Mama tried to push her away, but Coreen refused to let go. They were in this together.

A flash of clarity replaced the dandelion seeds in Coreen's mind. "Thank you, Mr. Howard."

"What? What are you talking about, you stupid girl?" He swiped the tears and snot across his face. His eyes were bloodshot and wild, like her daddy's used to be after a late night drinking. He looked crazy as he paced back and forth with the gun aimed first at her and then Mama.

"I said thank you. You saved me. He planned to rape me next."

He snarled. "You're lying. You's his daughter. He wouldn't touch you."

"He told me so. The day he died, he told me when he come home he was gonna show *me* how to be a woman. I didn't know exactly what he meant then—I knew he planned something bad—but now I know. If you hadn't killed him that day, I woulda gone through the same thing as your daughter—and my mama."

Mama stared at her with her eyes wide.

"So thank you that you saved me."

"Coreen," Mama whispered and wrapped her arms around her.

"No. It's a lie. You're both lying. And I'm gonna blow your lying heads off." Mr. Howard wobbled a little. He raised the gun and closed one eye. "Just like I did him."

He aimed at Mama. Coreen screamed and covered her eyes. Instead of an explosion, she heard a metallic bong and a crash.

She opened her eyes. Mammaw stood in the doorway with a black iron skillet in her hand. On the floor in front of her, Mr. Howard lay in a heap, out cold as kraut.

"Well, is somebody gonna call DeWayne before I have to do this again?" Mammaw leaned over and picked up his shotgun. "I reckon he's gonna have a whopper of a pump knot on his head."

"Mother, how'd you do that?" Mama jumped off the couch and gingerly stepped around the body.

"What'ya mean? I sneaked up behind him and whacked him with my skillet."

"But it's heavy."

"Honey, it's my hip what causes me problems. My arm's strong as always."

Mama laughed and slapped her leg before hugging Mammaw. Coreen tiptoed around Mr. Howard to the telephone and dialed the sheriff's office. Death had surrounded her this week, but this was too close. One thing she knew for sure, she wanted to live.

Chapter 43

Sunlight danced through the leaves of the old maple tree. Sarah stood underneath and stared up at the one leaf transformed to red orange. Fall would be here soon. Could she be like that one leaf? Could she change—for the better?

She climbed the ramp to the front porch and sat in a rocking chair. Did she make the right decision? Her fingers tapped on the arms of the chair as she rocked. Butterflies danced in her stomach.

The screen door slammed. Her mother and Coreen came outside and sat in the rockers on either side of her. They all rocked. Silence.

Coreen stopped. "Mama, are you excited about going to Aunt Shirley's?"

"I guess. And a little nervous. I ain't been to school since … I's your age." Sarah glanced at her mother. Her eyes looked red as she stared at the maple tree.

"Was that DeWayne I saw out here a little while ago?" Her mother leaned back in the rocker.

"Yep." Sarah smiled to herself. Nobody needed to know he said he would miss her and to hurry home. She sure wouldn't tell her how she struggled to tell him good-bye. Sarah rocked faster. "Mother, you sure you're okay staying here with Coreen while I'm gone?"

Her mother nodded. Then cleared her throat. "Yeah. It's a fine idea." A tear sparkled in the corner of her eye. "I'm really proud of you for what you're doing."

"Me too, Mama. I'm proud of you." Coreen patted her mama's arm and smiled.

Sarah sighed. "I hope it's the right thing. I know I need to find training for a job I want to do. I don't want to be stuck doing something I'd hate the rest of my life—like cleaning people's houses." She gave her mother a sideward glance. "I want to do more than survive. I want to do something … fun."

"I told Mama she should get a job as a detective since she did so good at figuring out Mr. Howard killed Daddy." Coreen grinned.

"You don't want no dangerous job." Her mother furled her brow. "Sarah, you need to do something like working in a store or maybe an office. Something safe."

Sarah rolled her eyes. Her mother couldn't help herself. "Mother, please. It's my life now. I'm so tired of people telling me what I should or shouldn't do." She reached for her mother's hand and held it in hers. "I wanna—no, I *need to*—make decisions myself for once. I might make the wrong one, but I don't care. At least it'll be my decision, not somebody else's." She placed her mother's hand against her cheek. "For once in my life, I want to do what I think is right without worrying about getting knocked down. I guess it took almost dying to muster the courage to try."

"Mama, I think you deserve to be happy. I'm proud of you."

Sarah smiled and put a hand on Coreen's cheek.

"I'm trying to be helpful, Sarah." A tear rolled down Mother's cheek. "I don't wanna force you into something you don't want."

"Good. 'Cause I've decided when I get to Shirley's, I'm gonna check out all my options and decide on my own what I'm gonna do. And then, well, we'll just see about then."

Coreen's bottom lip trembled. "Mama, you *are* coming back, ain't ya?"

Sarah's thoughts jumped to DeWayne and the way his eyes drew her into his heart. The warmth of his hands as he held hers. She had nearly changed her mind about Cincinnati. But whatever the future included, it had to be on her terms. "Don't you worry none. I'll be back."

Two car horn beeps drew their attention to the driveway. Shirley screeched to a halt. She climbed out of the car and joined them on the porch. Shirley hugged Mother and then Coreen as tears streamed down their faces.

"I guess this means you told 'em, sis. Glad I didn't have to do it for you." Shirley sat on the settee. "Tell me about what's been going on since the flood. You selling any tombstones, Mumsie? Coreen, you been hanging out with Betty Anne?"

Sarah rocked as her family chatted about their new lives and how happy they were. Her mind drifted as she stared up at the mountains. Funny how she always thought they never changed. But they did. Leaves changed color and fell to the ground, flowering trees and bushes bloomed and produced fruit, fog hid them from view as if they'd disappeared, and sometimes pieces crumbled and rolled down the mountainside and crashed below.

She smiled. Inside those mountains ran seams of coal. Coal that must be dug out to be worth anything. Coal that stained you black and dirty from your struggle to free it. Coal that only had value when burned.

Her life was much like the mountains. No matter what changes she went through, how many landslides threatened to destroy her, or how much coal she must dig, she vowed to stand firm.

"Here, Mama. A fresh fried apple pie before you go."

Sarah smiled as she took a pie and bit into it. "Mmmm. Good job, Coreen."

After every pie disappeared from the plate and they heaped compliments on Coreen, Shirley turned to Sarah. "Are you ready to go?"

"Already?" Coreen pleaded.

"I'd like to get home before dark." Shirley hugged Coreen. "It'll be okay."

"I gotta get my things. They's in my room." Sarah went into the house. Her stomach screamed and fought to get out. She was really going to do this. Golden rays of sunlight spread throughout the house. She breathed in the sunshine. Leaving turned out harder than she expected. She didn't think her heart would ache.

Sarah picked up the grocery pokes filled with her belongings and walked back through the house to the front door. She stopped inside and heard Shirley talking to her mother and Coreen.

"I love you, Mumsie. We'll give you a call when we get home so you'll know we're safe. Now, don't cry. I'm gonna take good care of her. It's a good thing."

"I love you, Aunt Shirley. I wish I could come too, but I know Mama needs to do this on her own. I'm gonna miss you both great big heaps."

"I'm gonna miss you too, precious girl. You be good, help your mammaw, and work hard on them grades so you can get a scholarship and go to college in a few years, you hear?"

"I will. I'll work really, really hard. I promise. Mama'll be proud of me. And you take good care of my mama, okay? Bring her home to visit when you can."

"I will, baby."

Sarah walked back onto the porch as three sets of eyes dripped tears. Shirley took a couple of the bags and carried them to her car.

"Mama, I'm really gonna miss you."

The tears Sarah had held back for so long raced down her cheeks. She put down her bag, stretched out her arms, and drew her daughter to her in a tight embrace. She whispered in Coreen's ear, "I'm sorry I hurt you so much. I really do love you."

"I love you too, Mama."

* * *

A hint of cooler air drifted across the porch and teased Coreen's hair as she and Mammaw rocked. Her tummy tickled. School started tomorrow. Funny how she hardly remembered her old life. Maybe her dreams had whispers of hope after all. She rubbed the gold heart. And just maybe there's a God too.

"Well, Co-reenie, my girl, it feels a tad cooler today, don't it?" Mammaw licked the end of her pencil and wrote something on her grocery list.

"Yep, Mammaw. I think fall's a'coming. It's about time, don't ya think?"

"Ummm-hmmm." She added something to the list.

"You 'bout done with that shopping list, Mammaw? I won't be able to carry it all."

"Don't you worry none. Now I wrote string beans down here. Make sure they's fresh. I need a mess big enough to string up shucky beans for Thanksgiving and Christmas. Make sure they ain't limp."

"I love shuck beans. I hope Mama comes home to eat some." Coreen admired the pretty houses with green grass, trees, and bushes on her street. She even smiled at the fog still lying on the mountains around them. "It's a lot different here, ain't it—I mean, isn't it? Except for the mountains, of course."

"There's lots of things different. You changing how you talk before you start up in your new school?"

Coreen looked down. "Well, I thought maybe since I don't live in a coal camp no more, I should learn to talk a little more like a city girl—so I'll fit in better."

"Uh-huh. As long as you don't start getting too uppity."

"I'm not trying to be uppity—just normal. You know?"

"I know." Mammaw added something to the list. "Betty Anne teaching you how to talk proper?"

"A little bit. Mostly I been watching the TV and listening to how they say stuff. Sometimes they sound kinda silly." A fly buzzed by. Coreen stopped rocking. "Mammaw, you think Mama's happy up there in Cincinnati?"

"As happy as she can be anywheres, I reckon."

"I miss her. Hard to believe it's already been three weeks. We was—were—getting to where we could understand each other."

"Being apart's good for figuring things out. She'll come back a better woman. You wait and see."

"At least she wrote to me." Coreen rocked and thought about how quiet living with Mammaw had been. She liked not getting yelled at or hit. "D'ya think she'll be gone long?"

"We'll have to wait and see." Mammaw gave her a wink. "I reckon she'll want to come back pretty quick. DeWayne's been keeping in touch with her right regular."

Coreen wrinkled her forehead. Why would talking to DeWayne make her come back sooner? Unless maybe she wanted to study to be a detective after all. That would be exciting. Whispers of hope for Mama too.

"Well, here ya go. That's all I can think of for now. Grab my pocketbook in the house and I'll give you the money. Make sure you don't dillydally. I need some of this for our supper."

"I'll hurry, Mammaw. It'll be hard, but I'll close my eyes when I walk past the library."

"How 'bout ya just look the other way instead? I don't want you smacking into nobody or falling in the street and getting runned over by a car. It might squash my groceries."

Coreen chuckled and rolled her eyes. "You're silly, Mammaw. And I love you a great big bunch."

"I love you too, Coreen—a great big bunch."

Chapter 44

The massive stone building stretched in front of Coreen and blocked out the mountains beyond. Her stomach churned. Rapid deep breaths made her head spin. She'd be so embarrassed if she threw up on her first day of school. With one hand on her stomach, she forced herself to slow her breathing. Arriving students flowed around her, greeting each other by name, waving with smiles and giggles. Some trudged toward the door in a stupor, probably wishing they were still piled in their beds. Coreen stood in a fog as the blur of new shoes and clothes passed.

"Hi, Coreen."

Coreen smiled with relief. "Betty Anne. Finally, somebody I know."

"Are you nervous?"

"Scared to death. I never been in a school this big before. I don't know where to go or what to do." She fought back tears.

"Come on, I'll show you around."

Coreen followed blindly as Betty Anne linked arms with her and they walked up the stone steps to a heavy red wooden door and pulled it open. Footsteps echoed on the wood floors as they climbed the first set of stairs to the main floor. Coreen's head swam as they made their way down the hall through the throngs of students.

"This is the office. You sign up for your classes here. Don't forget choir. You'll love Miss Woods."

They entered a drab room that smelled like the library.

"There's Miss Woods. I'll introduce you." Betty Anne dragged her across the room to a woman about her mama's age, with dark hair to her shoulders. "Hi, Miss Woods. This is my friend, Coreen Shell. She's new and you're going to want to meet her. She has a gorgeous voice."

"Hello, Coreen." Her voice sounded like a lullaby. Coreen envied her deep blue eyes. "I planned to search you out. Mr. Adkins told me you have the most beautiful voice he's heard in years. I'm definitely looking forward to having you in the choir this year."

Miss Woods' smile warmed Coreen's face with delight. Her fingers went straight to the heart hanging around her neck. Another whisper—no, a song.

"Thank you, Miss Woods. I'm excited about singing in the choir. I love to sing."

"Well, come on, we gotta get you signed up," Betty Anne said. She waved. "Bye, Miss Woods. See you in choir."

Coreen remained in her foggy state during most of her time in the office. She vaguely heard someone talking to her about math, science, English, and especially choir. She didn't understand talk about quarterly exploratory classes, except her first one would be speech and drama.

Betty Anne grabbed her by the hand and dragged her to the door. "We're all set, Coreen. I'll show you to your first class. Here's your schedule."

When they walked into the hallway, Coreen noticed color and bright light she hadn't seen before. Beautiful bright color. Hope. A new adventure beyond her dreams.

The words to her song sang in her head.

Above the fog, the sun still shines,
Beneath the mist the mountains stand.
Don't matter none how dark your life seems,
Because the fog is in God's hand.

Made in the USA
Coppell, TX
29 April 2021

54744241R00152